THE BULLET
STOPS HERE

LOOK FOR THESE EXCITING WESTERN SERIES
FROM BESTSELLING AUTHORS
WILLIAM W. JOHNSTONE AND J.A. JOHNSTONE

The Mountain Man

Luke Jensen: Bounty Hunter

Brannigan's Land

The Jensen Brand

Smoke Jensen: The Beginning

Preacher and MacCallister

Fort Misery

The Fighting O'Neils

Perley Gates

MacCoole and Boone

Guns of the Vigilantes

Shotgun Johnny

The Chuckwagon Trail

The Jackals

The Slash and Pecos Westerns

The Texas Moonshiners

Stoneface Finnegan Westerns

Ben Savage: Saloon Ranger

The Buck Trammel Westerns

The Death and Texas Westerns

The Hunter Buchanon Westerns

Will Tanner, Deputy U.S. Marshal

Old Cowboys Never Die

Go West, Young Man

Published by Kensington Publishing Corp.

LUKE JENSEN
BOUNTY HUNTER

THE BULLET
STOPS HERE

WILLIAM W.
JOHNSTONE
and J.A. JOHNSTONE

PINNACLE BOOKS
Kensington Publishing Corp.
www.kensingtonbooks.com

PINNACLE BOOKS are published by

Kensington Publishing Corp.
119 West 40th Street
New York, NY 10018

Copyright © 2023 by J.A. Johnstone

PUBLISHER'S NOTE: Following the death of William W. Johnstone, the Johnstone family is working with a carefully selected writer to organize and complete Mr. Johnstone's outlines and many unfinished manuscripts to create additional novels in all of his series like The Last Gunfighter, Mountain Man, and Eagles, among others. This novel was inspired by Mr. Johnstone's superb storytelling.

First Printing: August 2023
ISBN-13: 978-0-7860-4988-2
ISBN-13: 978-0-7860-4995-0 (eBook)

10 9 8 7 6 5 4 3 2 1

Printed in the United States of America

CHAPTER 1

The Keating Saloon was considered one of the worst in El Paso, and El Paso was no shrinking violet of a town. The border community boasted numerous drinking establishments, gambling parlors, and whorehouses. Men dying in the street was far from uncommon. The town stockyards were often filled with stolen Mexican herds preparing for the profitable drive north. It was not an atmosphere for the faint of heart.

Keating's Saloon fit right in, and its main claim to fame was cheaper-than-average alcohol. It was a place of brooding drunks, quick tempers, and low, back-shooting men. Its one and only claim to culture was Orville and Maddy.

Orville had been kicked in the head by a mule as a small boy. It was widely agreed that this kick knocked out what few brains he had, crossed his eyes, and somehow made him a piano player *par excellence*. In addition to that talent, for twenty-five cents, Orville would bite the head off a living chicken, a considerably less artistic endeavor.

Maddy was two hundred and fifty pounds of robust soiled dove. She had a ham-fisted right hook that had put more than one aggressive customer ass over teakettle. She held little compunction about using the straight razor or pepperbox derringer tucked into her garters, and this was as widely known as Orville's talent at the piano. However, Maddy was a cheerful drunk for the most part and stayed drunk most of the time.

She held a monopoly on the clientele of the Keating Saloon.

At the moment she stood on a groaning table, skirt hiked up over her hips and showing colorful bloomers as large as ship sails as she shook her ample backside in time to Orville's piano playing.

"Drink that rot gut, drink that rot gut!" she howled in a fair passing singing voice. *"Drink that red eye, boys, it don't make a damn wherever we land!"*

A crowd of vagrants and petty crooks had gathered around the dancing mountain of a woman and were stomping their feet and clapping their hands in time to Maddy's dancing. Orville finished banging out the tune and grabbed the half-empty mug of murky liquid next to him.

Tilting his head back, the sometime carnival geek drank in big, greedy swallows. He drank so fast the brownish liquor poured down the sides of his cheek and stained his shirt collar even more than it already was from the grime on his neck. Finishing the glass, he burped happily.

Besides piano playing and oral chicken decapitation, Orville had another job. He came to his feet, a short, scrawny man with greasy hair and a bum leg, and picked up a dirty pitcher from beside the piano and began searching the bar. Whenever he came upon the dregs of an unfinished drink, he would dump it into the pitcher. Behind the bar was a large bucket with the words *Mule Piss* scrawled on it.

The more adventurous or desperate of the Keating Saloon customers could purchase a glass of the recycled alcohol for pennies. Passing out at a table or the bar counted as finishing your drink and Orville always found enough beer, rotgut, tequila, and sour mash to add to the Mule Piss barrel.

As he worked, men loudly toasted Maddy as she continued

to shake her bottom. They cheered louder when she turned and shook her overly ample bosom as well.

Not every customer was entertained by Maddy. There were several serious drinkers in the place. Men who sat down and steadily drank until they passed out. They went about it like a laborer going about his work, and some scowled at being distracted from their task.

There was another kind of customer in the Keating as well. Men who were uncomfortable in more law-abiding or upscale establishments. Establishments that, say, kept a good working relationship with the marshal.

Two such men stood at one end of the bar, backs to the celebrating crowd cheering as Maddy produced one plump breast from her shirt. These two men were talking to each other and clearly didn't want to be interrupted. They had the hard eyes of veteran gunhawks and big irons rode on their hips, tied down and within easy reach of their hands.

The Whatley brothers, Timothy and Eli, mostly made their living from wet stock: rustled Mexican cattle or horses driven across the Rio Grande into Texas. Darker rumors circulated around them, as well. Whispers about stagecoach robberies where no witnesses were left behind. Back shootings of men who'd crossed them or beaten them too handily in cards.

So far their luck had held and there was never enough proof for them to be brought in by the law, much less brought up on charges and hanged as they surely deserved.

Tim Whatley was a gangly skeleton of a man with one wandering eye where his father had brained him with a piece of firewood as a boy. He carried a grudge about his looks because other than the eye he would have been considered handsome in a rough, frontier way. Men who happened to stare at the wandering eye were apt to find themselves struck with the butt of Timothy's revolver. Men who made jokes about it sometimes went missing.

Eli was lean as well, with bowlegs and a Texas handlebar

mustache of such epic proportions it looked like an opossum was hibernating on his upper lip. Tim was the talker; Eli was a brooder with a reputation for back shooting.

"Gotta take a leak," Tim said.

Eli grunted in response.

Tim, his mind on his business, turned to walk out the back door to the stinking outhouse set behind the saloon. Just as he did, Orville, carrying the Mule Piss bucket, came around a nearby table. The two men collided and the bucket flew out of Orville's grasp. The piano player stumbled back as the bucket bounced off the rough hewn plank floor.

The noxious liquid inside spilled out like a river over-flowing its banks and splashed across Tim's boots. Maddy, who'd seen the whole thing, stopped dancing. An expression of frightened horror gripped her face. It took a moment for the drunken crowd cheering her to realize something was wrong. The clapping died out and the men turned, taking in the scene immediately.

Those who felt they were too directly behind the shaking Orville backed out of the way. Silence settled over the bois-terous saloon in a dark cloud. All eyes went to the rigid and silent Tim Whatley as he looked down at his soaked boots. The smell of cheap beer and rotgut rose up, filling Tim's nose.

"Ah, jeez, mister." Orville breathed. "I sh-sh-sure am s-s-sorry!"

With a sound of groaning wood and several deep gasps for breath, Maddy climbed down off the table. Behind Tim, Eli Whatley reached into a brine-filled jar and pulled a hard-boiled egg from it. The sound of the shell cracking as he busted it against the bar seemed very loud in the pregnant silence following Orville's stuttered apology.

"Orville didn't mean nothing, Tim!" Maddy protested as she came up. "Don't you hurt that boy!"

Tim looked down at his pants. They were wet from the

knee down and reeking. His boots gleamed with the noxious liquid. He looked back up at the trembling young man. His hand came to rest on the butt of his pistol.

"I said don't you hurt that boy—" Maddy started yelling.

Tim's hand left the butt of his pistol in a blur and streaked toward the whore. His knuckles struck her in the heavily rouged bow of her lips and rocked her head back. The blow landed with a sound like a drover's whip popping. Maddy stumbled, hands flying to her mouth where a trickle of blood began flowing.

Tim's hand returned to his gun butt in the same blur of motion, and this time he filled his hand with the big iron. It came out of the holster like a snake striking and the metallic *click* of the hammer cocking sounded loud as the slap to the nervous onlookers.

Still looking at shaking Orville, Tim leveled the pistol at the big woman. Her eyes crossed slightly in an unfortunate parody of Orville's as she regarded the cavernous muzzle.

"Oh, lordy," she whispered hoarsely. "Please don't kill me, mister. I'll give you a freebie if you like."

Maddy was fierce and given her druthers she would have dealt with some cowpuncher pointing a gun at her in an entirely different manner. But the Whatleys weren't cowpunchers. They were legitimate hardcases. Tim Whatley was too fast and too ruthless to try.

"Stop talking, Maddy," Eli advised.

He bit into his egg and began chewing noisily. His chin was shiny with the dribbling liquid from inside the egg jar. He was an open mouth chewer and bits of egg stuck in clumps to his crooked yellow teeth.

Maddy slowly backed away, hands up. Once she was safely away, Tim, still regarding Orville with an unreadable face, lowered the hammer and reholstered the gun. His hand remained resting on the pistol.

"That was stupid," Tim said. "I'm wet, dammit."

"S-s-sorry, Mr. Whatley," Orville repeated.

His eyes were wet with unspilled tears of fear. He swallowed once, hard enough that his large Adam's apple made a dry clicking sound. He was so frightened his knees began shaking.

"You made the mess," Tim Whatley said. "You clean 'em."

"Yessir!" Orville replied.

He was obviously relieved. Cleaning the boots was a better outcome than he had any right to hope for.

"I'll just get the bar rag!" Orville said, eager to please.

There was the blur, too fast for onlookers to see fully, and then the pistol was out and the hammer cocked, muzzle pushed into a startled Orville's belly. The slow-witted piano player looked down in confusion.

"Mister—" he began.

Tim cut him off, voice hard. "You ain't touching my boots with no nasty old bar rag, idjit."

"Sir?"

"You're going to use your tongue."

The words hung between them for a moment as Orville tried to work out the meaning.

"My tongue?" he finally asked.

The gun moved as Tim Whatley punched it into Orville like a spear. The barrel rammed into Orville's gut and the air escaped him in a rush. Fighting to breathe, the gasping Orville fell to his knees.

"Yes, your tongue, idjit!" Tim snarled. "You're going to lick my boots so clean you can see your damned stupid face in 'em." His grin was savage. "Get to licking, or I'm gonna gut shoot you right here and now."

"Gut shot is a painful way to go," Eli observed, nodding solemnly as if he had just uttered something profound.

Eli had finished the egg and was leaning against the bar like a spectator at a burlesque show. His hand now rested on his own pistol and he casually eyed the bar patrons, daring someone to try and stop the show.

Tears spilled down Orville's face as he lowered himself to his knees before the smirking Tim Whatley. The Mule Piss had mixed with the grimy sawdust and dust on the saloon floor to form a disgusting mud. Orville's pants were instantly soaked in the muck as he knelt.

"That's it," Tim said, voice low and hard and utterly devoid of mercy. "You lick them boots like your life depended on it, idjit."

"'Cause it does," Eli added.

He was grinning, in obvious high humor. He'd seen a similar situation play out before. They'd swung down into Mexico looking for Apache scalps to sell in Ciudad where the bounty was high following some raids.

Apaches had proven difficult to track and were known to be dangerous. To save themselves time and unnecessary peril they found an isolated *granja,* or homestead, out in the flat lands.

The family had been poor and armed with a muzzle-loaded rifle that proved unreliable. Tim had made each family member—father, mother, teenage sister, and young brother—lick their boots. They'd done it because they believed it would save their lives. The Whatley brothers had found this comically stupid of them.

They tied the father to a fence post next to the goat pen and forced him to watch as they beat his wife and daughter repeatedly. When they were done they shot each one in the chest, starting with the boy and working up to the sobbing father. Then they took their scalps, pulled them into the pitiful dwelling that served them as shelter, and lit the place on fire.

When they tried selling the scalps to the Mexican authorities, the military officer in charge of the bounty program had instantly realized the scalps belonged to Mexican citizens and not wild Apache raiders. This had instigated a race for the border that they had just barely won.

All in all, it had proven a less than profitable endeavor. Nevertheless Eli had never forgotten the intense pleasure of making another human being lick his boots. He'd felt like a king. He missed that feeling.

"You lick these boots real good, idjit," Tim urged. "Go on!"

Trembling and crying, Orville leaned forward, head cocked to one side so he could locate Tim Whatley's boot with his crossed eyes, his tongue poking out like a strip of uncooked pork. Satisfied, Tim uncocked and reholstered his pistol.

"That's about enough of that," a new voice said.

The voice was unhurried, calm. It could have been commenting on the weather.

As one, both brothers turned with incredulous looks at the man who'd just entered the saloon. The batwings still swung a little, slowly, behind him.

Neither Whatley brother liked what he saw. The stranger was tall, with the lean build of a man built for endurance, and dressed all in black, although the layer of trail dust on his shirt and trousers gave them a gray cast. Two gleaming Remington revolvers rode on his flat hips. He stood easily, casually even, thumbs hooked behind the buckle of his gun belt, Stetson cocked back on his head. With the light behind him, it was difficult to make out any details about his face.

"I don't know who you are," Tim Whatley snarled, "but you picked the wrong saloon to stick your nose in."

Eli stepped up next to his brother, hand on his five-shot Colt revolver. He didn't have anything to add to Tim's warning, but he nodded gravely, like a parishioner in a pew agreeing with the preacher's fire-and-brimstone message.

"Well," the stranger said softly. "I have you at an advantage, then. You're Tim Whatley and that's your horse's ass of a brother, Eli. Together you two are worth six hundred dollars to the city of Ciudad, which, given the particular nastiness of your crime, seems low, in my expert opinion." The man shrugged. "But Ciudad is right across the river, not too far to haul your stinking hides, and the pesos they pay off in will spend just fine."

"Bounty killer," Eli spat just before the Keating Saloon exploded into a frenzy of violence.

The bystanders stared in stupid wonder as the gunfight erupted. The stranger's hands dipped and came up filled with the Remington .44 revolvers. His thumbs clicked back the hammers.

Orville froze where he was and Tim stumbled over him as he drew his own pistol. The loud, harsh *bang* of the stranger's first shot sounded like a thunderclap in the smoky room and the stench of gun smoke filled his nostrils.

A neat red hole appeared in Tim Whatley's chest and the hardcase stumbled backward, coming up hard against the bar with a look of quizzical shock on his face. Eli had always been the faster brother, and he got his gun out and level, the flat of his hand reaching to fan the hammer, by the time the stranger's second Remington spoke.

Because Eli was faster, this shot was more rushed, and the heavy-caliber slug took him high in the stomach and folded him over like a book closing. Eli grunted and blood rushed out of his mouth. He was a stubborn bastard, and his hand reached his hammer, pushing it back.

The stranger fired again as Eli's hammer fell. The outlaw's shot went low and wide, the last act of a desperate, dying man. The stranger's third bullet took Eli Whatley in the forehead and blood misted red out the back of the man's skull.

Both men landed with heavy *thumps* on the floorboards and their pistols clattered down beside them. The stranger twisted at the hips, cocking back both hammers simultaneously, and covered the crowd in case the owlhoots had friends with big ideas.

To a man the startled onlookers, shocked into sobriety,

held up their hands, showing they offered no offense. Slowly,
the stranger's temper cooled and he lowered his pistols, un-
cocking the hammers as he did. When the big irons slid into
their holsters, everyone in Keating's Saloon gave a sigh of
relief.

Maddy, in a somewhat frightening rush, given her not inconsiderable girth, rushed toward the man. She didn't give
him a chance to speak but instead crushed him into a hug so
fierce he was left slightly dizzy.

"Thank you, mister, thank you!" she said. She looked at
him and added, "Why, hello!" because his somewhat craggy
face, while not handsome, possessed a rugged power that
many women found attractive.

Orville came slowly forward, gratitude on his face. Some
memory of how to express that gratitude must have stirred
in his brain, because he stuck out his hand and said, "I . . . I'm
m-m-mighty obliged to you, sir."

Most people in El Paso wouldn't have shaken the hand of
someone like Orville. More than likely, they would have
drawn back in revulsion if he'd offered it.

Not this stranger. He clasped Orville's hand, nodded, and
said, "Don't mention it, son. Somebody would have gotten
around to killing this worthless scum sooner or later. What's
your name?"

"I'm c-called Orville, sir."

"Pleased to meet you, Orville," the stranger said. "My
name is Jensen. Luke Jensen."

CHAPTER 2

Luke Jensen reined in his horse.

Around him East Texas pines pressed in, the twilight bringing a gathering gloom and thickening shadows. The sun was gone from the sky above the tops of the trees. The branches held the heat of the day trapped down low in the woods, and Luke's dark shirt clung to him, made even darker by sweat. The air was thick with the astringent, gin-like smell of the pines.

Removing his black hat, he swept his sleeve across his forehead, soaking up the perspiration clinging there. His hair was lank with sweat. The humidity here was far different from farther west, out on the frontier where the air was dry as an old skeleton. What it reminded him of most was Georgia during the war, back when the Yankees burned Atlanta.

Luke didn't think much about the war these days. It had ended badly for him. But it had started him on the road to a new life.

He drank from his canteen and eyed the sandy trail his horse stood on. Dried pine needles littered the ground in a soft carpet. He saw the track of another horse in the soft soil. He was getting closer. His job was hunting men, and this search was reaching its finish. He was glad, because it had been a long ride from El Paso and the money he'd collected on the Whatley brothers was just about gone.

Jack Davies was wanted for the brutal treatment of a girl in Plano, up close to Dallas, and the murder of a gambler in Nacogdoches. He'd escaped the rope and disappeared back into the pine barrens his family called home. The Rangers were needed up in the Panhandle, chasing Comanche raiders, and south along the border, battling *bandidos* from the other side of the Rio Grande, leaving them stretched too thin to run down a lone rapist and murderer. That left local lawmen, none of whom were keen on taking a posse of tenderfoot townsmen into the piney woods after the Davies clan.

The bounty grew to five hundred dollars and that was enough money to put Luke on the trail.

Luke studied the woods as he lowered the canteen. With the coming of evening the birds had grown still. Squirrels and chipmunks no longer scurried through the underbrush. The silence grew oppressive. The last town was a four-hour ride west. He was alone in these woods.

The horse nickered, and he soothed the animal without conscious thought. Something was wrong, something had changed in the woods. His life could depend on finding out what it was. He stared through the branches, searching for the source of his unease.

Up ahead, the trail curved and disappeared behind a tangle of blackberry thorns. His head came up in recognition. Smoke.

He smelled kindling burning close by. Cautious now, he dismounted. Drawing the Henry rifle from its saddle sheath, he stood quietly, ears pricked for the slightest sound. He worked the action carefully, seating a round in the chamber.

"Let's just see what's what," he told the horse.

Putting the butt of the rifle against his hip, Luke took the reins and began slowly leading his mount forward. With every step the smell of wood smoke increased. Now he smelled something else, something fetid, and a fouler odor beneath that.

The smell reminded him of Georgia as much as the humidity had.

Luke frowned in disapproval.

Someone had skunked a load of 'shine.

Quality moonshiners cleaned their copper lines and drums. They didn't let old fermentation residue sit in the boilers. Only lazy varmints with no appreciation of good liquor would do something so criminally lackadaisical.

Stepping quietly now, Luke led the horse off the trail. He laid the animal's reins across a low branch and began slipping through the piney woods like he was hunting whitetail deer. Each footstep was carefully placed to avoid snapping a fallen branch or catching a root.

He had a rough direction on the smoke and he angled toward the scent, moving carefully to keep the trunks of trees between him and where he anticipated the source of the smoke was located. In the next step he discerned the outline of a building through the branches and froze before sinking to one knee.

His heart beat faster as adrenaline leaked into his body. There was a sense of tingling anticipation that came with his approach to the building. Sudden violence was a looming possibility. The world narrowed to what was in immediate reach of his senses.

He felt the weight of the rifle, the humidity soaking his clothes, the soft, almost imperceptible droning of insects buzzing around him. The sharp, acrid aroma of wood smoke, the stench of the poorly cleaned still. Now he detected the murmur of voices as well.

He slowed his approach even further. Each step was a dance. He lifted his foot high and then slid it down toe first to ease beneath forest debris, rather than crunching through it.

He was cat dancing, like an Indian raider. Slinking forward, he turned sideways and slipped between two tamarack pines and came around a sprawling gooseberry bush the size of a stagecoach.

The rundown shack of an old cabin sat in a little clearing.

In the dirt yard sat a good-sized still. Copper lines twisted and snaked from fifty-gallon tin boilers to the condenser. The main structure of the still sat on top of a Dutch-oven-style furnace that a man was steadily feeding kindling into.

The figure stoking the fire looked to be in his late fifties, no shirt under a pair of worn bib overalls, and not wearing any shoes. A shapeless Confederate cavalry hat was crammed on his head, and his grizzled beard spread across his chest in tangled knots like the arms of a squid.

Something rustled against the wall, and Luke looked over, seeing a heavy logging chain bolted to the cabin's foundation. At first he thought it was a dog at the end of the chain, then realized it was a young girl dressed in burlap and rags.

Just then Jack Davies stepped out of the house in bare feet and wearing only patched trousers so filthy they were encrusted with dirt. It didn't take a Harvard doctor to see the resemblance between Davies and the older man. They were kin. Maybe father and son, maybe only uncle and nephew, but kin all the same.

Luke shifted, keeping his eyes moving.

Where there were two there could be more. He considered the situation like an officer about to commit troops to battle. Davies said something and both men laughed. The grunts of cold humor came out like animalistic growls. The chained girl flinched. A mosquito whined in his ear but Luke remained motionless, calculating the situation.

There was no garden. There was no barn, or cow pen. The shack seemed less like a homestead and more like a hunting cabin. Something originally built to take advantage of late summer and fall hunting, and then later used to house the still.

There was also the matter of the girl. Even in the backwoods, keeping a young girl shackled to a shed would raise eyebrows. Luke doubted even the most backward of hill folk would do this so openly at their own homes.

That was good. It meant there was less chance of their womenfolk and young'uns being here. This was a 'shine camp.

Luke continued scrutinizing the situation before him.

A few feet from the still, next to a double bladed axe, a 10-gauge side-by-side shotgun leaned against an old stump. The old man would go for that. Davies had a Colt single action army revolver tucked in his pants. The pistol looked very new and well oiled.

Walking past the shackled girl, Davies kicked her hard. Both men laughed as she cried out. Pausing to spit on her, Davies walked to the edge of the little dirt clearing and started urinating. He and the old man continued talking, but their voices were only murmurs at this distance.

Frowning, Luke continued formulating his plan.

He decided he couldn't risk confronting the two men until he was sure no else was in the old shack. He was going to have to get in closer and take a look.

He rose, moving slowly, gun held ready. Easing through the underbrush, he approached the cabin as the two men continued their conversation. The girl remained motionless against the cabin wall.

His foot came down on a small clump of sawgrass next to a Tamarack pine. From out of the grass a spooked quail exploded in a flurry of wings. He jumped back, startled. In the clearing next to the shack, both men spun to look in his direction as the bird flew away.

Luke's plan went up with the bird.

"Someone's out there!" Davies shouted, drawing his pistol.

The old man lunged for the 10-gauge shotgun, eyes wide, tobacco-stained spittle spilling down his beard. For an instant, Luke remembered his mama telling him *If you want to make God laugh, tell him you have plans.* Whatever he'd intended was now no longer an option. There was nothing left but letting the guns do their deadly work.

Lifting the rifle, Luke stepped sideways to get a clear shot just as the old man reached the shotgun. Davies saw the flash of motion and leveled his pistol, thumbing the hammer back.

Luke and Davies fired at the same time.

A .45-caliber bullet sang past Luke's head and smacked into the tree next to him, throwing splinters of bark.

His rifle went off at the same moment, the butt plate kicking back into his shoulder. Seeing Davies stagger, he realized he'd hit the outlaw and quickly worked the lever action before swinging back toward the old man with the shotgun. By the time he turned, the old man had his firearm up and ready.

Luke threw himself to one side as the man fired. The 10-gauge boomed like a cannon and buckshot cut through the underbrush. Landing hard on his side, Luke rolled behind a twisted oak tree. A blast of buckshot pellets snapped branches and struck his arm. He began bleeding.

Cursing, he fired the Henry rifle, worked the action and fired again, attempting to give himself cover as he rose to aim more carefully. In the clearing the old man had fallen back toward the house, the shotgun broken open as he fed new shells into the chambers.

Still out of position, Luke chanced a shot at the old man. The round went wide and hit the house and the old man ducked through the doorway and inside. Spinning, Luke worked the action again, counting the rounds left in the magazine. Bringing the muzzle up, he searched for Davies.

The outlaw, holding one hand over a wound in his stomach,

fired at Luke. Lead buzzed past him, forcibly reminding him
of the battle of Atlanta for one horrible moment. Davies staggered to one side, firing wildly.

Glass shattered and Luke saw the double barrels of the old
man's 10-gauge break through a window. Dropping the
Henry, he threw himself backward, filling his hands with
the Remington .45s instead.

The pistol in his left hand barked three times, and he drove
the old man and his shotgun out of the window. The pistol in
his right fired twice and Davies screamed and stumbled as a
bullet tore through his thigh. He fired at Luke, and the hard
packed ground next to the bounty hunter spewed dirt.

Firing left-handed into the shack's window without looking, Luke straightened his right arm and aimed that Remington at the spinning Davies. The outlaw lifted his pistol and
pulled the trigger. The hammer fell on a spent shell.

Luke's pistol roared and bucked in his hand.

Gun smoke hung thick as fog in the little piney clearing.
Through the haze he saw his shot take the man in the chest
and blood spurted in a red lasso that splashed the East
Texas dirt.

Davies went limp as an old coat, and Luke turned from
him. Rolling to his side, he thumbed back his hammers and
pointed both pistols at the shack door. The old man, eyes
burning with crazed intensity, emerged from the building, an
old cavalry saber in his hands. He shrieked a rebel yell as
he charged.

Both of Luke's trigger fingers tightened. The pistols went
off at the same time and the reports trip-hammered across the
top of each other. The bullets struck, tearing through the filthy
overall bib to smack into flesh. The old man came to a stop,
saber held above his head.

Luke watched him, lost in the moment. He saw the shock
and growing dismay spread across the old man's face. In the

instant before he crumpled, Luke knew in that moment the old man understood he was dying.

Then the man's eyes went gray as a worn pair of long-handle underwear and he fell.

Luke sat there for a moment feeling the adrenaline leaking from his system. The man's dead eyes stared at him.

Looking over, he checked where Davies lay just to be sure and found the outlaw actually looked to be conscious. The wound in his arm had painted his flesh with blood. Luke eyed the ground where Davies' last bullet had gone and found it was less than two inches from his head.

When he lifted his head, he saw the terrified girl looking at him with huge eyes.

"I need a damn holiday," he muttered.

Rolling over, he stood, pistol ready. Davies made a gurgling sound low in his throat. Luke walked toward him, taking note of the man's wounds. The outlaw wasn't going to be trying anything. He had moments to live, at best. Coming over to him, Luke went to one knee.

"Davies," he said. "Look at me."

The outlaw rolled his eyes toward Luke. The bounty hunter saw nothing but hate in the man's gaze. Blood bubbled in the corners of his mouth. When he spoke the man's words came out slow and slushy.

"Go . . . to . . . hell . . ."

Luke smiled.

"Yeah, I know, Davies. I'm the no-good killer who put an end to you. You don't want to tell me a blasted thing. I don't blame you, but"—he rested a finger against the dying man's chest—"listen to me. I may have killed you, but I'm for the law. You knew someone like me was going to be coming. Wasn't me, it'd have been someone else. I never betrayed you." He paused for effect, making sure he had Davies' full attention. "Reed betrayed you. He threw you out as soon as things got tough and you wound up here. Reed's alive and well and laughing right now, knee deep in whores and rye whiskey while you're here dying. You owe him. Tell me where he is."

This was exactly the way to reach a man like Davies. Appealing to his better angels was a fool's errand. Petty vengeance was something the man understood. With his dying breath the man sold Reed out.

Now Luke had a lead to follow.

CHAPTER 3

The line of riders crested the ridge and followed the old deer trail down into the desert valley. It was early morning and the sun was a harsh yellow sliver behind them, casting their shadows out in front so that the riders seemed like giants astride an endless landscape.

They were hard men, well armed and well mounted.

There were Mexicans in their ranks, and several Apaches. One of them was a black man who'd started out as an escaped slave. He'd grown so used to killing to keep his freedom he saw little reason to stop now. The white men were a motley crew, all of them on a one-way path to the gallows.

Despite their different backgrounds, the men held three things in common. They didn't care for honest work. They liked being feared, and enjoyed doing the sorts of things that got them feared in the first place: theft, kidnapping, assault, murder. Finally, they followed their leader without question.

Samuel Melichus rode at the front of the outlaws. Abnormally tall, he was as lean and wiry as a badlands coyote. His stirrups were let out as far as possible, and his legs trailed down to either side of the horse. In the saddle, he sat a full head taller than the next man. Like the coyotes, he thrived by raiding on the outskirts of civilization.

Half Ute, he didn't belong fully to either the white man or the Indian world. Yet, because of his heritage, he found he could move in both. As such, he'd established a network within the various bands of the Apache along the Mexican border region that allowed him to sell slaves at will. South of the border, a stolen woman or child could fetch three times what a stolen horse paid north of the line. Children were easiest to transport over the hard terrain.

They took women as well; the men needed entertainment, though the line between woman and girl seemed a thin one to them and one crossed often enough.

As for Melichus, he cared little for such things. He liked hiding gold and some of the finery he stole in a remote cave in the Mule Mountains. He liked gambling. He liked killing. Let the others waste their time on whiskey and screaming women.

Unfortunately, he wasn't a lucky gambler, and he never won unless he cheated, and he refused to cheat because he felt it displeased Old Spider Woman. Once, after chewing peyote buttons with a Navajo witch, the goddess had come to him and told him it was wrong to cheat at white man's games. She hadn't said why, and she hadn't said if he should play those games or not, and he'd been so blasted out of his skull at the time he'd forgotten to ask.

Despite taking both peyote and mescaline numerous times since that experience, Old Spider Woman had not spoken to him again. Still, he remembered. He did not cheat and he did not win. So he raided.

Coming out of the rising sun they approached Affliction, Arizona.

Affliction began life as a poor Mexican village annexed into the growing United States. The soil was too rocky for many crops and the villagers herded goats for the most part. But it had a natural spring and a well-built public fountain.

Copper had been found in the foothills two months ago, starting a rush, and that fountain had proved pivotal in crossing the Sulphur Springs salt flats. Now the place was in full boom and the original inhabitants of the hamlet left to survive on the margins. The nearby mountains were being raided for lumber and buildings thrown up around the existing tent city.

More people arrived every day.

But there was no law yet, and it wasn't near as crowded as boom towns could get. Still, a lot of money and copper were flowing through the tent city. Melichus had gone in to look over the chances of hitting a fat mule train and left thinking that the entire place could be taken.

To do it he'd convinced the White Antelope band of the Mescalero Apache to provide him with fifteen extra fighters. The grim-faced Apache warriors frightened many of his men, but Melichus only needed to keep them alive long enough to pull off the brutal raid.

There were people up and about, even this early. A boom town didn't sleep. But Melichus determined the vast majority would be in bed, drunk or sick with hangovers at this early hour. His men would strike fast and kill them in their beds. A brutal sneer tugged at the corner of his mouth as he anticipated the slaughter.

Behind him he felt the men's tension grow as they neared the tent city set up among the old adobe houses and Catholic church. They were hungry for their kills and for their women. They were hungry for their stolen copper.

As the first of them passed the sign declaring this place Affliction, Arizona, a man stepped out of a tent. Shirtless, he pulled suspender straps up over his shoulders. He sported a great handle-bar mustache and salt-and-pepper hair, his face deeply lined by exposure to the desert elements. Above the elbows, and from the neck down, his body was a startling fish-belly white.

He eyed the dirty, heavily armed men with drunken derision. Hawking up phlegm he spat into the dirt.

"Who the hell are you lot supposed to be?" he demanded.

Melichus lifted the 8-gauge he carried just behind his saddle horn. The man's mouth fell open and his eyes grew to comical proportions of surprise. In the early morning the *click* of the hammer going back was loud as a thunderclap.

"No—" the man started saying.

Melichus fired.

The shotgun roared and his horse reared, whinnying angrily. The buckshot slammed into the man's face and neck from less than ten feet away and his head disappeared off his shoulders in a spray of red mist and a slurry of flesh and bone and brain matter. The dead man's still-pounding heart began squirting blood from the ragged wound of a neck as the body fell.

The raiders took this as the general signal to attack and galloped hard into the town. They threw themselves from their saddles or rode their horses straight through sleeping camps. A redheaded whore stumbled out of the tent the man had emerged from. When she saw the headless body she began shrieking.

Melichus rode forward and slapped her down with the heavy barrel of the shotgun. She collapsed in a heap and he dismounted to tie her. Men stumbled drunk or nearly blind with hangovers from their beds. They were butchered.

Half of Melichus's raiders remained mounted, charging in among the tents and buildings. Laughing, shouting men drove horses into tents and trampled the people sleeping inside them. Gunfire exploded in a terrible racket, chorusing with the frightened barking of dogs and screams of the victims.

More figures stumbled from under the flaps of tents. One man leveled a double-barreled 12-gauge and a white raider named Copperfield shot him in the back. The miner fell dead. A woman dressed only in stained bloomers ran screaming into the street. A Mexican bandit, laughing like a lunatic, shot her twice and she fell.

Seeing pure profit wasted, Melichus turned his murderous

rage on the Mexican and fired the other barrel of his 8-gauge. His horse, already spooked by the first discharge, neighed loudly and sprang away as the second shot boomed. The tightly bunched buckshot struck the Mexican in the side and knocked him to the ground, where he didn't move.

Leaving the hysterical woman bound behind him, Melichus began stalking through the chaos. The miners were well armed but the shock of the ambush was complete. Disorganized and terrified, they put up only sporadic resistance. Several tents already burned, and black smoke began trailing up into the morning sky.

His men who were still mounted rode through again, knocking more bewildered victims to the ground. The raiders didn't use just firearms, a great many wielded machetes and hatchets and long bowie knives. They attacked the wounded with vicious joy and blood-smeared corpses began littering the ground. One of the Apaches began taking scalps, and a second came out of a burning tent holding a nearly newborn infant by one leg.

Whooping, the warrior threw the squalling child under the hooves of racing horses. The child's mother, a dark haired teenager in a ripped checkered dress, came screaming out of the tent in time to see her child die. Howling, she flung herself at the Apache, but he clubbed her over the head and quickly hogtied her.

One of the whites had been a cavalry officer in the war; Melichus didn't know if it was North or South and didn't care. That hadn't been his war. The man had a saber left over from his time in the military, and as two other raiders held a struggling old man between them, he ran him through and laughed as blood sprayed.

A man in filthy boots and dungarees with only the top of his red long-handles showing, came out of one of the old adobe houses. He turned toward Melichus, a shiny new

Peacemaker in his hand. Melichus yanked a battered navy Colt from his belt, and they fired at the same time.

Melichus's hand was far steadier, and the man crumpled in front of the door to the adobe house.

As the Ute half-breed approached the fallen man, an eleven-year-old boy sprang from the house and began running. Melichus uncoiled like a striking snake. The barrel of the Colt slammed into the back of the boy's skull and he dropped. Using leather thongs, Melichus bound him quickly and left him in the dirt next to his father's corpse.

Smoke hung thick in the air now, and Melichus could no longer see the end of the street. He continued walking through the bedlam, brooding on Old Spider Woman's curse that he could not cheat at gambling. After a raid like this, the men liked to gamble their shares of the loot. A good gambler could triple his take or more as the fools drank and made wilder and wilder bets.

Melichus wasn't a good gambler.

He saw a gut-shot man leaning against the side of a building and recognized one of his raiders. As he walked up, the man, a boy really, a *Tejano* of about nineteen or twenty, looked at him hopefully.

"*Estoy herido,*" he said in Spanish. Then again in English, "I'm hurt."

There was no room for the wounded once they fled this raid. A man who could not ride, who could not help drive captives or stolen horses, was no good to anyone.

Melichus didn't slow as he approached the boy. The light of hope died in the boy's eyes as he saw the outlaw leader's face. He made no attempt to save himself as Melichus shoved the barrel of the navy Colt under his chin and pulled the trigger. The boy's head jerked as the round punched through his skull in a hammer blow.

As the body dropped away, Melichus lost his hearing. Suddenly he felt very far away from himself, as if he were a ghost walking out from his own body. Everything around him receded, the screams, gunfire, angry shouts, burning buildings, howling dogs, everything drew away from him as if he were flying down a long narrow canyon and leaving it all behind.

A figure emerged from the smoke and Melichus gaped in fear.

The figure was Indian, shirtless, dressed in buckskin breeches and loin cloth. On his feet there were deer hide moccasins adorned with the beadwork of a Navajo shaman. His bare torso was streaked with paint and he carried a feathered stick in one hand.

Coming to a halt, the figure turned toward Melichus and lifted his hand to point at the outlaw. The figure's face was covered in a buckskin mask under a plume of eagle feathers. The mask was blackened by sacred charcoal, save for several white markings: a full moon for a mouth, a crescent moon in the center of his forehead, and what Melichus knew (though not by that name) was the constellation of Pleiades on his left temple. The mask had no mouth opening inside the moon and behind the eye holes there was only darkness.

"Haashch'ééshzhiní," Melichus whispered.

Haashch'ééshzhiní, called Black God by the tribes and bands of the Southwest.

Black God was the rival of Old Spider Woman. He was the god of fire and the deity of bad witches. Haashch'ééshzhiní could bequeath the vile gift of skinwalking upon a disciple. Some believed he enjoyed human suffering, others that he simply didn't care.

Either way, he was not a benevolent god.

As Melichus stood in the middle of the battle, Black God told him what he must do if he wanted to lift the curse of Old Spider Woman and be good at gambling again. He told

Melichus how to dance with the dead and learn their secrets. He told him of dark ways that led to power.

Turning, Black God walked into the smoke and disappeared.

In a sudden rush of consciousness Melichus was back to himself. He took the big horse pistol lying next to the dead Tejano, and he turned toward the church. Before all else, he needed to kill the friar.

Then he must build a great fire as an offering to Black God.

CHAPTER 4

Mississippi River

Luke Jensen sat across from the woman. She had his full attention.

At the table with them sat three other gamblers. The game was five card stud. The bounty hunter was aware of the others on a purely professional level. Despite his studied detachment, the woman was getting under his skin. He was thinking about her when his mind should have been focused on the game.

The dealer gave each player two cards. One face down, the other up. His showing card was good, the queen of diamonds. Face neutral, Luke bent the corner of his hole card to see what it was. Expressionless, he let it rest and leaned back in his chair.

He had the top up card at the table.

As the highest showing card he began the betting. Frequently five card stud was played with set limits per bet to speed play. This was a no-limit table, however, meaning players were free to drive up the pot as much as their funds allowed.

He met the woman's eyes as he pushed his starting bet to the middle of the green felt-covered table. His wager sat in a pile with the rest of the other competitors' opening bets.

The redhead watched him, face beautiful and impassive.

She smoked a cigarillo as she waited for everyone to finish placing their bets. A shot glass of good whiskey sat in front of her on the table, untouched for the last five hands. A gold locket hung from her graceful neck and sat askew in the curves of her décolletage.

Luke was pretty sure she wore it to be distracting, which, he had to admit, was more effective than he liked. She cocked a bemused eyebrow at him, and he realized he'd just been caught staring. He smiled ruefully and glanced at the other players.

The high-stakes game was being run in a side parlor off the main gambling salon of the *Southern Gentleman*, a stern-wheeler paddleboat currently making the run from St. Louis to New Orleans at pleasant speed. Even now the rhythmic thumping of the paddle wheel churning the river could be heard under the music, the riot of alcohol-driven laughter, and the boisterous conversations in the main salon.

Luke fit in here. Instead of the dark shirt and trousers he wore when he was on the trail, tonight he was dressed in a tan suit with a vest, white shirt, and dark brown cravat under it. He enjoyed wearing nice clothes, although most of the time his work required more functional outfits.

The dealer, a house employee on the riverboat, looked questioningly at Luke. He nodded and the man dealt another face-up card to each of the players. Luke received a second queen, the spade. He felt the tension inch upward around the table. There were still plenty of deals left in this round, but he was the only one showing a good hand at the moment.

Again he had the highest card showing and made the first bet. The others would have to match his wager or fold. Of them, only the woman also held a hand showing strong up cards: a pair of sevens, diamond and club.

Luke considered the table. To his left sat a tall man with slicked-back hair and a handlebar mustache waxed into wicked points. He dressed the part of a dandy, from his ruffled silk shirt, tailored black suit, and undone bow tie down to his expensive boots and the pearl-handled, silver-inlaid Colt .45 Peacemaker.

He gave his name as Brent Westin, though Luke suspected this was an alias. The man had a subdued Georgia accent and an air of genteel conceit that Luke, a Southerner himself, had always associated with Deep South plantation owners.

The man across from Westin was his opposite in every way. Clearly an Easterner in his seersucker suit and bowler hat, Joshua Hascomb spoke with a Boston accent. Barely five foot, six inches tall in his low-ankle dress boots, he was built like a water barrel. Well groomed lamb-chop sideburns grew into his walrus mustache. More rings adorned his fingers than those of the woman sitting beside him.

Luke had little use for Yankees of any sort. However, in general, his mood was presently a good one. He'd been winning for the most part over the last several hours, and this made him inclined to overlook any shortcomings in the people whose money he was taking.

Westin, on the other hand, had been fighting a losing streak. His drinking had increased on pace with his losses. Luke suspected that if this kept up and Hascomb said the wrong thing, Westin might decide to revisit the battle of Appomattox. He found these sorts of tensions kept life interesting.

The woman sat between Westin and the last player. She'd given her name as Vina Delacroix almost certainly a nom de plume. Her accent was absolutely French, but Luke suspected it came by way of New Orleans. It didn't matter; her reputation as a successful madame had proven sufficient to bypass the usual men-only policies held by Eastern gambling establishments.

The frontier had pushed so far out after the war that Luke only nominally considered St. Louis as the proper West. Out West, saloon girls gambled or even ran faro and roulette tables. Successful madames could hold more power than the mayor and frequently did exactly as they liked until the encroachment of civilization pushed them farther west or back into socially acceptable habits.

Luke had known more than his share of successful madames. Enough for him to guess at how expensive Vina's dress, the same emerald green as her eyes, must have been. This was fine. A whore's money spent just as good as any other when it was in his pocket. Who was he to judge?

Besides, her presence made the game more interesting. To say nothing of the fact she'd been one of the only players to give him a run for his money so far. He wouldn't underestimate her.

Behind her, a burly red-haired Irishman, whose name Luke had gathered was O'Toole, hovered. He leaned casually against the bulkhead, cleaning his nails with a pocket knife, but his eyes never remained at rest. With the broken nose and scarred knuckles of a prizefighter, he was built like a blacksmith, but dressed like an Eastern dandy: frock coat, trousers, vest, and bow tie paired with dapper low cut boots and a derby as fine as Hascomb's.

There was a .44-caliber Colt army revolver in a cross draw holster on his waist. The big man wore it with practiced indifference.

The other player threatening to overtake him was one of the men Luke was in St. Louis to find. His name was Jack Garth and he rode with Frank Reed.

Garth didn't know it yet, but Luke was here to claim the five thousand dollar bounty on Reed's head. The only reason he hadn't taken him into custody or killed him trying to resist was because he had several confederates, just like Garth, worth on average four hundred dollars apiece themselves.

All told, he stood to make quite a bundle off Frank Reed's outlaw gang. In the meantime, he didn't mind taking some of the owlhoot's plunder through honest cards. It gave him as good an excuse as any to keep close to the man until his boss showed himself.

Only Garth wasn't completely accommodating in this. He and Delacroix and Luke had been essentially waging a three-sided battle to clean the others out. Garth, a transplanted Texan, dressed the part of a successful cowboy with expensive Stetson, bolo tie, and rattlesnake skin boots paired with his gray trousers and frock coat.

The man could afford nice clothes, Luke considered, with his share of the thirty thousand in bureau funds Reed had tortured out of an Indian chief responsible for overseeing government subsidy programs on an Arkansas reservation.

The gang, on the run after the Arkansas job, had split up and intended to meet again in Baton Rouge before moving into Texas. Following Davies' instructions, he'd found Garth, who was now Luke's ticket to Reed.

For now, Luke would bide his time until they reached Baton Rouge. Gambling was as good a way as any. He raised his first bet by fifty dollars and pushed the chips to the middle of the table. He picked up his own whiskey glass and drank half. As it burned its way down his throat, he watched the other players for their reactions.

Garth's jaw tightened. Delacroix bit her lip softly. Westin rubbed the silver signet ring on his middle finger with his thumb. Hascomb stroked his mustache with one chubby finger. One by one they matched his bet. The pile of chips grew larger.

Despite being well past midnight, the main salon remained busy. Travelers playing for smaller stakes crowded that room. Their chatter and drunken laughter hummed in the background. A piano player banged out "Buffalo Gals" as three dancers in layers of petticoats kicked their legs, revealing their bloomers.

Thick clouds of smoke clung above the revelers' heads.

Servants in white linen outfits moved among the throng dispensing cigars and drinks and rich meals.

It was, Luke reflected, *Babylon on water.*

As he watched, a floor boss led several men around to each table to secure the house winnings and transport them to the vault built into the bulwark at the back of the parlor. It looked like a lot of money.

The croupier dealt the fourth card. Luke had a seven. He now showed two pair. Hascomb didn't bother hiding his disgust. He threw his cards at the dealer and lit a fat cigar.

"Fold," he said.

No one looked happy, but with Westin that could be a bluff. Based on his four showing cards, if his hole card was a heart then he was looking at a flush, a strong hand. Luke knew he'd be willing to match and raise any bet, either because he actually had a heart, or because he was riding a daring bluff.

Garth had a pair of eights showing. There was a small chance he was looking at three of a kind. He showed no signs of folding despite this. Luke wondered what he was playing at, there was little point throwing good money after bad in such a situation.

Delacroix's situation was more intricate.

She showed three of a kind. Three eights and a four. Her three of a kind beat his two pair as it stood now. If she had a four·in the hole she was sitting on a full house; however, it would be of less rank than Luke if his hole card allowed him to build a full house as well. Sevens and queens beat eights and fours. *If* he had that proper card.

On a more interesting note, if her card was an eight then she'd obviously just won the table.

He looked up and saw her watching him, trying to read him like some yellow print newspaper. Luke smiled. He held up his whiskey and quietly saluted her. She returned the gesture and they drank. She may not have distracted him from poker, Luke realized, but she was still a very distracting woman.

Luke pushed in his bet and casually surveyed the room again.

He frowned.

Jesse Stuart stood across the room. Stuart was a big fleshy man, red-faced and sporting a paunch that hid the buckle on his gun belt. He had a schooner of beer in one big hand and was watching the house team secure the money from the tables.

Jesse Stuart was Frank Reed's right-hand man. He was a walking thousand-dollar bounty on two legs, and a known killer. But if Reed was on his way to Baton Rouge to rendezvous with his gang and ride to Texas, why was Jesse Stuart here also?

Something was wrong.

Luke scanned the gambling salon yet again. The sound of the dancing girls, merry piano playing, and raucous crowd faded away. There, to Stuart's right on the other side of a craps table, was Squint Harridan.

The Tennessee ridgerunner had learned his skills as a cavalry scout for General Longstreet and then Nathan Bedford Forrest. He lost an eye at Chancellorsville and now wore a black eyepatch. Waking from the wound, he found himself in the Point Lookout prison.

The degradation he suffered there at the hands of Union troops turned him even more murderous than he'd been before the war. Now he was a killer without compunction.

Luke kept himself very still, tension burning through his body like sheets of lightning leaping through the clouds. He counted two more known members of the Reed gang. In doing so, he realized that he by no means knew all of the potential outlaws by sight or description. There could be a dozen more, or fifty more, and he might not know it.

Things had escalated quickly.

Reed used a revolving roster of wild Texas gunhands and Civil War veterans that shrank and expanded with the size of the job to be done and the amount of heat coming down on them. Luke thought knocking over a riverboat casino was a pretty damn big job.

How many would you need to take this boat down? he wondered.

Quite a few.

Big job, big payout, though. Two guards with double-barreled scatterguns watched the men putting the table winnings into metal lockboxes to be taken to the cage. A third shotgun in the cage. Two bouncers armed with six-guns. The pit boss, or floor manager, would most likely have a hold-out weapon, but he wasn't paid to fight and might or might not have courage.

The captain and first mate were most likely armed. But one was in the pilothouse and the other in his room. It'd take them a moment to respond and they'd be expected and accounted for in the plan. Reed might have men waiting to take over the pilothouse.

That left the customers as the wild cards in the plan. Not everyone was armed. Luke guessed less than half. The Mississippi had a wild reputation and knives still settled gambling disputes along its waterfronts in the shadier establishments . . . but this was no longer the wild frontier where men like Mike Fink had earned his reputation as a brawler and riverboat man. Still, there would be more guns against Reed's men than for.

But only in numbers, Luke knew from long experience. Not every man carried a gun. And not every man who carried one had the disposition to use it. And of those willing, even fewer were capable.

Still, he thought, *this plan is foolhardy.*

Which only made the situation more dangerous.

"Sir?" the dealer said.

Luke turned to him in surprise, bringing his thoughts back to the present. Everyone at the table was watching him expectantly. He cleared his throat and adjusted his jacket as he settled back in his chair. In adjusting his jacket, he made it easier to reach the handles of his Remingtons.

"I'm sorry," he said with an easy smile, "say again?"

"Your wager?"

Suddenly he spotted Frank Reed entering the salon. There was no mistaking the wanted man. He had pistols in his hands.

Luke opened his mouth to speak and everything went to hell.

CHAPTER 5

The *Southern Gentleman* shuddered.

The steamer rammed hard into something, and the force of the jolt reverberated through the hull. The vessel groaned under the sheer brunt of the impact. In the salon, women screamed and men shouted as they were tossed off their feet. Drinks spilled, liquor bottles crashed to the floor, gaming tables upended, and chairs bounced away like dice.

In the high stakes parlor, Luke fell backward, arms windmilling. He'd been expecting something, but the riverboat running aground hadn't been it.

The dealer stumbled backward, the backs of his legs running into the low railing and he tumbled over like a drunk falling down a flight of stairs. His squeaking protest was lost in the general clamor. The other players went over as well, including Garth. Delacroix gasped as she landed on the suddenly canted deck.

O'Toole had been thrown down as well, and he rushed to his feet to help her.

Despite being thrown down, Garth had obviously been expecting the impact. He reacted quickly even as Luke drew his right-hand Remington. The outlaw yanked his Peacemaker clear of its leather and walloped the rushing O'Toole in the side of the head like a carpenter driving in a stubborn nail.

Everything happened at once.

The meaty *thwak* of the impact caused Luke to cringe in sympathy. O'Toole went down like a pole-axed steer in a Chicago slaughter pen, eyes rolling to whites. The Remington was clear of its holster and Luke thumbed back the hammer. Behind him, in the salon, shots rang out in rapid succession. Rough male voices demanded the stunned crowd *freeze!*

Garth was already in motion. Yanking the off-balance Delacroix to him, he put his gun to her head.

"Drop it!"

Luke froze. It had been ugly luck that had thrown the woman into the outlaw's lap. Behind him Reed's gang was shouting orders, demanding cash, trying to ride herd on the crowd and get them under control.

Garth grinned, face brutish and ugly. "I said *drop it,* Luke Jensen. Mr. Bounty Hunter. That's right, I know who you are."

O'Toole groaned and staggered toward his feet. The action was complicated by the severe cant of the *Southern Gentleman.* Grabbing the railing of the low wall separating the parlor from the salon, a groggy O'Toole tried dragging himself upright.

"Not so fast, you big mick," Garth hissed.

He went to backhand the Irish bodyguard again, keeping Delacroix between himself and Luke. To Luke's amazement, Delacroix produced a pepperbox derringer from her waist sash. With his attention focused solely on the big Irishman, Garth didn't notice his hostage had suddenly armed herself.

Delacroix shoved the derringer under her arm and fired all four barrels directly into Garth's side.

The outlaw staggered in shock, surprise on his face to an almost comic extent. Then his pounding heart began pumping gouts of blood out in spurts that stained the money and cards scattered on the floor from the overturned table.

Delacroix lunged forward, breaking free from his grip, and

Luke fired as the already mortally wounded man turned toward the woman, trying to bring his pistol around. The Remington went off twice, barrel belching flame and gun smoke. Garth staggered as both rounds caught him high on the chest just under his throat.

The outlaw went over backward in a tangle of limbs and a woman started screaming. Across the room Reed's men began shouting furiously. A double-barreled shotgun went off just as O'Toole grabbed Delacroix and put his big body over hers. Double-aught buckshot buzzed through the air above Luke's head and slammed into the woodwork of the gambling parlor.

Luke rolled.

His brain tried processing what was happening. The outlaws had arranged for the riverboat to run aground or strike something suitably large as the initiation of a robbery. Prior to the impact, they had fanned out around the main salon so they could keep the crowd under control while a small cadre of their gang robbed the casino.

The outlaws in charge of the crowd had to go first. And where the devil had Reed himself gone?

"You good?" Luke yelled to Delacroix.

"She's fine!" O'Toole said. The Irishman's tone was half snarl.

"Get Reed!" Delacroix shouted. "I'm willing to split the reward, but we've got to be the ones to bring him down or every man with a gun on this boat will try and snake their way in."

"Good point," Luke said, not wasting any time at the moment over the revelation that Delacroix knew who Reed was and had her eye on the bounty, too.

He turned and brought the Remington up, scanning the chaos in the main salon. Just as he did an outlaw, bandanna up over his nose and mouth in a mask, stepped around an ornate pillar and cut loose with a sawed-off 12-gauge shotgun.

The boom of the shotgun thundered in the room.

A big-bellied man in a seersucker suit and ten-gallon hat went over backward. Luke had interacted with the man briefly, and knew he was a successful rancher from the Panhandle who'd fought the Comanche and Kiowa. The buckshot tore the Peacemaker from his hand and punched into his chest.

As the rancher went down, blood splashed the people nearby. One of the dancing women who'd taken cover next to him screamed, shrill and loud, as the man's blood painted her face. The outlaw thumbed back the hammer on the second barrel and swept the room with his smoking weapon.

Luke, O'Toole, and Delacroix fired.

The woman had snatched up Garth's weapon and her shot was half a heartbeat behind those of the men. The outlaw stumbled as the first two rounds struck him. Delacroix's bullet hit the owlhoot in the face as he staggered and he went down.

Luke was in that state of mind that he'd first learned to enter during the war. He seemed to see everything all at once and time slowed while his own body became faster, more agile.

Leaping the railing, he bounded out of the parlor. Some sixth sense made him drop and turn. Wood paneling cracked above his head as if by an axe blow. In front of him another outlaw had just fired. Cursing, the man readjusted his aim and brought his smoking barrel around.

Luke fired. His round caught the man high and to the left on his chest. He went over, limbs akimbo, a look of stupid animal surprise on his face. Luke was already moving.

A large body, big as a barn door, suddenly appeared in front of him. Bouncing into the man, he heard O'Toole cursing in what he assumed was Gallic. They both stumbled backward, jarred hard by the impact, and Delacroix knifed in between them with astonishing grace given her ostentatious dress.

The two men glowered at each other.

"Get out of my way!" they both shouted at the same time.

"You get out of *my* way!" they repeated in unison.

An outlaw emerged from the casino cage, a leather valise in one hand, Colt Dragoon in the other. He scanned the crowd of casino patrons all lying facedown, saw his dead compatriots, and leveled the big revolver. Delacroix was scanning the other half of the room where an outlaw had just ducked through a door.

"Reed!" she yelled.

All of this unfolded simultaneously. In her eagerness to locate and catch the gang leader she hadn't noticed the outlaw armed with the big horse pistol. She fired Garth's pistol and missed Reed. The Dragoon went off like a cannon.

Even as the outlaw emerging from the casino cage was drawing a bead, Luke was up and throwing himself toward the woman. Already in motion, O'Toole came in from his left. Caught mid-step, Luke was thrown to one side as the Irishman bulled past him.

Sweeping the woman into his arms, the two of them crashed through a card table. The bullet passed through the space they'd just occupied. The heavy lead round smashed into a support post and knocked one of the ornate lanterns used to illuminate the room to the floor. From his belly, Luke fired. The outlaw's leather valise jerked in his hand then his shirt billowed out as Luke's bullet struck him in the gut. He folded inward and dropped as the lantern glass shattered and flames caught hold of felt curtains.

"He's getting away!" Delacroix shouted.

"Stay out of my way!" O'Toole bellowed at Luke.

"You're welcome!" Luke yelled right back, furious.

The curtains were highly flammable and fire raced up the felt drapes. As the heavy fabric melted and came apart, hunks like dollops of flaming syrup dropped away, clinging to the wall, the floor, and overturned furniture. Wherever the burning clumps landed a new fire started.

This is bad, Luke thought.

He got to his feet and swapped out Remingtons. O'Toole and Delacroix were already chasing after Reed. He was torn between following them and helping the crew conduct an orderly evacuation and fight the fire. He felt partially responsible even though Reed had given him no choice.

The crew and guests were in danger as long as murderous criminals were threatening their lives as they tried to escape. The Reed gang had to be dealt with, even more than the fire. Holding up the fresh Remington, Luke thumbed back the hammer and followed the other two through the door.

CHAPTER 6

Black smoke poured from several windows, hanging in the air and choking Luke. He was amazed by how fast the fire was spreading. People spilled out of doorways up and down the deck. It was deep in the night, and beyond the pools of light generated by the *Southern Gentleman* it was pitch black.

The sound of the paddle ripping loose from its moorings came with a splintered crash loud as an earthquake. The boat, already canted at an acute angle by whatever it had run into, reverberated under his feet. The boat was coming apart.

He saw the emerald flash of Delacroix's dress through the milling people and began fighting his way toward her. There was a substantial reward at stake. Out of the night came the sounds of oars slapping water as a large rowboat slid into view.

It was filled with gunmen.

O'Toole began firing at them.

"Blast it!" Luke shouted.

The exclamation came out of him as he realized the Irishman in his impetuous haste had just made himself and Delacroix into targets. Three of the six men in the boat had lever action rifles and they opened up without concern for any noncombatants. Staccato strings of gunfire erupted.

Luke saw a dancing girl still wearing a feathered headdress and boa go down as a bullet struck her in the side. She screamed, the note clear and high. Whatever he thought of O'Toole and Delacroix, he wasn't going to sit still for that kind of murder.

He lifted the Remington and took aim. The outlaws had driven their rowboat up against the wrecked steamer. The riflemen were still trading gunshots with O'Toole and Delacroix. The Remington roared in his hand.

One of the outlaws jerked and flopped backward as his Winchester flew from his hands. He went into the muddy black water of the Mississippi and slid beneath the surface like he'd never existed.

One of the riflemen realized they were taking fire from a second direction and pivoted to face the new threat. Luke's next bullet caught him in the forehead and split his skull like cordwood. The red mist of a bloody halo sprayed the face of the man next to him as the .44-caliber slug burst out the back of his skull.

"Come on!" Delacroix shouted.

O'Toole put three slugs into the last rifleman as two other outlaws clambered up the side of the boat. Luke turned toward the pair and saw Reed had made it up a flight of stairs to the pilothouse at the top of the vessel. Luke had no clue what the outlaw was thinking.

He ran toward the stairs, now just a little bit behind the burly Irishman. Just as he reached the first step, a gunman wearing a bandanna as a face mask came out a side door. He had the leather valise from earlier.

Seeing Luke with a drawn weapon he turned, trying to bring his own pistol to bear.

Luke twisted and fired across his body. He rushed the shot and his bullet struck the wall inches from the outlaw. Rattled by the close call, the outlaw's aim was thrown off and the material on the sleeve of Luke's jacket plucked up as the round skimmed across the flesh of his arm like a hot poker.

He finished spinning, dropping to one knee, left hand

down for balance on the canted deck. The outlaw was trying to adjust his aim, fear in his eyes. A cold rock formed in Luke's stomach as he realized how close it was going to be. They thumbed their hammers back simultaneously.

They were so close Luke saw the man's hand shaking as they pulled their triggers. His own was solid as stone. The Remington blasted and he felt the recoil rock his wrist. The outlaw's bullet hissed past his face. He saw the man convulse as his own .44-caliber round struck home.

The bullet busted the man's sternum and cored through his heart.

Blood like clotted cream flew through the air and the man grunted at the impact. He slumped against the doorjamb as his knees buckled and his heavy pistol dropped to the deck.

At the moment of conflict, time had seemed too slow for Luke. It stretched like taffy, each second inflating until the blink of an eye or the beat of a heart lasted forever. Now it snapped back into place. He suddenly heard the cacophony swirling around him again.

Reed! he thought.

Remembering how Delacroix had armed herself, Luke decided to mimic her tactic. The chase was on and there was no time to reload. The four bullets in the outlaw's gun were free shots and that left the lesser amount in his own pistols as backups. At the range this gunfight was occurring, an unfamiliar weapon wasn't going to make any kind of difference at all.

Scooping up the fallen .44, Luke turned and leapt up the stairs. At the very top he saw O'Toole disappear through a doorway. There was shooting behind him, but as he looked over his shoulder all he could see were plumes of black smoke and the flickering yellow of flames as the fire burned through walls on the casino deck.

Reaching the top of the stairs, he jerked his head back as bullets sliced through the opening. Crouching, he risked a second glance around the corner. O'Toole and Delacroix crouched with their backs to him. The river pilot, a gray-bearded man in an officious naval-like uniform of dark blue, lay dead. His eyes showed, wide open and staring, his throat a ruined mess. Blood pooled on the floor.

Delacroix had dropped her confiscated navy Colt. It lay forgotten in the river pilot's blood. She must have taken the pilot's pistol because she was firing a Peacemaker in a two-handed grip as O'Toole rapidly reloaded his own pistol.

Reed was across the room from them, returning fire with his own gun. There was a cabinet built into the wall, and he was crouched behind that. In the enclosed space the booming of firearms was deafening. Gun smoke gathered in clouds and made the air hazy. The slant of the floor kept the footing uncertain.

"Behind you!" Luke shouted.

The last thing he needed was O'Toole or Delacroix, both of whom had proven to be exceedingly quick on their triggers, to get startled and turn on him.

"About bloody time!" O'Toole roared. His brogue had thickened with the excitement.

"Give it up, Reed!" Delacroix shouted at the outlaw between shots. "Your men are dead and you're trapped! It's over!"

"Go to blazes!" Reed hollered back.

Luke heard empty shell casings rattle on the floor by where Reed hid behind the cabinet. He saw his moment and rose. He was going to end this right now. His step faltered as the situation, once again, took a turn for the worse.

A stick of dynamite, fuse lit and spitting sparks, arched out from where Reed crouched. The outlaw had miscalculated the arc of his throw, however, and the burning stick bounced off the low roof of the riverboat's pilothouse.

It dropped like a rock right onto the chest of the dead pilot and lay there burning. Both Delacroix and O'Toole stared at the dynamite in shock. The night just continued spiraling out of control to greater and greater degrees.

Luke, fearing the other two bounty hunters would react too slowly, lunged for the dynamite. As he did, O'Toole and Delacroix both seemed to snap out of their shock. They lunged.

Reed threw himself backward to the other side of the narrow pilothouse and used a second pistol to hammer out four quick shots into the glass of the main window. It shattered immediately.

O'Toole and Delacroix collided, their bodies blocking Luke's. The three of them slammed together in a heap. Luke could no longer see the dynamite. Realizing he could do nothing to help, he threw himself backward. Reed popped up, took two steps, rested one hand on the counter, and vaulted through the open window.

Luke went back out the door on his rump, landing hard enough on the landing at the top of the stairs to rattle his teeth. Delacroix came up with the dynamite held in one gloved hand. The fuse had burned low. She couldn't throw it out the window after Reed for fear the crew or passengers had become trapped on the foredeck. She turned and threw it at Luke.

Luke watched it turn end over end as it arched toward him. Acting without thinking, he raised the gun in his hand and batted at it. The barrel struck the dynamite and sent it spinning to the side. As it did, the fuse winked out, meaning it had burned down to the primer. Tucking his head, Luke instinctively rolled away from the coming explosion.

The dynamite flew out over the edge of the boat and exploded just above the water. The *boom* pierced his ears in a thunderclap, and he immediately heard a ringing that muffled the other sounds around him.

He got up and grabbed the railing around the landing, momentarily dizzy from the concussion of the blast. He fell against the rail and looked down as he regained his equilibrium. The dynamite had blown apart the outlaws rowing the boat alongside the steamer. The boat was cracked and sinking. Bodies and parts of bodies were slipping beneath the black water.

Luke blinked.

We're in trouble, he realized.

They were in the middle of the river; it looked like a quarter mile or more to shore on either side. The initial explosion or impact had ripped open a hole that immediately sucked in thousands of gallons of Mississippi water, resulting in the sharp cant.

Now the boat was sinking. Fast.

"Are you all right?" Delacroix asked as she came toward him.

"We have to find Reed," O'Toole shouted.

The Irishman seemed much less concerned about Luke's health than the woman. He glared at Luke as if this situation were somehow his fault.

"No one gets paid if you keep blowing them up," Luke told him. "Plus the boat is going down so we'll all probably drown."

"The lifeboat! We can still get him!"

Delacroix announced this statement like a particularly bright pupil answering a math question.

"Where else?" Luke asked. Some of these big stern-wheelers carried lifeboats and some didn't. He recalled seeing one hung on the side of the *Southern Gentleman*.

He could hear again, the deafening effect of the explosion having worn off. Screams. Timber burning. The sporadic gunshot. Chaos still ruled on the riverboat.

"This was the stupidest, most ill-conceived robbery attempt I've ever seen," he said.

Delacroix darted past him. "No time for talking!"

Despite his misgivings, he immediately turned to follow her.

Vina Delacroix was a clear and present danger to herself and anybody else around her. Yet she had an energy that was nearly impossible to resist. He knocked shoulders with the bullish O'Toole once again. This time he'd been ready, and he dipped slightly as he struck the big Irishman, catching the other man off balance.

O'Toole swore as he fell backward, and Luke was past him and chasing Delacroix down the stairs and along the deck toward the bow. Luke reloaded on the move, fingers working automatically, the way they had done hundreds, perhaps thousands of times in the past. The moves were instinctive to the point of mechanical. First one pistol, then the next.

He caught up to where Delacroix stood at a railing looking down at the bow. He could tell now that the initial dynamite bomb had been placed in the stern by the paddle wheel and that was where the river water was rushing in. As a result, the bow jutted up at its sharpest angle here.

When this boat finally goes under there'll be some desperate people clinging to it right there, he thought.

Already passengers were flocking to the high point while another crowd milled in panic around the lone lifeboat. The long rowboat had been most frequently used to ferry passengers from locations with shallower docks and piers. It had been a good number of years since river pirates or hostile Indians had sunk a boat on the Mississippi.

Now the Reed gang was doing just that.

Luke came up to the railing, steadying himself with a hand as he stood next to Delacroix. The woman ignored him, scanning the knots of people milling below in panic. Funnels of black smoke rose behind them and the light of the fire reflected off the water. Luke turned from searching for Reed and looked toward the shores. If there were settlements nearby, perhaps they'd see the fire and send boats to help the survivors.

He saw nothing but dark countryside.

"There!" Delacroix shouted.

Cursing loudly, O'Toole came up behind them. Luke turned and looked in the direction the female bounty hunter was pointing. Reed had pulled down his mask and moved among the frightened crew and passengers as one of them.

"We have to get down there," Delacroix said.

"There are stairs on the port side, we can use those if the fire's not too bad," O'Toole said.

Below them, Reed reached the manual hand crane being used to lower the lifeboat. The outlaw seemed intent on making his escape. He also must have thought himself safe because he never once checked behind him.

"Forget about that," Luke said, though Reed couldn't hear him. "You people aren't safe to be around."

Holstering the Remington, he went over the railing.

CHAPTER 7

Luke hung by his fingers for a moment and then let go.

He dropped ten feet or so and landed on his heels. Because of the deck's pitch, his feet immediately slipped out from under him. Boots had served him well for much of his life on horseback, but the deck of a sinking vessel wasn't a good place for them.

He went down, bounced off the wooden deck, and began sliding. Rolling over, he slapped his left hand against the planks and pushed with his toes to stop his slide. He managed to get himself into an awkward all-fours position and started pulling himself clumsily up the slanted deck. Terrified people clung to the gunwales and railing above him.

Delacroix vaulted the railing, too. Her dress fluttered as she plummeted downward. Luke heard her yelp as she landed on the deck. He turned in exasperation to see her falling backward, arms windmilling. He made a desperate lunge and caught her flailing arm in time to keep her from pitching down the deck. A window just below them suddenly exploded from the building heat, and black smoke roiled outward.

"I got you—" he started to say.

Something heavy slammed into him from above, and he grunted under the impact. His head snapped down and his nose struck wood. He saw stars for a moment and couldn't figure out what had happened. His entire body felt as if he'd been busting broncs all day. The wind was driven from him and he wheezed for air.

"Outta the way!" O'Toole yelled.

O'Toole had jumped and landed on him. The Irishman must weigh over two hundred pounds, Luke realized. Dropping from that height, the man's weight could have busted Luke's ribs like kindling. As it was, his knee stiffened and throbbed.

"That's it," Luke snarled. He'd had enough.

O'Toole had rolled off him and now was in between Luke and Delacroix. The female was climbing up the side of O'Toole's body like he was some kind of oak tree. Luke had reached one of the numerous posts supporting the mezzanine from the main deck, and he grabbed hold like a mountain climber.

Reaching over, he hauled O'Toole back by his collar. The man squawked in surprise and flipped over onto his back where he began sliding down. Luke released his grip and swung a hooking punch into the side of the Irishman's head as he slid past.

The man's head snapped like a ball on a tether, and Luke felt the grim satisfaction of the solid reverberation up through his arm signifying a truly solid punch. O'Toole slid away, eyes rolled up and showing only whites.

Luke rolled over and pulled himself up to the post by both hands. Smoke filled the air around them, and he felt the heat of the fire growing from below him. He went to scramble up and found Delacroix pointing her confiscated pistol directly at his face.

"He'll die," she said. "Go get him."

Luke knew she was talking about O'Toole. "To blazes with him."

She slapped the pistol at the fingers of his left hand where they held on to the post. Luke jerked his hand away just in time.

"Hey!"

He thought about drawing one of the Remingtons. He was fast. He knew that, but she had the drop on him, and after the reckless violence he'd seen from the two of them, he wasn't willing to risk his life betting she wouldn't shoot.

"Go get him."

For the moment Luke didn't have a choice.

Scowling, he let go and began sliding and clambering down the deck. The smoke had grown thick as fabled London fog and orange licks of flame danced in the swirling black clouds.

He'd seen where O'Toole had rolled down, and he aimed for that spot, though it was now obscured in the haze. Smoke burned his eyes until they teared, and his lungs protested breathing it. He felt blindly and found the big Irishman's arm.

"Come on, you big galoot, up!"

Groggy, confused, O'Toole tried freeing his arm and angrily shaking Luke's grip loose. Luke held on. The fire was bad, getting worse by the second. He'd been so angry he hadn't given a second thought to the Irish bounty hunter's plight after he punched him. Still, the man didn't deserve to die in a fire.

Not yet anyway.

"Knock it off, O'Toole!" Luke yelled. "You've got to get out of the smoke!"

As if to prove his point, the smoke burned his lungs, and he began coughing. He suddenly felt light-headed and nausea twisted his stomach.

"Here!" Delacroix shouted from above. "Catch!"

Luke couldn't see clearly in the smoke. He looked blindly upward. Suddenly a life ring appeared. He managed to close his eyes right before it struck him in the face. He knocked it away, seething at how badly his night had turned. Ten minutes earlier he'd been winning at cards. Now look at him.

It was definitely getting hotter. The life ring was attached to a length of white rope and Luke guided O'Toole's hands to it. He shoved him upward.

"Climb!"

The Irishman began doing so, but he was slow and clumsy. Grabbing the rope, Luke started scrambling up behind him. Both men were wracked by hacking coughs, and their eyes streamed from the irritating effects of the smoke. The fire had engaged so much of the deck around them that Luke could no longer hear people shouting, only the sound of wood combusting at a faster and faster rate.

The deck grew more vertical by the minute as dark water continued pouring into the stern. It would have remained possible to scramble up by themselves, but the rope definitely made it easier. O'Toole was moving faster now, his head clearing. They were above the flames and the smoke thinned a bit.

The Irishman clambered onto the post where Delacroix had perched just a moment before. Feeling fairly certain O'Toole was less of a grateful-good-sport type, and more of a petty-vengeful-jackass type, Luke planted his feet, rose out of his crouch slightly, and drew a pistol while holding on to the rope with his other hand.

"Just keep moving," he said.

O'Toole looked murderous. His face was blackened by streaks of soot that had channels smeared in them from his tears. The effect did little to soften his rage.

I'm going to have to kill him, Luke thought.

He thumbed back the hammer on the Remington.

That didn't seem to calm the Irishman any. He drew a straight razor from where it had been tucked behind his belt buckle.

"Enough, Liam!" Delacroix shouted. "Let him up, I need your help!"

O'Toole glowered at Luke. "Later."

"Whatever you say, you big dumb potato-eating ox."

O'Toole scowled but put away his straight razor and began following the life ring rope to the bow railing where Delacroix waited. One second the man had been in enough of a rage to attack a pointed gun head-on with only a razor. The next moment he'd cooled off enough to return to the task at hand.

Delacroix had a firm grip on the man, Luke realized.

Holstering the Remington, he followed O'Toole up the rope. He reached the railing just as some of the deckhands released the ropes holding the skiff. It was already over-crowded with frightened people, including Reed, and it hit the water hard.

People were screaming for the boat to wait, but the men manning the oars immediately began pulling. Coming up to the railing, Luke stopped beside Delacroix, keeping one eye on the unhappy Irishman. The three of them watched as a smirking Reed rowed away. The outlaw was surrounded by bystanders and there was no way to chance a shot.

"I can hit him," O'Toole declared.

"No, you can't, and I'll knock you on down if you try," Luke warned him.

O'Toole started to reply, hand on his gun. Delacroix laid her palm on his arm and he stopped.

"Jensen is correct," she said. "It's too risky. We have to try and find the bodies of at least some of the outlaws we killed. I refuse to leave this catastrophe empty-handed."

Luke stared at her, not sure he'd heard her correctly. "You're insane," he said. "This thing is on fire and sinking. The bodies not being burned to a crisp are already in the water and floating away. And, oh yeah, we're still stuck on this blasted paddleboat!"

Around them men were leaping into the Mississippi to escape the flames. Luke didn't give them good chances of reaching the shore. This part of the river was wide and the current strong. He doubted most of the people fleeing the boat were good enough swimmers to make it.

There had been an element of absurdity to the way everything had unfolded, but this was shaping up to be one of the worst Mississippi disasters in a long while, Luke realized. His desire to run down Reed only grew as he realized there wasn't a thing he could do to help these people.

"We've got to swim," he told Delacroix.

"It's more than two hundred yards in a strong current," she protested. "I go in with this dress and I'm dead. You think you can make it that far in boots, loaded down with those hogleg Remingtons of yours?"

He cursed.

She was right. He looked around, desperate for any idea, no matter how unlikely to get him out of this jam. He coughed, hacking up the taste of smoke. Flames were crawling up the deck toward them.

He looked out in the river and saw items bobbing. He blinked in surprise. He'd just assumed the dynamite would have ruined any of the dry good supplies stored in the aft hold. This wasn't entirely true, as it turned out. He saw beer kegs floating past. They must have only been partially filled, but that actually made them more buoyant. He didn't need a personalized invitation.

"The barrels!" he yelled, and pointed. "Go now before they drift too far!"

He stepped over the railing and stood on the lip. The other two would either follow him or they wouldn't. He hooked his rawhide holster straps over the hammers of the Remingtons. His daddy would have horsewhipped him for treating a firearm like this, but he didn't see another choice.

He leapt without looking back. They'd either follow or they wouldn't, he reminded himself. He might be better off if they didn't. There was a small moment where he floated after he jumped, feeling weightless. The dark waters of the mighty

Mississippi rushed up beneath him, reflecting the orange light of the fire.

Then gravity took over and he plunged downward.

Holding his hands on the butts of his pistol to secure them, he struck the water feet first. There was a cold shock as the river swallowed him, then darkness. Above him the firelight played across the surface, and he saw the dark shapes of the barrels floating past. His boots filled with water, pulling him down. He fought to swim but he was slowing.

He kicked his boots free and shed his jacket, lungs screaming for oxygen. His vision grew spotty and narrowed as he thrashed his way upward. He broke the surface in a rush, gasping for breath. Three strong strokes and he was able to reach one of the kegs. He clung to it, panting hard from the exertion.

He looked up as he floated away from the *Southern Gentleman*. O'Toole stood outside the railing, silhouetted by the fire as columns of smoke rushed out over his head. Delacroix was cradled in his arms.

He hesitated, looking for a place close to the barrels. He looked ridiculous with his derby hat crammed down over his ears.

"Jump!" Luke shouted.

O'Toole scowled.

Then, still clutching Delacroix in his arms, he stepped off the sinking boat. She screamed all the way down. They fell quickly and hit the water with a loud splash. Luke saw another keg and lunged for it with one hand. He grabbed it and held on, waiting.

The current smoothed over the spot where they entered the water. It was as if they'd never existed at all. The flow of the river carried them farther from the boat. The pair didn't break the surface.

Luke swore, voice soft.

Then, abruptly, the two of them were there, arms flailing,

churning the water as they fought sinking below the surface again.

"Here!" Luke shouted.

They both turned toward him.

Luke saw a sputtering Delacroix had shed her dress the way he had his coat and boots. He imagined that by now her waterlogged undergarments, not so easily discarded underwater, would feel like bricks weighing the woman down. Her red hair lay around the pale beauty of her face in soaking ropes, her makeup smeared.

Her green eyes looked frightened, but she was fighting hard to survive. Behind her, O'Toole looked the worse for wear. Somehow the derby had stayed on, and now water poured off the brim in streams. The careful construction of his waxed mustache had melted, and he looked like a ginger-haired walrus. He'd shed his overcoat as well and still had one hand under Delacroix's arm, helping her stay up.

"Here!" Luke shouted again.

They looked and he shoved the keg toward them. O'Toole saw his intention and suddenly heaved with all his strength. The former madame yelped in surprise as she flew half out of the water. O'Toole was strong, and he pushed her to within inches of the barrel. She latched on, hugging it tightly.

O'Toole went under.

Luke blinked in surprise. They were already a hundred yards from the wreck of the *Southern Gentleman*. They were twice that from shore, at least. If the Irishman was too heavy to keep himself afloat, there wasn't much chance for him.

"Ahhh!" Luke shouted.

He jerked in surprise as an iron grip clamped on to his ankle from below. For a wild second he thought maybe a monster catfish or gar had latched on. His fingers skidded across the barrel as his grip slipped.

A second grip found his gun belt and he realized who it had to be. Fighting to keep from being pulled under, he reached down blindly and felt around. His fingers found hair. He didn't stop to consider, just blindly pulled.

O'Toole's face broke the water. Luke had him by one of those wild, ridiculously thick mutton chop sideburns and the man howled with pain. Grinning, he hauled the Irishman over to the barrel.

O'Toole glowered at him.

"You're welcome." Luke smiled.

CHAPTER 8

The Belladonna was a good old-fashioned Louisiana brothel.

A three-story, Victorian-style manor with red table lamps burning in the windows, it was situated at the very end of the commercial district just before the railroad tracks. On the other side of the tracks, less prestigious gambling houses, saloons, and whore cribs ran down streets little more than dirt alleys.

But the Belladonna was a proper brothel.

Adam's Ferry was a small enough town that the Belladonna was its only high-class establishment. Because of the ferry crossing into Texas, the town was busy enough that the established red light district was booming on a Saturday night. That part of town, Luke had learned, was called the Bottoms by the local residents. Here where he was, things were a little more quiet, a little more low key.

Luke leaned against an oak tree on the opposite side of the road from the Belladonna. From the Bottoms came the sounds of banging pianos and occasionally trumpets. The brass instrument wasn't something you heard that often west of the Mississippi, he knew, but this was Louisiana so, of course, there were players.

Beyond the music was the dull background noise of loud

revelers, punctuated occasionally by angry shouts and gunshots as pistols were fired in the air. About half an hour earlier a pair of deputies had come out of the Belladonna and wandered down to patrol the Bottoms. Their presence hadn't done much to quiet things as far as Luke could tell.

On this tree-lined street of respectable homes the evening was far more sedate. Cicadas droned in the background, lightning bugs danced above his head. This was the Deep South and the humid air carried the smell of lilacs and jasmine. Inside the Belladonna, someone was playing a piano behind the drawn curtains of the house.

He watched the house. Up the street in a one-horse buggy, O'Toole and Delacroix were parked. The night was close, warm and humid, but a gentle breeze carried in the smell of the river.

It had been only two nights since the sinking of the *Southern Gentleman*. They'd come out of the water near the road to Adam's Ferry and begun walking. Luck had been with them and they found the corpse of an outlaw Delacroix knew as Whitey Hack, caught in some branches near the shore.

After alerting people to the steamboat sinking, they pooled the money left in their pockets, bought a horse and went to get the body. They split the thousand dollar reward and set themselves up with new clothes and rented the buggy.

Then they went looking for Reed.

Delacroix turned out to have contacts with most of the madames between St. Louis and New Orleans, which, given her former occupation, made sense. Reed had shown up at Belladonna's and paid good money to remain hidden while enjoying the services provided.

Just as the robbery of the *Southern Gentleman* had been ill conceived and poorly planned, so were Reed's attempts at avoiding detection and arrest. The outlaw was clearly no genius. So far only luck and a willingness to kill indiscriminately had allowed him to prosper.

This was true of most outlaws, Luke had found. Few had the capability of the James-Younger gang, for example. Mostly they were immoral wastrels too lazy to work. It didn't make them any less dangerous when cornered, but it frequently simplified tracking them down.

That ends tonight, Luke thought.

In the two days that they'd been looking, Reed's bounty had increased substantially as multiple murder charges were added to his list of crimes.

The man was now wanted to the tune of two thousand dollars . . . dead or alive. Luke figured he had to be paying out a pretty penny in bribes to remain safe. The stolen government money from the reservation robbery would open a lot of doors in circles where the law wasn't universally respected, but it wouldn't last. If he wasn't caught soon he'd have to make his way to the frontier very shortly.

The front door to the Belladonna opened, and a tall young man with the build of a farm boy took his time coming down the steps. He stopped when he noticed Luke leaning against the tree. The man's hand went to the butt of his gun. There was a star pinned to his shirt.

Moving slow, Luke touched the brim of his hat.

"Evening, Deputy," he said.

The deputy nodded once and then walked away, heading down the street toward the other side of the tracks. Luke waited until the man had turned a corner and then nodded to Delacroix and O'Toole.

The Irishman gigged the horse and the buggy rolled down the street toward Luke. When they reached the front of the house, O'Toole pulled them up short, and Luke walked over as the Irishman helped Delacroix out of the buggy.

"You ready?" he asked.

"You don't have to worry about us," O'Toole said. "You just make sure you do what you're supposed to, cowboy."

Luke ignored the surly tone.

O'Toole had been moderately better behaved since Luke pulled him from the river, but the man simply had the personality of a porcupine. Both bounty hunters had already proven their willingness to engage in indiscriminate gunfire. By virtue of sheer unpredictability, Delacroix was possibly the more dangerous of the pair, though she at least could behave civilly.

The sooner I'm done with these demented fools the better, Luke thought.

"We'll go in and talk to the madame," Delacroix said. "You come in through the back as we discussed."

Luke nodded and started walking toward the back of the house.

The plan called for Delacroix and O'Toole to enter from the front, O'Toole serving as a bodyguard while Delacroix attempted to get the madame, whom she knew, to help them. Failing that, she was to create a scene and flush Reed out. Luke was to enter quietly, seal off the rear exit, and provide a surprise attack if things went wrong.

The best thing would be to find Reed pants down in a whore's room, Luke knew. He'd surprised more than one outlaw that way, though he'd also had it go bad a time or two. Hunting bounties was not a business of sure outcomes. As their recent adventure on the *Southern Gentleman* had proven.

Coming up to the back door, Luke gently tried the handle and found it unlocked. This made sense, often a town's more prominent citizens preferred more circumspect entrances into even top-shelf brothels.

Carefully twisting the handle, he eased into the house and caught a glimpse of the back hallway. A handcrafted board supporting a line of pegs for visitors' hats ran at eye level down the wall. There was a large coat rack. The floors were polished hardwood, and a dim yellow light burned in a wall sconce.

What really caught his attention, though, were the cavernous barrels of a sawed off 10-gauge directly in front of him. Instinctively Luke reached for one of his pistols. The sound of the hammers cocking froze him before he could wrap his fingers around the Remington's grips.

"Hello," the man holding the shotgun said. "Don't move. Don't even blink."

Luke kept his eyes open.

CHAPTER 9

It was the same deputy from earlier, the one who walked out the front door and disappeared around a corner. Obviously he'd doubled back, which meant he'd been onto them from the start.

What Luke didn't know for sure was if he was doing this because he was in cahoots with Reed, or for some other reason.

"Take out those fancy Remingtons and put 'em on the floor. The only thing between you and this buckshot is the half pound or so of trigger pull left on this 10-gauge."

"What's this all about, Deputy?" Luke asked.

The deputy ignored the question. "Drop the pistols or get a face full of lead."

Up close Luke saw the man's face was heavily pockmarked. Luke had made his living sizing up hard men, judging whether they were killers or not, and then dealing with them accordingly.

That this deputy would pull the trigger, Luke had no doubt.

"Do it. Drop them now. I get even a hint of some fancy Road Agent Spin and I'm cutting loose, so you should make me believe you aren't going to be stupid.

Luke sighed.

He was caught dead to rights. He swore that redheaded Delacroix was a jinx. Thinking of her made him wonder what was going to happen when Delacroix and O'Toole got involved. He didn't think his being at gunpoint would cause either one of them to hesitate in escalating the situation.

If they hadn't been so heavily involved in the *Southern Gentleman* incident he would have already been putting as many miles as possible between himself and the pair. But, like it or not, the Reed bounty had brought them together.

"Watch this," the deputy said.

Luke watched him as he laid his thumb over the hammers and then pulled the trigger back and held it there. Only the grip of his thumb kept the hammer from falling forward.

"I slip, you die. I get shot by you or anyone else, you die. I trip walking down this hallway, you die."

"That's a lot of dying for just one man."

The deputy lowered the sawed-off shotgun to his waist.

"Save the funny talk and start walking, Mr. Bounty Hunter."

Faced with little choice, Luke, hands held up, began walking down the hallway. The deputy followed a few steps behind. Luke felt the weight of knowing those barrels were trained squarely on his back.

He remembered the fiasco on the *Southern Gentleman*. He remembered the quail bursting out of the brush as he made his approach on Davies. Maybe someone was trying to tell him it was time to find another line of work.

As he walked toward the front of the house he saw a room accessed by two sliding doors. Based on where he'd seen the windows placed from the front of the house, he assumed they were heading toward the parlor.

On the left-hand side of the hall a staircase ran up the wall toward the second and third floors. As they passed it he looked up, wondering where Reed was.

He got his answer soon enough. As they neared the parlor, people started arguing in loud voices. The loudest voice belonged to Vina Delacroix.

"Susan Annie Jones!" Delacroix scolded. "You'd sell out one of your oldest friends for a few dollars? Shame on you!"

"I go by Julia Fontaine now," a woman's voice snapped. "Which you damn well know. And don't you sashay in here talking about morals after the way you threw yourself at Wyatt!"

"*Please*," Delacroix fired back. "I hardly needed to throw myself at him. He came all on his own free will. I guess he was tired of rolling in the gutter!"

As the deputy pushed him forward he heard a loud sound somewhere between a punch and an axe handle slapping a burlap bag of grain. He stepped inside just as Delacroix fell, her face bloody where a woman he presumed was Julia Fontaine had struck her with the barrel of a pistol.

O'Toole stepped forward and Luke had zero doubt he would have smashed Julia Fontaine's face without a second thought. In the same instant Luke spotted Reed, the man they'd all come to see.

I guess that tells me what's going on with the deputy, he thought.

As this realization ran through his head, Reed was already in motion.

The outlaw lowered the bottle of whiskey he was guzzling and quickly drew his pistol. He stepped behind O'Toole as the Irishman lunged toward Fontaine. The big Colt Dragoon smashed into the back of the Irishman's skull with a sickening *crunch*.

O'Toole dropped face-first on the floor. The hair at the back of his head was matted with blood.

Reed kicked him in the face.

Hard.

Despite sincerely hating the rival bounty hunter, Luke winced in sympathy. Delacroix looked more aghast at O'Toole's injuries than the blood that had made a scarlet mask across the bottom half of her face.

Luke turned his head over his shoulder, speaking back to the deputy.

"Pistol whipping a woman and ambushing a man from behind. You'll probably get the key to the town for courageous work like that, *Deputy*."

Bounty hunting was Luke's profession. When surprise attacks were called for he was the first one to set up an ambush. The frontier was a pragmatic place and he wasn't changing his views on that because he found himself on the eastern bank of the Mississippi for a change.

But he had a code. It wasn't just about the law, it was about what was right, about what it meant to be a man. There were things he'd never do, lines he'd never cross. Apparently the deputy, despite his tin star, felt differently. Luke assumed a good amount of the haul from whatever Reed had salvaged from the casino job had found its way into the man's pockets.

So he pushed.

He was trying to see if the lawman felt any shame in his choices. Seeing if being challenged caused him to get ornery. But when the man spoke his voice was so calm it was more threatening than if he'd yelled.

"The sound of your stupid voice is making my thumb tired."

So much for that angle, Luke thought.

Reed kicked the unconscious O'Toole a second time.

The Irishman shifted slightly, but barely moved under the impact. Delacroix hissed like a wet cat and threw herself across O'Toole. Laughing deep, belly guffaws, Reed reached down and snatched the frenzied woman by the hair. She squalled in outrage as he bent her head back and hauled her toward him.

Holstering his horse pistol, Reed slapped Delacroix across the face. Instinctively Luke stepped forward, but the deputy met the motion with the 10-gauge barrels and Luke stepped back.

"Move again and I'll kill you," the man said. "I'd have done it already because you don't listen too well, but we need that map, don't we?"

Luke blinked. Map? He mulled his response over for half a second and then played along with the idea, whatever it was.

"I suppose you do," he agreed.

"But next time you move I take a chance and blow your legs off. You don't need your legs to tell us where the map is, do you, bounty hunter?"

Luke said nothing.

In the middle of the room, in front of the cold fireplace, Reed backhanded Delacroix, snapping her head back a second time. The beautiful woman was looking the worse for wear at the moment. Dark bruises circled her eyes. Her nose and lips were swollen and bleeding. She stared hatred at Reed through narrowed eyes.

"I might just take this one upstairs," Reed told Fontaine. "Interrogate the spitfire out of her."

"Do what you want," Fontaine snapped, "but get that map."

She stuck the navy Colt in the pocket of her dress and sneered down at Delacroix.

"Well, little-miss-my-drawers-don't-smell, I guess Reed here is gonna learn you a lesson, isn't he?"

Delacroix glared at the madame and sneered right back. "Wyatt said riding you was like riding a swayback mule and you smelled like a barnyard in summer."

Fontaine screeched and lunged at Delacroix. "You lying whore!"

She grabbed Delacroix around the neck and began throttling her. Choking, the female bounty hunter snatched hold of the furious madame's hair and began ripping.

Reed boomed more laughter. He was having a great time. Throwing back his head, he howled in good humor as the women writhed on the floor screaming. They rolled toward him and, still laughing, he stepped back.

Mid step the heel of his boot caught O'Toole's limp body. The drunken Reed tottered, arms swinging wildly. He fell backward, the whiskey bottle flying from his hand.

The bottle smashed against the brick fireplace, spilling almost a full pint of hard grain alcohol on the floor. Luke sidestepped the floundering outlaw as he tumbled backward, just managing to keep his feet.

Reed stumbled, the horse pistol still clenched in his fist, and Luke stepped behind him. The deputy snarled and tried stepping to the side, lifting the sawed-off shotgun. Reed fell and fired into the ceiling. The big round went off like a bomb.

As the outlaw fell clear, Luke picked up the shrieking Fontaine and shoved her toward the deputy. He came away with the navy Colt from her dress.

The deputy stepped to one side and Luke fired just as he let go of the hammers. One barrel of buckshot blew half of the madame's face away. Blood and bits of skull slapped Luke's face like gravel flung in a gust of rain. Bits of brain sprayed the wall and decorated the liquor bottles on the shelf.

The second blast sailed past her and struck an ornate candle holder on the mantel. It flew off, wrenched into a twisted lump of metal. Candles tumbled free, three still lit. One landed on the thick carpet and smoldered.

The other two landed in Reed's spilled whiskey. The liquor burst into flame and ripped across the hardwood where it merged with the pool of kerosene. The kerosene went up like a brush fire in summer and in the next moment the curtains were blazing.

Some of the flaming liquid and still-burning ashes from the curtains splashed Reed and ignited. Reed began screaming. Smoke immediately began filling the air. A line of blazing liquid spread toward the unconscious O'Toole like lava flowing from a volcano.

The deputy dropped his shotgun and went for his pistol. Luke straightened his arm and thumbed back the Colt's hammer in one smooth motion. There was less than ten feet between them when he fired. The deputy was quick. He had half drawn his revolver by the time Luke fired and blew away the bottom half of his face.

Screeching, Reed struggled to his feet.

His left arm and back burned like kindling. Swinging the Dragoon blindly, he triggered the horse pistol and it boomed twice. Luke ducked as Reed flailed with his pistol and Delacroix flung herself to the floor where she began crawling madly for the deputy's body. Flames ran up Reed's back and reached his collar.

In the next instant his hair went up like a match head.

Shrieking, arms windmilling, Reed raced from the room. Luke made to follow and Delacroix screamed. Turning, he saw her dress had caught fire. More than that, an entire wall of the room and all the furniture were now burning.

Without thinking, Luke holstered his pistol and went to the woman who was busy trying to slap the flames out with her hand. He produced his hunting knife as he went to one knee. Grabbing her dress at the waist he cut and yanked, stripping it off of her as she struggled.

She scooted clear of the burning material, both of them coughing harshly. The room was oven hot now and they were sweating freely. He blinked, momentarily mesmerized, as the pale skin of her legs appeared.

Vina Delacroix had beautiful legs.

"O'Toole!" she shouted. "I'm not strong enough to carry him! Get him, I'll go after Reed!"

Before he could argue she was on her feet with the deputy's pistol in her hand. She still wore ankle-high, hook-and-lace boots, and with her hair now wild as a thicket, she looked more like an escaped mental patient than the poised woman he'd seen so far.

"Fine!" he snarled.

He was furious. She'd started giving orders and expecting them to be followed as if she were part of some aristocracy instead of a madame turned near-lunatic bounty killer. He looked at the unconscious lump that was O'Toole. He looked heavy.

Fire rushed toward the helpless man as Luke sheathed his knife. He grabbed O'Toole by the back of his coat and heaved, pulling him away just as the fire began licking at his pants leg. The smoke billowed, and the writhing, hungry flames transformed the room into a chamber of hell. Fire raced across the ceiling as he drug the Irishman into the entryway hall.

He spotted neither Delacroix nor Reed.

"Fire!" someone shrieked above him.

From upstairs he heard women screaming, men shouting. Customers and whores, all in various stages of dress and undress burst through doors and crowded the second floor landing. Luke twisted, looking both ways to figure out where Delacroix might have gone. In the parlor, windows exploded.

He saw the front door hanging open and went in that direction, still dragging O'Toole. He stepped into the night and saw townspeople running in the direction of the brothel. He had no doubt that a sizable portion of the town's male population was in terror of what was happening. Hauling O'Toole, he went down the porch steps and left the man clear of human traffic on the grass of the yard.

From the front he saw flames exploding from blown-out windows and licking up the outside of the three-story house. Smoke hazed the air in an irritating fog, making him cough.

"It's the damn riverboat all over again!" he cursed.

Gunshots barked from the side of the house. Luke drew his

Remington and started running in that direction. He heard high-pitched shrieking. Then a third pistol shot.

Coming around the corner, he saw Delacroix standing in the middle of the street, bare legs spread for balance. She had her stolen pistol in both hands and a smudge of gun smoke hung above her head in a dirty halo.

Crawling in the middle of the street was Reed. His jacket still sputtered with flames though most of it was soot black now. His hair was no longer on fire. The head looked like a patchy mess of melted candle wax.

Two holes soaked crimson with blood had blossomed in his back. Mewling in agony, he continued dragging himself forward. Luke froze. He didn't know if he should stop Delacroix from murdering Reed, or if killing the outlaw was now a mercy.

He opened his mouth to shout, and Delacroix fired.

The round caught Reed in the back of the ruined mess that was his head.

He jerked as if caught hard by a pick handle, and a piece of his skull the size of a saucer blew free and struck the street.

Blood and brain and bits of bone splashed the gravel of the road, and the outlaw lay still, so much dead meat and nothing more.

Delacroix turned to face him. She looked in shock, blood splattered, eyes wild, hair in tangles, clothes ripped. She held the smoking gun in her trembling hands.

"Easy," Luke said. "Easy. It's over. You got him."

She blinked once, as if coming out of a deep sleep. She blinked again and Luke saw she recognized him now. Slowly, she lowered the gun.

"I guess you heard him talk about the map," she said, voice flat.

"Yeah, I did."

She sighed. "Damn."

Then the town marshal and his deputies came for them.

CHAPTER 10

They looked back to the burning bordello. Once again, it reminded Luke of the *Southern Gentleman*'s end.

They seemed to have a knack for setting things on fire, he thought.

The two-story structure was fully engulfed. As the building collapsed into a riot of flames, it began looking more like a giant slash pile fire at the end of some farmer's orchard. The inferno roared and crackled. The heat of it washed over them almost a block away. The fire's glare illuminated the night into day and smoke hung thick in the air, stinging eyes and lungs.

"Well," Delacroix said, "gosh-darn."

Coughing, Luke turned to look.

"Yeah," he muttered, "gosh-darn."

A bucket brigade had started up to help the town's volunteer firemen. Out of a knot of concerned citizens came a group of men. This crew wasn't concerned with the fire, Luke saw. Most of them carried rifles or shotguns as they approached. Two of them peeled off and yanked an obviously woozy O'Toole to his feet.

The Irishman was still in a bad way from the blow to his head. He couldn't stand on his own and was only kept on his feet by the strength of the men holding his arms. The bounty hunter turned his head and puked on the grass.

The rest of the group approached Luke and Delacroix. Firelight glinted off their badges and made shadow masks of their faces. The man leading them was a bulldog; short, deep chested, stubby legs, and sagging cheeks. Unlike the rest of his posse he didn't carry a long gun. His pistol, a Remington like Luke's, was still holstered.

The town marshal walked up and stopped. The deputies fanned out in a half circle to either side of him. The muzzles of their weapons weren't exactly pointed at Delacroix and Luke, but they were held up and ready. No one looked friendly.

The bulldog marshal stood with shoulders squared and hands on hips. In addition to a toothpick tucked into one corner of his mouth, he had a wad of chaw in his cheek and he spit a stream of brown juice into the dirt by Luke's boots. The top of his hat came up to Luke's nose.

Luke sighed. This wasn't going to go smoothly.

"Marshal—" he began.

"What in tarnation happened here?" the marshal interrupted.

"As I was saying—"

Delacroix talked over Luke. "This here is *the* Frank Reed, the villain responsible for the sinking of the *Southern Gentleman*. We're turning him in for the reward."

The marshal squinted at her. He moved his toothpick from one side of his mouth to the other. Still studying the disheveled, half-naked woman holding a navy Colt, he spit a second stream of juice onto the road.

"That so?"

"It is."

Luke crossed his arms in front of his chest and waited. He could see what was building and knew he had no influence over how it turned out. Delacroix and the marshal stared at each other like two bulls in a field. He suspected Delacroix was more stubborn, but he also knew the marshal had sharper horns.

In the background, O'Toole had finally regained his senses. Finding himself separated from Delacroix and in handcuffs had soured his mood. The two deputies struggled to keep hold of him.

Luke didn't think O'Toole should fight. One more blow to the head and the Irishman might not ever wake up. It was unlikely he'd fully recovered from Garth's blow before Reed had laid him out. The man likely needed a good long rest unless he wanted to end up dribbling permanently out of one side of his mouth.

So far the local law enforcement seemed exactly the sort to hit you over the head for resisting.

The marshal took his toothpick out and jabbed it at Reed's corpse. Without looking, he called out to one of the posse members.

"Jake, check that there dead body. Tell me if it matches the wanted poster we got on Reed."

"That's my man your deputies are abusing," Delacroix seethed through tight lips. "I must insist you release him at once; he's done nothing wrong."

"That a fact?"

"It is."

"Maybe this isn't the time for you to be insisting on anything, Miss . . ."

"Vina Delacroix."

"Yes, well, as I was saying, maybe this isn't the time for you to be insisting on anything Miss *Delacroix*."

"It is usually best to speak to dullards as forthrightly as possible, lest there be no mistakes."

"Good Lord," Luke muttered.

He opened his mouth to intervene, but the marshal talked over him.

"And maybe what you're needing is a good spanking, Missy Delacroix."

"Do you know how many men offer to spank me in a week? Please." She arched an eyebrow. "If and when I decide to get spanked, I can assure you it won't be by a sawed-off tin star and his pack of smelly apes."

"Maybe," Luke said, "Miss Delacroix, you could possibly shut up?"

"Marshal," the deputy named Jake said.

He stood by the burned and caved-in head of Reed. He was the youngest man here, maybe not out of his teens, Luke realized. A scattering of bright red pimples sprinkled his neck. He dropped the ruined head and wiped his hands clean on his vest.

"Yeah, Jake?"

"Maybe this is Reed, maybe it's not. The whole dern head is burnt worse than the inside of a chimney, and the face is missing from the eyes up." He swallowed, looking green. "This man's own mother wouldn't recognize him."

"So what we have is a potential homicide."

"Reckon so."

Luke stepped forward, cutting off Delacroix, who looked ready to spring at the man's eyes with her nails.

"Marshal, I think we got off on the wrong foot— "

"Take another step and die, mister."

Every rifle and shotgun muzzle were up and instantly trained on them. Luke stopped moving. Finally realizing this wasn't the time for acerbic barbs, Delacroix impressed Luke by doing something he knew she rarely ever did. She shut up.

The marshal continued.

"I got a body with the head shot to pieces. I have *the* finest establishment for sporting women this town has ever seen going up in flames, and a missing proprietress whom I currently hold an extreme fancy for come evening time. Top it all, I got me a deputy who I can't seem to locate." He spat between Luke's feet. "So what we're going to do is head on down to the jail and let everybody cool off until I've sorted this all out to my satisfaction."

He's not going to be happy when he finds his deputy and his favorite whore are both permanently out of business, Luke thought.

Delacroix opened her mouth to protest but the marshal held up a finger. The sleepy look was gone from his eyes now. They glittered in the light of the flames.

"One word out of you, little vixen, and by God I'll gag you." He spat in her direction. She looked at the brown slime clotting in the dust with disgust. "You just try me and see if I don't."

"We'll work this out, Vina," Luke said. "Just be patient."

She looked at him for a long moment, face impassive. Finally she opened her hand and let the Colt fall to the ground. She purposely dropped it in the scummy mud formed by the marshal's tobacco juice. Whoever had to pick it up would get a handful of spit.

"You are a grade A hellion, you know that, lady?" one of the deputies muttered, looking at the spit-slimed handgun.

Delacroix smiled.

"She knows," Luke told him. "Believe me, she knows."

CHAPTER 11

Arizona Territory

The sun was a white smear in a pale blue sky. Melichus had his men mounted and ready in a small arroyo beneath the low ridge he sat on. In front of him, railroad tracks cut across the desert. To the east, down the track about a mile, the Great SouthWestern Railroad engine came chugging into view pulling a long line of cars behind it.

A gnarled and grizzled veteran crouched in the rocks beside Melichus. Zeb Graver had been one of the first mountain men, traveling with both Kit Carson and Jim Bridger at different times.

His skill with a .50-caliber Sharps had served him well during the war when he'd operated as a sharpshooter. Drifting west after Appomattox, he fell easily enough in the outlaw path.

Right now he had leveled a .30-caliber Sharps on a rock and aimed for a target the size of a man's head one hundred yards out. Easy shot.

"You got it, old man?" Melichus asked as the train raced toward them.

"I got it," Graver snapped. "Jes' lemme *con-sir-grate,* darn it!"

"Better not miss. The boys'll be real mad if you don't hit that dynamite."

"I ain't gonna miss!"

"Better not."

"I said I won't!"

The train rushed through the final approach trailing black smoke behind it. Its chugging sound echoed off the hills and plateaus and filled the little valley with raw mechanical noise.

"Shoot, old man!" Melichus yelled.

Graver slapped his trigger instead of giving it a gentle squeeze. The .30 cal. went off, acrid gun smoke hazing the air. Down on the track sparks flew as the bullet ricocheted off the metal.

"Damn you!"

Graver cocked back the breech and fed another .30-caliber round into the chamber. Behind him Melichus hooted with laughter.

"You're losing your touch, old-timer," he howled.

Graver felt sudden sweat soak his shirt. It wasn't from the heat. If he missed this shot and failed to stop the train it *would* go poorly with him. These were not men prone to forgiveness.

"You'll miss," Melichus shouted.

Ignoring him, Graver sighted again.

Sweat stung the old scout's eyes; his heart beat fast against his ribs. He'd fought every Indian tribe in the Southwest. He'd fought the damned blue bellies. He killed men in shootouts with sheriff's posses and vigilantes. This should have been easy. He'd hit smaller targets at three times this distance.

Unless I really am slipping, he thought. *Drat that Melichus!*

Graver pulled the trigger as the train hurtled past the dynamite. The .30 cal. rocked back into his shoulder. More gun smoke rose in a cloud around his head, but he knew as soon as he fired that he'd hit his target.

Down on the flat valley floor, the dynamite exploded, ripping the rail line apart and bucking the engine into the desert. An engineer, or stoker, flew from the locomotive's open cabin. The body twisted in the air loose as a rag doll and slapped the earth hard. The man didn't move again.

"Go!" Melichus roared.

The outlaws charged out of the arroyo at full speed, splitting up into columns as they rode for the train. Several cars just behind the engine had tipped and lay on their sides in the dirt. Several more were upright, but had been yanked off the track. Passengers from out of the rear cars had appeared. Their terror was apparent even at this distance.

Melichus walked his horse close up to Graver. He showed his teeth to the old scout. Someone who didn't know him better might have confused the expression for a smile.

"You just made it, old-timer. I'd practice more if I were you."

Melichus turned the horse and galloped down the gravel slope toward the wrecked train. Graver watched him go. The man's hands clasped the Sharps rifle with white knuckles. It'd be easy enough to bring Melichus down.

Forcing air hard through his nostrils to calm himself, Graver lowered the rifle. If he didn't get down there quick he'd miss out on the best women. Loot was shared and doled out by Melichus, but women were first come, first served. He hobbled quickly toward his horse.

Melichus held the Colt Dragoon in his hand as he rode down on the train. A volley of shots erupted from some of the middle cars and his men converged on them in a rush. Bullets chewed the outside of the train car to splinters as they unloaded.

Men shouted. Women screamed. Cracking gunshots banged out staccato rhythms.

A fat man in a brown suit and too small derby took off

running down the track toward the caboose. Melichus shot him in the back. The man stumbled and tripped and went face-down on the gravel embankment next to the train. Melichus saw a face in a window; the flash was too quick to tell if it was an adult or child, male or female. He blasted the window and saw a halo of blood splatter.

He grinned. Raiding was good. So what if he rode with whites and Mexicans? He got them to kill their own. Whites and Mexicans were still being killed. *Haashch'ééshzhiní* the Black God claimed the souls of the dead killed in his name.

Hopping up the steps at the end of a car, he climbed up.

A young woman, barely out of school and in a gingham dress appeared in the doorway. Her eyes were wild with fear, hair blond as daisies. She shrieked and Melichus slammed the Dragoon pistol down on her head.

She dropped dead or unconscious to the floor. Either way, as long as she was warm, the boys would be happy enough.

He entered the car braced to attack. No one fired on him initially. He saw an old crone in her Sunday best, hair in a bonnet, holding a big black Bible in both hands as she prayed, eyes shut tightly. Drawing his knife, Melichus cut her throat as he passed.

A conductor, unarmed, cowered in the corner. His terror disgusted Melichus. He didn't waste a bullet on him, either. The knife went in and out. The conductor gurgled more than he screamed as he died.

Coming out the other door, Melichus saw a man standing with his back to him. The train passenger was wielding a Winchester lever action and trading shots with the outlaws.

Extending his arm, Melichus killed him with a shot to the back of his head from less than a foot away. The man dropped, skull cracked open. Holstering the Dragoon, Melichus took the .30-30 for himself. He worked the action, satisfied by the metallic *click-clack* of a round seating.

He jumped to the other coach and climbed the metal

ladder to the top of the railroad car. He was exposed but felt no fear. The Black God danced with him, so bullets could not find him. The battle and chaos swirled to either side. From his elevated position he shot three passengers, two men, one of whom was actually fighting, and a woman.

Quick and fast. These were the laws of raiding. Melichus had chosen a payroll train heading to the mining camps in the foothills to the west. The loads of silver and copper coming back down would be more valuable, but far heavier.

He just needed to find the express car.

The shooting was already petering out. The surprise and violence of the blast had taken a lot of the fight from the passengers, most of whom had never been gunhands of any sort to begin with. Now the men looted the dead and tried to assault as many women as possible before they had to flee.

Melichus hopped to another car and traveled down it. Usually the express car was in the first three or four coaches behind the engine. Those had all been upended and spilled across the Arizona desert like playing cards on the floor of a saloon.

One of the men, a half-Mex, half-Apache slaver named Ortega, climbed on top of a freight car. The door was still shut. Melichus saw it was the express car, just as they had figured during their reconnaissance in El Paso. Two more of his men climbed on top of the train and the three of them began working the door with a long crowbar they'd taken during an ambush of a miner's camp in the White Hills, along with several good mules.

Melichus heard muffled pistol reports from inside the car, and his men jumped back as bullets cracked through the door. The raider grinned.

"Forget that pry bar," he shouted at Ortega. "Blow it."

Ortega snarled at one of the men standing near him, and the man immediately clambered down and went racing toward a group of outlaws eyeing an old woman dressed in the dark dress and bonnet of a Quaker.

From up and down the length of the train the screaming had mostly stopped. Women and children could be heard crying, but it was a hopeless sobbing now, not shrieks of terror. The fighting and running were over; the passengers still left alive understood this. Melichus had seen it many times before. The captives had given up hope. Occasionally a pistol shot rang out, marking another random execution.

The man Ortega had sent for the dynamite came hurrying back, a tight bundle of TNT in his hand. He tossed it up, and Ortega snatched it out of the air while the second outlaw emptied his pistol into the railcar's wooden sliding door.

Whoever was trapped inside immediately responded with a barrage of their own. Bullets shot up through the door and whistled past the outlaws to disappear in the pale blue sky. Using a lucifer match and his thumbnail, Ortega lit the TNT bundle and wedged it in between the railcar door and the handle.

Immediately, he turned and sprang off the car, hitting the ground light as a puma and rolling with the impact. Melichus turned his back and tucked tight against the blast. There was a quiet moment as the fuse burned down, punctuated by a woman screaming, then a single pistol shot followed by silence. Then, with a deafening roar, the dynamite went off.

The explosion left plumes of pitch-black smoke smothering the area. The blast ripped the wooden sliding door open, and as far back as he was, Melichus was still thrown onto his backside by the force of the detonation. Dazed, he saw the man who'd brought the dynamite to Ortega being catapulted backward under the force. He hit hard, then sat up in an abrupt jerking motion.

The man started screaming. Melichus blinked, saw that the man's arm was missing at the shoulder, blood spurting wildly from the wound. Ortega lay facedown on the desert, unmoving. Black smoke covered the open doorway.

"Those idjits." Melichus snarled as he stood.

His men came running from all directions and formed a loose circle around the maimed man. Furious, Melichus drew the horse pistol. The man screamed. The outlaws looked at him with dumb fascination.

"Get out of the way!"

Melichus waved his arm at them and the men backed away. The injured man realized what was happening even in his agony and wildly clutched at the legs of the men backing away from him. He tried to articulate words but it was impossible.

Melichus thumbed back the hammer and aimed. The man looked up at him in terror and managed to get out a word around his cries.

"Please—"

Melichus shot him.

The heavy round slapped into his chest and cored through his body. The report of the shot was muffled in Melichus's ringing ears and he didn't hear the bullet's impact, but the outlaw jerked like a kicking mule and then immediately went still.

"You lazy idiots get in that car and get me my damn money box!" he roared. "Now!"

The outlaws sprang to obey.

Melichus watched with satisfaction as the men clambered up the overturned railcar, waving the hanging clouds of smoke away as they did. Ortega had gotten up and was stumbling toward the rest of them, clearly unsteady on his feet.

Melichus resisted the urge to shoot the Indian. The man was too good a tracker, plus he had connections for moving slaves with both the Apache and Mexicans that were too good to squander.

The outlaws shouted down into the smoke-filled car,

yelling for whoever was in there to give themselves up. No one answered.

There were two Johns in the gang, Tall John and Dirty John. Dirty John was on the coach now and, leaning over, he fired twice into the smoking opening. The bullets ricocheted wildly and zipped back out.

Satisfied, Dirty John and a Mexican vaquero named Juan who'd turned outlaw after killing his mistress's husband, jumped down into the coach. Melichus climbed down off his railcar and walked up to join the men waiting to see what Juan and Dirty John found.

The captives' screams were entirely done now. No one but his men moved in the desert around the wrecked train. The last of his men were finishing up their assaults. The victims had been reduced past tears to shell-shocked silence at this point.

Surveying the passengers' vacant eyes and hopeless expressions, Melichus slapped a big outlaw called Texas on the shoulder. The man looked more like an Oregon Territory logger than he did a Texas cowhand, with thick black hair and a wild bristling beard on a husky, big-boned frame.

"We ain't taking slaves," Melichus told him. "Get a couple of the boys and finish off the captives."

Texas grinned, revealing a blackened dead tooth. His shiny eyes shimmered with amusement in the unforgiving sunlight. He looked happy at the idea of killing what was left of the passengers.

"I'll take care of it."

"Good."

Melichus turned back to the smoking train. He worked his jaw and his ears popped in a sudden rush, allowing him to hear clearly again. A thick steamer trunk with an oversized padlock was pushed out of the smoke and landed like a rock on the track. Immediately Juan and Dirty John climbed out of the car, eyes streaming and coughing from the smoke.

Grinning, Melichus headed over to the strongbox. The outlaws knew better than to mess with it until he'd made his decisions. The box was overly big, it'd take two men to tote it, but one of the dead miner's burros could carry it with little problem. Pleased, he studied it.

"Open it," he snapped.

Ortega had gotten hold of the shovel used by the engine tender to feed the boiler. He went to break open the lock but Texas snatched the tool from him.

"A skinny little runt like you ain't gonna break that lock," he taunted. "That's a man-sized lock, gonna take a man to knock it open."

Ortega spat like a mountain lion and cursed in Apache. A foot-long bowie knife appeared in his hand. Texas spat tobacco juice at him and held the shovel up like an axe.

"You want to try and cut me? Come ahead then!"

Ortega made a feint, and Texas danced back, agile for a big man. He made to swing and Melichus fired his pistol into the ground between them. Both men jumped back in surprise. Melichus pointed his smoking pistol at Ortega.

"Kill him on your own time." He turned the gun on Texas. "Open the box."

Glaring at one another, the two men separated. Ortega sheathed his blade as Texas went to work on the steel lock with the shovel edge. Melichus stood by and calmly reloaded the Colt Dragoon.

Metal rang on metal once, twice, three times. On the fourth blow the lock came apart and Texas tossed the shovel aside. The men jostled around nervously, wanting to crowd in and look but eyeing Melichus warily.

Melichus strode toward the strongbox, smoking pistol still in his hand. Overhead the buzzards were gathering. They floated quietly above the carnage, the sun a pale yellow orb above them.

Melichus kicked the broken lock clear and toed the lid

back. The strongbox was stuffed with US federal money. Bundles and bundles of the stuff. The men began hooting and cheering. Juan and Dirty John hooked arms and started dancing a jig. Several of the outlaws pulled their pistols and fired them into the air.

"Load up and let's go!" Melichus shouted.

He was happy. He took what he wanted when he wanted. This had paid off well.

Texas and Ortega were going down the line of prisoners, cutting throats like butchers in a slaughterhouse. Women and children died crying and begging and praying. Blood soaked the sand. More buzzards gathered overhead.

In ten minutes the outlaws had loaded up and ridden into the hard gravel and cactus waste of the desert valley. The buzzards swung lower as the smoke from the dynamite began to clear. The sun burned down, baking the ground and the steel and rotting the flesh. The bodies would be rancid inside of an hour.

A little while after the outlaws had ridden off, something bumped inside the railcar that had held the strongbox. A pair of long, very thin arms appeared out of the hole, and a young man in his twenties with buck teeth and carrot orange hair cautiously pulled himself free.

The man's clothes were blood splashed. He'd been shot at least twice that he knew of, but in the smoke he'd escaped further notice, though he'd almost asphyxiated. His name was Jamie McCreavy, and he was a Tennessee boy. Too young to have fought in the war, he'd gone west at fourteen to escape the life of a tobacco sharecropper.

He stood for a moment, watching the buzzards begin landing just outside the killing ground. Lip trembling, he slowly lowered himself down and hugged his knees. He saw a woman lying dead with her skirts thrown up over her head and her body exposed. She still clasped the hand of the dead little boy lying by her side.

McCreavy buried his head and sobbed into his arms.

CHAPTER 12

Adam's Ferry, Louisiana

Events unfolded rapidly after their arrest.

O'Toole remained groggy and confused. Luke suspected only his inherent stubbornness kept him from inadvertently spilling the wrong information under questioning. Delacroix pitched a long and loud fit that he needed further medical inspection, and finally, mostly to shut her up, the town doctor was called in.

While that was happening, a young Mexican boy who swept up around the place and ran errands came in. Delacroix got him to bring her a pencil and piece of scrap paper by showing him her breasts. The kid looked like he was on the verge of passing out from overexcitement when she bared them, and Delacroix, impatiently, let him get a good look before covering them again. He ran off to get the items she'd asked for.

"You just made that kid's day for the next ten years," Luke told her.

She shrugged. "Desperate times call for desperate measures."

Several of the whores who had fled from the Belladonna admitted under questioning that Reed had indeed been at the bordello and that their madame was working with him. They did not mention the deputy, which Delacroix had predicted, so when interrogated both Luke and she remained firm that the deputy had stumbled in at the wrong moment and been killed by Reed.

Though curious about why Delacroix had needed to write a note, and to whom, Luke knew better than to ask. Delacroix enjoyed her secrets, and he was tired and in little mood to get the rough side of her tongue. Deputies came back to the cellblock and checked on them intermittently, giving them dark scowls before wandering off.

Those men had to know the deceased deputy had been crooked, but it served everyone's interest to pretend otherwise.

The Mexican kid returned, and Delacroix pulled one of the relatively new-to-the-nation twenty-dollar-denomination bills from under the neckline of her dress. The boy's eyes grew almost as wide as when they'd beheld her naked breasts. Today had turned into a matter of lifelong memory for the youngster.

"What's your name?" Delacroix asked.

"José," the kid answered.

He looked at her chest, mesmerized by the seeming possibility that her breasts could magically reappear. Delacroix snapped her fingers, drawing his gaze up to her eyes.

"Here, José. Pay attention. Take this to the telegraph office and give it to the operator. Pay the bill out of this twenty dollars and then keep the change. There will be plenty of change. But you bring me the receipt to prove you sent it, and I'll let you take another gander at my sweet honeydew melons. You *comprende* honeydews, boy?"

"*Sí,*" the boy replied in a very solemn voice. "*Chi chis.*"

He pantomimed breasts by holding his hands helpfully in front of his chest to show he understood. Sneaking a peak at Delacroix again, he moved his hands out, making his imaginary breasts bigger. Under different circumstances, Luke thought he might have laughed until he cried.

"You like *chi chis,* boy?" Delacroix asked.

"Sí!" Jose nodded.

"Then send the telegram! *Vamanos!*"

Luke blinked and the boy was gone. He regarded the former madame with curiosity. "Is O'Toole playing up that head injury? Did you two work this out in advance just in case something happened?"

"Yes and no," she replied. "Whenever we find ourselves being entertained by some podunk local yokel, one of us tries to draw attention so the other can find a way to get a telegram out to our employers."

"O'Toole flashes his chest to errand boys and keeps twenty dollars paper money in his bosom?"

She laughed. It was a genuine laugh, and to his surprise, he found he liked the sound of it.

"Something like that," she said. "They take your makings?"

"Sorry, I don't smoke except for the occasional cigar, and I don't have any on me. I haven't replaced the ones ruined by that dunking in the Mississippi."

"Darn, I could really use a smoke. I was hoping you had some that didn't go up in that inferno."

"I'm noticing that things have a tendency to meet their fiery demise when you and that Irishman are around."

She shrugged. "It's like the Frenchman explained, you can't make an omelet without breaking some eggs."

Something she'd said suddenly fully registered with Luke.

"Employers?" he asked. "You're working *for* someone?"

Who in the world would hire a pair of trigger-happy gunhawks like these two?

Settling back on the bunk in her cell, she arched an eyebrow at him.

"Indeed we are," she acknowledged.

She had been given someone's hand-me-down dress to cover her legs, and her skin was still soot stained and her hair wild.

They met eyes for a moment.

"Who might that be?" he asked, referring to her employers.

"Well . . ." she drew out her answer. "We're more like what you'd call independent contractors. But most of the time we work for the Pinkertons."

Luke blinked.

A Chicago outfit, the Pinkertons were the largest detective agency in the country, and their agents roamed the West, providing security, hunting outlaws, and collecting bounties. Whatever he'd thought Delacroix was going to tell him, this wasn't it. The Pinkertons carried with them a veneer of respectability he didn't associate with the odd, murderous pair.

Then again, the Pinkerton agency's reputation also had a dark side that spoke to an almost militant ruthlessness. Now, ruthless, on the other hand, was something Luke associated very strongly with the redheaded madame and her lug of a mick.

"That's who you sent the message to? The Pinkertons, in Chicago?"

"To the regional office in St. Louis, but yes, to them. Very soon that sawed-off lunkhead of a marshal is going to receive a telegram informing him that legal representation is on its way. That's usually enough to scare them into releasing us."

"I take it you've done this before."

Delacroix grinned.

"Indeed we have, my handsome friend, indeed we have."

Sighing, Luke sat down on his bunk and shook his head. He leaned back and put his hat over his eyes. There was nothing to do now but wait.

And briefly mull over the fact that Vina Delacroix had just called him handsome.

The boy returned with his Western Union receipt and got his peek at Delacroix's feminine charms. Not long after that, the marshal got a telegram as she'd predicted. When he came to release them his face burned dark from his glowering.

"I'm releasing you on your own recognizance," he announced as if the idea had sprung fully formed from within his own head.

"Because it turned out everything we told you was absolutely true?" Delacroix said this using her sweetest, *gosh ain't I just the most charming Georgia peach you all have ever done seen?* voice.

Luke saw the marshal grinding his teeth in fury. Which told him exactly how much influence and political pain Pinkerton detectives could wield.

"Just don't leave town anytime soon," the marshal ground out.

Good luck on that, Luke thought..

"Yes, Marshal," he said.

"Why, of course not, *Marshal,*" Delacroix said coyly.

She somehow made the word *Marshal* sound absolutely filthy while maintaining an innocent expression on her face.

Luke hid a laugh as he watched the man's ears turn red and then choke on his dip as he accidentally swallowed it.

Their belongings were returned to them. As they gathered themselves together they learned the doctor had insisted O'Toole remain at his office overnight to ensure there were no lingering effects from the concussion.

"That shouldn't be a problem since you're not going anywhere, right?" the marshal snickered.

Luke knew Delacroix and O'Toole would stick around exactly long enough to collect their money and not one minute longer. The marshal could delay that, but if the Pinkertons actually sent a St. Louis lawyer then they'd most likely make enough noise to prevent any kind of warrants or further incarceration.

The West was changing, Luke reflected.

"We'll be at the finest hotel this boil of a town has to offer, getting a meal and a bath," Delacroix informed the man.

That is not, Luke noted, *the same as promising not to leave town.*

The marshal seemed too tired of their company to push the issue. Luke buckled on his guns and they stepped outside before the man could change his mind.

Delacroix looked at the street, which was coming to life as the morning grew later. Wagons hauling sacks of dry goods and lumber rolled past. They heard hammers ringing on anvils. Every man strolling by on their way to some labor or business deal did a double take when they saw Delacroix. Standing next to her, Luke felt a little too scrutinized.

No wonder O'Toole is surly all the time, he thought.

"I believe you and I were having a discussion before we were so rudely interrupted," he said.

Delacroix put her hand on his arm, letting it linger there as she spoke.

"I have to check on O'Toole," she answered. "Let me do that and I'll meet you at the hotel and I'll tell you whatever you want to hear."

That's a lie, he thought.

He was positive Vina Delacroix never told anyone the complete truth, let alone whatever they wanted to hear— unless it served her interest to do so.

"And how exactly do I know you'll show up?"

He wasn't sure why he even cared, but there was more to this woman than met the eye, that much was for sure. Delacroix gave him a small, playful smile.

"Because," she said, "there's no way I'm leaving you to collect all the money on Reed's bounty."

"*That,* I can believe."

"See you soon, Jensen."

She turned and walked toward where they'd been told the doctor's office was located. Luke watched her go, smirking at the men rubbernecking and the Good Ladies of the town scowling with disapproval.

Whatever this business with the map is, he thought, *I'm not sure it's worth it.*

But try telling that to his curiosity.

CHAPTER 13

Luke ate a meal. The hotel restaurant made a grade-A beefsteak, and he devoured it with baked beans and cornbread. When he finished, he paid for hot water and a tub to be brought to his room along with a good bottle of whiskey.

After everything that had happened, he thought he deserved some relaxation. He soaked in the tub with his eyes closed. He pondered again if it was worth dealing with loose cannons like Delacroix and O'Toole, whatever this "map" business turned out to be.

Halfway through the bath, he made up his mind. Once he got his share of the Reed bounty he was headed west. He'd ride through Texas. Plenty of bad men roaming Texas with good money on their heads.

Satisfied, he took a swallow from the bottle of whiskey and edged down deeper into the water and sighed in contentment.

The door to his room swung open. It was supposed to have been locked. Luke sprang up in the tub in the blink of an eye. Filling his other hand with the butt of one of his Remingtons, he thumbed the hammer back and leveled it on the doorway.

Delacroix entered the room smiling gleefully.

"Surprise, cowboy!"

Sighing heavily in the manner of a long put-upon beast of

burden, Luke uncocked his pistol and set it back on the chair. He sank down into the water again.

"How did you get in here?"

"I usually get my way."

She stepped inside, shut the door behind her, and locked it again.

"Did you show another kid your *chi chis*?"

"No, it took all of two dollars," she said, and laughed.

"I'm flattered you spent even that much money on me," he said. "I think. The real question is why?"

Stepping forward Vina Delacroix slipped out of her dress. She'd put some forethought into this encounter because she was naked as the day she was born underneath. The dress formed a puddle of soft cloth at her feet.

Luke blinked.

He'd always liked redheads. He couldn't imagine that a woman this beautiful made the same amount of money hunting bounties, even high-end ones, for the Pinkertons that she could have made whoring. It seemed impossible.

She sauntered over to him and took the bottle from his hand and downed a long swallow.

"Why?" she replied. "Well, it's been one helluva last few days and I'd like to have a bath, some good whiskey, and maybe get to know a cowboy who can, ah, stay in the saddle."

She laughed at his expression. It was a good sound. He realized he was staring at her with the same look of stupid amazement and adoration as the kid from the jail and forced himself to relax. Delacroix took another slug of whiskey and dipped a toe in the bathwater.

The casual manner of her sinfulness was starting to have a clear effect on Luke. He didn't bother trying to hide it.

"What about O'Toole?" he asked.

Delacroix slipped into the tub and threaded her long legs between his.

"Oh, O'Toole is not up for any of those things right now," she answered. "He well and truly got his bell rung."

"I mean, what happens if O'Toole finds out?"

She looked him in the eye and grinned.

"Oh, he'll most definitely try and kill you. I don't know if you've noticed, but he's kind of a hothead."

Luke jerked up in surprise as one of her feet went exploring under the water.

"Pretty jumpy," she noted. "You aren't afraid of O'Toole, are you?"

"Nowhere near enough to kick you out of this tub."

"Good."

Taking her time, Delacroix moved toward the other end of the tub.

Yep, Luke thought, *I'm definitely getting away from these two once I get my money.*

CHAPTER 14

Arizona Territory

The train sped along, driving deeper into the furnace-hot badlands and leaving tattered banners of black smoke trailing along behind it as it went.

Luke Jensen sat with his hat over his eyes. The rhythmic sway of the locomotive and the unrelenting boredom made him sleepy. Unless he planned to start drinking in the middle of the afternoon, taking a nap was his best option.

He was headed to Copper Butte, Arizona Territory. A band of border raiders led by a Ute half-breed named Melichus was carrying out bloody raids, and the bounty on his evil hide had grown to well past five hundred dollars. Throw in the rest of the gang, and bringing them to justice would result in a mighty nice payday.

According to what Luke had learned, Melichus managed to parley his mixed ancestry to form a mixed gang of Apache renegades, Mexican *bandidos*, and white outlaws. They had set the southeastern part of the territory ablaze with slaughter, assaulting women, and looting.

Luke figured their biggest mistake was robbing and derailing the trains of the Great Southwestern Railroad Company. The GSRC had deep pockets, and with the reward money coming from their coffers every bounty hunter and gunhand in the West was heading to Arizona to try their luck.

Most of them wouldn't be worth a damn.

The few with skillful reputations would undoubtedly try to form large posses because of Melichus's numbers. *Good luck tracking Apaches through the desert,* he thought. *They'll see you coming for days in a large group.*

There were calls for the US Army to deal with the problem, but they were stretched thin across the frontier, and recent tensions with Mexico had maintained their focus away from common outlaws, no matter how successful those desperadoes might be.

Luke figured if he rode out by himself he'd have a much better chance of tracking the outlaws without being seen. He'd figure out the rest once he cut their trail. He always had.

"Tickets!" a drunken voice shouted. "Tickets please!"

Luke sighed and pushed the brim of his Stetson up. At the far end of the carriage the conductor had entered. The man was tall, cadaverously thin, with the flushed cheeks and swollen nose of an alcoholic. He wore a great walrus mustache that grew into thick lamb-chop sideburns that framed his face. His neck looked like it'd be better suited to a goose, in Luke's opinion.

Luke took the opportunity to survey his fellow passengers.

The train car was fairly crowded, and currently the only passengers riding were men. It was hot as a frying pan and the carriage had begun stinking of unwashed bodies. Most of the rough crowd looked like hopeful miners looking to cash in on the Arizona copper boom. He saw a lot of wild beards, sturdy boots, and guns.

Two of the passengers stood out. They both wore derby hats and brown suits with string ties, along with brand new cowboy boots. They were not the sort of boots worn by poor cowboys or struggling miners.

Everything about their demeanor and appearance shouted greenhorn and dude.

One of them was an old-timer sporting long blond hair, the skin of his hatchet blade of a face burned brown. His suit looked almost painfully new even though it was obviously travel-worn at this point. He had a fighter's hands, with gnarled and scarred knuckles.

His partner was nearly a full head taller than himself, even sitting down. Whip thin, he looked exceedingly dapper in his suit. There was an expensive leather rifle case leaning against the train window next to him.

As Luke watched, the older man, who sat facing him, removed a silver flask from his coat pocket. He held it aloft for a moment, toasting Luke when their eyes met. Luke nodded in recognition. Upon meeting those pale blue eyes, Luke modified his first impression. Despite the suit, this was no dude. Maybe green to the West, but not a man to cross lightly.

The conductor stumbled up to the two men, eyes bloodshot. Up close Luke saw the man's front teeth were false, overly large dime-store dentures. He had a disturbing habit of clicking them in and out of place as he concentrated on punching the offered tickets.

The thin man regarded the swaying conductor with a bemused demeanor. The older man had a look of disgusted annoyance on his face so severe Luke idly wondered if he was going to hop up and give the drunk a thrashing. Oblivious, the conductor belched and gave them back their tickets.

He was preceded by the smell of whiskey and stale cigars as he approached Luke. *Click-click* went the false teeth. His uniform was heavily wrinkled and looked like it hadn't been washed in a fortnight or longer.

"Ticket please," the man said as he burped.

Luke offered up his ticket as raw alcohol vapor washed over him. He wrinkled his nose in disgust. It made him long to be on his horse, which rode in a stable car, and out in the open air. The heat notwithstanding, he was glad to be on the frontier again.

The train lurched hard, metal wheels screaming on steel rails. The carriage shuddered as if caught in an earthquake. Luke had a sensation of tilting and sliding, and then the train came to an abrupt stop.

Caught off guard, he was thrown forward into the next seat. As he bounced back, the conductor went flying backward, his face comically terrified. Luke slammed back into place, his head snapping hard. Incredulously, he watched as the conductor's false teeth flew out of the man's mouth and landed in his lap.

Disgusted, and acting from pure reflex, he quickly stood, letting them fall to the ground. He wobbled on his feet, off balance. He had a horrible momentary flashback to the wreck of the *Southern Gentleman*. The train was listed hard to one side, just as the riverboat had been. Men jostled each other, cursing, as they tried to find their feet. The conductor's long arm came up and grasped the edge of a wooden bench seat.

Fascinated by the bizarre display, Luke watched the drunkard like a spectator would a street performer. The conductor regained his feet, face twisted in a furious scowl.

"Everyone calm down! Calm down!" he roared. "I said calm down!" he continued repeating this at full volume when everyone around him ignored his outburst. "This big iron son of a gun has just jumped the tracks a bit. Happens all the time!"

Speaking with a distinct British accent, the taller of the two greenhorns addressed the conductor.

"That's all well and good," he said. "But how do you intend to get the train *back* on the track?"

That is, Luke thought, *a fair enough question.*

His own thoughts were mostly with his mount, however. Edging out into the aisle, he began pushing his way toward the door at the front of the coach. He felt like a man climbing a steep hill as he navigated the canted train car.

"We're not that far out of Copper Butte," the conductor assured him. "We'll send one of the brakemen into town to get help."

"To blazes with that," the fair-haired old-timer growled. "We'll get our horses and take ourselves."

Luke was mildly surprised the men had brought mounts with them. Apparently there was more to those two than their expensive valises would at first indicate.

Still, none of his business.

None of the horses were hurt, though they were spooked and more than ready to leave the stable car. Luke, a big miner, and the blond-haired man lowered the ramp and the horses came out easily, eager to be standing on earth again.

The tall dude approached Luke.

"Malcolm Talbot," he introduced himself. "I and my friend are strangers to these parts. You don't happen to know the way into Copper Butte by chance?"

Luke shook the man's hand. "Luke Jensen," he said. He indicated a cactus and sagebrush dotted rise about a hundred yards away. "If my sense of direction is still working I'd guess the stage road is off that way."

"What if it's wrong?" the blond-haired man asked. He didn't smile when he said it.

Luke regarded him. "It's not," he said flatly.

"Forgive my companion," Malcolm Talbot interjected. "The heat doesn't agree with him."

"Maybe Arizona isn't exactly the place for him then," Luke said.

Talbot smiled. "Just so, just so! Let's be friends, shall we? Mr. Luke Jensen, allow me to introduce my companion, Argus Collins."

Luke nodded. Collins nodded back. Neither man offered to shake hands with the other.

"Well, good luck to you gentlemen," Luke said.

He picked up his kit, including his saddle, and walked his horse a short distance away from the derailed train to begin saddling the animal. Instead of doing likewise, Talbot and Collins entered into a hushed conference.

Luke didn't bother trying to overhear, but it was apparent that whatever Talbot was saying, Collins didn't like it. Ignoring them, Luke ran his hands over his mount checking to make sure the animal wasn't injured. He spoke to the horse in low, soothing tones. As far as he could tell, the animal was fine.

As he was readjusting his saddle, Talbot and Collins walked up to him.

"Gentlemen." He nodded.

"Mr. Jensen—" Talbot began.

"Luke's fine."

"Yes, well, okay. Luke. Smashing."

Talbot trailed off and coughed, clearly uncomfortable at the idea of moving so quickly to such informal interactions. To his amusement Luke saw Collins actually roll his eyes in frustration at the Brit's overly proper way of speaking.

"Spit it out, Malcolm," he muttered.

Talbot sighed but then pushed on. "Would you care to ride with us, Mister, er, Luke?"

When Luke hesitated Talbot pressed forward.

"My associate, Mr. Collins—"

"Argus," Collins interrupted.

"Argus," Talbot corrected and continued, "believes he may know you by reputation."

Luke was on guard. Bounty hunters had the potential to make enemies, especially among the relatives of the men they'd brought to justice, dead or alive. Luke had brought more than his share of bad men to justice. He was well aware that there were those who didn't regard this highly.

"That so?" he asked. He finished cinching his saddle.

"Manhunter, right?" Argus asked.

Luke sized him up, taking a moment before answering. Finally he nodded once, a curt motion.

"I suppose," he said.

"You know Arizona?" Argus asked.

"Well enough," Luke admitted. "But not like a local or an Indian scout, if that's what you mean."

"I represent the Pinkerton Detective Agency," Talbot announced. "We are forming a posse of interested and hopefully experienced manhunters to take after a train robber."

Luke sighed. This wasn't good news. It meant people were going to get in his way. He could imagine an army of Pinkerton mercenaries riding roughshod across the local population, sticking out like sore thumbs and being about as effective as they were against the James boys up Missouri way.

"I have some experience with your company, Mr. Talbot," he said. "I didn't like it."

"Money's good," Argus said. "Split for an actual veteran gunhand is more than fair. That Melichus sonofabuck is riding with an army. You won't be able to run him down the way you have some others."

"I've fought armies before," Luke told him. He swung up in the saddle.

"That's just the kind of experience we need!" Talbot declared.

His enthusiasm went unnoticed by both Luke and Collins. Both men ignored him.

"I can't have you getting in my way," Argus said.

"Right back at you," Luke replied.

Sensing the growing tension, Talbot stepped forward.

"Luke, let me propose a simple idea."

"What's that?" Luke asked.

"Ride with us to Copper Butte," Talbot answered. "If by the end of that ride I haven't convinced you, then no harm. I buy you a drink and we go our separate ways. But at least hear us out. I believe the Pinkertons to be in possession of certain information that you are unaware of."

Luke sighed. He thought about a certain trigger-happy redhead who was the personification of trouble in a dress. Surely not all Pinkertons could be that insane. The outfit did have a passing reputation for success.

Besides, they were already riding in the same direction.

"Fine," Luke agreed. "We might as well ride into town together."

CHAPTER 15

A few hours later, riding down through a stretch of ponderosa pines, they found the wagons.

Luke held them up as soon as the buckboards came into view. There were three of them shoved together and two were burned down to almost only the metal supports. One of them, while severely charred, was more intact than the others. The smell of smoke hung on the air, but by the looks of the wagons the fire had died out a bit ago. Only a few misty tendrils still curled up from the wreckage.

Collins shifted uncomfortably in the saddle. Talbot opened his mouth to ask a question but Luke cut him off with a gesture. Those wagons provided perfect bait for a trap, and the little clearing surrounded by the piñon stands was a good place to spring that trap. Luke scanned the trees.

There was the slight stirring of a breeze through the evergreen needles. The motion created a rippling effect through the top half of the pine grove. Down closer to the ground nothing moved. No chatter of a chipmunk, no bird calls or cicada buzz.

Finally Talbot could stand it no longer.

"Apaches?" he whispered.

Luke lowered his arm and pulled his Henry rifle clear of its boot. He didn't like riding with a round in the chamber, but they were currently far into dangerous territory, and he thought it the better option should he need it in a hurry. He worked the lever action.

"Could be," Luke said. "Maybe Apaches, maybe Melichus and his men."

"Could it be Geronimo?" Talbot asked.

His fascination was evident in his voice. The Apache war leader's celebrity put his name on everyone's tongue, but despite the Brit's near childish and macabre fascination with the famous killer, Luke had to admit it was possible. They were in the Chiricahua range.

"I was told on the train that Geronimo had surrendered and was on the reservation," Talbot continued.

Luke shook his head, eyes still studying the pine trees.

"His surrender means nothing. He leaves that reservation whenever he feels like, then it's so hard to catch him they offer him peace just to get him to stop raiding."

That news seemed to rattle the normally reserved Talbot. Geronimo had become the most feared individual in the West. Luke figured he'd earned the reputation fairly enough. The wily Apache had run General Crook a merry chase, and there was now something like a $25,000 bounty on the Indian's head.

That kind of payday could set a man up for life, but Luke didn't expect he'd ever collect anything like that.

Luke studied the horses. More sensitive to smell, they would grow nervous if they scented Indians. So far, the horses stood patiently, flicking an ear now and then.

"Let's go see what happened," Luke finally said.

Following Luke's lead, the other two men rode with their rifles out. Smoke hung around their heads, trapped by the low hanging branches. They came upon the first corpses lying off the trail only a few yards from the wagons.

The bodies belonged to two men now stiff with rigor

mortis. Their limbs were rigid as planks and their expressions as unmoving as plaster masks. The mouths were frozen open, showing protruding tongues, and their unblinking eyes bulged from their sockets. The sides of their bodies closest to the ground were black from settled blood.

The horrific wounds they had suffered were easy to see.

Luke swung down from the saddle, holding his Henry ready. Collins dismounted as well and without being told began scanning the trees, providing cover as Luke investigated the dead bodies. Talbot drew a handkerchief and pressed it against his nose. The stench of death was considerable. The droning buzz of flies was nearly deafening this close to the bodies.

Luke rose from his crouch and began advancing, scanning the area for more corpses. He found the woman and girl after a few minutes. What had happened to them was ugly. It filled him with a cold, heavy rage that left him seething.

He heard a low, gasping groan from behind a fallen log, and he whirled, rifle at the ready.

"Look sharp," he told the other men.

Stepping carefully, he advanced toward the sound. As he came around the log, he saw a man in a filthy, blood-stiffened serape laying facedown on the pine needle carpet. Flies crawled across him the same as they had the mutilated corpses of the family, but as Luke studied the body he realized the man was still breathing.

Carefully, he walked around the body, his muzzle down but aimed generally toward the wounded man even though he didn't seem to be any sort of a threat.

"Got us a live one," he said.

"Good or bad?" Collins asked.

"Bad, I think," Luke said. "He's not dressed like a farmer, and he appears to have been hit by a load of buckshot."

Talbot, still holding his handkerchief to his nose, walked over. Using the toe of a boot, Luke heaved the man over. He'd been shot in the head at close range. His flesh was peppered with gunpowder burns, and the side of his head furrowed deeply where the ear had been blown off. His face on that side was a mask of bruising and dried blood. Flies had laid eggs in the gruesome wound and now maggots squirmed there.

"Someone tried to blow his brains out once he was down," Luke decided.

"That is Fernando Juárez," Talbot announced. "Bounty worth $200 and a known associate of Melichus."

Luke looked up at him. It seemed impossible that Talbot could have known that. Even if the rendering on Juárez's wanted poster had been perfect, the man's face was horribly deformed by the point-blank round he'd taken. Still, Talbot had said it in such a matter-of-fact tone that Luke felt inclined to believe him.

"You seem pretty sure of yourself, Talbot," he said, "given the circumstances."

As he spoke the bandit gurgled wetly in his throat and opened his eyes. The bullet must have struck at an improbable angle and glanced along his skull. It was a minor miracle he was still alive, though it was obvious he wouldn't survive.

"It is my job to recognize bad men," Talbot said. "So I do."

Again the man said it with such flat-voiced assuredness that Luke was inclined to believe him. He turned to the gasping bandit.

"Well then, Fernando," Luke said. The situation reminded him of his exchange with Davies back in the piney woods of East Texas. "You're a dead man. And even if I were inclined to try and save you, which I'm not, you'd just wind up swinging from a rope anyway."

Fernando Juárez began blinking rapidly and trying to form words. Fresh blood spilled out of his mouth. Luke shook his head at the attempt to talk. He made a sharp cutting gesture with the edge of his hand.

"Enough. Here's the deal, and from where I'm sitting it's pretty generous, so, *mi amigo*"—he leaned in—"I have a bottle of laudanum in my saddlebags. I can ease your pain. Hell, take the whole damn bottle, I don't care. Just tell me where Melichus is going."

The man seemed to be struggling with the decision, and Luke placed a single finger on his heaving chest for emphasis.

"He left you to die. You going to just let that go?"

The man ceased his struggling. Finally, he laid a hand on Luke's arm, pulling him closer. He whispered something and Luke nodded.

"What did he say?" Talbot asked.

"Affliction," Luke answered.

CHAPTER 16

Following smudges of smoke on the horizon, Luke rode up over a rise and saw the town laid out in the harsh glare of the sun. It wasn't much, a stagecoach road running in a scar from where he was, down through the town and out the other side where it disappeared into the furnace-like wilderness of the Arizona border region. Three dirt streets cutting across the stage road formed the town, such as it was.

Fernando Juárez had not lied with his final words, it seemed. Thirst for vengeance was the most understood emotion among men with no moral code, Luke had found.

Luke studied the town, taking a moment to get the lay of the land before he rode down into it. He'd left it up to Talbot and Collins to notify the authorities in Copper Butte, but he'd pointed out that having a scout to pin down Melichus's location before a larger group could be brought into action might be their best chance in this situation.

His shirt hung damp with sweat, dark circles under his arms and clinging to him in the arid heat of this wasteland. Shifting in the saddle, he breathed in sage and the animal stink of his horse. The mount had been hard used coming out of the Mule Mountains and crossing Sulphur Springs Valley.

The town had been a Mexican settlement first, and it

showed in the numerous adobe buildings. There was a church with a square bell tower and a little cemetery behind it. Crumbling houses lined the side streets. With the influx of miners from the north, a more typical brand of frontier construction had sprung up: the tent city.

From where Luke sat, he saw large numbers of the tents had been reduced to tatters or blackened by fire. Smoke-seared canvas sheets lay collapsed between armies of busted wooden poles. Trouble had come to the town.

He saw a corral, large barn, and livery stable. A hotel, two saloons, and a mercantile. An assayer's office sat next to what he thought might have been a small jail.

He lifted the reins and prepared to nudge his horse forward when he noticed the buzzards. They'd been in the pale sky all day, but that wasn't unusual in this country. Something was always dying and going to rot. Buzzards had to eat the same as anything else.

The big, hooked-beak vultures glided on silent thermals above the town. Some primal instinct stopped Luke short. He turned his gaze back to the sun-blasted buildings of the town. On first glance he'd assumed most of the residents had been at siesta. Now he looked more closely.

No one walked the streets or lounged in the shade of the buildings. No one drew water from the fountain. He didn't see a dog or a horse anywhere. His gaze swept back toward the public stables. The corral stood empty. A tumbleweed blew down the street, branches stiff as dried bones.

Uneasiness stirred in his gut.

Still, there was only that emptiness. No obvious threat presented itself, and the horse needed rest and water. Reaching down, he grabbed the stock of his lever action Henry .45-70 and loosened it in the scabbard where it had settled during travel.

"Come on," he told the horse as he heeled it into motion.

With his shadow stretching out behind him to improbable lengths in the brutal sunlight, Luke rode into the town.

A cluster of houses nestled on the outskirts. Luke eyed them warily as he rode up. He left one hand resting on the curved handle of his Remington pistol. As he rode past, raglike curtains hung limp in dark windows left open against the heat.

A desiccated wind lifted, stirring the tattered lengths of cloth. Rough grit lifted off the hardpan and made him squint as it stung his face like shrapnel. In the near distance, the disharmonic caw of a crow blasted out into the quiet. His horse snorted in irritation and tossed its head. Luke patted its neck in a reflexive soothing action.

His gaze ran over the buildings as he drew closer to the town. Off to one side he saw a lizard clinging to a wall, crouched in the narrow shade of a windowsill. The silence grew oppressive as he rode forward and he tasted dirt in his mouth.

After passing the last of the houses leading into town he came to a sign made of wood salvaged from some old buckboard, seemingly thrown up as an afterthought. It read:

WELCOME TO
AFFLICTION
ARIZONA TERRITORY

A desert tarantula, the same tannish-brown as the grit and rocks, scuttled past the horse. Luke looked at the scurrying arachnid in mild disgust. He was hardly squeamish, but the ghastly things were so big . . . all those legs moving in an undulating rhythm like gears in a cotton gin. This time of year the desert was filled with them.

He had only the vaguest recognition of the town of Affliction. Believing the town had been a Mexican or Spanish settlement first, he wondered what name it had gone by before the miners discovered copper deposits nearby.

The hot breeze shifted slightly. The corroded metal of a weather vane squeaked as it moved from south to west. The new direction of the wind brought the sudden stench of death. The horse smelled it and nervously danced from side to side, whinnying in protest.

"Easy," he said.

The horse settled after a moment and Luke urged him forward. Snorting, the animal walked with its legs stiff. Pulling the Henry repeater from the saddle scabbard, Luke worked the action.

He rode forward with the butt resting on his leg, muzzle in the air. Up ahead he saw the town fountain, another indication the initial charter for the settlement had likely come from the Emperor of Mexico. Wanting to water the horse, he rode toward it.

Something creaked on the scrap-wood porch built in front of a small mercantile store. Luke twisted and lowered the Henry, but then let out a pent-up breath. The bone-dry breeze stirred a rocking chair perched next to an old barrel. It rocked gently in the breeze.

Now that he was closer he saw obvious signs of violence. Here, toward the middle of town, he saw bullet holes pockmarking the adobe plaster and rough wooden planks. Doors hung open where they'd been kicked in. The glass windows in the one or two businesses prosperous enough to have them were all smashed in. Shattered glass glinted in the sunlight. The sunlight scintillated here and there off the brass of spent shell casings.

Luke reined in the horse and dismounted. Tense, he began walking. The jingle of the horse's tack mixed with the soft sigh of the wind and errant creaking of the rocking chair. A crow squawked again. This time the bird's caw was answered by another. He looked up. The buzzards hovered overhead.

Every rooftop, every gaping door or shattered window became a source of potential attack. Letting the horse have its head, he moved to one side of the street to reduce his exposure. His hands gripped the rifle, and his sweat stained the wood dark.

He walked slowly past the storefronts, stopping at the saloon. The smell of gunpowder lingered in the air. The astringent scent irritated his nostrils. He looked through the doorway. Tables were overturned, great gouges were ripped out of the bar and walls from shotgun blasts.

Hearing the buzzing of flies, he squinted, looking closer. On the floor, and splashed across the legs of overturned chairs and upended tables, he saw dark stains. Blood. The flies buzzed around the maroon blemishes, their droning filling the ruined room.

The blood was fresh, but had congealed into a film as it soaked into the wood. From experience Luke guessed it was a day old at the very most.

The whole town? he wondered. *Everyone here slaughtered?*

It didn't seem possible, yet he'd seen many horrors in his long career pursuing outlaws from one end of the West to the other. Certainly the men he tracked were capable of it. He stepped back from the door and saw his horse walk to the fountain and drink. Luke ran his tongue across his own parched and cracked lips. He'd been rationing his water for the last two days and his throat was raw. Sweat stung his eyes as he started walking again.

Beyond the fountain where his horse drank stood the town's church. The building was constructed from white adobe. The church was the center of the community. A sick suspicion drew him there. Stepping out into the sunlight, he'd begun walking toward the building when his horse suddenly screamed.

He spun, bringing the Henry rifle around. His horse, throwing its head wildly as it neighed, collapsed. It lay in the dust, belly heaving, tongue lolling. He didn't hear a gunshot or see some Apache arrow sticking from the animal. Vomit ran out of its mouth and stained the ground. White foam lathered its muzzle.

Crossing quickly to the fountain, he scooped a handful of water and sniffed it. Something was there, but the smell was far from overpowering. He touched a little with the tip of his tongue. Immediately he spat it back out and flung the dregs away.

Poison.

His horse, two days without more than sips of water, had plunged its head into the fountain and gulped huge draughts. In this heat, even with pure water, that was dangerous and could lead to paralyzing cramps. But in that thirsty state the animal might well have ingested gallons of the tainted liquid.

The horse's eyes rolled in agony. Its stomach heaved in and out as its body tried expelling the poison. Anger searing a white hot knot in his chest, Luke drew one of the Remingtons and put a single round through the horse's head.

He was unmounted now unless the stable had a horse tucked away in one of its stalls. Luke strongly doubted that. This was not a good turn of events. He holstered the .44. Some cold-blooded snake had poisoned the public fountain. It didn't get a lot lower than that.

He turned his attention back to the church. He was sure whoever was responsible for the doom that had come to Affliction was long gone, but he still approached the building warily. He heard the flies as he came closer. The breeze had died and the smell of smoke hung thick on the languid desert air heavy with afternoon heat. It almost overpowered the miasma of death. Almost.

The double doors of the church hung limply, scarred by fire. The droning of flies was approaching a cacophony and the death-stink made him gag. He put his bandanna up over his nose and stepped up to the entrance.

What he saw turned his stomach.

He had no idea how many people were in the pile. More than two dozen, less than a hundred, maybe. They were heaped in a mound and the wooden pews had been used as kindling. The sides of the walls and ceiling were black with soot. The adobe construction had turned the building into a sort of Dutch oven and the bodies had melted into each other.

He'd smelled burnt flesh before and in the confined space the familiar sickly-sweet smell overpowered him. Gagging, he stepped back out.

Fighting the urge to vomit, he pulled his bandanna into place over his mouth and nose. Once he'd collected himself, he stepped back inside. He studied the room, ignoring the stench and the deafening drone coming from the clouds of black flies crawling over the charred corpses. It was a horrendous sight.

Blackened facial flesh pulled back from grimacing teeth. Eye sockets peered emptily where the eyeballs had melted. Arms locked in rigor mortis stretched out, forever frozen in time. Clothes and hair had been burned away, ears and noses were shapeless lumps like hardened wax on the sides of a candle. He saw signs of violence. Skulls and rib cages splintered where bullets had smashed into them like clubs. Teeth lay scattered across the floor like dice. Here and there limbs were no longer attached.

In his mind it was easy to reconstruct the scene. The attackers had herded their victims into the place and then poured a continuous fusillade of bullets into the tightly packed crowd. Luke reckoned it must have felt like it had gone on forever. Then the raiders had walked among the dead, busting the pews into kindling and throwing the pieces across the bodies. They'd splashed kerosene around then tossed in a lit match while the wounded screamed for mercy.

He stood for a moment, considering. His mind played over the horrid scene he'd just surveyed.

"There were only the men," he muttered into the silence.

Maybe there could have been a woman's cadaver mixed in there, he couldn't be totally sure in that mess. Yet all the bodies he'd seen had been too large for children and almost certainly too large for a large portion to have been female.

The women and children were missing.

"The Apache pay for slaves," a voice said.

Luke looked up into the massive muzzles of a double-barreled 8-gauge shotgun.

"Don't be stupid," the man holding the shotgun said.

His eyes seemed to beg Luke to do exactly the opposite.

The man stood on a narrow platform at the top of an inexpertly crafted spiral staircase leading to the bell tower. Like the church, the stairs were cramped and spoke of a time, a hundred or two hundred years ago, when Spain ruled the region. The 8-gauge looked like a cannon in the man's hands.

As tall as Luke, he was rattlesnake lean with a hatchet nose and greasy black hair swept straight back from his craggy features. A scar turned one lip up into an ugly sneer, and his cheeks were brutally pockmarked. The reddish-copper of his skin testified to his heritage. He wore the clothes of a Mexican vaquero with a bright, multi-colored serape draped across his narrow torso.

"Melichus," Luke said.

Luke's hands hovered near his waist, inches from the butts of his Remingtons. The bounty hunter knew he was fast. He couldn't have survived this long if he wasn't. But was he faster than a leveled shotgun with the hammers cocked back?

Probably not. Probably there was no *probably* about it.

He eyed the ground out of the corner of his eye. If he were

forced to dodge he'd end up in a pile of greasy burnt corpses. It was an unappetizing thought. So was getting blown in half.

The man grinned, revealing several gold teeth.

"I know who you are, too," he said. "The infamous manhunter Luke Jensen. Your reputation, like mine, is growing. We're actually not so different."

"The devil we aren't."

"We both kill for profit." Melichus's grin grew. "I just make more money at it than you do."

Luke knew he had to keep Melichus talking. He had no pretensions that the Ute half-breed was going to fire. It was only the man's innate sadism that had kept Luke alive thus far. From a position of superiority, Melichus felt safe enough to inflict fear, to mentally torment his potential victim.

If Luke was fast, and lucky, that arrogant cruelty might be enough to save him.

He gestured toward the pile of dead bodies next to him, watching to see if Melichus's eyes followed the motion. The outlaw was too savvy for that. He kept his attention focused on Luke.

"I think you've got me pretty well beat when it comes to murder. Besides"—Luke twisted his foot slightly, surreptitiously grinding it into the floor to find purchase for a spring—"where are all your men?"

"They're taking the women and children to their new lives as slaves to the Apache or the old Mexican dons who run vast ranching empires like feudal lords."

"Then why are you here instead of with them?"

Melichus lost his smile. His eyes glittered, serpent-like. When he spoke, it was in an intense hiss, and the muscles of his jaw clenched and unclenched.

"I like spending time with the dead," he said. "They tell me secrets."

Distracted by the cavernous barrels of the 8-gauge, Luke hadn't at first noticed Melichus's hands. Now he saw they were stained red, glistening with blood that smeared the stock of the shotgun. His canvas trousers were stiff and black with the stuff.

"My mother was Ute," he said. "A *bruja*. You know that word?"

"Spanish for witch," Luke answered.

Calmly, he eyed the barrel of the shotgun. It hadn't been cut down and the muzzle was a full choke. Full choke tightened shot spread, improving the range and increasing accuracy at a distance. In contrast, a sawed-off shotgun exploded shot wide, catching everything in front of it but not much good past the distance of a room's width.

Luke was close to Melichus, well inside the range of mushrooming shot when the 8-gauge fired. It wasn't much, but it was something. He'd have to drop the Henry. This was going to be pistol work.

"She taught me many secrets," the kill-crazed outlaw went on. "How to become a wolf by wearing the skin of my kills. How to fly and become invisible. This is why no one can catch me. Not the white men. Not the Mexican army." He flashed the ugly grin again. "And not you!"

Even as Melichus was shouting, Luke was in motion. Dropping the lever action Henry, he threw himself to the left, pulling the right-hand Remington clear of leather as he did. Searing pain flashed across the right side of his body and peppered his bicep so sharply he barely kept hold of the pistol. The 8-gauge's boom was deafening inside the close confines of the church.

Luke hit the spongy corpses on one shoulder and felt the skin of one seared corpse split apart under his weight. Hot juices soaked his shirt and ashy skin clung in ratty strips as he rolled forward. The Remington came up as Melichus shifted, swinging the long barrels of the shotgun toward Luke.

Luke fired.

Three fast rounds banged out of the handgun, but the angle

was wrong and the shots were rushed. One flew wide, another cracked the banister of the spiral staircase and exploded it into splinters. That bullet ricocheted at the impact, and the shirt at Melichus's right shoulder puffed up, instantly stained with blood. The outlaw swore in shock and stumbled.

The third round slammed home into the shotgun.

Sparks flew and the buttstock came apart in the outlaw's hands. Melichus threw the useless firearm from him and raced for the top of the stairs. Luke rolled, trying to come to his feet in time. His side was on fire, and his own hot blood ran slick down his side.

The stench of burned corpses overwhelmed him in a poisonous miasma, and he stumbled, gagging. Pushing off with his left hand, he choked on bile as his fingers plunged through the skin of a dead body. He fought his way to his knees, firing two more rounds after the fleeing Melichus to lay down cover as he tried to stand.

As he came to his feet, he snatched up the Henry and pointed the muzzle at the top of the stairs. A trapdoor leading into the bell tower stood open. Though the 8-gauge lay on the floor in pieces Luke knew the outlaw had to be well armed besides the shotgun. Going up those stairs after him was suicide.

Keeping his muzzle on the opening, Luke shuffled to the door. He bled freely, and his clothes were smeared and stained with pieces of dead bodies and fire-charred skin. Gore caked the hand he had used to lever himself upright. He heard a muted scuffling and suddenly realized Melichus had no intention of holding the high ground where his field of fire was so limited.

Luke sprinted for the door.

He burst out into the blinding sunlight and spun, sweeping the Henry toward the roof. Melichus didn't appear, but Luke heard boots shuffling on the red tiles. Running wide around the side of the church, Luke broke out into the desert from the border of buildings enclosing the town square. He ran.

A picket fence of worn wooden slats stuck up in spears from the hard soil. He hurdled the fence and landed inside the town's graveyard. Wooden crosses ran in uneven rows toward where a small wind-worn statue of the Blessed Virgin Mary stood. The ground thudded with his footsteps as he raced toward the back of the church. He caught a flash of motion and saw Melichus leaping from the roof.

He fired, the round kicking a chunk out of the adobe wall. Melichus, stumbling in surprise, lurched around the corner. Panting in the unforgiving heat, Luke vaulted the cemetery fence on the other side of the graveyard.

A snarl of pain ripped from him as cactus stabbed at his leg when he landed. Suddenly Melichus appeared around the far corner and fired a heavy .44-caliber revolver. Working the lever-action Henry from the hip, Luke went to a knee and cranked off three rounds, driving the outlaw back behind the church.

A covey of sage hens exploded off the ground in a flurry of wings and terrified cooings. Instinctively Luke spun toward them and leveled his gun. They fled past his head, wings pumping. He spun back toward the church, sure that Melichus would use the distraction to attack.

He threw himself to the ground, expecting a barrage of fire to erupt. The tense moment stretched, drawing Luke's nerves to a painful tautness.

His ears still rang from the gunfire inside the church, and he was acutely aware of the sun beating down on him. Sweat ran freely and pooled in the small of his back. Blood seeped from his wounds into the sandy earth beneath him. As his panting slowed, the smell of raw desert sage filled his nostrils. Stalks of yellow cheatgrass rippled stiffly in the hot breeze.

Staying low, he scooted sideways, trying to see past the corner of the building without exposing himself. It was an impossible task and his stomach twisted with anticipation as he hurriedly cleared his line of fire.

He didn't see Melichus.

Using the church as cover, he raced forward and took a position at the corner of the building. The sun was a blinding glare in his right eye. Quickly, he ducked around the corner. He caught a flash of movement down the street as Melichus disappeared between two buildings.

Dripping in his own sweat and blood, Luke ran forward. He crossed the street in a dead sprint and threw himself up against the side of a building to stop his momentum. Panting, he risked a look.

A bullet whined by, blasting splinters from the structure inches from his face. He jerked his head back and ran to the other side of the building. A narrow passage cut between that and the next buildings. Henry rifle up and ready, he made his way down the alley.

Two horses had been left behind the structure, presumably to eliminate the temptation of the poisoned fountain on the brutally hot day. One was loaded down with burlap sacks of what Luke presumed was loot. Melichus was in the saddle of the other.

He reached for the reins of the packhorse where they were tied to a fence post and fired the .44 with his other hand. The bullets whipped past Luke to either side of his head. Leveling the Henry, he fired and saw Melichus jerk as blood spurted from his shoulder.

Snarling, the outlaw whirled the horse and took off, riding low in the saddle and leaving the packhorse behind. Luke fired and missed as the outlaw cut behind a shed. Cursing, Luke ran toward the remaining horse. The animal's back was loaded with slings and sacks and saddlebags. The looted wealth of Affliction, Arizona, was stuffed inside them, Luke realized.

He wasn't interested in wealth.

The desire to deliver vengeance burned inside him hot as the desert sun. Pulling the sheath knife from his belt, Luke hurriedly cut the belly strap running under the horse. Everything fell to the ground and Luke jerked the reins free. He wished he had time to take the saddle or retrieve the one from his own dead horse, but he didn't.

Ride now, ride hard. The thought drove him.

His world had narrowed to a single focus, killing Melichus. He no longer noticed the heat, or the wound in his side, or the blood soaking his clothes. This wasn't about the bounty, though that was how he made his living. This was about anger and hate and justice.

Images of the burned corpses flashed through his mind. The sound of his horse neighing in agony as the poison churned through his guts like razor blades. Luke seethed with fury.

The packhorse tried shying away from an unfamiliar rider, but Luke wasn't having it. Gripping the reins tight, he swung up onto the horse's bare back.

He rode hard around the shed where Melichus had disappeared, and as he emerged once more into the main street, he saw the priest.

The man's robes were shredded tatters from bullwhip lashes, but there was no mistaking the cassock for anything else.

The man was tied facedown in the dirt, arms and legs cruelly bound by rawhide thongs to deeply driven wooden stakes. The bonds cut deep into his flesh, and his hands and feet were ghastly, swollen and black. The friar's back was a flayed, bloody mess, coated with hordes of crawling flies.

Luke muttered a shocked obscenity.

The brutality stopped him cold in his tracks.

The friar heard him speak, and lifted his head enough to turn his face toward the sound of Luke's voice. Luke recoiled. The man's face was covered with red stinging ants. They scurried across his features in a frenzy. His eyes were clouded with them and they scurried in and out of his nose and his mouth.

"*Mátame,*" he whispered in a voice so hoarse the words were almost unintelligible. "*Mátame,*" he whispered again.

Luke was hardly a master of the Spanish language, but he knew quite a few words and phrases the way anyone who spent any time along the border would pick them up. He understood what the friar was saying, what the friar was begging for.

"*Kill me.*"

The man struggled to speak again but could manage only a gargled moan.

Luke looked toward the desert where he knew Melichus was fleeing, even now. He swore in frustration and dismounted. Moving quickly to the man's side, he used his knife to cut him free and remove the cruelly twisted bonds.

Working furiously, Luke put his hands under the friar's armpits and hauled him bodily away from the madly swarming ants. Steeling himself, Luke rolled the groaning man over and saw that the priest's captors had smeared his face with syrup or molasses to attract the insects. He noticed the line of ants trailing off into the brush.

Hurriedly, Luke began wiping them from the man's face, digging them out of his eyes and nose, slapping them clear of his cheeks and hair. As the flesh on the man's face was revealed it showed lumpy and red from the thousands of bites, swollen to the point of gruesome distortion.

Hurrying back to the pile of goods he had cut off the second horse, Luke found the water skin he'd noticed. He snatched it up, went back to the friar, and began rinsing the rest of the stinging ants from him. The man had lain helpless so long that he'd soiled himself and he stank horribly.

Luke didn't know if he could save the Mexican priest, but he had to try. Melichus would have to wait.

CHAPTER 17

There was an adobe house nearby, and Luke took the padre there to get him out of the sun. The place had been ransacked and looted, but the raiders hadn't spent much time in such an obviously impoverished home. A rope bed with a straw mattress remained, and Luke got the priest onto it.

The man was delirious from agony and exposure and Luke barely understood half the things he said. It sounded mostly like he was praying and wondering where the *chiquitos* were. Beyond that, Luke had little way of knowing. He knew the man had to be cleaned and his wounds tended to.

Most of all, if he were to live, he'd need water.

Luke searched the town, taking time to bring Melichus's horse to the corral where the raiders had overlooked the water in the trough. He tasted it, and beyond being brackish, he detected nothing wrong with it. He found no medical supplies. Whatever had been there had been taken, but he found enough clean linen and clothes to make bandages from.

By being persistent and methodical, he was actually able to acquire a fair amount of potable water that had been overlooked in the buildings. Luke remained torn. Melichus had captives and their fate was assuredly bad, yet the friar was on the verge of dying without help, and the man was right in front of him.

But every moment he delayed played on his nerves, winding him tighter and tighter until he thought he might explode from the tension. He wondered why no one from some outlying homestead or ranch had come into town. But he realized that in a community this small it could be days, possibly weeks before outside people came through.

During this time the priest remained unconscious, breathing shallowly in a ragged and labored rhythm. The only time he gave any sign of life was when Luke used whiskey to disinfect the open, oozing wounds on his back where the whip had flailed him. Despite that pain, he did not regain consciousness, only shifted slightly and moaned.

After cleaning the man's wounds and bandaging him, Luke took a look at his own injuries. Buckshot had peppered his side and right bicep. He shuddered as he thought about how close the charge must have come. The bulk of it had passed between his body and arm as he leapt away.

In a career full of close calls, he'd just had another, he realized.

He tended to his own injuries as best he could and felt reasonably confident that he would avoid any infection. He gritted his teeth as he poured whiskey over the gunshot wounds. The pain was agonizing enough that he began fearing for the friar even more because of the way the man barely stirred when Luke had done the same to him.

Leaving the priest to sleep, he went to check on the horse. After giving it some grain from the bin in the stable, he took his saddle and bedroll from his dead mount and carried it back to the building.

The sun was sliding down in a bloody red disc behind him as he went in, casting a long shadow before him. The air hadn't yet begun to cool off, and he was still sweating freely. He'd begun talking to the tortured man even though the friar still couldn't respond, but he'd heard speaking to them was good for unconscious patients.

"Hey, padre," he said. "Sun's going down, it should be getting cooler soon."

He didn't expect an answer, but suddenly he noticed how quiet the man lying on the bed had become. There was an unnatural stillness to his body.

"No," Luke said, his voice dull.

He hurried to the priest's side and checked for signs of life. "No, no, no!"

The man was dead.

He'd let Melichus gain half a day's ride with no chance to follow him now until morning. He'd given the murderous raider almost a full day and the padre was dead anyway.

Stomach clenching with frustration, Luke pulled the blanket over the man's face and went to see if there was any whiskey left. As he walked back toward the saloon, he scanned the desert. The horizon was lit up as the last bit of the sun slipped away.

He would get Melichus. What had started out as an impersonal business matter now felt like a steaming boiler inside him, driving him toward their confrontation. Come what may, he'd face the man. The Pinkertons were going to be out of luck on this bounty, he decided with cold certainty.

"I swear it," Luke told the empty desert.

CHAPTER 18

The ground was baked hard as stone. It would have taken more time than he had to spare to bury the priest. So, the next morning, he tucked an old Bible he found into the man's hands and left him covered by the blanket, an anonymous body in an empty house in an abandoned town.

It was the best he could do.

He was on the trail as soon as the sun was high enough. At dawn and twilight the sun cast long shadows over impressions on the ground, bringing them into sharper relief. He cut Melichus's tracks easily enough, and after not much riding they merged with what must have been the trail of his gang and their captives.

Luke was not an expert tracker, though he possessed solid hunting skills. Unlike some of the Indian scouts he'd seen, he doubted he could track a deer across shale. But following a gang of outlaws loaded down with stolen loot and captives hardly proved difficult. He got on their trail early and kept on it.

It wasn't long before he realized they were heading toward the southern range of the Mule Mountains, undoubtedly to meet up with Apaches. A few hours later he came upon their campsite, the extinguished fire still holding some heat.

They'd built a fire. That meant they were feeling comfortable, Luke figured.

What he didn't know was how close a natural water source might be. Men like Melichus and those he rode with had little compunction about riding a horse to death. Despite their value, horses were considered an expendable resource. They would kill one mount, take one from their remuda of stolen horses, and ride it to death as well if it gave them a lead on any pursuing posse.

The only thing he had going for him in this chase was the captives. The gang simply couldn't move as quickly pushing women and children along.

The Sonoran Desert lifted up out of the valley, and he saw Chihuahua Hill rising out of the badland like a fist. He entered a maze of chaparral and rode through as the plants grew larger until the bushes were high as houses and their sage perfume hung rank in his nose. He used the distant peak of Mount Ballard as a rough guide and pushed carefully through.

He found plenty of signs in the powder-soft dust between the brush and, after a little while, a deer trail cut his path and he saw that the raiders had taken it. Luke rode the narrow trail at a slow pace. He felt closer now than he had before, though it was only a feeling.

He paused and pulled his canteen free. The water was unpleasantly warm as he drank sparingly, but it was enough to knock the dust from his throat. He lifted his hat and rubbed one arm across his forehead, eyes searching the brush. The chaparral pushed in on the sides of the trail and clawed at him. Luke made a mental note to check himself thoroughly for ticks when he finally stopped.

He followed the trail as the foothills grew steeper. Now he was in a land of deep coulees and shale rock ledges. Wiry sagebrush clung to cracks in the stone. Above him a hunting hawk circled. Craning back his head, Luke squinted into the sun. He was near the top of a mesa, and the last little bit of path was more goat trail than anything else.

A nearly sheer drop plunged away to one side, while to the other a jagged cliff face rose in a wall. It was as tactically untenable a position as one could find in these hills, Luke knew. He needed to push through quickly.

The horse jerked beneath him and in the medium distance a rifle cracked.

His mount went to its knees and Luke threw himself from the saddle. Hitting the ground awkwardly, he rolled into a sprawling prone position. The spike-like needles of a beaver tail cactus patch speared into him and he cried out in surprise. The horse went over and lay still, blood gushing from its neck.

Suddenly the ground beneath him gave way in a waterfall of gravel.

He shouted in surprise as he began sliding down the hill. His foot caught on a root, and his momentum jerked him over his own legs so that he was sliding headfirst. His hands scratched for purchase but could find none.

The sky spun above his head and abruptly there was no ground beneath him. Arms windmilling, he fell through the air. Striking the ground he bounced hard and began rolling. He lunged for a bush as he catapulted past but missed it.

Again there was the sensation of nothingness followed by the bone jarring impact of landing after a fall. He felt as battered as a losing boxer. He managed to get to his back and was able to grab hold of a bush just as he rushed toward another lip.

Gasping, he held on tight.

Flat on his belly, Luke looked wildly around. He needed to find cover, but he now had little idea of where he was in relation to Melichus. The branch broke and came away in his hand. He began slipping and he fought to stop his slide but could find no purchase.

He shot over the edge of the ridge like water flowing out of a culvert. Arms and legs flailing he plunged downward. Landing with a bone jarring *thud,* he gasped as the air was driven from his body. Wheezing, he fought to breathe, dust clogging his nose. His body ached but was too numb for him to tell if he'd broken anything.

He struggled onto his knees, then fought to stand. Chest heaving with the strain of breathing, he looked around. He'd fallen a long way, he realized. In short enough bounces that he wasn't dead but . . .

The body of his horse came thundering down the side of the mesa.

Throwing himself against the rock wall, Luke barely missed being struck by the thousand-pound animal body. The horse hit the ledge and bashed through it to continue rolling down the precipitously steep slope.

The sandstone cracked and then crumbled directly under Luke's feet.

He scratched at the rock in front of him but couldn't grip anything as the ground gave way fully and he fell again. He plunged downward. Twice he slammed into rocky protrusions that bounced him around. The skin along his arms and body was scraped clean by the jagged gravel and his wounds began bleeding again.

He was thrown backward as he struck the ground, and he came up against the carcass of the horse. His body screamed from the abuse he had taken, and dimly he realized he'd lost a boot somewhere along the way. Head to toe he felt as if a crew of burly miners had taken axe handles to him.

The sun blinded him, and he slowly put a hand up to fight off the glare. He thought that despite the pain he would be able to move. Slowly, he rolled over.

Dirt kicked up near him, followed almost instantly by a rifle report. Luke threw himself sideways and scrambled behind the body of his horse for cover. Two more rounds struck the dead animal, and the shots echoed out over the foothills. Instinctively, Luke drew one of his Remingtons, both of which had somehow made it through the mad tumble without falling out of the holsters.

Another shot hammered through the stillness and Luke cursed as he saw the round strike his canteen where its strap had wrapped the horn of his saddle. The container jumped three feet into the air and began bleeding his water. Just looking at the precious liquid draining into the dust made him thirsty.

"Bounty hunter!" Melichus shouted.

The outlaw's voice echoed, seeming to come from every direction at once, the sound so disembodied it could have come from the desert itself. The sun beat down hard against Luke's back.

"Bounty hunter, you have come here to die!"

"In a pig's eye," Luke muttered.

He didn't sound entirely confident to his own ears.

He needed to worry about Melichus's men circling in on him. He had to assume the outlaw wasn't alone. Just below him a line of gravel lay spread out in an arroyo where rain runoff had carved a channel in the earth. If he could make that he might be able to belly crawl out of the area and regroup.

He looked for his rifle but the Henry was gone. He cursed. Blood from some scalp laceration dribbled into his eye, blinding him. He shoved dust against the side of his head to get it to clot. He couldn't wait. He had to seize this chance to escape.

His body was stiffening from the multiple brutal impacts. If he didn't act soon, it was unlikely he'd be able to move quickly enough to survive anyway. Gritting his teeth, he threw himself backward and began rolling.

The ground thudded with the impact of heavy-caliber

rounds, and the rifle reports boomed down the mountainside. Dirt shot up in spumes like geysers, and he rolled off the lip of the coulee. Grunting, he fell two feet and landed among the stones.

Then he began crawling.

CHAPTER 19

Luke knew he'd escaped mostly because the outlaws hadn't pursued him that hard. They had captives and horses to move south of the border and didn't want to waste time on one man afoot in the Sulphur Springs Valley. Let the desert kill him. That was what they'd think.

Forcing himself to his feet, he struggled forward. He'd have preferred to hole up during the heat of the day and travel at night, but there was no cover to be found. If he were going to bake in the sun, he might as well be walking toward help if he could find it.

Once he used a stick to rip open a barrel cactus and drink what was inside. It was unappetizing, but wet. Wet was good enough. Other than that lone drink, he went thirsty.

He was exhausted by the time the sun slid down beyond the horizon, but without means to make a fire he knew he'd only shiver in the frigid chill of night as the cloudless sky sucked all the heat away from the desert floor. He continued walking.

In the night coyotes followed at a distance, waiting for him to drop. Their yips and barks floated to him from out of the darkness. During the day buzzards circled overhead. His lips dried and split open and bled then dried again. He walked with legs stiff and heavy as lead.

He had the pistols, but he realized he was more hurt than he'd thought because with his head throbbing and fuzzy he couldn't hit the few jackrabbits he saw. Finally he killed a rattlesnake and ate it raw, hungrily lapping at its blood.

He slept where he lay but continued crawling in the morning.

Not long after the sun came up, Luke rested. He was growing weak again. Dehydrated, he was starting to lose focus. Coming out of a sort of exhaustion stupor, he realized he didn't know how long he'd been crawling completely lost in his own thoughts.

It was a dangerous oversight.

He was surrounded by thick growths of crepe myrtle and yarrow. Lean desert bees hovered and darted above the plants, their buzzing a soft drone in the forge-hot air. His throat was tight with thirst, and his shirt was wet with sweat as much as blood, so that the soaked cloth stuck to his prickly flesh.

He heard footsteps on gravel.

He turned his head slowly in the direction of the sound and heard several more footfalls. His hand began sliding downward toward the butt of one of his Remingtons. He settled his palm on the worn grip just as he heard a second pair of footsteps join the first.

"See the varmint?" a rough male voice asked.

"He was dragging himself clearly enough," the first man answered. "But then he crossed a patch of shale. I'll cut the trace again soon enough."

"He was bleeding like a stuck pig. He ought to be easy enough to find."

Luke silently cursed.

The voices were coming from only a few yards away. He realized that to see him, the hunters would be looking into the sun, and it was only that glare that had kept him undiscovered, nestled under the desert plants. He needed to strike fast because his luck couldn't hold for very much longer.

"Here," the second voice called out. "I found more blood."

"Where?" the first voice demanded.

The footsteps began approaching the place where Luke was concealed. Through the interlocking bristles and branches of the yarrow and crepe myrtle plants he saw two men appear. Their faces were furrowed in concentration as they intently studied the ground.

Both were white men. One wore a shapeless Confederate cavalry hat and the other a rain-warped Stetson. The Johnny Reb had a tangle of white, puckered scar tissue on one cheek that Luke guessed came from taking a 4-shot pepperbox derringer blast to the face. The man wearing the Stetson had a gigantic handlebar mustache that dropped down past his jaw.

Both men carried lever-action carbines in their hands.

Stetson's eyes scanned the ground, following a line of blood splatter like a trail of crumbs. His eyes swept up and met Luke's through the branches of the yarrow. The man's mouth dropped open in surprise.

The Remington boomed in Luke's hand. Once. Twice.

The slugs caught the man on the left side of his body and jerked him backward so that he stumbled over his own feet and went down heavily. Luke exploded up off the ground, battered body screaming in protest at the sudden motion.

The Confederate veteran rammed the butt of his weapon into his hip and spun toward Luke. On one knee, Luke's hand shot across his body and he began fanning the Remington's hammer. The .44 cracked three times, the barrel jumping wildly.

Fanning the hammer was extremely inaccurate, but the scar-faced man was within arm's reach as Luke began firing, and all three rounds struck him in the gut and chest. The man cried out under the repeated impacts and blood halos misted out behind him as one or more of the rounds went through him. His knees buckled and he dropped.

Luke shot him again, emptying the cylinder, then holstered

the smoking pistol and drew his second Remington. The echo of the gunfire was still spinning across the desert like thunderclaps. The sound would carry for miles, Luke knew.

Shifting left, then right, he checked for further outlaws but found none.

No matter, the others in Melichus's band would hear the shots and be alerted. If the men didn't return in a timely fashion, someone might be sent to check on them.

On the other hand, Melichus might have sent the two back to track him but then used the opportunity to drive the captives deeper into Apache territory.

Luke holstered his pistol and reloaded the empty one before claiming the dead men's rifles and ammo. He took a waterskin off one and drank deeply. Moving as quickly as he dared, he began backtracking the two dead outlaws.

After half an hour he found where they'd hobbled their horses. The mounts had more water, bedrolls, and some beans and hardtack. It would be enough to get him away.

He closed his eyes for a moment in relief when he saw the animals. In his line of work, he had long since accepted the idea that he'd probably die violently. But crossing the divide while trading shots with outlaws was entirely different than dying by slow inches from thirst and exposure in this desert hell. That would have been a hard fate to swallow.

Luke rode through the day, moving slowly to spare the animals. He checked his backtrail often but detected no pursuit.

The next morning he came across the railroad tracks. He settled in to wait. The Great Southwestern Railroad ran frequently, carting copper out and eager would-be miners in. A train would be along shortly, by tomorrow at the latest.

He figured he could wait that long.

CHAPTER 20

As the name indicated, Copper Butte, Arizona, was riding a copper strike. Unlike Affliction, however, the boom hadn't run out yet. Also unlike Affliction, the boom didn't seem to be even close to dying out. Luke stepped off the train and walked into a busy main street filled with wagons hauling freight and dry goods back and forth.

Droppings from the armies of horses and mules in the town lay so thick on the street it was dangerous to walk without keeping a sharp eye out. Men slept off drunks in the alleyways between buildings. Piano and accordion music spilled out the doorways of the too-numerous-to-count saloons. Dogs barked loudly at passersby until they were kicked to silence.

Men went about heavily armed, mostly unwashed, and rarely sober. Whores hung from windows, calling down to any man or boy walking by. Outside of those dancehalls and brothels, women were very scarce on the ground.

Luke walked into the controlled chaos, hunting down the town marshal or county sheriff's office. He found it sandwiched between an assayer's office and a dry goods mercantile. Stepping up onto the wooden sidewalk in front of the building, he went in to check who was available.

He entered a plain room with a desk to one side and a line of cells at the back. Next to a chair, an unlit pot-bellied stove stood across from the desk. On one wall hung a gun rack filled with various rifles, on the other an area reserved for wanted posters.

Despite the tumult and the frenzied celebrations outside, it was still fairly early in the morning. Coupled with the higher elevation, the temperature was comfortable for the moment. After the hardpan and the hellish heat of Affliction, Luke appreciated being able to enter a building without feeling like he was stepping into an oven.

Normally Luke would have been keenly interested in those wanted posters. They were his bread and butter. Not this time.

A tall thin man sat lounging behind the desk. He wore a beard, and a sheriff's badge was pinned to his chest. His boots were up on his desk, and he studiously cleaned his nails with a paring knife as Malcolm Talbot pleaded with him about something. At Luke's entrance the Englishman looked up, then stopped in mid-sentence.

"Luke!"

The sincerity of relief in the man's voice surprised Luke. He nodded at Talbot.

"You made it here all right, I see," Luke said.

"This the fellow you were so worried about?" the sheriff asked.

Talbot beamed. "It is!" He frowned slightly as he took Luke in. "Though he's perhaps a tad worse for wear."

Luke lifted a corner of his mouth in a small, rueful smile of acknowledgment. "Yeah, I got rode hard and put away wet," he admitted. He turned to the lawman. "Sheriff, you've got a slaughter up Affliction way. I've been in town. There's nothing left but dead men and animals. I figure Melichus took twenty, twenty-five captives. Women and children. Ran them off toward the Mule Mountains."

"You know where Melichus is?" Talbot's eyes shone bright with interest.

"I know where he was," Luke said. "And he's moving with an army of owlhoots and killers all across Arizona. He's got to be stopped."

"There!" Talbot announced, voice ringing with vindication. "Now will you give me the Indian?"

Luke blinked in surprise at Talbot's sudden swerve in topic. He looked at the sheriff, but the man studiously cleaned his nails and refused to look up.

"If what this hombre says is true," the sheriff drawled, "then this isn't a matter for a posse. This is a matter for the army. The army is relocating the Jicarillas up to Fort Defiance along the New Mexico line. The red varmints is being a mite uncooperative. I've already tried telegraphin' for assistance and been turned down." He looked up from his knife. "Twice."

Talbot inhaled sharply, visibly frustrated but containing himself. "So my cohort is the last, best option. But in order to be our most effective we need a tracker. Apparently this Kiowa boy you have, Walks-the-Horizon, is the best."

"You going to track an Indian, an Indian is usually best," the sheriff agreed. "But this one here," he gestured with the knife at Luke, "already told you where that rascal Melichus is. Tracking a platoon of wild injuns and bad Mexicans hauling a bunch of captives shouldn't be too hard."

"You don't seem very concerned about those captives," Luke said.

He felt himself growing annoyed with the man. Law enforcement on the frontier was always a mixed bag. Of late, he'd been dealing with too many ornery lawmen, it felt like.

"It's the army's job to fight bad Injuns," the man answered. "I ain't goin' off into no durn Mule Mountains against a platoon or better of hardcases with the sort of posse I can muster from around here. I feel for those captives, I surely do, but getting myself and fifteen men killed riding into Apache territory ain't the answer."

"No," Talbot agreed. "It isn't. We are. But in order for us to do our job, we need this Charlie Walks-the-Horizon."

The sheriff sighed. Clearly put upon.

"I can't," he said. "Charlie struck a white man. He has to sit in jail until the circuit judge comes. I let an Indian out after having struck a white man, I might as well start lettin' Mexicans get away with it. The town'll have my job in two seconds, and the next fella to wear this badge won't say boo when the lynch mob shows up."

Luke opened his mouth to offer an argument, then closed it again. He hadn't come here to hire a tracker. He'd come here to tell the authorities about Affliction. That was done. Now he needed a meal, a bath, and to get a good night's sleep and reoutfit. Then he'd see after Melichus himself.

To his surprise, however, Talbot also didn't argue. He merely straightened his coat and nodded.

"I understand your position, Sheriff. You do seem to be in a tight spot. I hope you'll have a good day." Turning to Luke, Talbot addressed him. "Luke, I think we're most likely sharing a hotel, so why don't you let me buy you a drink?"

Luke nodded, sensing the Englishman held some ulterior motive. He nodded to the lawman.

"Sheriff," he said, with a lot more respect in his tone than he actually felt.

CHAPTER 21

Luke and Talbot stepped out into the growing bustle of commerce and activity in the street. Talbot lit a pipe as they walked the few short blocks to the hotel, which was less than a year old and beautifully built. Like the rest of the town, it was swarming with activity.

On the porch in front of the establishment, a busty blonde in a tight red satin dress, straw bonnet with brilliant scarlet sash, holding a parasol watched as a large black man hauled in a steamer trunk and several leather suitcases from a buck-board. Heavily lipsticked and rouged, she twirled her parasol and openly sized up Luke.

"Ma'am," he nodded.

"You're a tall one." She smiled.

"Hands off, Daphne," a familiar female voice snapped.

Luke barely managed to conceal his surprise as a strong feminine arm slipped around his and pulled him close so that his triceps was nestled firmly against the pleasant swell of a not inconsiderable breast. Breathing in, he smelled jasmine.

"Vina," he said in surprise.

"Vina," the blonde said. She spoke the name like she'd just bitten into a lemon.

Luke felt such a strong sensation of dejá vu at the sight of

Vina Delacroix that he began to worry the hotel might end up in flames around him.

"Luke Jensen and I have some very important business to discuss," Delacroix purred. "I can't have him distracted by an easy roll in the hay with a second-rate soiled dove."

The other woman spat like a cat, eyes narrowed, words slipping out in an angry hiss. "I wouldn't go thinking you're so high and mighty. I was in El Paso when you—"

Delacroix let go of Luke's arm and leapt forward. Luke stumbled back in amazement. The female bounty hunter grabbed the other woman by her bright yellow tresses and clawed at her face. Daphne responded with wild swinging slaps as they struggled.

"Ladies, please!" Talbot implored.

Ducking under her flailing arms, Luke caught hold of Delacroix around her waist and plucked her up off the ground as Talbot clumsily attempted to insert himself in front of the other furious woman. Delacroix twisted and struggled in Luke's arms, her body lithe and vigorous against his. The motions brought vivid memories of a different sort of exertions to his mind.

"Blast it, Vina!" he shouted. "Stop this before we all end up in the hoosegow!"

"I will not be disrespected by a whore of *her* caliber!" Delacroix snapped as she writhed in Luke's grip.

What in the world does that even mean? he wondered as they wrestled.

"*My* caliber? *My* caliber!" the other woman shrieked.

"Luke, take her upstairs!" Talbot pleaded as he struggled to stay in front of the furious woman and block her path to Delacroix.

Shouldering the redhead like a sack of potatoes—an extremely soft and shapely sack of potatoes, he corrected—Luke carried Delacroix through the open doors, across the lobby, and began climbing the stairs. He reached the landing as, below him, Talbot managed to get inside and close the door in the angry blonde's face.

"Will you calm down before I have to spank you?" Luke demanded.

"Put her down, now."

O'Toole spoke the words with a definite edge to them. The Irishman's tone held the dark promise of violence. Dumping Delacroix unceremoniously onto her feet, Luke turned to face the other man. He held up his hands, showing they were now empty of the madame turned bounty hunter.

"Get that burr out from under your saddle, O'Toole," he said. "I'm all finished doing your job."

"You know, Jensen," O'Toole seethed, "I've had just about enough of your smart mouth, you son of a—"

Argus Collins leaned against one wall watching the unfolding events like a spectator at a sporting event. He shook his head in bemused disbelief.

Like two bulls in a field, the men came toward each other. Delacroix, suddenly the voice of reason, threw herself between them, shoving hard against each man's chest in an effort to hold them back.

"Stop it, you pig-headed mules!" she shouted.

"I'm sending for the sheriff!" the desk clerk shouted from the bottom of the stairs.

"Talbot!" Delacroix shouted again.

O'Toole scowled at Luke, not quite willing to physically move his partner-in-crime out of the way. Seeing the man's restraint, minuscule as it was, helped Luke accustom himself to the reality of the situation.

He muttered to himself more than to anyone else, "I don't know what in tarnation you're even doing here."

Hair still wild from her own scuffle, Delacroix beamed up at him.

"Getting rich, Luke. Getting rich."

CHAPTER 22

"I'm leaving," Luke muttered. "There has to be another hotel in this town, and I'm finding it."

"Luke, wait!" Delacroix protested.

"Good riddance," O'Toole said.

Pretty sure he knows what happened between me and Vina, Luke thought.

All the better reason to get as far from the unstable pair as possible. Mixing business and pleasure was always ill-advised in his experience, and he doubted any bounty was worth this much potential trouble.

As he went down the stairs, he saw Malcolm Talbot calming the desk clerk using a combination of soothing words and a gold double eagle. The twin-pronged tactic appeared to work. With his bewildered and annoyed manager taking a last frowning look up the stairs, the man retreated to the safety of his desk.

"Mr. Jensen," Talbot said as he turned toward Luke.

"Look, Talbot." Luke held up his hand. "I *know* those two. I don't want anything to do with a bounty involving them. They're trigger-happy loose cannons who attract trouble and turn normal plans into fiery explosions."

"We are a touch boisterous, it's true," Delacroix said, and smirked from the top of the stairs.

"He can't keep up and so he's jealous," O'Toole said. Standing next to Delacroix, he folded his arms across his wide chest and glared down at Luke.

"Talbot," Collins said as he came up beside the other two, "how is this going to work if our group ends up killing each other before we even leave town?"

Talbot took Luke by the arm and leaned in close. He had an air of desperation about him that surprised Luke. Of course, if anyone could take an unflappable Englishman and reduce him to nervous uncertainty, it was Delacroix and O'Toole, Luke realized.

He let the man speak.

"The bounty on Melichus is considerable," Talbot said quietly. "But that's not why we're after him. Or not the *only* reason why, anyway. I'm telling you that outlaw is sitting on the location of enough gold to make us all fabulously wealthy, ten times over, and he doesn't even know it. Luke, it's more money than you could make in a lifetime of bounty hunting."

Luke frowned. "That's a lot of money," he allowed.

"Yes, it is," Talbot agreed. "And look, you're going after that vicious animal anyway, aren't you? I saw your face when you told the sheriff about what had occurred in Affliction. You're not letting Melichus get away with what he's done."

That's true enough, Luke admitted to himself.

"One drink," Talbot said. "You might as well reject our offer in full command of the facts."

"One drink," Luke agreed.

"I knew you couldn't stay away," Delacroix said, laughing.

"Great," O'Toole said. "Just wonderful."

He didn't sound like he meant it.

Talbot paid the hotel clerk to send a runner to the telegraph office with a message for his bosses back in Chicago. After

that, he collected a bottle of top-shelf whiskey, and the group
of bounty hunters convened in his suite. Putting some distance between themselves in chairs scattered around the
suite's sitting room, they eyed each other warily. Delacroix
smoked a cheroot and O'Toole a cigar as Talbot poured generous portions of the whiskey into glasses.

Luke savored the whiskey and studied the others. O'Toole
glowered. Delacroix, smirking, arched an eyebrow at him.
Collins kept sliding his gaze between Luke and O'Toole. He
seemed genuinely curious to see how this was going to
unfold. Talbot studiously packed his pipe and then struck a
match.

Luke sighed. In negotiations it was often said that whoever
spoke first lost. However, he wasn't even sure he wanted to
win in the first place and didn't feel like playing games.

"Look," he said, "you want to go up against a group the
size of the one Melichus has, you've got two ways to go
about it. Either overwhelming force, or sly, like you're hunting bear. From what I've seen, you don't have enough guns
to take him head on, and you're too many to whittle his numbers down quiet-like."

"Yeah, well." O'Toole sneered. "It ain't just about some
murdering skunk of an owlhoot is it?"

"This is about the map," Luke said.

O'Toole didn't answer. His jaw settled into a hard, clenched
line. He obviously didn't approve of Luke knowing so much.
Delacroix didn't seem to share his reticence as she immediately answered.

"You've seen Melichus," she said.

It wasn't really a question, but Luke nodded, curious as to
where this was going.

"Did you see his horse? Did you see the saddle he used?"

Luke paused for a moment, reflecting on the battle in
Affliction. He thought about Melichus racing into the desert.

He remembered the hard yellow sunlight reflecting off the silver conchas.

"Sure," he said. "It was a Mexican saddle. Worth sixty dollars if it was worth two bits. Silver conchas, fringe, inlaid, a real showpiece. Obviously plunder."

Talbot leaned forward, eyes bright with eagerness. He stabbed the stem of his smoldering pipe toward Luke, emphasizing his words with hard little jabs.

"I knew it! That saddle did, indeed, cost sixty dollars, twice as much as a normal one. It was commissioned from a Mexican leatherworker in Tombstone by one Timothy Lejeune. That saddle is the key to all of this."

Sipping his whiskey, Luke leaned back.

Through the window, he heard the sounds of the bustling town. Men shouting, the clatter of wagons going down the street, doors opening and closing, the distant music of a piano in some saloon, and the ringing of a hammer on an anvil. Normal, regular life was unfolding out there. It was a life built on personal grit and hard work, a life he well understood.

Maybe he wasn't one to become a farmer or try his hand at ranching. He preferred his nomadic existence and the challenges of a frontier life, but he respected the people who were building this country. He liked to think he was doing his part as a defender of those people, a guardian. Sure, he worked for money, lawmen worked for money, a man had to eat . . . but he chose a life dedicated to running down the gun-wolves who only took and never gave, who only destroyed and never built.

He wasn't sure where treasure hunting fit into all of that. Yet, he could tell by the palpably rising excitement in the room that this wasn't some old wives' tale. Whether or not there was gold at the end of this rainbow, he didn't know. What he did know was that the people sitting in front of him *believed* there was.

He sighed, made his decision, and asked the question.

"Explain what's so important about this saddle? If it's got a map carved into it, how come Melichus hasn't snatched up the gold already?"

Delacroix clapped her hands together and made a small sound of satisfied mirth. This brought to mind the other sounds she made when satisfied. Luke firmly pushed *that* distraction out of his head. He looked at Talbot, scrutinizing the man.

"Hand tooled into that saddle, starting at the gullet and spreading across the flap panel, is a map. Lejeune had it put there."

"Ignoring the questionable logic behind that," Luke said, "where exactly does this map supposedly lead?"

"When Juárez was defeated by Díaz, and Napoleon the Third began pulling his military and colonial infrastructure out of Mexico, they also made sure to collect as much wealth as possible," Talbot explained.

Luke nodded. He had a cursory understanding of Mexican politics, same as any American who earned a living on or near the border. Juárez was left running the government of Mexico when the US used diplomatic pressure to ensure the French pulled out from the country in 1867. Juárez had sought to solidify executive power and had proven very unpopular with the working classes. Diaz seized control in '77. However, the French withdrawal had been neither orderly nor without violence, especially in areas west of Mexico City proper.

He nodded to show Talbot he understood the broad strokes, and the Pinkerton continued.

"Lejeune was an infantry officer," he explained. "He served as a captain to a company of French Foreign Legion tasked with bringing an enormous payroll of gold out of Sonora."

"Define enormous," Luke said.

"According to the ledger kept by the Legionnaire quartermaster," Talbot answered, "approximately eight million francs."

"That's over a million and half in U.S. dollars," Delacroix interrupted. "Just sitting in a cave in a cannon in the Sonoran Desert."

Luke frowned.

"Where in the Sonoran Desert?"

The Sonoran Desert was mighty big. It stretched from north of Tucson southward to below Sonoita. Crossing it was not done lightly. Evidently Talbot didn't have an answer to Luke's question, because he just cleared his throat and looked down at the glass of whiskey in his hand.

"The Mexicans aren't going to be happy with American treasure hunters trying to claim their gold," Luke went on.

Talbot nodded vigorously. "Too right, old man, too right. We shall have to avoid the Mexican army patrols at all costs."

"While hiding from the Apaches," Luke added, his voice dry.

Talbot nodded, a little too cheerfully, Luke thought, given the risk they were discussing.

"What's the matter, Jensen?" O'Toole asked. "Are you losing your nerve?"

"Any man who thinks he's got nerve because he isn't afraid of Apaches is someone who'll be scalped before morning," Collins said in rebuttal.

O'Toole glowered at Luke as if he'd made the comment instead of Collins.

Luke ignored the Irishman. Still regarding Talbot, he continued. "And we're supposed to find all this gold while running down one of the most elusive and meanest outlaws the territory's ever seen."

"Don't make it sound impossible," Delacroix pouted. It was her best sultry voice and it sent shivers down Luke's back.

"And how big is the Pinkerton group going to be?"

At this Talbot actually looked abashed. "Yes, well, this isn't exactly a Pinkerton-sanctioned endeavor."

Luke was mildly surprised to hear this. He'd had Talbot pegged as a company man, through and through.

"So allow me to sum up," he said. "You're mounting an illegal armed incursion into Mexico during a time of heightened border tensions. You're pushing deep into Apache territory during an Indian war. You're running down a mass-murdering outlaw and his gang who know that area better than anyone other than Geronimo."

Talbot opened his mouth to protest, but Luke steamrolled over the top of him.

"In order to pull off this feat of monumentally bad decision-making, you're taking along"—Luke began holding up fingers as he made his points—"yourself, a Chicago bureaucrat by way of England with no frontier knowledge, a madame turned lunatic arsonist, her bowler-hat-wearing fancy boy who, I admit, is okay in a scrap, but is no horseman, and an Indian tracker who is currently in jail and likely to hang at the end of a lynch mob's rope. Collins has experience on the frontier, but that experience will be blunted by your own lack of it. Also, your biggest contribution in a situation like this, the resources you can get from the Pinkertons, won't be available because, oh yeah, you're intending to keep this secret from the world's best known detective agency." Luke looked at Talbot. "That about the size of it, Mr. Talbot?"

Talbot had the good grace to look dejected. Delacroix wasn't burdened by such restraint. Collins studied the rim of his whiskey glass. If he was troubled he didn't show it.

"Yeah, that pretty much sums it up," Delacroix agreed, again way too happily, given the gravity of the discussion. "Well, you forgot one thing."

Luke regarded her. "Pray tell, Miss Delacroix."

"You," she said. "We're going to have you. You've already found Melichus and shot it out with him once, and he, as you rightly point out, knows this territory better than anyone short of Geronimo. You lived to talk about it, and you plan on going back out after him anyway."

"Also," Talbot had found his voice, "while you are correct in suggesting that my employers are not fully abreast of the *entire* situation, they are fully supportive of our first major hurdle, running down and exterminating the outlaw Melichus. For that part, you will have Pinkerton-provided aid in the form of experienced gunhands. Several of them are veterans of the Indian warriors and men long accustomed to frontier hardship."

"Come with us to get Melichus," Delacroix argued. "You can decide the rest later."

Luke opened his mouth to tell them to go kick rocks. He didn't want any part of their madness.

"Unless it seems scary," O'Toole suggested. "I wouldn't blame you for not wanting to go."

"I'll be ready to go in the morning," Luke said. He knew he was rising to the Irishman's bait, but he couldn't help it. He got to his feet and continued, "Now, I have a certain former peer of Miss Delacroix, whose acquaintance I'd like to make." He put on his hat. "Gentlemen, Miss Delacroix, if you'll excuse me."

He left them with their mouths hanging open. That response was satisfying, perhaps childishly so, but still satisfying.

After that he found the blonde called Sophie and found her amenable to polite discussion.

Several polite discussions, in fact.

CHAPTER 23

Collins proved a capable quartermaster. Better, or at least more imaginative, than Luke initially expected. Talbot had chosen well in that regard. Their mounts and tack were all top-notch. He'd replaced the rifle Luke lost fighting Melichus with a new lever-action Winchester and outfitted Walks-the-Horizon with the same.

The Indian, finally released from jail, wore comfortable-looking moccasins, threadbare canvas trousers, and a tan button-up shirt that looked brand new. His long silver hair was held by a beaded leather strap away from a face worn to deeply etched wrinkles by the sun and elements and time. His eyes were pale brown and lively though he talked seldom. In some weird sense, his eyes looked much brighter and younger than those of the rest of him, Luke thought.

Besides tack, mounts, and provisions, Collins had also purchased a surprise.

Lashed to the burro he bought to carry their supplies was a crate of dynamite. Looking smug, Collins opened the box and showed them how he'd modified the sticks of TNT.

"Old Walks and I did it last night," he told them.

He stepped back, and the others crowded in to look. O'Toole grunted in mild surprise and Delacroix nearly squealed with delight, clapping her small, gloved hands together with excitement.

"Good Lord," Talbot muttered.

Luke inspected the dynamite. Collins and Walks-the-Horizon had slathered each eight-by-one-and-a-quarter-inch stick with tannery glue and liberally applied finishing nails. All the wicks had been trimmed for quick detonation as well. Weighing less than half a pound each, the blast of a single stick of dynamite was enough to blow a stubborn tree stump out of the ground. When that kind of force exploded with this dynamite, a lethal haze of nails and nail slivers would scatter to devastating effect.

Luke remembered the Belladonna brothel going up in flames. He vividly recalled the *Southern Gentleman* ablaze as it started sinking. Dynamite in O'Toole's and Delacroix's hands just couldn't end well.

"Great . . ." he muttered under his breath.

Delacroix, hearing him and misunderstanding his intent, happily nodded in agreement.

"Isn't it just?"

Ignoring her, Luke turned to Collins. "We're doomed, you know that, right?"

Collins shrugged, then shot a stream of tobacco juice into the dust.

"We got owlhoots, Apaches, and maybe even Mexican army patrols if we're forced to dip much farther south. We'll need every advantage we can get."

"I can see you haven't worked with these two before," Luke said, voice dry. "They're going to be using that TNT to run off snakes and coyotes. They're lunatics, I'm telling you."

"*Tres* hurtful, *mon amour*," Delacroix protested sweetly.

"Kiss my Irish butt, Jensen," O'Toole growled.

Collins looked at Talbot. The Englishman shrugged. "This entire venture is lunacy, but we're doing it anyway."

Walks-the-Horizon grunted. Everyone looked at the Indian scout. The rough-hewn man extended his arm to the south.

"Melichus went that way."

Luke burst out laughing as the town bustled around him. Obviously Melichus and his band were to the south.

"Let's get it done," he said.

CHAPTER 24

They rode south through the sage and chaparral. They rode under a blistering white sun through stands of cheatgrass yellow as summer wheat. Their shirts clung to them, soaked with sweat from the frying-pan heat, and the dust of the ancient road, like chalk, billowed up and coated them until they seemed pale as apparitions.

Walks-the-Horizon ranged ahead from the start. They spent the night on a mesa in the protection of a saguaro cactus forest. When they looked toward Mexico, they saw the flickering flames, large as match strikes in the far distance, of other campfires out in the waste. When the sun came up in the morning, they rode down into the desert past cliffs of sandstone the colors of coral and marmalade.

They rode until their water turned brackish, cooked just short of boiling inside their canteens. The chalk clinging to their clothes turned to grime when their sweat dampened it and then it dried again, hard as shale, in the noon heat. Walks-the-Horizon would appear throughout the day, sitting astride his horse above some arroyo.

Tarantulas and Gila lizards darted between prickly pear and barrel cactus as the hooves of the mounts hammered gravel and the branches of creosote brush whipped the riders' chaps. The arid wind lifted grit off the hardpan and flung it in their faces so that they rode with their heads down, brims of their hats turned low, and bandannas hiding their noses and mouths.

They wanted to make time, so on the second day Walks-the-Horizon led them off the stage road and through narrow ravines where rattlesnakes sunned themselves on flat piles of tabletop boulders. They rode without water for twelve hours and made a cold camp in a dry creek bed where slinking coyotes watched them from the safety of the darkness, eyes yellow. Their yips and howls went on all night and no one slept well.

By the next day, Talbot, Delacroix, and O'Toole were hurting. The Sonoran Desert was unforgiving, and the part Walks-the-Horizon had chosen to reduce travel time was brutal. They were entering Yuma County and moving toward the Pajarito Mountains, in the heart of Melichus's territory.

They had run out of water the previous night and faced another eighteen hours in the unforgiving heat without it before they would reach the Gila River. That long without water for both humans and horses was a grueling ordeal that would test their endurance.

As before, Walks-the-Horizon ranged ahead, but not as far as earlier in the journey. They were nearing the mountain range and, just beyond that, the border. When, in the late afternoon, the scout rode up and told them he'd found a spring in an arroyo in the foothills, everyone was relieved.

What he told them next was decidedly less reassuring.

"Apache sign," he said. "I make it six, maybe eight warriors."

"This far off the reservation," Collins said, his voice grim, "can only mean bad news."

"Is it this Victorio?" Talbot asked, referring to a well-known Apache.

Walks-the-Horizon shook his head. "I do not believe so.

I do not feel his power. I think it is young raiders looking for horses."

"Fantastic," Delacroix said.

"Still dangerous as hell," Luke said.

"Stinking savages die the same as Mexicans," O'Toole muttered. "Same as anyone."

The big Irishman spoke in a confident tone, but he was scanning the rocky rim of the arroyo and the open desert as he did, Luke noticed.

"You see any sign of homesteaders?" he asked the Indian scout.

Walks-the-Horizon nodded. "I think miners. There were heavy wagon tracks going south. Deep ruts like the trail had been used coming and going for a while."

Luke studied the sky, looking for vultures. He didn't see any. His mouth felt as dry and gritty as the sandy gravel covering the ground. A thick layer of the white, chalk-like dust covered his dark clothes, turning them gray.

"Apaches or no," he said, "we need water."

That settled that.

Walks-the-Horizon led them into the spring as twilight began deepening across the desert. It took a supreme effort of willpower not to simply throw themselves at the pool of fresh water. They needed to stay sharp to ensure that the thirsty horses didn't become colic from drinking too much, too fast.

Eventually they settled in for the night. Luke remained vigilant and saw that Collins did as well. An oasis like this was a known location. The likelihood of unwelcome visitors seemed a very real possibility. Luke kept his rifle close to hand.

Desert cicadas trilled from out of the darkness. A great horned owl screeched as it swooped and plucked a bat from the air. From farther off a desert lobo howled, calling for its pack. Nothing answered the plaintive cry, the beast was alone.

They'd reached the Gila soon enough, though they were all parched and worn out at the moment. Walks-the-Horizon told them they'd cut as much as five or six days' travel off the journey by cutting through the open Sonora.

"Have you seen any more signs?" Collins asked the Indian. "Not just Melichus's raiders, but the others."

"What others?" Talbot asked.

"White Mountain Apache," Luke answered. "We're in the *Apacheria* down here. Or what's left of it. The White Mountain Apache consider everything south of Mogollon Rim into the northern Mexican Sonora to be theirs. It's another reason Melichus didn't take this route even though it might have saved him a week of travel. There's no way he was going to drive a herd of stolen horses and a line of captives through this region. That would be too much temptation for the Apaches."

"Victorio is no Cochise." Collins smoked from a clay pipe, the coals orange in the dark. "But he's still an Apache, and he hates Melichus for stealing one of his wives in a raid several years ago and selling her to the Mexicans."

"If Melichus comes into this territory, Victorio will hound him to death," Walks-the-Horizon said. "But if Melichus can get into the Gilas from the east, he ought to be all right because when Victorio was a boy, he was told by a medicine woman, a bruja, that his spirit will wander blind forever if he's killed in the Gila range."

"Why?" Delacroix asked.

Walks-the-Horizon shrugged. "Who knows why witches say anything? But still, best not to cross them if you can help it."

"You think Melichus came through here from the east?" Luke asked.

"No."

Walks-the-Horizon's reply was flat and confident. Luke

believed him. He doubted even a novice tracker would miss the sign of a group that large coming through. Certainly not an expert tracker like Walks-the-Horizon.

"He entered the hills ten miles east of here but did not come this far," Walks-the-Horizon continued. "He's going for one of the river canyons before he pushes further south in Mexico."

"How close are we to the border?"

"Few miles, no more. The way the Pajaritos run it can be hard to tell," Collins answered.

"If the Apaches are raiding," Luke pointed out, "that could mean we'll have to deal with the Mexican army."

"They're no fans of American bounty hunters in the best of times. Now with the tension between their country and ours . . ." Collins trailed off.

"I was led to believe that, depending on the officer in charge, we could expect arrest," Talbot said.

"Followed by a long walk in heavy chains to Chihuahua for a date with a short rope," Collins muttered. "We *do not* want to cross paths with the Mexicans. No matter how an encounter like that turns out, our endeavor will effectively be over."

"What in blazes is that?" Delacroix spoke up.

All of them except for Walks-the-Horizon turned to look. In the late twilight, an orange glow showed above the saw-toothed top of the canyon. A column of black smoke lifted to the sky like an unfurling flag.

"It's the young raiders," Walks-the-Horizon informed them. "They found whites."

CHAPTER 25

No one wanted to rush to their own death, so they crested the lip of the little canyon carefully to avoid silhouetting themselves in the light of the skull-white half moon rising in the sky behind them. Once over the ridge, they saw flames engulfing a series of lodgepole and tamarack pine cabins inside the crumbling adobe walls of an ancient presidio.

Walks-the-Horizon pointed, carbine in hand. "The Spanish built it," he said. "First soldiers, then monks. The Spanish left and Comancheros moved in to trade slaves with the Apache. The Mexican army drove them out and miners moved in."

Luke grunted as he surveyed the scene, garishly lit by the light of the leaping flames. This land was wilderness, but people had been here for a long, long time. Indians forever. The Spanish for centuries. Now whites struck with the fever for silver. The land was wild, the land was bloody, but the land was not empty.

Squinting, he looked across several brush-choked gullies to the bottom of an escarpment on some minor tributary of the Camotain River. Nothing moved down there. He saw no horses or men. There were no war cries or gunfire, just the bonfires of collapsing buildings.

Talbot, apparently forgetting he was the one nominally in charge, looked to Collins and Luke.

"Are we going down there?" he asked.

"We better see if there are any survivors," Collins said. He didn't sound optimistic. "Besides, maybe we get lucky and the yahoos who did this are actually linked to Melichus's larger group somehow."

"You want to go traipsing down through those gullies in the night with a war party sneaking around?" O'Toole sounded incredulous. "Are you crazy?"

"Scared?" Luke asked.

"We have to see," Delacroix said quietly. "If someone is alive we can't just leave them."

"Besides," Collins added, "we may have one thing in our favor."

"What's that?" Luke asked.

"You know of any group of miners who doesn't travel with plenty of whiskey?"

Luke nodded. It was likely.

"You think the savages will be drunk?" Talbot asked. He seemed horrified and amused in equal measures.

"Sure." Collins nodded. "Redskins can't pass up the firewater, right, Charlie?"

Luke glanced at Walks-the-Horizon, seeing how he was taking the casual disrespect. He hadn't made up his mind about whether to trust the tracker yet, but so far he'd been as good as his word. He didn't see how insulting the man to his face could help.

The Indian's expression remained impassive. Turning from the group, he looked down on the burning buildings again.

"If the raiders are young, yes, you are right," he said after a moment. "If they have a good leader, an experienced leader, then no. They will not be drunk."

"There's enough moonlight to travel by," Collins said, talking directly to Luke.

Luke nodded. "Let's go see what we see."

* * *

It took the better part of three hours to break camp and navigate the terrain. Getting in a hurry in a situation such as this would be plumb foolish. Rushing could get a man killed . . . unless speed was the only thing keeping him alive.

They paused in the tree line at the top of the escarpment above the ruined presidio. Below them, the flames had died down to glowing embers as the last of the pine logs burned away. Black smoke smudged the broken-plate face of the moon now directly above them. It fogged the air around the adobe ruins, and the group clearly smelled the acrid stench from their position.

Around them now was silence. Nothing stirred in the pines. Even the crickets had fallen quiet. It was still enough that the popping of burning wood was clearly audible even this far from the presidio.

Closer now, they saw a dead horse on the edge of the clearing. It wasn't an Indian pony and still had a battered old Spanish-style saddle cinched around its body. Walks-the-Horizon slipped away and the group waited for him to finish his reconnaissance while they scanned the ruins for signs of life.

"That saddle look right to you, Jensen?" Collins asked.

"It's a saddle," O'Toole scoffed. "How's it supposed to look?"

"It's a Spanish military saddle," Luke said, voice grim. "That's not some prospector's rig. That's Mexican cavalry."

That startled Talbot. "Mexican? The Mexican army is this far north?"

Collins spat, disgusted by the turn of events. "First of all, Mr. Talbot, we ain't exactly what you'd call 'this far north.' We're pretty far south actually. And secondly, the border has a way of getting real, real vague out here in the Sonora."

"Wonderful," Delacroix muttered.

At that moment, they heard the sound of hooves walking through bush, snapping twigs as they approached. As one the group turned, weapons ready.

"Easy," Charlie Walks-the-Horizon called out, voice soft. "I found a horse."

Lowering their firearms, they watched Walks-the-Horizon lead a nervous little sorrel into their group. It also wore a Spanish military saddle. A bullet had grazed its right shoulder and the blood had crusted over. Its eyes rolled in fear as Walks-the-Horizon led it in, but it followed along docile enough.

Collins walked up and inspected the brand mark burned into the cantle panel. He swore and spat again.

"No doubt about it," he said. "Mexican army."

"So that settles it," O'Toole said. "We avoid this whole mess. We got a bunch of fighting heading our way, no need to risk getting shot up by wild Injuns just to help some greasers."

"However indelicately put," Talbot said, "Mr. O'Toole may have a point."

"That still doesn't explain where everyone is," Luke pointed out.

CHAPTER 26

They worked their way down the butte carefully, weapons ready. The air turned bitter from the acrid smoke, and leaping shadows played across the gravel as they drew closer to the burning structures.

"Wait here," Collins told Talbot and Delacroix.

Before either of them could protest, he held up his hand.

"We need you to stay sharp," he said. "The Apache are still in the area and maybe even Mexican cavalry."

He turned to the others.

"Let's fan out and move once through the ruins. Sound good?" He stopped talking and frowned. "Where in blue blazes is Charlie?"

The group looked around. The expression of confusion on everyone's faces would have been amusing in a different context, Luke realized. At the moment there was nothing funny about it at all.

The raiders didn't shout as they struck from ambush. One moment they were not there and the next they were. The group shouted in anger and surprise and fear as the Apaches hurtled through them. Bodies swung around each other, gunfire exploded, and the momentum carried the bounty hunters apart like flotsam on the surf.

Luke stumbled back as a silent, black-eyed warrior fired

a bolt action rifle at him from the hip. The rifle boomed and he felt the wind-rip as the heavy bullet creased the air a foot to the side.

Without thinking he twisted and dove, rolling over one shoulder and coming up in a crouch inside the crumbling ruins. From somewhere beyond the adobe walls and still burning fires, he heard a military bugle chirp wildly, unleashing a flurry of brassy notes. In the next moment he caught the thunder of hooves on the ground, but then in the moment after that he was fighting for his life.

Luke spun as instinct warned him. An Apache warrior rushed out of the shadows, bone-handled knife plunging down toward the bounty hunter. Luke's arm swung up and blocked the Indian's, stopping the blade mid-swing, but the impact knocked both of them off balance.

Stumbling backward, Luke came up hard against the adobe wall. He grunted, body straining against the Apache's. He tried bringing his pistol up, but the warrior's grip was clamped tight as a vise on his wrist.

Teeth gritting with the strain, Luke brought his leg up, knee hunting for the other man's crotch. The Apache turned his hip and took the strike on the outside of his leg. Eyes burning, the warrior snarled and leaned into his knife, driving the point closer to Luke's neck.

Luke spat in his eye and the warrior faltered for just a moment. Luke shifted and drove the heel of his boot down on the other man's moccasin-shod foot. Toes broke and the Apache howled in shock and pain. Luke twisted his wrist hard and yanked his gun hand free. The Apache quickly sprang backward, but Luke fired before he could get clear.

The muzzle flash lit up the night between them, illuminating the warrior's face as two .44-caliber bullets struck him in the belly. The Indian fell to his knees, and Luke, back still pressed to the ruined adobe wall, lifted his leg and kicked the Apache in the chest.

The Indian went flying backward and flopped in the dirt, blood pouring in streams from his upper abdomen. Panting from the exertion, Luke turned and began making his way through the maze of crumbling walls and loose debris.

A Mexican *soldado* ran through the crumbling remnants of a doorway. His long-barreled bolt-action rifle was held up in both fists and was topped by a two-foot-long bayonet. Blood dripped from the blade and ran down the stock over his fingers in crimson rivers. Luke had no idea who the man had just stabbed. He looked frantic, almost mad with some combination of terror and rage.

Sensing Luke, the man spun in his direction.

"We're friendly!" Luke shouted.

The terrified *soldado* swung his unwieldy rifle toward the bounty hunter, but Luke easily beat him. Given no choice, Luke fired. The Remington barked and blood splashed the man's tan uniform. He staggered backward, eyes glassy and rifle tumbling from lifeless fingers.

A Mexican officer, saber bared, sprang screaming from the same crumbling doorway. Luke turned but the man was on him, and he dropped his pistol to catch the officer's sword arm in both his hands as the saber swept down. He staggered beneath the man's momentum and was forced hard up against the ruins of another wall.

"We're not against you!" he shouted. "*No quiero pelear!*"

The officer screamed at him in rapid-fire Spanish, far too fast for Luke's rudimentary linguistic skills. The man's eyes were wild with hate and spittle flew between them from his lips as they struggled. Luke realized the man was already bloody from some previous combat and knew he must have been driven nearly mad by the intensity of it.

For a moment, both men strained hard against each other, then Luke began slowly pressing the saber back. From somewhere nearby to his right, he heard Vina Delacroix scream.

The sound was sharp, cutting through the night with perfect clarity.

Luke braced himself against the wall, still locked in the struggle to control the saber with the Mexican officer. Braced, he threw a knee into the man's midsection. The officer grunted under the impact but remained engaged. Luke stomped his toes, then buried his knee in the man's gut.

The Mexican gasped as the air was driven from his lungs, and he folded over from the blow. Getting him off balance, Luke shoved hard and the man went over backward like a tripped up drunk and fell. Luke quick drew his second pistol and fired twice, pinning the officer to the ground with both bullets.

Panting hard from the exertion, Luke sensed motion as he went to reclaim his fallen pistol. He spun in that direction but an Apache had leapt onto him from above. They crashed to the earth, the Indian warrior on top of him, trading post hatchet decorated with blue and red beadwork now hammering down.

Luke tried bringing his pistol up as the Apache crashed into him but was driven into the ground too quickly. His gun hand was forced into the dirt, trapped under his body. He grunted hard as the forefinger of his left hand, caught in the Remington's trigger guard, bent painfully backward.

He got his other arm up and stopped the falling hatchet, but the club-strike of the handle against his wrist instantly numbed his arm. He threw a wild, desperate elbow into the Apache's jaw, once, twice, three times. The impacts of his blows reverberated back up his arm as they landed with teeth-rattling force.

Unseating the warrior, Luke bucked like an irate bronco, snarling with pain as his bruised trigger finger slid free of the pistol. Spinning inside the Indian's clinch, he managed to wrap the arm of his injured hand around the warrior. Unable to grip with the hand, he cinched their intertwined arms tight, immobilizing the hatchet for the moment.

The Apache tried striking with his free hand, but Luke tucked his chin and took the blows to the top of his head. The warrior was like a wildcat in his grip. While the Indian raider tried raining blows, Luke concentrated on wrapping both his legs around one of the warrior's.

He'd grown up wrestling with his brother and cousins. Such contests of old-school wrestling were common among the rough-and-ready Ozark mountain folk he'd grown up with. Having secured control of one entire side of the Apache's body, he waited for the flailing warrior to overextend himself.

In the next moment it happened, and Luke exploded into action, heaving with his hips and twisting hard. The Apache squawked in surprise as Luke spun him over and ended up on top, straddling the man's hips. The hatchet was lost in the somersault and Luke saw where it came to rest barely two feet from the struggling men.

Driving his forehead down, he smashed it into the Apache's nose. The warrior's nose burst like a tomato, and his eyes went dull. Numb hand functioning just well enough to grasp, Luke snatched up the hatchet and went at the Apache's head with the blade like a woman beating dust from a rug.

The blows dashed and strewed blood wildly, painting Luke, streaking the ancient adobe, making sticky mud in the dust. Chest heaving like a man carrying a heavy load, Luke staggered to his feet. He saw one of the Remingtons and quickly picked it up.

Stabbing bolts of pure agony lanced through his left hand from his broken finger. He looked down and saw his trigger finger was canted like a tree branch. Bringing up the pistol in his good hand, he looked around. He found himself in the eye of the storm, momentarily out of the desperate fighting.

Remembering Delacroix's scream he hurriedly attempted to find some solution to deal with his injured finger. Seeing buckskin fringe on the Apache's breeches he used the edge of the bloody hatchet to slice several free. Working quickly, alert to the possibility of another attack, he rapidly lashed the broken finger to the next two on his hand.

The pain of straightening the finger brought tears to his eyes, and his breathing came in short, sharp snorts as he forced himself through the pain. Finger immobilized, he awkwardly holstered one of the Remingtons and retrieved the other.

From beyond the section of ruins penning him in, he heard gunshots and the sound of men screaming. Apaches screeching war cries, *soldados* cursing in terrified Spanish. Delacroix did not scream again.

Thumbing back the hammer on his .44, he pushed deeper into the rubble.

Coming through a narrow passage, he almost fell over Collins. The grizzled old veteran lay against a wall. There were two Apache dead at the old man's feet. Blood had poured down around his face from a head wound, turning his features into a scarlet mask.

Just beyond him a wall had crumbled away and Luke saw open desert. Talbot and O'Toole stood back to back, Delacroix between them. Both men had dead Mexican soldiers in front of them. An Apache lay a few feet away, bloody knife still clutched in his dead fist. Delacroix bled heavily from a wound in her arm.

"This is crazy!" Collins shouted. Despite the gore covering his face, he wasn't dead. "The Apaches were drawing in the Mexicans and now the Mexicans think we were with them!"

"We've got to get out of here!" Talbot yelled.

Two Mexicans came around the corner of the ruins, Springfield rifles held at port arms, long bayonets gleaming. As a single organism, all four of the Americans turned and fired. A buzzing hornet swarm of lead smashed into the soldiers with merciless accuracy and lethal force.

The men jerked like marionettes falling free of their strings. Blood burst from their wounds in streaming rivers. The soldiers stumbled backward and fell, their cries lost in the echoing pistol reports.

Suddenly Walks-the-Horizon was with them, running fast. Talbot went to shoot the Indian, but O'Toole slapped his arm, shouting, "No!"

"Run!" Charlie Walks-the-Horizon yelled. "They've taken the horses, run!"

It was the most Luke had ever heard the man speak at once. He turned back toward the adobe ruins and saw more Rurales. *To hell with that,* he thought.

"Go!" he shouted.

The others were already running, even Collins, and as a group they hit the tree line.

CHAPTER 27

The woods grew heavy with hawthorn and pine, twisting oak, and time-worn alder. Birds called from far back among the gnarled, twisting trunks. Shadows hung thick, split at odd intervals by bars of hard sunlight swirling with dust motes. Small animals scurried through the tangled brush. Silence bled through like a stain.

The path was ancient, marked by deep ruts driven into mud by heavy cart wheels, flattened in the middle by the steps of human, horses, oxen. The trail seemed to wind through the past as much as forest.

In the uncertain light of false dawn Luke crept forward. Slipping through the trees, he walked silently on a bed of fallen pine needles through a forest now devoid of bird calls. The hair on the back of his neck and along his forearms lifted.

Step, scan. Step, scan. Luke realized he was gripping the Winchester too tightly and relaxed his hands, letting pent up breath escape through his nose.

The valley mouth was only a little way ahead. There was a line of dense brush grown up around a haphazard pile of storm-fallen pine snags. They were stacked like a kid's game of pick-up sticks. Lifting his leg, Luke eased around a stump and set his foot down carefully.

A bit of motion caught his eye.

Turning his head in that direction, Luke saw a branch quivering, then like a mirage coming into focus, Luke saw the soldiers.

Thirty or forty *soldados* crouched in the trees, silent and still, waiting for the bounty hunters. They were kneeling in the heavy brush, using the fallen trees for cover. They faced into the clearing where the narrow valley mouth was located. Their discipline was good, but once his eyes adjusted it was easy to pick out their tan caps. Some wore high-peaked gray sombreros, and Luke frowned as he caught sight of them.

Moving as slowly as possible, Luke turned sideways so he could easily scan both directions. He edged backward until he was able to put a line of trees between their line of sight and his. Luke saw the group crouched, Charlie Walks-the-Horizon bringing up the rear, Delacroix at the front next to O'Toole. Just behind them Talbot and Collins watched Jensen intently, looking for some clue about what was happening.

Delacroix's wounded arm was bound up, and another bloodstained bandage torn from the redhead's petticoat was tied around Collins's head, the white fabric forming a sharp contrast with his deeply tanned face.

Luke said in a low voice, "Thirty-five, maybe forty."

"Mexican army then?" Collins asked.

"Yes," Luke confirmed.

Delacroix swore under her breath. Luke went on, voice grim, "Standard rifles. But I saw their uniforms. There are two kinds of troops along the border. *Activo,* which are militia, less well armed, less trained. Then there is the *Permanente,* regular army. Better equipped, better led."

"Let me guess," O'Toole said, "these are *Permanente*."

Luke nodded. "Worse than that, some are *Rurales*. President Diaz recruited bandits to police the interior. They're better armed and paid than the regular units and even more ruthless. They have Henry repeating rifles instead of Spencer breech loaders." He paused. "It also means they could have a mule team hauling a Gatling gun. The US companies running Mexican mining and railroads gifted them on a case-by-case basis to help coordinate fighting the southern Apache and to put down labor disputes. We've got to be ghosts or we're not making it out of here." Luke nodded toward Walks-the-Horizon. "They set up on our escape route. We need a new plan."

The Indian nodded. "We need to leapfrog them," he said. "Go further down the ridge. There's an antelope trail, rough but passable."

Luke looked at Delacroix and the rest of the group to see if they had anything to add. They didn't. This was what it was.

"Let's go," Luke said. "Arrowhead formation, Vina in the center. Me to the front, O'Toole and Collins on the wings." He looked to Charlie. "I need you walking drag."

Moving slowly, they took fifteen minutes to backtrack and swing wide around the ambush. They had to go wide enough to avoid any pickets the Mexican lieutenant might have set out. As tired and worn out as they already were, it was a grueling diversion in the unrelenting heat.

But if they wanted to live they didn't have a choice.

CHAPTER 28

Luke stopped the group with an upraised hand.

The path had come to the intersection of a stream that forked off into two separate branches. Under different circumstances it would have seemed idyllic. The brooks were damn near babbling. A mule deer, hide a ruddy rusty-brown, lifted its head from where it drank, displaying a rack of antlers large as a chandelier.

Nose quivering, it sniffed, scenting the wind. In a flash it was gone, waving branches and stalks of grass the only thing left to mark its passage.

One fork of the stream cut away from them and wound into the pine forest. The other ran up toward the opening of a small valley between low ridges. Charlie appeared next to him on the silent feet of an accomplished woodsman, which he was. When he spoke he was close enough that his breath was warm in Luke's ear.

Luke's stomach twisted. The only reason Walks-the-Horizon would have spoken so closely was if he thought Mexicans were very close.

"The valley," he whispered.

Luke nodded, indicated the route to the rest of the group, and they moved out. Putting the fork at his back, Luke followed the main branch of the stream back about eight yards before deciding it was a good place to cross. One by one, they crossed under the watchful eyes of the others.

Once across they began moving back toward a saddle in the hills at the valley mouth. Luke had lost sight of Charlie Walks-the-Horizon. The tracker had swung out to cover their rear and was out of sight. The group pressed on. Thinking he saw something, Luke ventured off the deer trail a little ways to look closer.

A bugle call broke the stillness.

The harmonic blast echoed out in piercing, undulating waves. Luke froze. Looking back he saw the rest of the group had frozen in place as well. Luke also realized that he'd become separated from the others by about twenty-five yards.

They were all on one knee as if someone had called a halt while Luke was still on his feet. He realized someone must have called a stop because they'd seen something he hadn't. Delacroix was halfway between the group and himself, next to an ancient alder tree. Both of them were at the opening to the valley, Luke a little farther in.

The world turned upside down.

The earth came up and slammed him hard. His hearing suddenly was replaced by a strange, far away ringing.

Explosion, Luke thought numbly. Dynamite? A cannon?

Dirt rained down around him and Luke realized he was sprawled on the ground, body aching. He saw Delacroix pushing herself up out of the grass, already checking for her weapons. His ears popped and sound returned in a rush. Forest debris, dirt, rocks, leaves, branches, all fell to the earth.

Luke looked for the rest of the group.

All he saw was black smoke. A billowing cloud of it covered the ground and rose into the sky. The breeze made little swirling eddies of it. His hands found a grip on his rifle. A figure staggered out of the cloud, stumbling toward him.

It was O'Toole.

He was in a bad, bad way.

The explosion had ripped his jaw off his face. The bone dangled down in a grotesque parody of a human face. Smoke poured from his back and all of his equipment had been ripped away, clothing shredded. His left arm dangled far lower than his right. He stumbled and Luke saw the limb was barely attached by just a single rope of twisted skin and sinew. Luke patted his own body for injuries and miraculously found none.

Luke looked at Delacroix.

She also seemed uninjured, though struggling to gain her internal equilibrium. She held her weapon in a death grip. She turned and Luke realized that, like O'Toole, her clothes and gear belts had been split open in the back. Luke thought the alder, now smoking, had protected her from much of the blast.

Stumbling, Luke came down the hill and took her by one shoulder.

"Help O'Toole!" Luke told her.

He gave her a shove, blinked, and the woods came alive with motion. O'Toole was deep in shock, he hardly reacted as Delacroix reached him and tried pulling him down. Movement drew Luke's eyes as several Mexican *soldados* streamed out from around the smoking alder. They were only steps away from Delacroix.

Pivoting, Luke brought the carbine up and opened fire. Delacroix turned, almost supernaturally fast, flinging O'Toole down with one hand while firing her weapon with the other.

Her carbine opened up and Delacroix laid down a withering hail of fire at near point blank range. The first five *soldados* were swept to the ground under the force of the fusillade. Rounds struck them, puffing out their tan uniforms and sending geysers of blood splashing into the air.

Firing wildly, the last three *soldados* retreated behind the alder.

As that happened, on Luke's left a larger element of regulars rose from hiding on the nearest hill at the valley opening. Twenty or twenty-five *soldados* sprang their assault.

Luke saw the Gatling gun then.

This is how I die, he thought.

Luke dropped his rifle and snatched up O'Toole's without conscious thought. Behind him Delacroix opened up with her revolver as Luke worked the lever action, seated a round in the chamber and began firing. He didn't know how many of the group were still alive, all he knew for sure was that Delacroix and himself were the only ones firing.

Where was Collins? Where was Charlie Walks-the-Horizon?

As the larger group of Mexicans charged forward, Luke realized with something like panicked hilarity that the soldiers hadn't actually pinpointed Delacroix and himself. They were charging the site where the main part of his group had been struck.

That was how Luke now thought of them: his group. He didn't like most of them. But he'd made an agreement, same as swearing an oath. Talbot could go to Hades, this was *his* group.

As the *soldados* swept down Delacroix and Luke caught them from the flank. Ambushing the ambushers as they ran past.

Their gunfire hit the running figures in hammer-strikes of fury. They split them, knocking bodies flying. At such close range the bullets struck the Mexicans like high-speed meat cleavers.

Luke felt a tight grin split his face as he heard their screams. Those few, mad seconds were a complete slaughter. Luke led a leaping regular with a pistol in each hand, then triggered a string of rounds. The man ran into the bullets and went spinning off as his skull came apart.

Not every *soldado* hit was killed. The wounded dropped into the tall cheatgrass and vegetation. What was important was that they'd broken the attack momentum. Luke turned and saw Delacroix firing two rounds, hitting a *soldado* drawing a bead with his rifle. Luke dumped the lever-action rifle and grabbed up another.

It took several long moments for the *soldados* to realize where the gunfire killing them was actually coming from. One of the soldiers screamed a warning to his brethren before Luke shot him.

The group turned and began firing.

But Luke and Delacroix's counter-ambush had divided them, shredding their cohesion so that they were an uncoordinated mob. The ones farthest from them were firing through their own people. Finally a sergeant or officer took charge and they withdrew en masse.

The initial haze from the explosion had begun dissipating. The Mexicans had overrun the other's position, he saw. Delacroix and Luke hurried down to the group. There were enemy dead mixed in with the bodies of his people. Luke shot two wounded as they tried crawling away. Delacroix killed three more.

"Holy Mother of God," Delacroix said.

Luke had nothing to add to that. The ambush site was an abattoir.

O'Toole clung to life, his eyes rolled, but with his jaw gone he could only moan and grunt. Collins's shirt had been blown off his body. He was lean, each muscle etched against a near albino-white skin except for his arms below the elbow which were burned deep red.

Covered in his own blood, he had maybe a dozen bleeding wounds on his body. Despite the damage, he may have been in the best shape of anyone else. He was actually trying to stand.

Talbot and Walks-the-Horizon were in far worse shape.

Luke could actually see Talbot's intestines, glistening in the hideous wound that almost separated his body in half. Charlie had a dent in his skull that was shockingly deep. Luke didn't understand how he still breathed.

"Delacroix," Luke said, "the Mexicans are pulling back."

"Good."

Maybe a minute had passed since the Mexicans had withdrawn into the tree line. As soon as the officer got a handle on the situation they'd return. The Mexican soldiers had the numbers, clearly. Luke did not think they could survive another assault.

"Come on, friend," Luke said to a half-conscious Charlie Walks-the-Horizon. "Let's get you out of here."

Luke got his arm around his neck and stood the man up. He hissed in pain but did not cry out. With Charlie Walks-the-Horizon still leaning heavily on him, Luke grasped Talbot by the back of his collar. Talbot had to be dead, as badly as he was wounded, but Luke wasn't going to leave him behind. He half carried, half dragged them both across the rocky stream bed and toward the other bank.

Luke wanted a natural barrier of some sort, any sort, between them and the next assault.

His lungs burned, his legs ached. Each step was a fight through adrenaline-induced exhaustion. He dug down deep and kept pushing, always pushing. Nearly spent, he managed to get the two men to relative safety behind some fallen trees.

Delacroix knelt and helped Collins to his feet. Stumbling across the stream, they collapsed next to Luke in the new concealed position. Luke's and Delacroix's eyes met.

"I'm going back to get him," she said, meaning O'Toole.

"I'll go," Luke said. "See what aid you can give these men."

She nodded.

While he scrambled to bring O'Toole in, Delacroix quickly began giving what aid she could. She tore more fabric from her petticoat and used it to pad Talbot's abdomen, keeping the slick, blue-gray coils of his intestines inside his body where they belonged. She crossed his arms over the pad, which was rapidly becoming blood-stained, and hoped they would stay in place.

She wrapped Charlie's head as best as she could. One of his pupils was grotesquely large, the other the size of a pinhole. He was unconscious, shivering violently, his breath coming in gasps.

There was a wet, gurgling sound to those breaths that made Delacroix look for another injury. She found a hole in his chest beneath his arm. The white of his ribs showed through. His clothes, like everyone else's, were bloody scraps.

Delacroix looked around as Luke laid O'Toole down. Blood was everywhere. It painted the yellow grass scarlet and made muddy pools in the dirt. Though the Irishman's chest rose and fell in an uneven pattern, his eyes, wide open and bulging, stared blindly out. Flies crawled across him, feasting on the gore. As with the others, it was astounding that he was even still alive.

Some men were stubborn that way. Life could be incredibly fragile, yet amazingly resilient.

"Here they come," Delacroix said in a low voice.

She swung the Winchester around and took up a position on the ground. Her sheer will to never admit defeat impressed Luke in a way that had rarely happened before. He twisted around and followed her line of sight. Across the creek, the Mexicans were coming down the hill. His heart sank. A three man crew was pulling along the Gatling gun on oversized wagon wheels.

Behind him O'Toole eased air from his lungs, softly gurgling blood. It was his death rattle. Luke had heard enough of them to recognize them. He looked over. The Irishman's chest was still. The mountain of a man lay quiet.

"Be at peace, brother," Luke said softly.

"We should get to the top of this hill behind us," Delacroix suggested, voice ragged. "They need high ground."

Surprised by her seeming indifference to O'Toole's death, Luke looked at her. Her face was deathly pale and tears streamed from her eyes in unbroken rivers, but her expression, though grim, was determined. This was not the time for mourning.

Luke shook his head, getting his mind on her suggestion.

"You want to drag everyone up there?" he asked.

He realized she was so pale not only from grief, but also from blood loss. She'd been wounded, too.

"No choice," she said. "We can't stay here."

Luke nodded.

Just then the underbrush above them began shaking and they heard a large group coming down the slope toward them. *Soldados* appeared between the trees, spreading out and moving fast.

"Oh, we are in trouble," Delacroix whispered.

Luke had to agree.

CHAPTER 29

They were caught between two forces. Going to his belly, Luke scooted forward and pushed aside some vegetation to scan the ambush site just beyond the stream. The pickets stalked back and forth, trying to find some sign of Luke's group while others methodically collected their dead and wounded and started dragging them off to whatever they considered safety.

Why should they hurry? Luke thought. *They have us surrounded.*

One of the Mexican soldiers found a blood trail. It wasn't hard to find. Shouting at the others, he called over reinforcements. A *soldado* discovered O'Toole's Henry rifle and held it over his head triumphantly.

A lieutenant barked orders, and the Mexicans began following the trail of blood, moving with more urgency. The three-man Gatling crew pulled the gun into place and blocked the wheels.

The officer barked something, and two men crossed the stream, looking for them. The group was hidden from view, but the amount of blood spilled on the ground ran like scarlet flags indicating the route they'd gone.

As Luke watched, one of the scouts stopped, face to the breeze, eyes darting. He suddenly moved to the left and vanished behind some tall grass growing on top of a short, sharp rise in the ground. Luke looked back, found the other scout. The Mexican squatted frozen, attention focused off to his left flank.

The officer had wandered down to the bank of the stream. He was looking at the blood-splattered gravel. Luke realized it was the precise place Delacroix and Luke had carried the group across.

The man crossed the bank, a carbine held ready in his hands. His line of travel would take him directly toward where the group was hiding, Luke realized. Silently cursing, Luke eased up and slid back from the line of bushes. He needed to keep everyone in sight.

The scout Luke had lost track of suddenly reappeared. His head popped above the grass, and he began moving in Luke's direction. He stopped, hunting for traces of the group.

If he discovered them and called out, it would bring the full weight of the Gatling gun down on them. Luke felt sure they couldn't survive another attack. They'd die here in this remote valley, and he doubted their bones would ever be found.

Luke saw the grass was bloody and beaten down from bodies being dragged over it. A schoolboy or drunk preacher could have followed the tracks.

A cold wash of calm spilled through him. His focus sharpened. As the Mexican soldier crept closer, Luke didn't even move his head for fear of giving away his position. His eyes followed the man's approach until he was almost on top of the group.

Creeping forward, the soldier disappeared behind the greasy leaves and thickly intertwined branches of a line of elderberry bushes. Slowly, Luke rolled onto his side, torn by indecision. Luke feared if he fired on the scout, the others would unleash hellfire.

And where was Delacroix?

The scout slipped around a clump of bushes and fallen trees and suddenly froze, body rigid. He had found the group. Throwing back his head, he yelled and broke into a frenzy of rapid-fire Spanish.

Luke bolted up and snapped off two shots. Both rounds hammered into the man and flung him to the ground.

The other regular, lying down by the streambed, saw Luke pop up and began shooting wildly. Even as he fired, Luke was turning toward him. Flame geysered from the Winchester's muzzle. The rifle rounds punched through the Mexican and Luke saw blood splatter outward in a mist.

Startled, the Mexican army officer turned and began firing his pistol in Luke's direction. Bullets burned through the air around him and Luke hugged the ground. The rounds made a series of *hiss-spat* sounds as they cut the air inches from his head. Luke pushed so deeply into the ground he was breathing dirt.

That was the cue. The entire Mexican army patrol on the far slope opened fire. There was no other target but him. The air flew fast and thick with bullets. The Gatling gun roared. Luke had the slight advantage of elevation, but that was the only cover available. There was nothing but prayer and tall grass between him and them. Great gouts of earth erupted around him, the deadly fusillade seeming to last forever.

Then suddenly it stopped.

Using the elevation to his advantage, he played one of the limited cards he had available to him. He rolled to his back and pulled one of the nail-covered TNT sticks from the bandolier at his chest. He popped the sulphur head of a lucifer match with his thumbnail and lit the dynamite.

Stretching out his arm, he hooked the improvised bomb across his body and down the gentle slope. The stick tumbled end-over-end, its lit fuse sparkling brightly.

Men screamed in Spanish as it landed among them before the dynamite exploded. The roar blasted outward, spewing the slender spikes of the finishing nails into a hail of deadly shrapnel.

Soldados cried out in anguished screams. Seeking to shift the momentum, Luke pulled a second stick of dynamite free.

A man came over the lip of earth and sprang toward him, carbine held over his head like a club. Dropping the dynamite, Luke drew and fired as the man came down on him. The muzzle of the Remington slammed into the Mexican's chest and Luke pulled the trigger again.

Momentum carried the body into him and Luke was momentarily pinned by the weight. The pistol was ripped out of his hand, almost breaking the finger trapped in the trigger guard. That would have been a disgusting development, unable to fire a gun with either hand. Grunting under the impact, Luke's free hand was already at his knife.

Even with three fingers lashed together, Luke snatched the bowie free and began wildly stabbing at the man. Luke hit him six or seven times, spilling hot blood over himself before he realized the man had gone limp in death.

Panting, he shoved the corpse away from him and sat up, reaching across his body to draw his second revolver as he looked for where the first Remington had fallen. Finding it in the blood-splattered cheatgrass, he quickly holstered it, thumbing back the hammer on the pistol in his other hand.

Still cursing, Luke looked toward the ambush site. He saw a hellscape. A grass fire burned, gaining momentum, pushed up the slope by the wind. Thick, caustic smoke spread out across half an acre of land. Shadowy figures moved in the smoke, rushing back and forth. The firing had tapered off. Bodies lay strewn on the ground like forgotten children's toys.

Damn Delacroix, he thought, *fire wherever she goes.* It almost made him want to laugh.

"Delacroix!" Luke called.

"Here!"

Luke sighed with relief. Hurrying over, he found her

giving first aid to the group. Collins and, amazingly, Charlie Walks-the-Horizon were conscious.

Charlie looked *wrong*.

A human wasn't supposed to have a skull like a broken eggshell and still live. But when the Indian looked at Luke his eyes were alert. The two men appeared able to move under their own power, but Luke knew that was all they'd be doing. And go where? They were all dead men walking, he knew.

This carnage was throwing him back to the war and the horrors he'd lived through as Sherman pushed south relentlessly.

Operating in a daze of exhaustion, Luke shouldered Talbot while Delacroix helped Collins to his feet. Swinging wide, they began moving toward the back of the valley. Charlie got up and began following them like a child obediently trailing his parents.

They had to flank the Mexicans, who were between them and the way out of the valley. Holding his recovered Winchester in one hand, Luke staggered through the pine woods. His lungs burned and his legs ached. Talbot's weight settled into his torso like a sandbag, making it difficult to draw breath. Luke was huffing and puffing so hard his teeth ached.

Keep going, Luke thought. *Keep going.*

The wounds left by the clash stung and wept blood, sapping his strength. His clothes were stiff with all of it.

Luke thought of his brother. Smoke Jensen never gave up, no matter what the odds against him. One time he had gone into an abandoned town where nineteen killers were holed up and had gunned down each and every one of them to gain the revenge he sought. No normal man would have even attempted that.

He thought about his sons, as well, the sons he hadn't known he had until a few years earlier. Ace and Chance had found themselves in plenty of bad scrapes, and somehow they had come through those dangers. His blood ran in the veins of those Jensen boys, Luke reminded himself. When the Good Lord made *all* the Jensens, He didn't put any back-up in them. They were fighters, all the way to the end. To the last breath.

And all that mattered was here, was now. One foot in front of the other . . . until the time came when he could strike back against his enemies.

And that's how you survive, Luke told himself, *one step at a time.* His boots squished with blood on every step, He felt it oozing between his toes.

"Luke, we need to stop," Delacroix told him. "Collins's tourniquet has come loose, he'll bleed out."

"Okay," Luke said immediately.

He realized he hadn't even known how close Delacroix was to him. That was frightening. He was too exhausted. His thoughts were cloudy.

Going to one knee, Luke laid the Englishman out gently and checked to make sure he was still breathing. Somehow, despite the hideous wound to his midsection, he was. Charlie Walks-the-Horizon, moving as if in a fog, stumbled and sank to the ground nearby. Luke knelt and drew in several deep breaths. He just needed a moment to collect his thoughts, he told himself. Then he would be all right.

He didn't get that moment.

A wall of bullets ripped out of the trees to their left. They cut through the air and buzzed past Luke. A round nicked his shoulder. He stumbled in surprise. Tripping over Talbot as he tried to get up, he lost his balance and fell. As he rolled over onto his back, he lifted the Winchester in both hands and fired out from between his legs. The booms came like thunderclaps.

Delacroix spun around from where she'd been tightening Collins's bandages. She brought her Winchester up and cut loose, sending a flurry of return fire into the tree line. Luke saw several *soldados* drop, drilled by the slugs spraying among them. The rifle ran empty. Luke tossed it aside and drew the right-hand Remington from its holster.

A lot of lead was flying. He was shooting by instinct at movement among the pine branches and trunks. He couldn't be sure he was hitting most or even any of his targets, but they couldn't afford not to return fire for risk of being pinned down.

Three bullets flew in and struck Delacroix. Her body arched as if struck by lightning and she screamed. She dropped to the dirt. Her blood gushed into the grass.

Luke was up and moving. As he reached her, he snatched the carbine off the ground beside her. Turning, he lit up the tree line, firing from the hip. A Mexican soldier broke from cover and bounded toward him. Luke lifted the rifle butt and jammed it into the pocket of his shoulder. Leaning his head down against the stock, he sighted down the barrel.

He breathed out and squeezed the trigger. Worked the action, fired again.

The man collapsed nose-first into the uneven ground.

Dropping the rifle, Luke pulled one of Collins's fragmentation dynamite sticks from the bandolier, lit and hurled it. The dynamite bounced off the splintered trunk of a tree and landed in the middle of the scrambling squad of soldiers.

It detonated. Razor sharp shrapnel tore through the woods as smoke from the explosion hung in a pocket. Gunfire ceased and Luke saw two *soldados* running away through the trees. Neither carried rifles and one of the men was missing an arm below the elbow.

Luke lay still for a moment, catching his breath, before drawing Delacroix's Winchester back to him. He heard Mexican officers screaming orders and crashing through the brush in the middle distance. He still didn't know where that Gatling gun had gone. That frightened him most of all.

Panting, he rolled over to look at Delacroix. She was one of the strongest people he knew, Luke realized. The most indomitable. She lay without moving, leaking blood from her wounds. Her face was relaxed, as if she was asleep. Luke could see the little girl she'd been once reflected in her calm features.

Luke inched toward her. He reached out to touch her neck. His fingers shook as he pressed them into her skin. There was a pulse. It fluttered weakly beneath his touch, but it was there.

"You stubborn fool!" Luke laughed.

Luke squeezed his eyes shut with relief. But when he opened them again he realized how little hope they had. Collins could walk, but that was it. Charlie Walks-the-Horizon had his head down, mumbling to himself. The tracker's features were caked with blood. Talbot's chest rose and fell in shallow pants, but that was the only sign of life left in the man. By all rights, he should have been dead a long time ago. Luke looked around. They were not in a good defensive position.

"Collins," Luke said.

The man looked at him. He was breathing in shallow pants, mouth hanging open. His face was a mask of blood and gravel. Delacroix had put dressings on his open wounds, but they were soaked through with blood. He was the only one who could help.

"Help me try and conceal everyone," Luke told him. "I know you're weak, but even a little cover might buy us some time. We've got to find better ground."

Collins nodded. He showed his teeth. At first Luke thought he was snarling but then realized he was trying to smile, to let him know he'd do his best. Luke touched his arm and nodded, then moved out.

CHAPTER 30

Carrying the carbine, Luke rose and began looking for a place they could make a stand. Some of the soldiers from the patrol were still between them and the valley mouth. Luke began moving toward the Mexicans, or at least part of them. He didn't know what he was looking for, but knew he'd recognize it when he saw it.

Boulders, fallen trees, depressions in the earth, anything that could provide cover from sustained enemy fire. As Collins moved up the slope toward the valley, Luke scanned behind him, checking potential avenues of approach and fields of fire.

Luke was lucid, but pain and exhaustion and blood loss had given everything a hallucinatory feel. Collins was stumbling in among the trees now, he could hear him breaking brush, but Luke was momentarily alone. Checking his wounds, he realized he'd bled through his makeshift bandages.

He stumbled onto a little cliff face with several boulders and windfall trees knocked down around it. He turned and looked behind him; he had good views toward the places he considered likely avenues of approach.

He sank to his knees, catching his breath. He began automatically reloading his weapons without conscious thought. He thought he should tighten his bandages before returning to the others. Inhaling deeply through his nose, Luke scanned the woods. A lone *soldado* emerged from behind a tree, rifle in his hands. Luke lifted the carbine but held his fire.

In the next moment, five more *soldados* followed. The last one wasn't carrying a rifle. He had a 10-gauge shotgun with barrels that looked as large as cannon muzzles. He wore crossed bandoliers across his torso and shotgun shells glittered in the loops, hanging from his stocky frame. The group obviously thought they weren't close to Luke's people because they were moving too fast.

Luke shifted his aim to the shotgun man.

Surprise, Luke snarled silently.

He opened up. His first round struck the man's chest and spun him off his feet. Luke shifted his fire left to right and killed two more. The rest dove for cover and began returning fire. Again the air around him was alive with the wind-rip of near misses. It was like his head was stuck in a swarm of lead hornets.

Luke ducked low and the rounds slammed into the deadwood and rocks around him. Through a gap in two rotting logs, Luke spied one of the remaining soldiers. Luke trained his sights on him, squeezed the trigger and shot him.

As the man fell, Luke sensed motion to his right. Two *soldados* sprinted toward his position, bayonet-mounted rifles in their hands. Operating on pure instinct, Luke swept up the carbine and shot them.

Crack-crack. Thump-thump.

They fell. Gun smoke hung in a haze now and his shoulder was sore with the recoil of the fighting. The merciless Arizona sun beat down.

Dragging himself up, Luke staggered back down the hill, wounds still leaking blood. The carbine felt impossibly heavy, his limbs were made of wet sand, and he couldn't catch his breath. He felt like he was receding, slipping toward sleep.

Luke couldn't find the others.

"Collins!"

Luke shouted it, because why not shout? What possible difference could it make at this point? The enemy had them located. Dizzy, he stumbled and went to his knees. He began using the rifle the way an old man uses a crutch.

That was stupid, he knew. Dirt would clog the barrel. He tried to stand without it and couldn't. Suddenly he saw some of the group.

Gathering the others had cost Collins. He was deathly pale from blood loss. They looked at each other, close as brothers. Luke nodded in respect. He nodded back. Luke looked around. Delacroix was conscious. Talbot was conscious. Charlie Walks-the-Horizon was conscious still but just as remote. Luke crawled over to Delacroix.

"You okay?" he whispered. It was a stupid question, but he had to ask her something.

"S-s-sure," she gasped a little.

Her hands, fingers like iron claws, reached out and grasped the front of his blood crusted shirt. She pulled him closer. Luke leaned in. She stank like blood. Like the rest she was conscious but couldn't walk on her own. Delacroix hadn't told him to go to blazes. She was more severely wounded than he'd feared.

Luke couldn't carry them all at once, that was impossible. He'd have to move them one at a time. Luke crawled back to Collins. Collins had taken a round through the thigh at some point. It was a mangled mess. He'd tied it off himself but there was no way it'd support weight. Luke grabbed his shoulder.

"I found a place we can defend from," Luke told him. "But I'm going to have to drag everyone there. I can only do it one at a time, shot up like this. Understand?"

Collins nodded, then gasped out. "We're done for, you should go if you can. You know that. You're being a fool."

"Ah, hell," Luke said. "I don't have any place to be."

He crawled over to Delacroix. Her eyes followed him but her head didn't move. She opened her mouth to speak and a bubble of blood bulged out. It popped and blood spilled over her chin. Luke took her pistol out, made sure it was cocked, and then wrapped her hands around it.

"I have to go one at a time," Luke told her. "I would never leave you."

She blinked once in acknowledgement. Luke's throat tightened as he realized just how close to death the woman was, but he felt her hands grip her weapon with renewed strength. There was fight in her still.

"You're strong," Luke told her. "Just be strong for a little longer, okay?"

She nodded once and he left her, crawling back to Collins. "This is going to hurt," Luke told him.

He cried out softly as Luke put him over his shoulder, but that was the only sound he made. Luke pushed himself to his knees then stood and began walking.

Once again, his world narrowed down to one step at a time. He staggered among the pine trees heading toward the rocks. Time lost all meaning. He wavered in and out of lucidity.

"Here."

Luke didn't register the word at first. He blinked out of his stupor. He was in a stand of lodgepole pine trees. Collins was a weight on his shoulder. Luke was soaked with his blood. There was just so much damn blood.

"Here," he repeated.

Luke blinked. It was his own voice. He was at the position. As gently as he could, Luke went to a knee. Setting down the carbine, he lowered Collins to the ground as gently as he could.

"I'll be back," Luke said.

He rose to go.

Suddenly, without quite understanding how he had gotten there, Luke was on the ground next to Collins.

Something's wrong, Luke thought. *What? What's wrong?*

Luke was on his side, in the dirt. He couldn't think. He wasn't unconscious but he was unable to gather his thoughts. Something had happened; he didn't remember deciding to lie down. He had collapsed without even being aware of it happening.

I should sit up, Luke told himself.

Using one arm, he pushed himself into a sitting position. His legs were crossed in front of him, and he smelled cooking flesh and smoke. His head spun and he slumped forward. In the next moment his stomach turned over and he vomited.

Blood gushed into his lap. He was puking blood.

"Oh no," Luke muttered to himself. His voice gurgled. *I'm going to die.*

Luke looked down. There was a smoking hole in his chest. He oozed blood. He hadn't just collapsed. He'd been shot.

When had *that* happened?

Working one handed, every motion an eternity, he pulled out his bandanna and began wadding it into the small hole in his upper chest.

Keeping pressure on the wound, Luke awkwardly worked the rifle sling loose and wrapped it around his body. He pulled it tight and sloppily tied it off to keep the cloth in place. It wasn't as tight as it should have been, but he couldn't get a good enough purchase. He leaned back.

His hand found the butt of the Remington and pulled it clear.

"I'm going to just catch my breath," Luke explained to himself.

"There's no time," he argued. "Hey? Who could've shot me?"

He looked up.

Three *soldados* in a triangle formation with a lieutenant trailing them approached. They stepped out of the woods and started walking in his direction, rifles ready. Luke had fallen back among the large, shiny leaves of a laurel berry bush. He was sprawled out, partially hidden behind a lodgepole pine sapling.

Luke studied them as they approached, taking shallow breaths. They were in a defensive formation, but weren't moving like they were nervous. They were almost strolling toward him.

They think I'm dead, he thought.

They walked up on him and stood in a line. One of them spat on his body as the rest lowered their rifle muzzles. When Luke opened his eyes wide and lifted the Remington it shocked them into stillness.

Their eyes bulged as Luke swept the pistol up.

He was less than ten feet away, point-blank range. The .44-caliber round left the barrel, and the booms of his firing penetrated the fog choking his brain, and Luke snapped back fully to reality.

Two of them dropped, one of them almost decapitated by the bullet that had caught him in the neck. The third turned to run, and Luke put two in his back. He swung his pistol around to fire on the trailing lieutenant, but the officer was gone. Luke caught a flash of his uniform among the trees as he disappeared.

Luke remembered Collins.

He looked over. Collins lay very still with his eyes closed. Luke couldn't tell if he was breathing or not. Didn't matter. Luke had made a plan. He was sticking to the plan. Using a branch to drag himself up, Luke staggered forward, each footstep jolting his wound. It was hard to breathe. The pistol felt heavy in his hand, like an anchor dragging him down.

Luke stumbled in and out of the trees like a drunk. He

wasn't moving stealthily, he was just moving, blundering through brush, tripping over roots and branches. As he continued bleeding, he experienced his consciousness as if it were floating above his body at the end of a kite string.

He stopped. He didn't know why. Blinking, Luke looked around stupidly. The group lay at his feet and he sank down to the earth. Luke looked at them. He was still in the best shape of anyone. He wanted to take a nap. Head nodding, he closed his eyes.

They snapped open again as he forced himself awake by sheer force of will.

Luke opened his eyes. He took hold of Talbot. He wasn't going to be able to pick him up. Fine, Luke would drag him by his collar. Luke found he couldn't stand. Fine. In a sort of fever dream Luke dragged the Englishman while crawling. Exhaustion caused him to blink, long and slow, and when he opened his eyes he was suddenly at the hiding place in the trees. He couldn't remember making the trip.

When Luke laid Talbot down next to Collins, he nearly collapsed. How had he gotten here? He tried again but still didn't remember making the trip.

In that state of semi-consciousness, Luke crawled back for the rest of his group.

Luke looked at them. Walks-the-Horizon was still. Delacroix looked furious. That seemed like a good sign. Luke wanted to take Delacroix next. She seemed capable of firing her weapon. Luke realized with a start that she had a compound fracture in her left arm. The bone stuck out of her skin like a broken branch.

"How'd I miss that?" Luke slurred his words. He pointed at her arm.

"You're stupid," she told him.

She tried to smile. It was ghastly.

Taking her belt, Luke transferred some of the ammunition and her dynamite sticks to his own belt. Using the stripped-down belt, he made a loop to put over her neck and maneuvered her broken arm into it to keep it from moving around as much as possible. Once she was at the hiding place he'd try to stop the bleeding.

Luke snatched her by her collar and began crawling. She chided him and told him to be careful, but she didn't have the strength to complain for long. It took every bit of her concentration to keep from screaming as Luke dragged her over the broken ground.

Luke had no idea where the rest of the soldiers were now. He couldn't grasp how much time was passing. It was darker than it had been earlier, but that was all he could tell. There were too many clouds to see the stars. Delacroix finally passed out.

Luke made it to the hiding place just as the Gatling gun opened up, the bullets shredding the branches and sawing at the tree trunks around them. The horrible, deafening chatter of the weapon welled up, grew into a wave that washed Luke away into utter blackness.

CHAPTER 31

When he came to, it was like a fever dream. He hung limp in the grip of two men. Rough male voices speaking Spanish milled around him. They weren't being gentle, and he knew he was in pain but it felt far away, as if he were watching someone else suffer.

"¿Queda alguno vivo?"

"Todos están muertos."

"Tirar las claras en una pila."

There were men bustling around him, and he heard the clatter of rifles on slings and the sound of animals, horses or mules, he wasn't sure which. He smelled rank manure somewhere close by and was nearly gagged by the press of hot, sweating bodies. He smelled blood.

Surreptitiously, he found his lip with his teeth and he bit down hard to pull his mind away from the sharp agonies lancing through his body. But even as he did so, he realized that he felt, essentially, whole. He'd been wounded badly before, knew exactly how that felt. He was better than that right now.

His clothes were glued to his skin by blood, and he figured the fact that he was bathed in it was why the Mexicans thought he was dead. But he was weak as a kitten, and the jostling jerked his head around on his neck. He couldn't take the rough handling.

He felt a wave of vertigo and his eyes rolled up in his head and all was black once again.

The next time, Luke woke to the sound of flies.

The buzzing filled his ears. As he tried to open his eyes, he found them nearly glued shut, and he had to strain to part the lids and eyelashes. His skin was sticky and tight, and the air rasped in and out of his lungs in short, shallow breaths, rattling in his aching chest.

The glare of the sun met his eyes, and he moaned softly in pain. Heat had settled over him in an oppressive blanket. He blinked, giving his eyes time to adjust to the hard-edged sunshine, and as he did he realized he couldn't just hear the flies, he felt them as well. They scuttled across his face. Disgusted, he shook his head in reflex and the droning exploded in volume as the carrion bugs buzzed in protest.

Agonizing bolts of pain lanced through his temples so sudden and sharp that he gasped. He lay still for a moment, the flies forgotten. As he winced, his olfactory senses seemed to switch on like a piece of disused machinery. Suddenly the agony of his head was replaced with a fresh new hell.

He gagged as he inhaled the stench of rotting flesh. The scent of death filled his nostrils and clung there like mud to the bottom of a boot. His stomach revolted and his gorge rose in his throat, acidic and vile. He coughed, suddenly choking, and turned his head to the side so he could vomit.

The pain was less overwhelming now, more tolerable. His eyes adjusted to the daylight, and as the bile rushed over his parched lips, he saw around him for the first time. His hand went to his holster in a sudden, reflexive snap and found it empty.

He was in the shale of a slight escarpment. Prickly pear and brittlebush poked up from the gravelly soil. The sky was a cloudless, anemic blue. Down the hill he saw dottings of pine trees and the south fork of the river where the battle had taken place.

Laid out on the slope next to him were the bodies of his group. O'Toole. Collins. Talbot. Delacroix. Their broken, mutilated bodies had been arranged in a line. Flies crawled across eyes grayed with death. Their ashen faces were streaked with clotting crimson and black-scarlet stains soaked their clothes. Their flesh, the muscle and skin and sinew, showed the trauma they'd endured in a ghastly display.

He whispered, not even fully aware of what he was saying. It might have been a prayer.

He realized in an abrupt rush of understanding that this was the work of the Mexican *soldados*. Apaches wouldn't have laid them out in such an orderly fashion, and they'd have all been scalped long before now. He also realized the soldiers must have thought he was dead as well, or surely he'd be in chains tied behind a mule for a long walk to the nearest town where, with little pomp and circumstance, he would have been propped against a wall to serve as target practice for a firing squad.

He heard the crunch of gravel and reacted out of pure instinct. He dropped back into the position he'd awakened in and closed his eyes. Calling upon his courage and mental discipline, he slowly exhaled and made his body limp. Flies settled on him like a living shroud.

"Dios mío! Apesta, compañero!"

Footsteps came closer, kicking loose scree down the incline in little avalanches of pebbles and jagged shale. Luke carefully moved the fingers on his left hand, just enough to check the holster on that side. Just as he'd assumed, that Remington was gone, too. He flexed his calf. The boot knife was still there. He could feel it. Likely the soldiers in charge of dragging him up here had been exhausted from the battle and unfocused after so much fear and rage and adrenaline. They'd missed the knife.

A knife wasn't much good against guns, and he didn't have a clue yet how close the rest of the Mexicans were. Still, it was better than nothing. It was, in fact, a start. The footsteps stopped just down the slope from him, the men arguing in Spanish.

He opened his eyes a fraction, looking out from behind the screen of his eyelashes. Two squat soldiers in the tan uniform of the northern Mexican militias stood down the slope, about six feet from the bottom of his boots.

They argued over who was going to wrap the bodies for travel and who was going to stand guard in case the Apaches returned. Luke frowned as he caught a familiar name in the jumble of rapid-fire Spanish.

Melichus.

He strained to hear over the buzzing flies, afraid to move in any way. Mentally, he willed his tensed body to relax, to appear limp and loose in death. The men weren't paying attention to him. He was so much dead meat rotting in the sun to them. Breathing shallowly through his nose, he tried making out what they were saying.

He started in surprise when he realized what they were talking about. Quickly he relaxed again, hoping they hadn't noticed the reaction. One of the men looked over at him. The man's eyes, muddy brown and squinted against the desert sun, ran across Luke's limp form.

Flies crawled across Luke's face as he lay there. They scurried over his eyes and lips, exploring the recesses of his nostrils. Every fiber of his being revolted at the disgusting, featherlight scurrying. His brain screamed for him to sit up and dislodge the disease-carrying bugs from his face.

But to do so would mean death. Luke lay still and suffered.

After a moment, the Mexican soldier hacked up some dust and spat on Luke's pants before turning back to his compadre. He grunted his consent to something the other man said that Luke didn't understand, and the two of them began walking down the escarpment toward where Luke now saw a burro loaded down with supplies. The animal stood tied to a clump of chaparral.

Once they were several steps away, Luke couldn't stand it anymore, and he risked snorting hard, clearing the flies nesting inside his nose. The protesting flies rose and hovered in a black cloud, then descended once more onto his face.

The Mexicans think we're with Melichus, he thought.

The subsequent shootout, even though they'd started it themselves, would have done nothing to change their minds on that account, he realized.

They butchered four people on a wild assumption, he thought angrily. *It's by sheer damn luck I survived, and if they learn that fact they won't waste any time dealing with me like any other outlaw.*

His choices were stark. Give himself up and be executed or fight his way clear. If he wanted to live there really wasn't a choice. The Mexicans had brought this upon themselves, because there was one thing Luke knew for certain: Melichus was still out there, driving those captives to a life of slavery.

Moving slowly, Luke began to twist and inch his hand toward the knife in his boot.

CHAPTER 32

One of the soldiers came up the hill. His name was Pedro Juarez, and he'd been born and raised in the Sonora. A rifle was slung over his shoulder and slapped the back of his thigh as he walked. The weapon was a .50-70 US Springfield, a souvenir of the War Between the States, part of the arms shipments that flowed south across the border now that the French had pulled out of the country.

He stopped down at the line of corpses and regarded them thoughtfully. He cocked his head as he mentally made his way along the line. His eyes stopped when they got to Delacroix. He grinned, a big toothy smile that showed the greenish tint to his teeth and the black rot around the gums.

He walked closer and looked at the woman. She'd been torn apart by bullets, but he could still see the swell of her breasts through her bloody shirt. Her eyes stared off, unseeing, directly into the sun, covered in a patina of gray so that the eyeballs were clouded to the sheen of pearls.

It was a waste the gringo woman was dead. Pedro had never been with a white woman. Just whores in Hermosillo. Once also with an Apache woman they found when they raided an old camp. She'd been left behind and sung her death song as the soldiers approached. She'd been very old and he hadn't enjoyed himself all that much.

With a woman like this redhead it would have been different.

He snuck a look around. No one was watching. The lieutenant was consolidating their ammo and arranging for transport of the wounded men. He'd been left to stand picket on this side by himself. Everyone else was over the rise of the escarpment.

He licked his lips. Nervously, he bent down and ran his hands across the soft shelf of the woman's breast. He shivered in delight. He stood again, wondering how much time he had alone. Gravel crunched softly behind him.

Startled, he turned to look.

Before the *soldado* could even begin to turn, Luke stepped up behind him and slammed his forearm around the man's scrawny neck, pressing hard and strangling the startled cry before it made it out of his throat. The soldier began to thrash. The knife from Luke's boot punched into the soldier's liver, six inches of Arkansas-crafted steel slicing through the organ.

The soldier convulsed in Luke's grip, muffled cries of terror vibrating through his throat and into the skin of Luke's forearm. The man's knees buckled. Blood poured from the wound. Luke yanked the knife back out then whipped it around in a half circle, driving the point up under the soldier's ribs and into his pounding heart.

The man stiffened once then fell limp, and Luke let him slide from his arms to land in a crumpled heap at his feet. The soldier's eyes bulged, filmed gray in death, and seemed to watch him as he looted the corpse.

He cleaned his blade on the man's shirt in two quick slaps and slid it home in the boot sheath. Hands free, he snatched up the Springfield and checked to make sure a round was chambered. Next he took the man's canteen and then his bandolier of ammunition.

He heard footsteps just over the slight rise. He was out of time. Desperately he looked for a place to hide.

Luck was with him. Just beyond the line of the bodies, the spring runoff had carved a shallow gully. It was choked with cheatgrass and creosote bushes. The Mexican was slight and not tall compared to the American and Luke yanked him up and shoved him into the gully and then threw himself down into the powdery, crumbling dirt next to the body.

This was far from a perfect hiding place. Luke froze, forcing himself to lie perfectly still. He heard the clatter of dislodged pebbles and shale as the footsteps of whoever was approaching set off mini-avalanches on the escarpment with each step.

He wished for his pistols. Tucked into the gully like he was, bringing the Springfield to bear would be extremely difficult. Slowly he began inching it forward from where it was caught between him and the gully wall. The footsteps came closer.

The rattle came in a hard, angry buzzing. It was a sound everyone in the West knew without question. Rattlesnake. Rattlers were rarely aggressive by temperament, but if they felt threatened or aggrieved, say by the bodies of two full grown men being dumped on them, then they would strike.

Frantic, Luke's gaze darted around, searching for the threat. The furious rattle buzzed again and it sounded like it was coming from under his damn nose. Cold adrenaline gushed through his system, and his heart began pounding in response. There was a motion to his left and his eyes darted there.

The agitated snake twisted in on itself, head still low, tail up and trembling. Its forked tongue slipped in and out of its mouth as it tasted the air. It was a Sonoran sidewinder, quick as lightning and potentially deadly this far from help. Luke froze, one hand wrapped around the Springfield's front stock.

The footsteps came up to the line of bodies. The person

walking went still and Luke knew the man had heard the sidewinder as well. He would be scanning his surroundings, trying to find the snake. In the gully the snake lifted its blunt, diamond-shaped head.

Operating on instinct, Luke reacted, using the barrel of the Springfield the way a matador uses a red cape. The snake immediately became fixated on the barrel waving close to it and turned its attention from the nearly motionless Luke farther down. The head rose and the serpent hissed as it revealed long curved fangs.

Luke knew his timing had to be perfect.

He jiggled the barrel slightly. The angry snake struck like a whip uncoiling. It struck the metal barrel of the firearm and bounced off. Instantly Luke struck. Sweeping the barrel back he pinned the snake against the hard earth.

The snake began thrashing wildly, but Luke pressed the rifle hard against it while his other hand came up and snatched the sidewinder right behind its head. Without conscious thought his arm whipsawed around and flung the snake toward the Mexican soldier now standing over the line of dead bodies.

The snake struck and bounced roughly, propelled directly at the soldier. Luke had tried to cast the rattlesnake up slope and slightly behind the soldier and his throw had been exceptional. The snake cut off the man's line of retreat and began aggressively crawling in its signature side-to-side motion toward the startled Mexican.

The man squawked and leapt backward. He fumbled with the carbine on his shoulder. Luke was up and on his feet. His foot found the lip of the shallow gully and he bounded forward. The Mexican realized he was never going to get his weapon free in time to escape the snake and instead turned to run.

His eyes bulged in horror as he beheld the blood-soaked

American before him. Luke drew the Springfield back and
slammed the rifle butt into his face. The harsh *crack* of the
impact followed hard by the wet sound of a nose being shattered and blood gushing. The Mexican's head whipped back
and he staggered.

Luke was on him like a hunting cougar, the rifle butt rais-
ing and falling without mercy. The second strike shattered the
man's jaw and drove him to the ground. Luke took the rifle
barrel up in both hands like the haft of an axe and brought it
down hard on the top of the man's head.

Behind them the sidewinder, locked in a sort of blood
frenzy, struck. The man didn't even respond when the snake
fangs punched through the soiled and sweat stained material
of his uniform to bury themselves to the hilt in his back
muscles. His brains were already leaking from a cracked-
open skull.

Luke, breathing hard through his pain and exhaustion,
panting with the effort in the unforgiving sun, stepped forward and stuck the barrel of his battered Springfield under
the snake and flung it back into the gully where it slithered
rapidly off.

He had to work quickly now. One of his wounds had
opened up and fresh blood was spilling down his side and
into his pants where it glued the material to his flesh. Clouds
of flies had erupted in angry swarms at the distraction of the
combat.

Moving sideways, still clutching the Springfield by its
bloody stock, he made for the place at the bottom of the escarpment where the soldiers had tied their mounts and pack
animals. He'd already killed their guard, so there was little to
do but run. Every moment was precious. He had to scatter
those animals after taking the best for himself.

If he could strand the Mexicans on foot they'd have no
choice but discontinue the chase. Even as he hurried, sliding

down little avalanches of shale chips and sharp gravel, his heart twisted in loathing at the idea of leaving Delacroix and the others behind. They wouldn't be buried and the thought of the redhead rotting in the sun until the vultures and bush rats and coyotes came to scavenge was almost more than he could bear.

But it was run or die.

So he ran.

CHAPTER 33

He managed to get mounted and secure a moderately loaded mule before scattering the rest of the Mexican horses. He headed out, relying more on speed than stealth at this point. He drove the horse north, back toward the mountains where he knew there was water and where he hoped the soldiers had suffered too many casualties to want to risk meeting more Apaches.

When he scattered the other mounts, he heard shouting and cries of near panic from the surviving Mexican *soldados*. He was partway over an open plain of cactus and sand headed for a small bluff when he heard the rifle fire.

Angry lead hornets buzzed past but none came too close. After a short, all-out gallop, when he turned to look, he could see where the bullets fell and struck the earth when he'd ridden outside their range. He was feeling light-headed and burned with a fever that had little to do with the unforgiving Sonoran sun.

He felt his wounds begin weeping again, seeping through the gnarled, scabbed-over injuries. He needed to cleanse and dress them properly. He also had to put as many miles between himself and the Mexican army patrol as possible.

The horses were trained military mounts. Once they'd

calmed they'd be relatively easy to round up. His hope was
that with some of their supplies gone they would return to bar-
racks to resupply and gather reinforcements. The Mexicans'
noses had been bloodied badly, and for every American or
Apache corpse laid out there had to be two or three *soldados*.

Four hours later, he reached the top of a mesa and looked
out over his back trail.

His lips were parched and cracked. He carefully drank
from a canteen off the gear of the stolen mule. Despite his
thirst, he slowly lowered the canteen. Out on the landscape
spread out like a tabletop below him, Luke saw three dots
break the horizon.

"You stubborn *pendejos,*" he coughed out of his dry throat.

He had the high ground, but they wouldn't be in range
until after dark. He couldn't hit what he couldn't see. Besides,
the Springfield had been used to batter more than one man.
The impacts were bound to have knocked the sights off. He
could try and adjust it, but without firing rounds he wouldn't
know if he'd fixed it or not.

He couldn't afford to waste the ammunition, and he didn't
want to alert the three men hunting him of where exactly on
the mesa he was. Even waiting for close range, he was taking
a chance of entering combat with an inaccurate rifle. Better
not to fight.

Plus there was the situation of the lost Remingtons. He
knew the *capitán* would have claimed the pistols for himself.
They were too nice to waste on a peon lucky to be armed
with a muzzleloader. No, his revolvers were prime pieces of
weaponry. The officer would keep them. Rank had its privi-
leges.

He gave the horse water. It pained him to have to give so
much up, but now that he knew horsemen were following
him he had to keep the animal in as prime a condition as
possible. He needed to get to that water in the mountains.

Resigned, exhausted, leaking blood, he hauled himself back up into the saddle and rode on.

At the foot of the mountains his vision began to darken and he swooned. He stayed in the saddle for another few miles on willpower alone. When he angled out of a stand of ponderosa pine and into the sun near the opening of a narrow arroyo, his eyes rolled up into his head and he fell forward like a man shot by a rifle.

The ground swept up and struck him with hammer force, and he moaned. Somewhere on his body one of his crusted-over wounds broke open, and hot sticky blood trickled out to make crimson mud in the dust. He moaned.

His heart beat hard in his chest as he struggled to push himself up. Dust clogged his nostrils as he inhaled under the strain. His limbs felt leadened and numb.

"Get up!" he ordered himself.

Arms trembling, he pushed hard against the ground, bunching the muscles in his arms under the strain. He barely lifted his chest free of the dirt before fatigue made him settle back down. He smelled the astringent odor of pine as his nose came to rest in a nest of old brown needles.

"Get up," he told himself again.

His body had to be reasonable. He wanted to live. To have any chance of living he needed to get back in the saddle. To get back in the saddle he had to rise. Simple.

He lifted his head as he dug his fingers into the warm earth and vertigo swamped him in an instant. He closed his eyes against the sudden flashes of pain lancing through his body. His arms shook violently as he pushed. He came off the ground and reached out for the stirrup nearest him.

He grappled it clumsily and the horse, unused to him, grew skittish and jumped away. The stirrup jerked from his weak grip. Luke went down again, burying his face hard in the ground. He lay there for a moment, panting like a man at the end of a long race.

"Get up," he begged himself.

He didn't move.

Just rest for a moment, he thought, delirious from the fever burning through his body like a brush fire. *Just a moment and then you'll get up.*

Just a moment . . . His eyes closed.

He opened them with a start. No way of knowing how long he'd been out cold. Long enough. Before him he saw a pair of bead-worked moccasins. He rolled his eyes upward but the figure stood with its back to the sun. All he could see was a black silhouette against the white-golden glare.

Apache, he thought. *I am dead.*

Luke's head sagged back into the dirt and rested heavily there. He fought to keep his eyes open but the battle wasn't even close.

The figure stood motionless for one long moment, weighing the man's life. It held the reins of the horse loosely in one hand. The mule had not wandered far. Turning from the unconscious Luke, the figure went over and picked up the Springfield. The rifle was in good shape.

Rifle. Horse. Mule. Trade goods. All these items added up to a nice chunk of wealth to any scavenger. The figure considered its haul, then sighed. Mumbling in disgust, it began searching for branches long enough to create a travois with.

CHAPTER 34

Several hours later, the Mexican officer and his sergeant came to a halt at the spot where their quarry had collapsed. They studied the tracks and spilled blood clotting the dirt.

"He's still badly injured," the sergeant pointed out. "He will die soon."

"That is not good enough!" the captain raged. "My honor has been insulted by this common brigand."

The two sergeants looked at each other. The captain's honor had been insulted by these white bandits who rode with Apaches and brought a whore along with them who'd turned out to be a savage fighter. However, he knew this wasn't the only problem. The command had been decimated. Sixty men reduced to fewer than ten, their horses driven off and the bandit responsible escaped.

Failure on this order was rewarded only one way in the Mexican army: stripping of rank, flogging, and being sent east to guard the prisoners working the salt mines beyond Caborca.

No. Much better to hound this bandit until they had his head.

The captain studied the landscape. He and his soldiers had ridden all through these mountains hunting Apache. He knew what lay before them. A narrow, winding canyon led back to the cliff dwellings of a Hopi village. Unless you could scramble and climb like a mountain goat, the only way out was back through the canyon. He doubted the man so wounded his men thought him dead (the idiots) would be climbing any cliff walls, no matter how he'd fought.

"If he rode with the Apaches and the Hopi helped him, it's possible he lives. We will not stop until I have the gringo's head."

Luke would never fully remember the next several hours. He held vague memories of his body shivering violently, wracked with fever. He realized at some point that the figure that had taken him was an old woman and that she made him drink bitter concoctions that seemed to make him feel better enough to sleep.

He spoke once mumbling "Apache, Apache . . ."

He recalled the old woman telling him in Spanish, *"No Apache, Hopi. Estás en la casa de los Hopi."* Then, more firmly, *"No Apache."*

"Men are coming," he babbled. *"Hombres, Mexicanos, soldados."*

But then he was back in Georgia at the end of the war, talking to another woman, this one young and beautiful, who had nursed him back to health once upon a time. Another time he had been left for dead by his enemies. This cycle of lucidity and fever dreams played itself out repeatedly. He woke once to pain in his torso and found he had been tied down to stakes driven deep into the earthen floor. The old woman was sewing his wounds closed.

When he started to cry out, she gave him a thick cloth soaked in whiskey to bite down on. He struggled briefly but was still too exhausted to fight. All he could do was lie there and suffer through it. Finally, she finished, and he was able to sink into a deep slumber from which he did not stir for many hours.

* * *

When he woke he found himself in a city of the dying. The old woman brought him beans and corn and medicine, though he never figured out why she helped him. In broken Spanish and crude trade language she told him the story of this pueblo.

"Once the Hopi flourished here," she said, "safe in their hidden valley and high in their pueblo houses. They grew maize and hunted antelope and traded their blankets and bowls with the Navajo and hid when the wretched ones, the Apache, came. But even with the Apache they traded.

"Then came the Spanish, and when they left, the Comancheros. But with the tobacco and iron tools the Comancheros also brought the plague, influenza."

Within two weeks all who were going to die, which was nearly everyone, did die. The old woman, Ciji, had been a new bride and mother then, she explained as they shared harsh tobacco out of an ancient Zuni clay pipe.

In less time than it took for the moon to pass from new to full, she was a widow and without her two little boys. Now the dozen or so survivors had grown old and would die here among their forgotten people.

Luke was quick to heal under Ciji's ministrations. His wounds scarred over and his strength returned as the days passed and became a week. As best he could tell, the woman helped him out of some combination of boredom and loneliness. It was just a guess, however, and he couldn't say for sure what her motivation truly was.

Once the fever broke and he'd grown strong enough to climb up and down the lodgepole pine ladder, he began moving around, fetching his own water, relieving himself outdoors. Bathing in the river that meandered through the valley.

There were other Hopi here, a dozen or so. They watched him with indifferent eyes. They offered him no harm, but he knew, unlike Ciji, they would have left him to die. He saw no young people, only elders, and he wondered if the reason the Apache had left them alone was because they were so obviously poor.

On the second morning after he was able to walk, he woke up feeling strong. His mind had already turned to Melichus and the captives. He worried at the problem and was just about to ask Ciji if she knew anything about the outlaw when Makyah, an ancient fossil of a man, appeared at the square opening in the roof of Ciji's house.

He spoke in a voice like gravel. Luke had no idea what the old man was saying, only that partway through his animated spiel he heard the Spanish word *soldados* and grew instantly alert. Done speaking, the old man regarded Luke with a sour expression before Ciji shooed him away.

For some reason, possibly no more hard to understand than a reduction of his pain, Luke noticed, truly noticed, her buckskin dress for the first time. It had been rendered bone white by some process he was unfamiliar with. She was a medicine woman of some considerable capability, he realized.

"What did that old coot want?" he asked, speaking Spanish. "Other than to give me the skunk eye, I mean. I heard him say *soldado*. Are men coming?"

"*Sí*," she answered. "While you healed, the Two Gun Captain waited at the valley mouth. Today more men have come. I think he was only waiting for them to come and get you."

"Two guns? Two pistols?"

Ciji nodded. He described the Remingtons, and she nodded again. He'd thought them lost and now it seemed providence was returning them to him once again. If he survived.

"How many men total?"

"Nine."

"I need a gun," he said.

CHAPTER 35

Outside the valley, Captain Llamosa looked over his men. None of them appeared particularly professional or enthused to be here. The ride across the Sonora from Caborca had obviously been rough. They look tired and burned by the sun and unhappy about going into a box canyon after a man who'd almost wiped out an entire platoon of their comrades-in-arms.

It is, he thought, too damn bad.

If he returned to garrison without the outlaw he might as well turn in his saber and return to his family in Mexico City in dishonor. This wouldn't be like the incident with the Cantina *puta* back in the capital; such failure as this would not be swept under the rug. He was going to get this *bandido*.

Besides, who knew? From what Llamosa had seen, the man rode with Apaches and whites, and was now cared for by other savages. Perhaps this was the feared Melichus himself. If he brought the man's head on the end of a cavalry lance he'd be hailed as a hero no matter how many enlisted men he got killed in the process. The territorial governor would likely put him in for a medal.

Juan Llamosa liked the idea of being adorned with a medal much more than he did the idea of returning home in disgrace.

His sergeant major rode up. The man had been with him for several years, since Llamosa had been a brand-new lieutenant fresh to the West and the northern border. Sergeant Major Jesus Sanchez was the iron fist inside Llamosa's aristocratic glove. He gave the orders and Sanchez was the bulldog who made sure those orders were carried out. He was a squat, hatchet-nosed figure of a man with ham-hock fists and a permanent squint who spoke little when he wasn't repeating Llamosa's orders.

"Get the men ready," Llamosa said without preamble. "We have the *bastardo* cornered and we're going in."

Sanchez grunted his acquiescence. Then asked, "The Indians?"

"As usual. Kill them and collect scalps. The governor appreciates being provided with Apache scalps to display."

Again Sanchez nodded. If he knew the Hopi in the cliff dwelling valley before him weren't actually Apaches, it didn't matter overly much to him. Turning his horse, he began barking orders for Llamosa, Sanchez, and the other seven men to line up for inspection.

The unit was in bad shape. The ride across the Sonora had been taxing on both man and horse. The cavalry soldiers drooped in the saddle, fatigued and thirsty. Their already deeply bronzed faces showed ruddy in the unforgiving sunlight and their uniforms were stiff with their sweat.

These were men long used to taking orders, so when Sanchez gave the command to form up they fell in despite any discomfort or weariness they felt. With Llamosa looking on, Sanchez put them through their paces. Sabers loosened. Pistols loaded and at half cock. Carbines primed and hammers set.

Spurs jangled as the troop took a stirrup and swung up into their saddles. First in the rank was Gomez, a gleeful little killer from the Baja peninsula. He loved saber work and had

mastered the art of racing even with a fleeing infantryman
and dispatching him with a single backhand swing in just the
Napoleonic manner he'd been trained when the French ruled
Mexico.

Next to him sat Miguel Alverez-Curiel, who was colloqui-
ally and exclusively known as Gafas, or Spectacles, because
of his oversized glasses. With the exception of Llamosa,
Curiel was the only man in the troop who could read and
write.

The brothers Esteban and Carlos were native to the
Sonoran Desert, coming from a hamlet just south of Yuma,
Arizona Territory. Though they'd joined the army to escape
crushing poverty, they would have fought the Apache on
their own if no one had offered to pay them. Apaches had
wiped out most of the men in their village and stolen the
children, including their sister, as slaves. Both their mother
and father had been killed in the slaughter. Just boys, they'd
only survived by hiding in the tall bushes down by the trickle
of a stream that bordered their village.

They did not bother distinguishing between hostile and
non-hostile Indians. Red skin was enough to mark them for
death in the eyes of Esteban and Carlos.

Lined up beyond them was Domingo, the marksman. The
oldest man in the troop, he was also the best shot. Upon
seeing him shooting in garrison, Llamosa had insisted the
man be made a part of his command. He carried a Springfield
rifle with the near unheard-of accoutrement of a Malcolm 6X
scope. Domingo proved so lethal with the scope, he managed
to keep the troop fed by hunting the highly elusive mountain
goats.

Once, during a raid, Llamosa had spotted two Apache
children running for safety more than half a mile away. Resting the barrel on his saddle, Domingo had killed them both
on the run. Impressive shooting.

The final two soldiers in the line, Bernardo and Simon,

had the distinction of competing not only for who was the youngest, but also the most stupid. Ugly brutes of men, in many ways they seemed more like brothers than Carlos and Esteban. What Llamosa cared most about was that they followed orders and did not shy away from killing.

These were the men he'd been given to hunt down the gringo who'd destroyed his platoon. Now that *cabrón* was trapped in the dirt huts of some vermin Indian tribe that should have been wiped out long ago.

Captain Llamosa's spirits were lifting. He nodded to Sanchez.

"Let's move out, Sergeant Major."

"Sir, yes sir," Sergeant Major Sanchez growled in response. When he spoke again his voice boomed out with the clarity of a pistol shot in a quiet room. "Mount up and prepare to ride!"

Unhurried, the troop entered the canyon.

CHAPTER 36

The line of cavalry troopers entered the canyon and came to a stop before the cliff dwellings. On the ground, an old man worked at tanning a bobcat hide, scraping it with long, careful strokes with a stone awl. He watched the Mexicans with hooded eyes, face impassive.

"You there, old man," Llamosa barked. "Do you speak Spanish like a civilized human?"

The man regarded them, and after a moment, nodded. *"Sí,"* he said.

"Where is the white man?" Llamosa pointed a gloved finger at him. "Do not lie. We know he is here."

"I will not lie," the old man answered. "I did not invite him here. He is not my guest."

"Then where is he?"

The old man turned and looked at the pueblo cliff dwellings, some six hundred years old, that rose up hugging the cliff face behind him. There was a long pine log ladder running from the ground up to the first level of buildings.

Llamosa followed his gaze, nonplussed. It was one thing to enter a village by force and root out a single man. It was quite another to try and find him in a vertical maze of ladders and openings. Especially a man such as this one had proven to be.

"No matter," Llamosa told himself. "Honor demands it."
He turned to Sanchez. "Prepare to search."

Sanchez turned to the men. "You heard the captain! Off
those horses and up the damn ladder, you miserable dogs!"

Luke assembled the Springfield in a hurried but practiced
manner. He'd taken the rifle apart and put it back together
several times to familiarize himself with the weapon and
ensure there was not even the smallest amount of grit present.
There had been no gun oil in the supplies he'd managed to
steal before fleeing.

The second time he'd done so, Ciji had appeared and
given him some oil.

"Gun oil?" he asked, confused how she'd come into possession of it.

She shook her head no. "Muskrat gland."

As soon as she opened the cork stopper on the little stone
phial, he'd known with only a whiff that it wasn't a store-
bought product. Still, it worked, and he lightly greased the
bolt and barrel before feeding a round into the breach.

Ciji appeared, a heavy bundle in her withered brown
hands. Luke regarded her with questioning eyes. He wondered again why she was helping him, but in the end decided
the whys didn't matter. He was in no position to refuse help,
and without this Hopi medicine woman he'd have been dead
by now.

"The men are here," she said, speaking Spanish. *Los
hombres están aquí.* "Take this."

Without ceremony, she thrust the heavy bundle into his
hands, forcing him to set the Springfield down. He took the
bundle and looked at her.

"It belonged to my man," she said. "He got it from the
Comancheros for many fine rugs."

Carefully, Luke unwrapped it.

He found a Colt Dragoon. The pistol was big, heavy, with a long barrel and five-round cylinder. A percussion revolver designed as a sidearm for cavalrymen, this model sported worn walnut grips. She didn't offer him additional ammunition. What he got was what he had.

He eyed the weapon, carefully running the chamber along his arm and counting the clicks to make sure it was loaded to capacity. A round was missing. Four shots then.

Four shots and the Springfield. It was far better than nothing.

"Thank you," he said.

"Kill the Mexicans." She spat. "For all I have done for you, kill the Mexicans. They do not bother to know the difference between Hopi and Apache. They kill us and take our hair and claim to have defeated some Mescalero warband. They are liars and cowards!"

"They're going to leave me very little choice," Luke said. "So I think you're going to get your wish."

At the foot of the pueblo before them, Llamosa halted his men as the last one climbed the first ladder. For a moment, they considered the rising structure before them, attempting to deduce the best way to approach it tactically. Already Llamosa felt the hair on the back of his neck rise as he realized what an advantage a sniper would have in this forest of adobe buildings. The ancient city wasn't just tall, it was deep as well, with the entire pueblo town built on a wide shelf that gave the dwellings depth.

He saw several faces peering out at him from the length of the cluster of buildings. All the faces were brown, so he paid them little mind. The buildings were far from uniform. Some rose as much as three times the height of others. The entire city was a series of ladder-connected platforms and bolt-holes.

"Pull that ladder up after us, Sergeant Major Sanchez," he ordered. "No easy escape for our quarry."

"Yes, sir."

"And Sanchez?"

"Sir?"

"Have Bernardo and Simon keep it close. We must not find ourselves without a ladder in this place."

"Yes, sir." Sanchez went on, "He knows we're here. There is no element of surprise in this."

Llamosa grunted his acknowledgment, already plotting how to best execute a search. He turned to Domingo, the marksman. "You come last when we move. Find good platforms and watch over us as we go room to room."

"Si, mi capitán."

"The rest of you spread out and stagger yourselves, carbines ready. We'll move slowly and methodically."

So saying, Llamosa drew one of Luke Jensen's fine Remington pistols and thumbed the hammer back. The cocking mechanism made a graceful, oily *click* as he thumbed it into position. The sheer artistry of the weapon made him smile. The pistols of an American gunfighter outlaw would certainly impress the ladies of Mexico City when he returned the triumphant hero.

The men, many of them obviously nervous, began moving across the wide mezzanine avenue between the first cluster of buildings. Their Springfields were up and held ready, hammers thumbed back. Their eyes darted and scanned the open windows looking for protruding rifle barrels. They warily watched the open squares that served as doorways, ready for a deadly gringo's head and shoulders to suddenly appear as he opened fire at close range. Llamosa counted the ladders he could see, determined to notice if any of them disappeared if he looked away even briefly.

The rifle report was a sharp *crack* that echoed like a thunderclap in among the stone and clay buildings. Blood splashed into the air like a glass of casually tossed wine and Carlos screamed, his shoulder jerking hard to one side as a heavy bullet found the muscle there.

Llamosa spun in the direction of the falling soldier and stumbled backward in surprise as the air inches from his face burned with the distinctive ripping sound of a near miss and a second rifle report echoed through the pueblo city.

Carlos fell backward and dropped, blood gushing from his wound to form a growing pond beneath him.

"Get back!" Llamosa shouted.

The men had fanned out as much as the terrain allowed and were preparing to return fire when he yelled his command. A third shot narrowly missed Sanchez and the big man squawked in frightened surprise as he threw himself flat.

In rapid succession, two more rounds blasted out, narrowly missing Bernardo until he managed to duck behind the corner of a building.

As close as those shots are coming, we'd be dead if he had a properly zeroed weapon instead of one of our stolen Springfields, Llamosa thought.

"How is he?" Llamosa demanded as Sanchez checked on the wounded Carlos.

"The way he's cussing he has to be okay," Sanchez said. "Esteban, bandage him up!" The sergeant major drew his revolver. "You want us to press in? Domingo can provide covering fire."

Llamosa considered the proposal but then shook his head. "No. He's got nowhere to go and it's getting dark. We've got time. We'll do this methodically."

He paused for a moment, mind working hard as he scanned the tall pueblo where he believed Luke was hidden. The American had the advantage of terrain here. They needed to drive him out into the open like animals fleeing a forest. . . .

Llamosa smiled.

"Fire," he said. "We'll smoke him out."

"The buildings are adobe," Sanchez pointed out.

"Yes, Sergeant Major, they are. But what do we have in our packs for night watch?"

"Kerosene," Bernardo said. "We have the flask of kerosene."

"We also have a stick of dynamite we took from the dead Americans," Gafas spoke up. "Smoke and fire."

"Make it happen," Llamosa said.

The men worked fast, one of them retreating down the ladder to retrieve the supplies from the mules. Jensen took a shot at him, but missed, and the soldiers were able to more fully narrow down his position. They stuck to the shadow of several buildings as they prepared their missiles.

"We throw the dynamite at the bottom, try to weaken the building," Llamosa instructed. "Then, when the explosion goes off and we know his head is down, move forward and throw the lanterns."

Domingo took a kerosene tin and, leaving it open, stepped to the edge of the narrow one-story pueblo hiding the army unit from Luke.

"Ready," he said.

Esteban lit his stick of confiscated dynamite. Immediately the rest of them unloaded their weapons in Luke's general direction in a firestorm of lead. In the midst of the fusillade, Esteban swung around the corner and threw the stick. He ducked quickly back around the corner, the signal for the rest of the men to take cover.

The burning stick of dynamite tumbled end over burning end in a high arc through the air. Striking the adobe wall of the pueblo it bounced back a few feet and dropped to the base of the building. It rolled to a stop against the adobe wall, fuse sizzling, sparks showering the hard packed clay around it.

The dynamite went off like a cannon blast, shaking the ground under the soldiers' feet. Black smoke billowed up from the site of the explosion. Domingo pitched the can of kerosene underhand and it sailed into the cloud of smoke.

A shot rang out, marring the wall inches from the Mexican soldier's head.

"Now the lantern!" Llamosa cried, eager as a hound on the scent.

Domingo lit the brass lantern and took it by the handle. He nodded, and once again the rest of the soldiers opened fire. Stepping around the corner, he hurtled the lit lantern after the spilling kerosene tin. The throw was perfect, and there was a *whoosh* as the lantern broke apart and the flammable liquid ignited.

Domingo went to step back and staggered as a single shot rang out. He fell over backward, nothing more than a sack of loose meat, and Llamosa saw that most of his face was gone where Luke Jensen had placed a single round between his eyes.

The soldier hit the ground heavily and lay very still, a pool of blood spilling out to form a pond around his motionless corpse.

"*Dios mios!*" Simon cried out.

"Add another mark against the American," Llamosa snarled.

"With Carlos wounded, we're down to seven," Sanchez said.

As always, the man spoke in a calm, near monotone voice. If the loss of his men or the precariousness of the situation bothered him, it did not show. His seeming indifference had a calming effect on the men, though it also reminded them how expendable he and the captain viewed them all.

Llamosa looked at the building where Jensen was making his last stand. He frowned. The dynamite had opened a hole about the size of a wagon wheel in the adobe and sent cracks halfway up the structure, but the smoke put out by the burning kerosene was minimal and not drifting in the correct direction.

"We wait for night," he said. "Then we rush him."

* * *

Luke Jensen stood back from the window and surveyed the warren of rooftops and narrow alleys running between the adobe houses spread out below him. Nothing moved, and the man he'd shot in the head lay where he'd fallen.

"I think they've given up on smoking me out," he told Ciji. "Though I hadn't realized we had any dynamite left."

He was speaking to the old Hopi medicine woman, but mostly he was thinking out loud, putting himself in the soldiers' place and deciding what he'd do if he were them. He ran through options before coming to his conclusion, uncertain as it was.

"I'd try and gain elevation for a marksman and then rush me once night falls," he decided.

"The moon tonight will be only a crescent moon," Ciji told him. "There will be clouds. I see them this morning on the horizon. It will be very dark at times."

Luke nodded. "That can work as well for me as it does for them."

"They are not as wounded as you. I gave you good medicine, but you are still hurt."

"Doesn't matter." Luke dismissed her protests. "I will outfight them. They never should have come here, after me; they have come to their doom."

Ciji cackled happily. "You are a warrior. They are not so much warriors, I think." She sobered for a moment to reflect, then added, "But they do have plenty of guns."

Luke sighed. "Yes. They do have plenty of guns."

CHAPTER 37

As twilight deepened, the Mexicans grew restless. Luke traded shots with one of them set back from the others, a designated sharpshooter for the group, he suspected, but both men missed. Then as the sun passed over the rim of the canyon plunging the steep ravine into shadow, the men began shifting, trying to push closer.

One of them got overconfident and exposed too much of his body as he slipped into the recess of a doorway. Luke stepped out to one side of the window and quickly lined up his shot. He pulled the trigger and his hammer fell. Nothing happened.

Misfire.

"Curse it!"

He moved to pull back and unseat the round when the sharpshooter took his shot during Luke's small moment of surprise. The Springfield round slammed into Luke's rifle, and the thing came apart in his hands. The impact knocked him flat and a piece of the shattered rifle opened a cut above his eyebrow.

"*¡Lo tengo! ¡Lo tengo!*"

"I got him! I got him!" rang out in Spanish. Below him, he heard the Mexican officer rallying his people, and he knew they were coming now. All his plans went out the window. He had time only to survive.

"Vamanos!" he shouted at the old woman.

He staggered to his feet, blinded by his own blood from the cut on his forehead. If they got into the building below him, they could hold it long enough to try smoking him out again. He had to avoid being cornered at all costs even if he held the high ground.

He wiped at the blood streaming down his face, rubbing it from his eyes until he could see again. He had to stop the bleeding or he could be blinded again at any moment. On his feet, he stumbled forward, crossing the room toward the hole in the floor where there was an inside ladder.

A shot rang out and another heavy slug burned into the room. It smacked into the adobe wall above Luke's shoulder and blasted out a crater the size of a man's head before traveling all the way through and out the other side.

Luke stumbled away from the shot, ducking low and pulling the Colt Dragoon clear. He had four shots, assuming there were no duds. The situation had just changed drastically against him. Survival suddenly looked like a much, much bleaker proposition.

"You must go!" Ciji told him, voice urgent. "Hide in the pens among the goats. Go!"

Still wiping blood from his eyes, Luke reached down and took up a handful of dust from where the rifle rounds had hammered the walls. Holding the loose grit in his hand he reached up and hurriedly packed his wound with it, using the dust to make a muddy crust and staunch his bleeding.

He stumbled to the open smoke hole, descended the ladder, and dropped down into the chamber below. Part of a several-room complex, this chamber held a door that led out into a courtyard facing away from the advancing Mexicans.

He scrambled up the ladder of a random pueblo and then kicked it over so it clattered to the ground like a forgotten toy.

Ducking into a square-carved window, he pushed back into the shadows and watched outward.

The Mexicans had reached the structure he'd just left. They swarmed across the surface like a squad of ants, ducking into openings only to reemerge, shaking their heads and each calling out "No" as they found each chamber, room, and niche empty.

Breathing heavily, Luke leaned against the interior wall. Four shots was what he had left. He had to make them count. Grim-faced with resolution, he pushed deeper into the adobe city.

Llamosa was furious once it became obvious that Luke had somehow escaped him. A careful search of the pueblo had turned up no one other than an old woman who either didn't understand Spanish or pretended not to. A search around the area revealed a series of blood drops showing that the American was injured, but not telling them how badly. That, combined with the remains of the rifle, told the captain that Domingo must have hit the man at least once.

He ordered his men to fan out and search the rooms closest to the initial building, but by this time darkness had settled in and they couldn't find a trace of him.

In baffled disgust, they finally returned to where they had the old woman under guard. After posting one man as a sentry, Llamosa regarded the woman.

"What is her story?" he demanded of Sanchez.

"Bah." The sergeant major spat in disgust. "The old fools left in this place claim she is a witch. She is called Ciji, and apparently she is the one who brought the American here. According to the toothless old pigs, he was badly hurt when he got here, but she nursed him back to health."

He faked a swing at the old woman. Ciji did not flinch away. Sanchez spat in disgust again.

"I know you speak Spanish, you withered crone!" he barked at her.

Ciji sat unmoving, offering no provocation but also refusing to speak. Her face was hidden in shadow as the room grew steadily darker with the coming of night.

Carefully, Luke slipped in among the goats. The Mexicans had positioned themselves in front of the only ladder down too quickly for him to circumvent them. For better or worse, they were stuck inside the nearly abandoned city together. That meant he couldn't afford to be seen, but he had to whittle down their numbers if such an opportunity presented itself.

Suddenly he heard men approaching just outside the building. They sounded relaxed, perhaps because Luke had doubled back to get here and they thought these buildings already had been checked, and thus were safe. They spoke Spanish.

"Don't let the captain catch you," one man warned.

"What he doesn't know won't hurt him," another man replied. "One cigarette, what can it hurt, no?"

Luke tucked the pistol firmly into the back of his pants. Flexing lightly at the knees, he leaped up, arms stretched out, and caught hold of the edge of the smoke hole with his hands. He hung for a moment, testing to see if the oak support beam could hold his weight. Satisfied, he muscled himself up and disappeared through the opening.

At that moment, a Mexican stepped through the doorway, ducking out of sight, and lit a cigarette. The match sparked, then caught, illuminating the man's broad, soft-featured face in flickering, yellow light. Luke dropped down behind him.

The flame from the match reflected briefly in the American's eyes. The Mexican looked up at the last moment as if he sensed something, and Luke unfolded like a snake striking. The match snapped off in the rush of air.

Grabbing the Mexican by his broad forehead, Luke snapped the soldier's neck back, exposing the big blood vessels of his throat and windpipe. The cold gray metal of Luke's knife traced a line across the man's throat. Blood rushed out over the man's uniform collar, absorbed by his shirt. The man's frantically beating heart sent additional geysers spurting up in repeated arcs from the cleanly lacerated carotid artery.

The Mexican crumpled at the knees, and Luke snatched the dead man's Springfield rifle out of his limp hands before it could clatter to the floor. He eased the body down and searched it quickly, unbuckling the equipment belt with an ammunition pouch from around the dead man's waist.

"Hurry up," the man outside urged in a low voice, having no idea that his compadre was dead. "Sanchez could come by at any moment."

Luke grunted in reply.

The man seemed frustrated by the response. Footsteps came close. Luke drew himself up against the inside wall. The goats seemed unfazed by the violence or spilling blood, something Luke hadn't anticipated. One of them bleated, restless, but the noise was not taken up by the rest of the animals.

Gripping the Springfield by the barrel, he gently laid it up against the wall, careful not to make a sound. The second man stopped just outside the door.

"Simon, hurry up, man!" he said.

Exasperated, the soldier leaned into the doorway, eyes hunting the gloom. Luke gripped his knife tightly, knuckles white on the hilt.

"Simon?"

"Pssst," Luke hissed.

Confused, the man turned in the direction of the sound. Luke's hand came out like a bear trap and closed on the man's rough uniform tunic collar. Grabbing hold, he yanked sharply and jerked the man off balance.

The knife came around fast, too fast to see in the dim light. The blade entered the man's body twice, puncturing both lungs. The soldier coughed blood and gasped in a wet gurgle as Luke ripped the second strike free. Rotating at the shoulder, Luke brought the knife around from overhead and slammed it home in the back of the soldier's neck.

He heard the distinctive sound of a pair of glasses being broken apart under his foot.

The Mexican instantly dropped to his knees and then collapsed facedown. His last breath escaped him in a rush of blood and a soggy death rattle. Reaching down to search him, Luke's hands found his primary weapon. In the darkness, the American grinned.

This man had carried a shotgun. It was like rolling everything on a single toss of the dice and coming up with a natural eleven.

Not wanting to risk his run of good fortune, Luke made the decision to relocate. He could try coming at them again but now from a different direction. He'd been lucky enough to score two quiet kills, but he doubted he would continue to enjoy the same good fortune for long.

CHAPTER 38

Watching as his men pulled the bodies of Gafas and Simon from the goat pen, Llamosa fumed with impotent rage. He looked out across the multiple levels of terraced pueblo houses and the orchard of smoke holes, air vents, windows, and doors. Any of the dark patches could be holding the gringo.

"Let's make the old woman talk," Sanchez suggested. "That crone has to know something."

"She'd only resist," Llamosa argued. "For whatever reason, she's loyal to that son of a whore. Go and grab the old man. He hates the gringo as much as he hates us. If these savages know where he's gone to hide, then he'll tell us before she does."

Sanchez grunted in obedience. Truth be told, he'd been hoping the old woman *would* try to resist the questioning. He didn't like how this manhunt was turning out at all. Exorcising some of the frustration he felt at finding two more of his men dead had seemed a good proposition.

No matter. The captain had spoken, and in the wilderness the captain's word was law.

"Go." He jerked his head at two of the men while Bernardo kept watch from the highest terrace roof above them.

The two men sprang to obey and returned in minutes with the withered old Hopi man in tow.

"The only way we leave," he told him, "is when we've killed the gringo. That means a house-to-house search. The sooner he's dead the sooner you're free of us."

Llamosa waited for the old man to acknowledge the truth of his words. After a moment the Hopi gave a grudging nod to show he understood. Satisfied, the officer continued.

"So I want you to get your people together and help us search. We'll initiate a systematic sweep of the town until we uncover the gringo's location!"

"This is your fight," the old man replied in halting Spanish. "Ciji brought this to our doorstep because her dream visions told her the white man was important. So be it. But the rest of us want nothing to do with your war."

The Hopi elder made his statement in a flat declarative voice. For him, the matter was settled. Let the outsiders kill each other. Llamosa found the old man's unflappability in the face of the death of his soldiers enraging. Snatching the elder up by his buckskin shirt, he shoved the barrel of one of the Remingtons under his chin and cocked the hammer.

"You pathetic insects are taking longer to die than anyone has a right to!" He said the words with such force that spittle flew from his mouth and sprayed the Hopi elder's face. "You can go back to your pathetic little animal lives as soon as we finish with the gringo. Until the moment that he is dead before me, I demand you and your people give me full cooperation."

He threw the old man back and lowered the hammer on his pistol.

"Demand as you will," the Hopi elder replied. His voice remained unconcerned, though he did rub his jaw where the muzzle of Llamosa's pistol had dug into it. Even that gesture seemed like a lazy afterthought.

Llamosa stepped back farther, seething with a cold, black anger. "Sergeant Major Sanchez."

"Sir?"

"Take this man outside where the rest of these pathetic beast-lovers can see, and encourage him to help us."

Soon the meaty *thwacks* of fists and boots and rifle butts on flesh were clearly heard. The Hopi elder grunted under each blow but steadfastly refused to cry out.

As they beat the old man in the relative safety of the lee of the covered goat pen, Llamosa considered his next steps by trying to predict the American's next moves. He didn't think the man would want to engage in another sniper exchange; that had proven too costly, though, in the end, he might have no other choice. As soon as he fired, if he was unable to move, then he would risk being pinned down by the Mexican soldiers' return fire.

That left maneuvering through the warren of rooms and alleys and terraces that made up the ancient pueblo city. One man could move more covertly than many men, but a single man could be driven like a jaguar before hunters until cornered. Cornered was where a jaguar was at their most dangerous, but it was also necessary to finish them.

Come what may, Captain Llamosa was consumed with the idea of finishing the American once and for all.

After a much shorter time than Llamosa had anticipated, Sanchez returned to report that the old man was dead. Llamosa sighed. He'd thought the villagers would have come out and offered to help to save the old man.

"Tell the men to form up. We go to corner the jaguar."

The sergeant major looked slightly puzzled but nodded his agreement.

Once the group—depressingly smaller than before—was assembled, Llamosa addressed them directly, forgoing his usual habit of having Sanchez reiterate his orders.

"The gringo is a wily fox," Llamosa told them. "He sur-

vived a battle that slaughtered his compatriots. He escaped
from the platoon charged with taking care of the dead. We
tracked him here and he's drawn first blood."

Suddenly Llamosa's voice changed in pitch and volume as
he became more agitated. "That ends now! He is one man!
We split up into two groups of three, and we search pueblo by
pueblo until we corner him. Once he's cornered, we'll come
together and flush him altogether."

His voice lowered into a low, ominous tone. "No one
leaves here until the gringo is dead." He pointed a finger at
them. "First man that falters, I will kill him myself."

CHAPTER 39

Luke watched the three soldiers as they passed below him. He hesitated to strike. Three could become six quickly enough, and if they managed to flank him in even a rudimentary pincer movement, he could find his position untenable, even with his confiscated weaponry and ammunition. Better to be safe and wait for a more promising opportunity.

He moved quietly, pacing his hunters, sliding in and out of smoke holes and square-cut windows, a shadow among shadows as he cut across terraces and clambered up and down ladders, ghosting through the searching Mexican soldiers.

Twice he stumbled upon some of the city's few inhabitants. They stared at him with wooden-faced indifference, averting their eyes as if he were simply a ghost that would dissipate on his own if only they didn't acknowledge him. He tried avoiding them as much as possible so as not to bring attention down upon them. He'd heard the soldiers beating on the old man and had started in that direction, determined to put a stop to it no matter the cost, when the infrequent cries had fallen off and he assumed the soldiers had given up.

It was easier moving along the alleys and avenues formed between the buildings and the areas where the terraced roofs ran in undulating patterns of high and low. However, it was also easier for his hunters to move through these areas in the same fashion, and he had no wish to find himself unexpectedly trapped in some cul-de-sac or handmade adobe cavern.

He heard a scuttling, rustling scrape behind him and whirled.

The shotgun swept around, and he brought the hammers back with his thumbs until they clicked into position and his fingers took up the slack in the smooth metal curves of his triggers. Tensed, he hunted for a target.

A long, green lizard scurried across the uneven wall, running away for several steps.

Sighing, Luke eased up on his triggers and uncocked the hammers.

He heard a murmur of conversation and turned away from the lizard. Down the street, he saw soldiers approaching his position. Nestled in tight against the cornice of a terrace, he watched through a chink in the adobe as the three halted before the structure and looked it over.

The sergeant major he'd heard referred to as Sanchez held his Springfield cocked and ready while he stood back, alertly watching their surroundings. His eyes scanned the pueblo rising in front of him for the slightest sign of movement. Pistols drawn, the two soldiers entered the house ahead of him. Once they called out that it was empty, Sanchez followed them inside.

Ear pressed to a narrow vent, Luke heard an occasional faint crash from within as they carried out the tedious business of examining each room of the building. Luke frowned as he considered his height advantage. He was going to have to take a risk at some point. A heavy jug-bowl used for water had been left on the terrace, forgotten and now covered in dust.

Taking out his knife, Luke began prying at the stones left around the outdoor hearth next to the jug. Working quickly, he worried the knife point into the crumbling adobe and prized the heavy river stones free. Quietly, he transferred the loose stones into the jug, making it even heavier.

The sound of voices reached the street again, and Luke sheathed his knife. Rising to his feet, he tried peering over the edge to see when the men stepped out into the street. Luck remained with him in that they had chosen not to emerge onto the rooftop themselves, presumably to avoid suffering sniper fire at his hands.

The grumbling voices grew clearer as they emerged. Time to roll the dice. If his timing was off, this could prove catastrophic. His feet set against the terrace, Luke braced his shoulder against the stone-filled jug and slowly heaved. Waist high and loaded down with stones now, the jug resisted his pressure at first, so he pushed harder, using the muscles of his legs.

With a sudden treacherous release of tension, the jug shifted outward and dropped. Thrown off balance by the sudden shift, Luke waved his arms wildly, tottering on the edge, close to toppling after the plummeting jug.

The three were just emerging from the doorway, grumbling in frustration. The sudden trickle of adobe gravel was the only warning the men got. One of them leapt to one side, rolling clear, as Sanchez ducked back through the doorway.

The third man, Carlos, mind perhaps dulled by the pain of a wound he had suffered earlier, looked upward at his companion's warning shout, wasting the split second that might have saved him. His scream had scarcely reached his lips before it was swallowed in the thunderous shock of the heavy crockery slamming into him and driving through to the street. The resulting crash was thunderous.

Sanchez glanced in horror at the scarlet-splotched heap of loose adobe and rock strewn before the doorway. Only the barest fragment of time had separated him from death in that moment, he realized.

"There he is!" the other soldier shouted. "Quick!"

The man had recovered from his shock just in time to see Luke regain his balance and dart back from the roof edge. Scrambling over the terrace like an ape, Luke dashed for the neighboring building. Not-so-distant shouts began answering the alarm being raised below him, and he had no desire to get in the open.

Another building rose up, hard adjacent to the terrace he raced across. Luke threw himself upward to clear the few feet discrepancy between the two structures and started across the steeper sloping roof. His ankle twisted and Luke skidded dizzily downward, hands clawing to secure a grip. His searching fingers found no purchase.

Helpless to stop his slide, Luke floundered over the edge and dropped back to the terrace roof just below him. Heart racing, he leapt up and began his climb again, thankful the fall was only a few feet rather than all the way to the plaza below.

A hunk of adobe next to him exploded as a rifle cracked below, the bullet passing only inches away. A second shot shattered a chunk of adobe under his fingers, but in the next moment he gained the crest of the roof and slid down the other side, out of sight for the moment.

This side of the multi-level structure abutted a building one floor less in height. Catching at a carved gutter line as he reached the edge, he lowered himself over the side and dropped lightly to the next terrace.

Angry shouts sounded closer now as his pursuers sought to close in, but Luke felt more confident. A ladder at the far end of the terrace led him down to an alley in the back formed by a rock wall to one side and adobe on the other.

Reaching the narrow avenue, he pushed through a dark doorway in an opposite building and vanished before Llamosa's men could circle from the other street. As they frenziedly sought to retrace his movements, Luke ducked through several empty buildings and reemerged some distance away. The dark avenues cloaked his escape.

Twilight deepened and was swallowed by the night. Across the dead city blackness settled like shadows in a tomb. No lights shone in the empty town. Starlight and illumination from the moon looked down on the ancient structures, their soft light no more than shading the night to gray.

The last of the Hopi villagers huddled in their pueblo homes, knowing death stalked outside their doors. Grim-faced men cast suspicious eyes over each segment of night-time city laid bare by the lights of their lanterns. Warily they searched for some new evidence of their quarry's presence. The smell of gun smoke lingered in the air.

Determined to put an end to this deadly match of cat and mouse, Llamosa grouped his remaining men together and ordered the search to continue. By lantern light he and his band relentlessly pushed through the city, hunting their prey through the now familiar streets and deserted buildings.

If this was to be a contest of endurance, Llamosa meant to give his enemy no chance to rest. Not even this deadly American could hold up against the strain of ceaseless skulking from one bolt-hole to another, never gaining more than a few steps on his pursuers.

Eventually he would grow weary and then careless. They would trap him and learn how well an exhausted fox could fight as the pack of hounds closed in to kill.

"I'll lay you odds the American has run by now. He's probably running as fast as he can for the desert right now!" Domingo growled, his surly temper worn thin from the hours of tedious and dangerous search. "He's probably sleeping in a ditch while we're wearing down the streets with our boots. He'd be a fool to stay here inside the walls dodging us all night."

"That's true enough," Bernardo pointed out. "Assuming he's running from us." Unease crept into the man's normal bravado.

"I do not think that is the case here. It seems to me the gringo is hunting us as much as we are hunting him."

"It is obvious enough by now that the American isn't exactly in full flight," Llamosa broke in, voice brusque. "We've known that from the beginning. He's still with us . . . staying just out of sight like a snake, waiting for a chance to strike at us. But his boldness will be his undoing, eventually. We'll wear him out before he does us. So shut up and keep your eyes open, I command you!" The captain finished the last in an angry bark.

Not daring to grumble, the soldiers concentrated on their search. Sanchez worked his way close to the normally flippant Bernardo.

"What's the matter?" he asked. "You haven't let this devil of a gringo get into your head have you?"

The other man glanced at him edgily, somewhat ashamed at how readily apparent his unease had been noticed by the sergeant major.

"I'm fine," he muttered. "This has just been a long day is all." Abruptly he paused, then started again. "No, that's not all of it. The American, this place, the damn Indians . . . I . . . I'll just be happy when we kill this man is all." His voice trailed off uncertainly.

Sanchez grunted something noncommittal. He was already sorry he'd asked. He needed the men sharp, not crying for sympathy.

As if sensing his leader's mood, Bernardo forced a smile across his face. "I'll be fine once we drive him into the open. This monotonous game of poking through a ghost town trying to flush out a snake is wearying, that's all. It's quite a strain on a man's nerves."

"The captain doesn't care about your nerves," Sanchez informed him. "And neither do I!"

"Yes, Sergeant," Bernardo said automatically.

"Good." Sanchez jerked his head in a nod. "Now, let's go find that gringo and put an end to this madness."

CHAPTER 40

Stealthily Luke raised the heavy trapdoor. Its dry, rotted leather hinges rasped, and he uneasily peered about the darkened storeroom. Satisfied that the sound had been too faint and that no one was near enough to catch the desiccated whisper, he grimly inspected the dank-smelling sub-cellar of a corn bin below, then replaced the trap over the opening. Whether the old tunnel still lay open was impossible to say without light, but at least the trapdoor had opened for him without disintegrating. He listened.

Silence.

The soldiers had not yet reached this building, although their lanterns had been drawing close to the seemingly abandoned structure the last time Luke had looked outside.

This entire section of the pueblo was a series of corn bins and storerooms, one vast warehouse of a looming structure abutted directly up against the cliff face on one side and built out from it.

The storeroom ceiling stretched high, and the wooden door closing the main entrance was immense. A system of chain and pulleys lifted the main door vertically along grooves cut into the jamb, sliding the heavy wood barrier upward and down by means of a capstan.

The heavy winch had the look of Spanish manufacture due

to the filigree and fleur-de-lis worked into the metal. For all Luke knew, the mechanism was as much as two hundred years old. Obviously the capstan had been acquired through trade with friendly conquistadors or perhaps gifted by friars in order to facilitate conversion by the natives to Christianity. Luke knew the Spanish had first come to the Southwest and Mexico more than three hundred years earlier.

In truth, it didn't matter where the pulley came from or how old it was, only what aid it could provide in his war with the *soldados*. He intended to exploit this for all he could.

The door stood open, raised upward to the ceiling as if left that way when the tribe grew too small through attrition to properly utilize such a large storage space. The capstan sat mounted alongside the front wall where a thick hemp rope strained from the winch, running along heavy pulleys jutting out of wooden brackets set into the girders of the pueblo building and then fastened to the massive door.

Luke inspected the fittings, making sure he was familiar with their operation. Then he drew his knife and crept into the shadow of some waist-high clay cylinder jars once used to hold grain. A desert rat darted away from his boot and scurried off into the darkness.

Luke's lips pressed into a thin smile as he saw the first flickers of lantern light streak the entrance and heard the shuffle of approaching footsteps and the low mutter of voices. Tightness of anticipation slipped from him and he relaxed. Cunning or foolish, he was committed to his plan now.

Closer came the light, the sound spilling into echoes when it bounced off the natural cliff face within. The light grew brighter. Figures appeared at the doorway. After a moment's hesitation, they entered.

Two soldiers stood just inside the door, lanterns raised, eyes narrowly scrutinizing the shadows just beyond as the two soldiers leveled their firearms inside. Luke pressed himself tightly against the wall, unseen behind the cover of the tall cylinder jars.

Two men entered, one holding a lantern, while the rest provided cover.

"See anything, Esteban?" Sanchez called from just outside.

"No. There's nothing here," came the grumbling reply.

The second man swept the muzzle of his Springfield around. Pressed into the shadows, Luke held the hammers of his shotgun back and took out the slack in his triggers. Now all he had to do was release tension and the hammers would fall. He forced his breathing to slow.

Just as the others moved to follow the first two inside, Luke, gripping the shotgun one handed, leapt from the shadows and reached the old Spanish capstan in a bound. Framed against the darkness by yellow lantern light, the blade of his knife flashed.

"There he is!" someone shouted.

A Springfield went off, the shot sounding like a cannon blast in the echo chamber of the storage room. Luke lashed out with his knife and severed the rope holding the great wooden door open.

There was a moment of improbable length and then with a dry, grinding snarl the mechanism released itself and pulleys began whining as the rope shot through their narrow grooves. The immense overhead door shook and then broke free of its moorings. Debris fell in a trickle then exploded like a bomb into the night.

The thunderous screech of metal on metal screamed out as the heavy door tore loose and hurled downward across the entranceway, momentum building to a point of blurring acceleration. The capstan shrieked on its pivot, spun like a gigantic top by the streaking rope. It swung widely, slamming into Luke, who stumbled and lost his grip on the shotgun.

Both barrels went off with a deafening blast and muzzle

flash lit up the gloomy cavern of a chamber. The door crashed against its sill like the gate of hell closing behind sinners. Caught by the inertia of its fall, the rope snapped short on the spindle and ripped the spinning capstan free of its smoking mounting. Wood drum and coils of hemp rope lashed across the warehouse like a thrashing snake, sending all three men flat behind cover.

Luke dropped the shotgun and pulled the Colt Dragoon.

Adobe jars shattered, sending ancient stores of corn and grain into the air, forming a choking cloud of dust.

Outside, chips of adobe pelted Llamosa and the other two as they leapt back from the collapsing barrier. Clouds of grain-dust and pulverized adobe clay blasted their faces and whipped at the lantern wicks as the door thundered shut.

"Sanchez! Bernardo! Left and right fast! Find me an entrance!"

Damn the man's cunning, the Mexican captain thought, *he's split us again!*

Inside one of the lanterns crashed, spilling kerosene across the adobe floor. The flammable liquid went up in a blaze, illuminating a swath separating the soldiers from Luke. The men, cursing, swept their rifle muzzles around.

Domingo, thinking he'd seen a shape, instinctively hurled his lantern in order to free up his hands to use his rifle. Luke dodged the missile and it shattered against the rock face of the cliff forming the wall behind him. Kerosene-soaked fragments spattered into the grain dust and it went up with a deafening *whoosh*.

Luke dove to the right, rolled over his shoulder, and came up with the pistol. He saw Carlos backlit by the burning dried corn. He fired once, unwilling to waste more bullets than necessary. The Dragoon jerked in his hand, and he saw the Mexican jolt as his round found a home.

Carlos staggered backward, stunned by the rapid turn of events. His feet tangled up in themselves and he fell. Screams ripped from his throat as the linen of his uniform blouse and greasy hair instantly caught fire. Shrieking, he rolled in agony even as he poured his life's blood out into the dust.

Instinct made Luke move. He swiveled around one of the remaining cylinder jars with lithe grace as Esteban's rifle fired.

Carlos, still screaming, somehow managed to regain his feet and stumbled blindly from the blaze. Tongues of fire danced over his hair and clothing. Blinded by the flames, flesh seared and blackened, he flopped across the storage room floor, smashing into objects in a hopeless effort to escape the unendurable pain. Driven to cover by Esteban's rifle fire, Luke ignored the burning man as he crumpled into a writhing, smoldering mass.

The fire gave Esteban time and cover to close with Luke. Rushing the American from behind, he knocked the pistol from his hand with a wild swipe of the breech-loading rifle. Though his bullet was spent the Springfield still made for an excellent club and the soldier brought it to bear.

Luke twisted sideways, narrowly avoiding a wild swing of the man's rifle butt. The metal butt plate of the shoulder stock clanked hard against unforgiving rock. Reeling back, Luke struck out, thrusting the blade of his knife for the other's side. But Esteban was quick and, with a sweep of his barrel, dislodged the knife from Luke's grip the same way he had the Colt pistol.

Shouting in rage, Luke stomped out with the heel of his boot. Striking the other man squarely in the chest, he drove him back. That gave Luke time to bend and snatch the fallen knife from the floor.

Behind him, he heard the Mexicans trapped outside shouting and then the sound of rifle butts hammering the wooden planks of the storage room door. Lengths of wood splintered into long strips under their blows.

The fire was spreading from one pile of desiccated corn

and grain to the next with devilish rapidity. The dried material was so combustible that it broke into flames with small explosions that sounded like gunshots. Everything was chaos as the door began splintering in earnest now.

Time was running out.

Esteban yelled in fury and swung his Springfield like a club. In a red fury, Luke avoided the attack and drove forward, knife plunging toward his enemy. The Mexican soldier dropped back, seeking to use the greater length of his rifle to better advantage, even if only as a bludgeoning weapon.

The fire was spreading, and the door splintered to the point that cracks had appeared in it. Esteban tried stabbing Luke with the barrel of his rifle, but the move was ill-timed and Luke avoided it, slapping the firearm to one side. Overextended, the soldier fell forward and the American struck before the other could parry effectively.

The blade tore through the man's side, slipping through the ribs and stabbing into a lung. Esteban toppled to the floor, eyes brimming hatred through the agony of his death. Bright, frothy blood burst from his mouth like water from a culvert. Rifle forgotten, he tried dragging his broken body to safety but died after only a moment of exertion.

Luke stepped back.

Already flames had engulfed the section where Carlos's body had lain. The door still held against the assault by the other three men, but the inside of the storeroom was ablaze, furnace hot, as flames consumed the grains and corn. Flames now had leapt over half the floor and in places the planks had given way to collapse into the shallow cellar.

It was difficult to breathe or even to see with the rapidly building smoke and heat. Hurriedly, Luke retrieved his pistol and started for the cellar stairs. He thought about firing a shot through the door but decided against it. It would undoubtedly slow them, and he stood a fair chance of hitting one of the three remaining men, but fair chance wasn't good enough when he was counting every bullet.

The short tunnel was his only escape.

Moving fast, he found the trapdoor still clear of flaming wreckage. Seizing the leather strap Luke heaved it open and descended the short ladder into the tunnel. Here the musty dampness of the bedrock was undisturbed by fire above. Though stale, the dank air was a relief from the burning smoke that choked the storage room.

As quickly as he dared, Luke passed through the tunnel, bent almost in half. He moved in utter darkness, hand held before him to avoid running full tilt into a wall. Twice he banged his head against the unforgiving roof, and a trickle of blood ran down from his scalp.

He was breathing hard and the wounds from the earlier battle pained him greatly, but he had little choice other than to keep moving. He'd done fine so far, but there remained three armed men bent on his murder, and he had an old cap-and-ball pistol with three shots left.

Rotting timbers sagged overhead, bowed down by the adobe and the weight of centuries. Dirt had trickled through to make soft ridges along the floor, and in a few places mounds of debris almost blocked the passage. Gingerly, Luke crawled over these crumbling heaps of dirt and mortar and adobe clay fragments. Clods and sand and grit fell over his back and legs, making a dark paste with the blood that flowed freely from his wounds.

At one point, a dull shock echoed through the short tunnel, followed hard by a muffled crash. The storage room must have collapsed, Luke guessed, nervously eyeing the tunnel walls. In the darkness it was impossible to tell if he was in danger or not. But by now he had come a bit of a distance beneath the flooring of several chambers, and the tunnel felt more secure as he approached the far end.

The floor rose, and after a moment's scramble his head

butted into a narrow post. His grasping hands found the post was one side of a ladder and eagerly he ascended. He came to another of the trapdoors and pushed it up to enter a cellar-like storage room, the twin of the one he'd just escaped from.

Three left, he thought.

CHAPTER 41

When smoke began streaming from cracks and openings through the storage room and the splintering door began emanating heat from the inferno within, Llamosa called a halt to their frantic efforts to break in.

"This place is doomed!" he pronounced, stepping back from battering the door with a Springfield. "Anyone inside must flee now or the smoke will kill them if the flames don't! Domingo and Esteban will shout through the door if the American hasn't killed them—and if he has, then we'll give him the choice of roasting alive inside or coming out to meet us!" He lowered his shouts, bringing his voice under control. "Either way he will be burning in Hell before dawn breaks. Spread out and watch for any bolt-holes he might slip through."

The two men he had left followed his orders. One of them kept an eye on the storage room's main entrance while the other made sure there were no vents or smoke holes or windows in this labyrinth of pueblo structures.

Clearly no one had escaped while they fruitlessly attempted to break down the door. Weapons ready, they watched vigilantly for a figure to stumble from the shroud of smoke and flame, blinded and coughing.

If it was the American who emerged, Llamosa meant to give him scant time to draw clean air into his lungs.

But the door did not open, and nobody appeared out of the smoke. No scorched figure stepped clear of the inferno. Crashes from within indicated the floor was giving way, and then came a ripping concussion as the storage roof, baked until the adobe cracked, collapsed ponderously upon the burning wreckage within.

A cataclysmic blast of flame and cinders leapt into the night sky, transforming the yet standing walls of the storage room into the cone of a volcano. Soon the main door crumpled under the heat, falling inward to reveal a blazing holocaust. The thick walls, one side the cliff face itself, stood red hot from the blazing furnace inside. Before this, the watchers ceased standing sentry.

"It's that gringo's funeral pyre!" Llamosa observed triumphantly. "He took two more good men with him, but they died as heroes of the army." He turned to accept Sanchez's congratulations. "Only three of us left. It's been a costly campaign to be sure . . . the most dangerous of my career, clearly . . ."

A rustle from the alley behind them abruptly drew their attention.

"Why, it's the witch," Llamosa announced, catching sight of her in the light from the blaze.

Ciji hung poised at the alley entrance, almost concealed in the shadow of a building. Firelight shone across her face and limbs as her dark eyes darted back and forth. She seemed to be summoning the courage to approach them, yet remained on the verge of flight. Considering her past treatment at their hands, this was an understandable hesitation.

"Why have you returned, old woman?" Sanchez asked. He sounded genuinely curious.

"Come out of the shadows, witch," Llamosa called magnanimously. "I have decided to grant clemency to your village out of the bountiful goodness of my heart. Come see the fate of the villain you protected and healed."

Sensing the leniency of the man's current disposition, Ciji stepped forward to join them.

"The white man is dead," the crone announced. "I dreamed of him before his arrival and remained connected with him by my medicine. I felt it when he was cornered here and when the flames took him. The white man is dead. You can take your men and go."

"Your witch's sight showed you his death?" Llamosa smiled, voice lightly mocking; he had little time for the superstition of savages. "I envy you. That is a vision I would have given much gold to have shared." He turned from her. "As for our departure, my men and I will ride on as soon as we've rested and reprovisioned. Run, fetch us tortillas and beans to go with our wine, and we'll be gone faster still."

"I'd take fresh air instead," griped Bernardo. "The smoke from this fire is foul. What did these animals keep in there besides grain?"

"We kept dried animal feces to burn during the winter when the trip to find more firewood grows more arduous," Ciji explained. Her tone seemed to indicate Bernardo was a little slow not to have understood this to begin with.

"Bah . . ."

The Mexican soldier strolled across the little plaza and looked over the edge to the valley below. His lean figure could be seen silhouetted against the dark skies as he paced back and forth like some sentry on watch.

Llamosa settled himself against a wall and stretched his long legs out before him. Dreamily, he smiled into the dying flames of the storage room, reliving the excitement of the past few hours and congratulating himself on his tactical acumen. In his mind he began constructing the report that would result in several medals if he worded it correctly. He looked over and saw Sanchez indicating for the old Hopi woman to go. The sergeant major, for all his inherent brutality, seemed to have found some measure of respect for her medicine and seemed intent on getting her clear of the scene.

Bernardo sighed, looking out at the piñon-filled canyon with its little creek. He was the last of the soldiers, the real soldiers. The captain and the sergeant major didn't count, they were loyal to each other above all else. The lieutenant had been different, he'd treated the men as if their lives had value, but he was gone, killed in the first battle against this gringo devil.

He turned.

A figure approached him along the wall, striding through the smoky haze as ominous as the angel of death. Menace radiated from the smog-wrapped figure. With something like childish horror, Bernardo realized who it had to be.

He cried out incoherently as he fumbled for the Springfield's slung muzzle up over his shoulder. He managed to get the rifle off his shoulder and up. Trembling, his thumb found the hammer and cocked it back as his finger wrapped around the smooth metal curve of the trigger.

In Luke Jensen's hand, the ancient Colt Dragoon boomed like thunder. Muzzle flash lit up the gloom, briefly illuminating his face like a lightning strike. The bullet crashed into Bernardo, cracking his ribs like dry branches under a big man's boots. The heavy-caliber slug tore into his pounding heart, and the muscle shredded under the impact. The bullet burned through and erupted out the other side of the dying man's torso.

Spinning, he went down, and Luke was moving forward, thumbing his own hammer back.

When Llamosa first heard the gunfire he stared at the scene of combat in disbelief. Then, through his astonished mind came the incredible truth—the gringo was alive! Somehow, some impossible way, the flames had not claimed his enemy.

"Sanchez!" he shouted. "Sanchez, he lives!"

Forgetting the old woman, Sergeant Sanchez spun toward the commotion. The hand axe came out from the fold of her robe in a flash. The metal head of the trade-good hatchet glimmered in the reflected firelight as she lifted it. With a wild prayer to a god that was ancient before the Spaniards came to this land, Ciji struck.

The blade bit deep into the back of Sanchez's head. His eyes bulged and crossed in surprise. The handle of the hand axe jutted from the back of his scalp. He stumbled forward a step as black-crimson blood gushed from the wound. Then his eyes rolled up in his head and he dropped. His heavy body struck the ground with a loud, meaty impact, and Ciji turned and slipped between two buildings.

Llamosa blinked, shrugging off his amazement at what he'd just witnessed. The right-hand Remington was out of its holster and up, but the old woman, who'd lived all of her years right here in this vertical labyrinth, was gone.

Realizing his true danger, Llamosa swung around. Luke was on the edge of his terrace, just beyond the light of the burning storage room that was already beginning to dim. Instinctively, Llamosa fired a shot from the hip, a wild chance that veered close enough to spoil Luke's aim.

With only two shots left, Luke couldn't afford to make a mistake. He dove to one side, throwing himself off one roof and down onto another. With his enemy driven back, Llamosa felt his rage take hold. His last two men were dead, but now the architect of their deaths, of his humiliation, was within his grasp.

Running forward, he veered off to the right and then jumped from his terrace to the next one. He caught a flash of movement, and the wall next to him exploded as Luke fired. Turning toward the crouched figure, Llamosa unloaded three times, sending a wild fusillade in Luke's direction.

Darting into a doorway, Luke turned to fire again, sure of his aim this time. The ancient Colt Dragoon exploded in his hand, the chamber coming apart instead of propelling the bullet toward his enemy. He yelled out in surprise and dropped the ruined pistol.

Seeing his chance, Llamosa darted into the building after Luke before the American could make his escape and somehow outmaneuver him yet again. Firing the one Remington empty into the black maw of the doorway, the Mexican officer drew the second and entered.

Luke had anticipated his actions and stepped to the side of the doorway, avoiding the wild shots, and placing himself ideally for an ambush. Llamosa came through the door, wild-eyed and panting with his rage, Luke's own Remington leading the way. Forming a knot with both his hands, Luke stepped around and brought his fists down.

He hammered the other man hard in the wrist and the revolver flew from his grip. Squeaking in surprise, Llamosa fell backward, stumbling over his own feet and back out of the pueblo doorway. Pulling his knife, Luke followed after the man.

Seeing the blade in Luke's hand, the other man grinned in sudden devilish delight. Reaching around to the black leather uniform harness he wore, the Mexican *capitán* pulled forth the long bayonet issued to all soldiers for use with the Springfield breech loader.

"You want to cross blades with me, *pendejo*?" he asked. "Then come and die."

Luke didn't bother to reply. Dropping into a crouch, he lifted his own blade up. It was answer enough.

Llamosa's silent lunge brought them together. Their blades clashed and locked, then Luke hurled the lighter man back. The blade in Llamosa's hand sliced empty air. They locked again. Blow upon blow hammered a vicious cacophony of death punctuated by the gasps for breath of the tired combatants.

A wild slash tore open a wound on Luke's right arm.

"You are not leaving this cursed place," Llamosa jeered, observing the fresh blood dripping down the American's arm.

Other wounds were tearing open under the strain of fighting, and fresh blood spotted through some of Luke's older bandages. Luke seemed to use the pain as a catalyst for his aggression. The more he hurt, the harder he fought. An apparent feint suddenly reversed directions and opened a cut on Llamosa's face.

The men struggled in silence now, voiceless save for panting breath and animal grunts. Llamosa was a shrewd opponent with wiry strength driving his somewhat long frame. In addition, he was relatively fresh compared to the fatigued, bleeding, and wounded Luke. Despite his physical issues, the American's endurance did not falter against the Mexican officer's attacks.

Relentlessly, the two men parried and feinted, slashed and thrust—each confident their attack would exhaust the other and soon bring an end to the stalemate.

Their blades locked hilts again. They strained against one another, man-to-man, blade-to-blade, then in the next moment they were thrown apart again. Llamosa's bayonet slipped past Luke's guard and stabbed for his side. Shoving hard, Luke twisted away and threw Llamosa back a step. As the captain fell away, Luke seized his wrist in passing.

Forcing the taut muscles of his injured arm to respond, Luke crushed the wrist in his grip and bent it back as his enemy lunged hard, trying to break free. Llamosa tried striking around to cut at Luke's hand, but he was able to dance away even as he wrenched. There was a ripping sound as the tendons and ligaments in Llamosa's wrist finally gave way and tore.

"Ahhhh!"

Llamosa cried out and swung his blade widely, frantic to relieve the crushing, ripping agony. Luke released his grip and jerked his arm clear. At the same moment, his knife flashed out at Llamosa's unprotected torso before the other could recover his guard. The powerful blow stabbed down through the Mexican officer's right shoulder opening a ghastly wound.

Luke's reddened blade gleamed and slashed again, catching Llamosa as he spun, hacking open the man's carotid artery. Blood geysered up as if from a fountain, driven by the panicked beating of his heart. Llamosa staggered backward, eyes wide in shock. He tried lifting an arm to staunch the flow of blood but found it too damaged to obey his commands.

Heavily, he dropped to his knees. Bent over with exhaustion, Luke focused on taking in as much oxygen as he could draw from the smoke-fouled air. Llamosa dropped his bayonet and used that hand to try and stop the cascading river of blood gushing from his neck wound as his other arm hung limp and useless. He was becoming paler with blood loss even as Luke looked on.

"I was never with Melichus, you stupid son of a whore," Luke said in his rough Spanish. *"Nunca estuve con Melichus, estúpido hijo de puta."*

Llamosa's eyes rolled up in the back of his head and he fell forward, facedown on the adobe terrace where he finished bleeding out as Luke Jensen looked on.

CHAPTER 42

When Melichus finally snapped and fell fully into the madness of his beliefs, he unleashed a firestorm of slaughter that consumed everything around him.

Haashch ééshzhiní was the Black God, the god of fire and death. He came that night to Melichus in a dream and his message was clear. If Melichus showed his faith then he would teach him how to fly like Father Hawk, how to disappear like Coyote, the trickster, but these were powerful magics, so the price to obtain them was high.

Rising from his bed, he took up his machete. The first kills would need to be quiet. Once he was started, he would kill the whites first. The Apaches would think it a fine joke, turning on the whites right before selling the captives. By the time they realized they, too, were sacrifices, he'd have their trust and could strike without mercy.

The woman he'd tied to the Joshua tree looked up at him, blackened eyes dull from the misery of her abuse. He stood above her, machete naked in his hand. She didn't even cry out as he cut her throat. Her blood spilled in a hot red rush, and Melichus felt her spirit leaving her body, feeding Haashch'ééshzhiní.

The Black God would eat well tonight.

Walking through the sleeping bodies, he went to Graver's

bed roll. The old man had once been a good marksman, but his skill was fading with age. He was not a prime gift to Haashch'ééshzhiní, but he would be the second of many.

Melichus stood above him as the old man snored in a drunken stupor. Blood dripped from the blade of the renegade's machete. Lifting it high, he brought it down and hammered the edge into the crown of the old man's skull. Graver's eyes shot open, but the skull was cracked deep, and the blade bit into the man's brain bringing instant death.

Three more times the machete fell, each stroke a prayer, and three more men died in almost complete silence. On the fourth kill, the captive the outlaw had raped into an exhausted slumber came awake at the sound of blade hacking flesh, and she screamed as blood splashed hotly across her face. With a single swipe of his arm, Melichus decapitated the girl, sending her head rolling through the embers of a fire, sparks jumping in rooster tails as it came to rest and the flesh began cooking.

Johnson startled awake and tried to claw his way out of his blankets.

"What in tarnation?" he managed to exclaim.

He was slow and stupid from drink and sleep, and he couldn't comprehend what he was seeing. Melichus swung again and sent the man's head rolling after the first. Now people were starting to stir all over the camp.

Pulling his pistol, he thumbed back the hammer and squeezed the trigger, the bullet catching a white outlaw in the chest as he tried to scramble upward.

"To me, brothers!" Melichus called in the language of the People. "Kill the whites! Kill them all!"

One outlaw lunged for a carbine leaning against a log next to his bedroll. The big revolver crashed, and the side of the man's chest caved in as if staved with a heavy club. Another broke and ran, and Melichus gunned him down so that he pitched forward dead into the blazing fire.

Everywhere white outlaws died screaming. Melichus stood in the middle of the carnage laughing. What better offering to the Black God than wholesale slaughter? Nothing. Flowing blood made crimson muck of the desert dirt, and the air hung heavy with the bouquets of gun smoke and ripped open flesh.

It stank of violence and death.

It was good. The Black God would be pleased.

CHAPTER 43

Luke Jensen rode up out of the gully and onto the rocky shale and shifting sand plain surrounding the city. He had no idea what the settlement was called. Ahead of him the town was lit up in the night like some frigate on an endless ocean. Even from half a mile out he easily heard the merriment and music of the celebration, all of it punctuated with the barking reports of firearms.

Above the small city bouquets of fireworks spilled across the sky in screaming streaks and brilliant explosions. It was *Día de los Muertos,* the Day of the Dead. The holiday was in full swing as Luke made it to the edge of the city.

The streets were packed with revelers, all dressed in some variation of skeleton attire and face paint. Brass bands played in a harmonious cacophony of trumpets and drums, piano music spilled from the well-lit doorways of taverns and restaurants. Drunken celebrants emptied their pistols into the air. Señoras and señoritas danced in the street wearing their dressiest finery and sporting brocade masks, escorted by gentlemen in mariachi suits with faces done up to resemble skulls.

Finding a stable that was still open, Luke boarded his horse, leaving his own hat with his tack and saddle. He didn't know how long the hunt for Melichus would take. All he knew was that the man was somewhere in all this teeming chaos and festivities.

As he walked down the street, he bought a gaudy serape and sombrero and promptly put them on. The serape covered the Remingtons. As he moved through the crowd, he considered what he knew about Melichus to try and anticipate the madman's actions.

He knew the man was deeply religious, or superstitious depending on your point of view. Whichever, he considered his worship of the Black God to be a very serious thing indeed. *Dia de los Muertos* was exactly the kind of holiday he'd celebrate. But where, that was the question.

The outlaw had all the money he could need. With the help of Ciji telling him of certain Indian paths through the desert, Luke had cut Melichus's trail once again and came upon the slaughter of the whites at the man's camp. He'd shed no tears for the murdered owlhoots, and he didn't bother trying to bury the remains he found. Let the desert be their grave and the buzzards their worms.

Despite his weakened, battered condition, though, he had buried the captives . . . at least the ones he was able to identify amidst the slaughter. He had set out to save them and failed, but this was one last thing he could do for them.

At a spring on the eastern edge of the Sonora, the Apaches headed north and a lone rider had continued farther east. By that time, Luke knew the raider's tracks as well as his own. The frontier was a wild, unforgiving place. The only law was the law made by good men with guns. He couldn't save the captives, not after the battle at the adobe ruins had left him in such bad shape. While he lay weak with blood loss and wracked with fever, they were lost. Not the first innocents consumed by the West and most certainly not the last.

But be that as it may, there was still the matter of Melichus. The outlaw headed east where his name carried less weight and his legend was less terrifying. Once it became clear which way the wolf was headed, it had become a race to catch him before the trail went cold. Luke rode day and night, pushing his horse as hard as he dared, until tonight he had seen the lights ahead of him and recognized instinctively that this was the end of the trail.

No matter how much gold Melichus might have in his pocket from the slave trade, he wouldn't feel at home in the higher class establishments. He might want to drink good liquor, but he'd want to drink in a dive where sudden violence wouldn't automatically result in the law coming in. A place where a dice game could turn into a knife fight in the time it took a man to take a shot of rotgut tequila.

Small parades and processions filled the streets. As the night wore on, the revelers grew more intoxicated, louder. The sound of firearms going off increased. Several times revolvers were discharged so close to Luke that his hands dipped toward his pistols of their own volition. In a rundown tavern, he was in the crowd as two drunk Mexican soldiers fought with knives over the affection of an ugly whore.

Finally, as night began giving way to morning, Luke entered a cantina at the end of an alley off a main thoroughfare. Slipping through the throngs of milling people, he ducked under the low door opening and entered the building. Here the festivities felt different, less celebratory and more raw. Most of the patrons weren't in costume, though loud laughter was the primary noise. Men diced at tables, a buxom Mexican woman in a low-cut dress ran a faro game.

A girl who didn't look much older than twelve waited on the customers, bringing clay pitchers of beer to the shouting men. On one table, two scorpions were being forced to fight as men laid wagers. The owners pushed the deadly little creatures into each other using the barrels of their pistols. Pesos and American two-bit pieces littered the surface.

Ignoring them, Luke began the same search he'd played out over and over again. Drifting to the back to try and remain anonymous, he carefully surveyed the room, looking for Melichus. In the shifting, aggressive crowd, he saw men sitting with their heads down, sombreros worn low on their faces, obviously not wanting to be noticed. None of them were the half-Ute outlaw.

One of the serving girls came into the room through a beaded curtain, and Luke realized there was a second room to the establishment. Edging in that direction, he tried taking a peek through the doorway before entering. He got the impression of a small but still-crowded section of the tavern where more people seemed to be playing cards than in the front.

He paused at the edge of the door, trying to search the faces of the card players. A waitress brushed past him in a scent of warm beer and petulia oil. Frowning, Luke stepped backward. A stumbling vaquero, bottle of tequila in one hand, slammed into him from behind, obviously staggeringly drunk.

The contact knocked Luke through the curtain in an awkward, attention-grabbing lurch. Luke looked out as every face in the room came up at the fresh commotion. In the middle of the room, Melichus sat at a table, a pile of pesos in front of him.

They made eye contact at the same time. Melichus's eyes grew wide even as Luke's hand dipped for his gun. Both men drew in sync with practiced ease. The waitress, oblivious to the danger, swung around, two beer pitchers in each hand, and stepped in front of Luke.

Luke stopped his trigger finger from contracting and tried to shove the woman aside. Melichus brought his .45 up and began fanning the hammer. Three shots cracked out like thunderclaps, silencing the entire establishment. One went to the left and flew past Luke to strike the ceiling. The second clipped the girl in the shoulder, and she screamed, dropping the clay pitchers with a crash.

The final shot caught her in the heart and stopped her screams cold. The girl jerked and crumpled backward into Luke, who caught her with one hand.

The patrons surged to their feet and began racing and fighting toward the door. Still holding the dead girl in one arm, Luke swung around and leveled the Remington. A mob of gamblers and drunken revelers pushed past him, filling the space between him and Melichus.

The half-Mexican, half-Ute outlaw was on his feet, backing away from the milling throng of panicked humanity. Extending his gun, Luke took aim as the man turned to run. Several vaqueros bumped into him, jostling him hard, and he staggered a step. When he got his equilibrium again and looked up, Melichus was by the window.

The eyes of the outlaw and the bounty hunter locked across the space. Melichus was snarling like a cornered animal. He had one leg through the open adobe shelf of the window bottom and was about to duck through. Thumbing back his hammer and operating on pure instinct, Luke took a shot.

The .44-caliber slug smacked into the wall next to the escaping outlaw, startling him. Melichus ducked under the frame and half fell from the window. Lowering the dead serving girl to the floor, Luke flipped a table and raced to the window.

He saw a narrow alley cutting between two more populated avenues. He spotted a donkey bucking wildly on the end of its tether and knew which way Melichus had gone. He could do nothing for the girl. The entire scene in the tavern had lasted at most three minutes from the time he entered, filled with unlucky breaks from start to finish.

Now an innocent bystander was dead at the hands of the renegade, and Luke knew the local authorities would just as soon hang a white man for the crime. He had little choice but to escape and follow Melichus.

He slid through the window, gun out, and headed down

the alley toward the upset burro. Skirting the trembling and braying animal, Luke came out into a dirt street. This lane was not as choked with people as some of the others he'd walked down, and he was able to get a good view in both directions.

Melichus had chosen speed over subterfuge, and he left a clear path of angry residents marking his passage as he went across the boulevard and headed for an alley mouth. Luke plunged into the crowd after the man, pistol out and in his hand. He knew he had at most minutes until the *federales* would start to congregate in the area.

Pushing through a river of skeleton-dressed men and brightly clad and masked women, Luke cut across the street. He reached the alley and came around the corner. Chunks of adobe exploded next to his head, and the report of a pistol echoed down the narrow lane.

Ducking back, Luke crouched lower and came back around the corner. Melichus darted away, and Luke took off running after him. They came out into the street again. This avenue wasn't quite as crowded but was still filled with party-goers. Fifty yards down the street Melichus was dragging a teenage boy off a horse, beating him in the head with the barrel of his pistol.

People shouted in protest as the outlaw swung up into the saddle. Luke extended his arm and took aim. A group of terrified people ran in front of him, and he was forced to hold off firing. Whirling the mount, Melichus saw Luke and wasn't as restrained.

The renegade fired twice, bullets burning past Luke like angry lead hornets and striking the ground with hard *thumps* that kicked up dust. Luke ducked toward a doorway to find cover. A shootout in the middle of a crowded saloon or street had never been his intention. His mind flashed on the fallen barmaid, and he added another tally to Melichus's bill of lading.

From the safety of the doorway, he peeked around the corner and saw Melichus flying down the street, whipping the horse for all he was worth. The charging outlaw sent revelers in all directions, making the shot impossible for Luke to take.

Luke swore. The murdering madman had escaped again.

Now he had to get out of town himself before he ended up swinging from a noose on general principle.

"We're not done," he told the retreating outlaw. "We are not done, I promise you that."

CHAPTER 44

"I go no further."

"What?" Luke asked.

"I go no further," the Yaqui scout said. "Beyond here is the land of the bad Yaqui."

They stood in the foothills of the Cerro Mohinora. The highest location of the Sonoran Desert, the extinct volcano reached over ten thousand feet high. Luke Jensen had never been this far south before, but Melichus had fled into Chihuahua and Luke had followed. This was the longest hunt Luke had ever undertaken, but Melichus's blood debt was simply too great.

If it cost him his life, Luke would bring him down.

"What do you mean, 'bad Yaqui'?" he asked.

The scout made the sign of the cross. The Yaqui religion, Luke knew, was a strange amalgamation of Catholicism brought by Spanish monks and the tribe's original spiritualism that flowed and ebbed between the two in a way indecipherable to outsiders. The Yaqui had fought the Mexican army to a draw for the last hundred years. They could be dealt with, but none of them were to be taken lightly.

If these were bad Yaqui that Melichus had chosen to hide with, Luke wanted to know about it. The scout seemed reluctant to talk of it with an outsider.

"The Black Mountain Yaqui," he said, indicating the volcano, "have turned their back on the ways of our people and taken up the Navajo worship of the fire god. Haashch'ééshzhiní's ways can be turned to evil."

Luke grunted. All he needed to know was that the Yaqui ahead of him were possessed by the same bloody fanaticism as Melichus. That made them fair game as far as he was concerned, if they tried to stop him. Fully outfitted now and healed up, Luke had come ready to wage war if need be.

Reaching into a saddlebag, he gave the Indian guide a pouch filled with silver coins, their agreed upon price. The man didn't bother to count it, an action Luke took as a compliment. Before the man left, Luke turned and regarded the way forward.

A great black shadow lay across the land, cleaving the red flame of sunset. He stared upward at the dark crag where it loomed against the dying sun.

Startled, he suddenly narrowed his eyes against the glare. He could have sworn he'd caught a hint of movement along the upper ridge as he looked on, hand held to shield his eyes against the glare. It was too far to tell if it had been a man darting for cover or perhaps a goat.

Shrugging to himself, Luke examined the rough trail leading up and over the brow of the crag. Impossible to a horse, it seemed at first that indeed only a goat could traverse it. Looking closer, he saw how handholds had been chipped into place at some of the more narrow overhangs.

He sighed as he realized that a great deal of his equipment and weaponry could not make the journey. He'd be reduced to knife and pistols if he wanted to make that climb.

"You won't go any further?" he asked the Yaqui guide.

"I am going north," the man said. "I will go west first to see the great water but I will return to my home."

"Suit yourself," Luke agreed. "But if you will wait with my horse one day I will give you half again as much silver."

The Yaqui looked dubious. The Indian looked very much like a man weighing out the price of silver against his own life. Luke waited, uncertain about what he'd do if the man simply decided to leave. At last he made his decision.

"Last spring is three hours back," he said. "I will wait one day there."

"Fine, that will work," Luke said.

Whatever was going to happen, Luke knew, for good or for ill, it would happen well within the time frame of a day.

"How will I get my money if the bad Yaqui kill you?"

"You'll have my horse and rifle," Luke pointed out. "That's a pretty fair price for a day of sitting beside a cool spring."

The Yaqui grunted his acquiescence. "*Via con Dios,*" he said.

"*Via con Dios,*" Luke echoed automatically.

The man was already leading Luke's horse away.

Tying down the Remingtons strapped to his leg and ensuring his knife was secured as well, without a backward glance he began the long, treacherous ascent. The path narrowed at spots until he could proceed only by turning sideways and scraping through tight spots perfect for ambush from above. Again and again he was forced to halt his upward climb and rest for a moment, clinging to a precarious cliff face.

Night fell swiftly and the crag above him became a shadowy blur in which he was forced to blindly feel with his fingers for the holes and man-made cracks which served as a rude ladder up this precipitous slope. Upward he struggled as the cliff bulged outward near its summit and the path ran only wide enough to stand on tiptoes.

If he slipped, he doubted he would be able to stop the slide. The physical strain wore at his hands and calves while his mind played tricks on him, envisioning over and over what the drop would do to him if he should lose his grip. Time and again he slipped, and he escaped falling only by a hair's breadth. He forced his fingers into rigid talons that ached as they supported his body weight. He concentrated on putting one foot in front of the other, the ledge no larger than a tightrope. His progress went slower and slower but at last he saw the cliff's brow splitting the stars a scant twenty feet above him.

In that moment, his mind flashed to the movement he'd seen earlier, and some instinct made him crane his neck and look up. A vague bulk, too large and too close to see properly, heaved into view, toppling over the edge and hurtling down toward him with a great rush of air.

Operating on blind instinct he flattened himself against the cliff face and felt a heavy, glancing blow against his shoulder. The incidental contact almost ripped him from the wall, and one foot was swept off the narrow path, sending an avalanche of gravel cascading down the mountainside. In the next moment he heard a reverberating crash among the rocks below. Cold sweat soaked his shirt and beaded his brow. He looked up, wondering if this was a natural hazard or some kind of ambush.

Luke Jensen was a brave man, but the thought of dying helpless as a sheep with no chance of resistance turned his blood cold. He swallowed hard against the building fear. But then a wave of fury rose up in him, smothering his apprehension, and he renewed his ascent with near reckless speed, legs driving hard into the rocky crevice as his hands scrabbled for purchase.

A second boulder didn't materialize, and nothing living greeted him as he clambered over the edge, rolled away from the brink, and leapt erect, pistol flashing smoothly from its holster. He stood on a shallow plateau that served as a sort of natural porch to a very broken string of sawtooth-ridged hills spreading to the west. The crag he had just mounted jutted out from the rest of the heights in a sullen promontory, looming above the desert below and serving as a barrier to the volcanic crater just beyond its rim.

Silence hung heavy in the cool air. No breeze stirred and no footfall rustled amid the altitude-stunted brush cloaking the plateau, yet the boulder that had almost finished him had obviously not fallen by chance or any sort of natural happening.

Who else occupied this highland mesa? he wondered. Ready for an attack, he studied the terrain around him. He felt the hairs along the back of his arms lift, and the sensation of being watched left his skin crawling.

Gun still in hand, Luke started forward. For a while, the only sound he detected was the soft swishing of his own legs as he moved through a field of yellowed cheatgrass. Occasionally, he stopped to scan about him when he came to rock formations or small stands of piñon and white pines. Nothing met his gaze except dry, prickly shrubs and silent promontories of wind-shaped rock and shale.

At last he came to a place where the mesa broke into the higher slopes, and there he saw a clump of white pine trees blocked out in crude geometric shapes by the thick shadows enshrouding them. He approached warily then halted as his gaze, growing accustomed to the darkness, made out a vague form among the somber trunks that wasn't part of them.

He hesitated, tensed, pistol ready. The figure remained still and silent. Carefully, he advanced, poised to react instantly if any attack came. The figure was too small to be that of Melichus but that didn't rule out one of his apparent Yaqui followers.

Finally, it was the odd slump of the figure's head that decided him. Drawing the second Remington, Luke walked closer. The shadows fell back to reveal the figure of a Mexican peon pinned to the bole of a large white pine tree by Indian spears. The man must have been pinned while alive and subsequently bled to death because the front of his body was crusted with a dark crimson stain.

His ears had been pinned to the wood of the tree by stone-tipped arrows, but the weight of his head had caused the lobes to stretch and begin tearing as the flesh decomposed. The jaw hung open and loose, swollen tongue lolling from the corpse's mouth.

Luke grunted. The meaning of the gruesome signpost was obvious. Beyond lay death. Luke shrugged mentally. There had been plenty of death already on this bloody trail leading him to Melichus's door. It had been a dark, winding road indeed. But he was near the finish now, he could feel it. Finally.

Pushing through the little copse of pine trees, he emerged at the foot of a rugged incline, the first of a series of ridges. As he went up the boulder-strewn slopes the moon rose, illuminating everything in a soft, bone-white glow. In its light the broken ridges and mesas loomed like the battlements of some grim, fairy-tale castle.

He moved, keyed up and alert, ready to whirl at the slightest indication and begin firing with the Remingtons. Despite his readiness, he was still surprised when the confrontation unfolded. He strode up the steep, narrow path, eyes searching like a hunting cat when he entered a section of strangely stacked rocks. The cairns formed a sort of natural stone grove, some of them reaching twice his height.

One instant the night was still and silent, and in the next an Indian had appeared from behind one of the cairns. He had the squat body structure and straight black hair indicative of the Yaquis, and he held a Henry repeater adorned with an eagle feather hanging from a blue-beaded string.

More movement from the left as additional Indians revealed themselves. Luke didn't hesitate. As the warriors emerged, he dropped and rolled across one shoulder. Coming up, he threw himself into the boulder field, keeping low even as a pistol filled his hand. A cloud covered the moon, plunging the eerie landscape into inky blackness.

Hearing a rush of feet, Luke spun and fired. A Yaqui, no

more than a dim shape in the dark, stiffened and came to a stop. Luke fired a second time then ducked behind a five-foot-tall cairn. The Indian crashed to the gravel, and a chorus of rifle fire lit up the night, bullets whipping past his makeshift barrier or striking rocks and ricocheting wildly.

Luke knew he couldn't afford to get pinned down. Scuttling across the broken ground and using his free hand to support his crouch, he tried circling around. Muzzle flashes lit up the night and then died away. He paused in the narrow space between two boulders, ears straining to detect the slightest motion.

"Jensen!" Melichus called out.

Luke remained silent. He thought the outlaw was only talking to trick him into revealing his position.

"You were a fool to come here, this is no land for a white man!"

Using the shouting outlaw's voice like a beacon, Luke began edging toward the sound. His only warning was the faintest scrape of moccasin leather on stone. Turning, he caught a flash as a Yaqui warrior in white coarse-woven pants and top hooked around an ancient cairn, Henry rifle in both hands.

Luke's hand flashed across his body and fanned his hammer, once, twice, three times. The Remington boomed, the shots stuttering hard on one another. The muzzle flash cast stark shadows against the stones. All three bullets slammed into the Indian, and he staggered under their impact.

The Yaqui fell backward, bounced off a boulder, and pitched forward onto his face. As the rifle slipped from dead fingers, Luke was already holstering his pistol and reaching for it. The body hit the gravel and bounced hard as the carbine came into Luke's grip.

Spinning away, he bolted past a forest of rocks stacked into cairns that had probably stood since before the Spanish had even arrived in this land. His shoulder struck one pile a glancing blow as he pivoted in among them. Unsettled, the cairn toppled with a clatter, stones cascading down in a rush.

He spun back the way he'd come as the night lit up with rifle fire. Bullets ricocheted wildly as he darted in among the rocks, knifing across the field like a fish in water. Stepping around a boulder, he honed in on the crash of a nearby rifle and caught a Yaqui gunman from behind. The Henry in the Yaqui hands crashed and the man went down. Cutting left, Luke darted in among the rocks.

He came upon a hogan. Hogans were traditional south-western domiciles made of earth and wood. This one was made from pine logs packed with dried mud. There was a round mouth of a door and a smoke hole in the top. He froze, crouched in the lee of a rock, and watched the building. It was far too dark to see inside. A horse nickered in the darkness, and Luke recognized Melichus's mount tied to the protruding eave of a support joist on the hogan.

His blood ran cold when he realized he must be very close to the outlaw now.

He heard men moving surreptitiously out in the boulder field. He thought he counted at least three distinct people, but there could have been many more. There was no way of telling which, if any, were Melichus.

A bullet whined off the rock next to his head and stone splinters stung his face as the bullet ricocheted away. Cursing in surprise, Luke fell backward. He struck the ground hard and bit down on his own tongue. Pain shot through his mouth and he saw stars.

Seething at the discomfort, he twisted in the direction of the muzzle flash. Firing the Henry from the waist, he worked the action, fired again, and jacked another round into the chamber. His first round caught a Yaqui low in the stomach, bending the man in half like a book snapping closed. His second round struck the Indian in the top of the head and dashed his brains out of his skull and splashed them on the rocks.

Melichus came out of the hogan firing a Greener double-barrel .12-gauge. The shotgun roared and shot peppered the boulder next to Luke. Several rounds of buckshot tore into his leg.

Firing once, Luke missed and tried firing again, but the rifle was empty. Melichus and Luke each threw aside their long guns and scrambled for their pistols. The renegade's face was a twisted mask of rage. Melichus fired at a dead run as he broke for the cover of the rock cairns.

Luke dodged and rolled away from bullets burned through the air where his torso had just been. Rolling to his belly, he snapped a shot, but Melichus was gone. Then in that moment the clouds parted enough for a bar of moonlight to illuminate the area. Light poured into the black mouth of the hogan, and Luke froze momentarily at what it revealed.

A blond woman, naked and bruised, with blood flowing from her nose, was bound by iron manacles to one of the pillared roof supports. She was looking directly at Luke, eyes wide with surprise and a sort of crazed, animal hope.

Luke pushed himself up, searching for Melichus. It was impossible to tell what the outlaw would do. Sometimes he fought, other times he ran. It seemed the man was governed by unknowable whims of aggression and cowardice that Luke couldn't get a mental handle on.

Luke made a snap decision that the hogan offered some semblance of protection to keep him from getting flanked and leapt into action. He jumped up and sprinted toward the doorway, boots pounding hard into the gravel as he leapt over a boulder and dodged around a rock cairn before throwing himself through the opening.

The woman was sobbing but seemed too distraught to form words as he entered. He landed heavily then turned, pistol ready. A Yaqui sprinted forward, a Mexican Army

Springfield held in his hands. Excited, the whooping Indian fired from the hip. The rifle cracked loudly, and the big-bore round speared past Luke's head before slamming into the back wall of the hogan.

Luke lifted his arm and sent two shots tripping out, one hard on the heels of the other. The pistol jumped and barked in his hand. Recoil lifted the barrel as the muzzle flash illuminated the hogan interior. Outside the Yaqui stumbled in surprise as two bloody patches blossomed on his white, homespun cloth shirt.

Uttering a choking cry, the man went down to his knees then pitched forward onto his face, the Springfield bouncing away as it fell from lifeless fingers. Luke's hands worked automatically in the moment of quiet that followed.

He dumped his spent and smoking brass, letting them fall to the hardpacked earth of the hogan floor. As if of their own volition, his fingers reloaded the pistol by feel even as Luke's eyes searched out through the door, ready to drop the pistol he was reloading and draw the second Remington at a moment's notice.

"Just hold on a little longer," he told the girl over his shoulder. "You just need to hold on a little longer."

"I w-w-wanna go home," she moaned.

"I promise," Luke told her. "I'll get you home."

At that moment, a muzzle flash sparked out in the night. Luke saw the flame bursts wink from the dark crevice between two boulders. Without thinking, he fired two shots, putting the rounds into the dark where he'd seen the muzzle flash. He couldn't know if he'd hit anything, but he knew he had to do something to protect the girl.

Turning in that stolen moment, he found where the manacles had been attached to the raw pole of white pine used to frame the wall. The Remington boomed in his hands. A .44-caliber slug, slow and heavy and powerful, cracked into the wood and blew the chain link apart.

With a gasp the woman—no more than a girl, really—let her arms drop and collapsed inward on herself. In that brief moment Luke saw how dozens of angry red welts adorned her slim white back, and fury burned in him.

"Stay low!" he commanded.

He spun in place as he heard footsteps racing toward the hogan. A figure appeared in the doorway, features no more than a black silhouette as he blocked out the moonlight. The *click-clack* of a round being seated in a Henry repeating rifle filled the hogan, drowning out the audible, metallic *click* of Luke thumbing back the hammer on his Remington.

The guns blazed and the hogan was illuminated wildly by the muzzle flash of both weapons. Luke missed. A deadly .45-70 took Luke on the outside of his shoulder, gouging a bloody fissure through the muscle there. Crying out, he fired a second time.

This round cracked the Yaqui's skull and sent him collapsing back out through the door of the hogan. Luke sprang forward immediately, heart pounding, breathing hard. He snatched up the Henry rifle and jacked a fresh round into the chamber.

Carefully, he peeked around the edge of the door, head down low. He saw nothing but boulders and rock cairns in a forest of stone. He heard rocks scrape and whirled in that direction, weapon ready. He saw nothing living but a dribbling little cascade of pebbles off a rock the size of a kitchen table.

"Let's finish this, Melichus!" he shouted. "You and me!"

Thinking he detected motion, Luke whirled in that direction. He saw the swaying of the low branches on a lone pine tree standing surrounded by boulders like a teacher by children.

"All you do is run, Melichus," he yelled. "Stop running for once, you cowardly dog!"

A bullet whined out of the darkness and struck the doorframe three inches above Luke's head. He jumped back as the wood exploded into splinters, and the gunshot report echoed through the fields of stone.

"He's an animal," the girl said, voice a whimper. "Kill him!"

"I'm trying, believe me," Luke told her. Changing positions he called out again. "You missed, Melichus, you red devil. Just like always. How many of your men have I killed now? More than you can count, I bet."

He waited to see if his verbal barbs found a home. The outlaw didn't answer. Carefully, Luke adjusted his position a third time and then risked a look out. Nothing moved. Above them, clouds began swallowing the moon again, casting long shadows over the area.

From his position, Luke saw where a collection of boulders, some big as horses, others the size of water troughs, were nestled together in a little collection like headstones in a graveyard. He thought if he could get in among them he might be able to maneuver more freely.

The run would be a dangerous ten yards, though. Still, better than finding himself pinned down here. Satisfied he had little choice, he pulled back inside the hogan. He looked at the girl. She stared back with terrified, fever-bright eyes. There were bite marks on her neck and breasts. It turned his stomach.

Melichus needed to be made to pay for everything. Everything. Charlie Walks-the-Horizon, Collins, Talbot . . . Delacroix. For that matter, even O'Toole deserved better than the way he'd been taken out. They hadn't ever really stood a chance against a full platoon of soldiers outfitted for battle. The Apaches working with Melichus had led them into a clever trap.

"Take this," he said.

Not taking his eyes off the doorway, he drew his left-hand Remington and passed it to the woman. Her eyes were wild, breathing frantic, and once she took it he wrapped his hands around hers before she could place her finger on the trigger.

"Look at me," he said, voice low and soothing.

She did as he asked, and he risked looking away from the doorway for just a moment.

"Calm yourself, it won't help if you end up shooting me. Make sure of your target before you fire. Do you understand?"

She nodded, a quick, furtive gesture that could have been essentially meaningless in her mental state. Luke tightened his grip.

"Say it," he instructed. "Say it back to me."

She swallowed hard and inhaled and the act of answering a question seemed to physically calm her.

"I'll make sure of my target before I fire."

Luke smiled to reassure her. "Good, honey, real good. My name is Luke Jensen, what's yours?"

"Sally," the young woman answered. "Sally Miller."

"Sally," Luke said, "I'm going to get you out of here, I promise. But in order to do that I'm going to have to go out there and kill that evil madman who stole you. Do you understand?"

She nodded.

"Okay. If I have to come back I'll call out, okay? You hear me call out my name, you don't shoot, all right?"

"I u-u-understand," she stammered out.

It was clear she didn't relish the idea of him leaving her. Still, she was being brave about it. Luke's respect for her nudged up several notches higher than it already was. Sally Miller was a survivor. That was good, he thought, because she was going to have to be.

"All right then," he told her. "I'm going to go kill him."

Sally surprised him by saying in a fairly strong voice, "He's got it coming."

That brought a laugh from Luke, a sound that he had never expected to hear again.

"He surely does."

CHAPTER 45

Luke darted out of the hogan at a dead sprint. Seeing the cluster of rocks ahead of him, he threw himself forward just as shots rang out from the opposite side of the boulder field. Bullets buzzed past him, close enough to feel them buffet the air. He landed hard, bounced once, and rolled into the rocks.

Another shot rang out and ricocheted off one of the table-sized boulders. Luke marked the location of the shots and began to visually map out his approach. He was going to have to circle around and try to keep an angle on the outlaw. A task easier thought than actually done.

Carefully, keeping the hogan in sight, Luke began crawling through the maze of rock. After he had gone a little way, he rose to his feet and proceeded in a crouch. He wove his way through the thicket of cairns and boulders, each turn capable of bringing him face-to-face with the deadly renegade.

One, two, three steps; pause, listen, inch forward again. Once he thought he heard the scrape of feet on gravel, and he froze, poised. After several long moments of hearing nothing he proceeded forward cautiously. He came upon the corpse of a Yaqui Indian he'd killed earlier. The man had died with his eyes wide open and staring. Blood had formed a coppery-smelling pond around his body. Carefully, Luke stepped over the corpse.

He was in a narrow passage between two lines of boulders the size of small houses. The clouds parted and moonlight like bone shimmered down, illuminating the scene in an otherworldly glow. He spun, hearing the swift beating of footsteps behind him.

Lit up bright as day, the shrieking Melichus raced toward him with .36-caliber navy Colts in each of his fists. The renegade's face was a twisted mask of blind rage and wild hate, the eyes burning with animal frenzy. Bullets shot past Luke to either side, the lead projectiles plucking at the cloth of his sleeves. A bullet sliced open a furrow along his ribs and another did the same on his opposite thigh.

Snarling, he dropped to one knee and brought the Remington up. The edge of his opposite hand found his hammer and fanned it until the pistol went dry. The gun roared and bucked in his hand, fouling the air with thick, acrid gun smoke.

The charging Melichus stutter-stepped as rounds struck him. Then he shuddered like a man in freezing water. The last bullet Luke fired cracked his forehead like an eggshell and tossed his brains on the rocks in an unceremonious pile. He pitched backward, boneless, flopping to the ground in an untidy heap, arms and legs akimbo as his eyes stared blankly up at the night sky.

Ears ringing from the cacophony of gunfire, Luke slowly stood. His chest heaved. He was alive. Melichus was dead. At long last, Melichus was dead.

Luke supposed that when he thought about what was home to him, he thought about his brother Smoke's ranch. He was a wanderer, but that ranch and the family living there were the closest thing he had to a home.

He had never traveled so far from home to hunt a man.

Hands working automatically, he reloaded the Remington. There could still be bad Yaqui around. He thought about the girl he'd found in the hogan, knew she would likely suffer from this experience for the rest of her life. He could only hope that by returning her she could heal. Killing Melichus couldn't undo the harm he'd caused, but it put an end to his reign of terror at last.

Suddenly a new thought flashed through Luke's mind.

The saddle.

CHAPTER 46

He found Melichus's black stallion in a small valley behind the boulder field. The basin formed a natural paddock and the saddled mounts grazed there. A winding trail cut down the mountain leading out onto the plain. The stallion stood out like a giant among the Indian ponies.

He dropped Melichus's corpse to the ground, and the girl, now dressed in stolen clothing, shied away from the body. Horses didn't like the smell of death and also shied but didn't go that far. He caught Melichus's mount by the reins and soothed him.

"Easy big fella, easy," he whispered. "Let's get that saddle off you."

After a time the horse was gentled enough to let him un-cinch it, and he hauled it off and flipped it over before putting it on the ground. Luke was eager to get started on the ride down. No more Indians had made an appearance yet, but there must be a village close by. Yaqui were not the wandering raiders Apache tended to be. They were far more likely to remain within easy striking distance of their homes.

Squatting down, Luke pulled the saddle blanket free and threw it aside. He stared down at the saddle. Abruptly, he threw back his head and began laughing. The woman looked

at him in confusion and not a little fear; there was an edge to
the laughter that seemed dangerous.

"Those dumb, stupid dreamers," he howled.

He wiped tears of laughter out of the corner of his eyes.
The inside of the saddle pads were made from sheepskin; any
map drawn on their surface would stand out in bold relief.

The saddle pads were bare. There was no map.

Luke looked over at the body of Melichus. The man had
lived by violence, and he'd sure as hell died by it as well.

"I guess the only treasure is what I'm going to get for your
mangy hide." Luke started laughing again.

It would have to do.

TURN THE PAGE FOR AN EXCITING PREVIEW!

JOHNSTONE COUNTRY.
WITH A DETOUR THROUGH HELL.

Legendary gunfighter Perley Gates
always fights on the side of the angels.
But in the East Texas county of Angelina,
the war is half over—and the devils are winning. . . .

In spite of his holy-sounding name,
Perley Gates is not his brother's keeper.
Even so, he can't refuse a simple request by his elder
brother, Rubin. Rubin is starting his own cattle ranch, and
he wants Perley to deliver the contract for it—through a
lawless stretch of land called Angelina County.
Perley can't blame his brother for wanting a piece of the
American Dream. But for the famed gunslinger,
it means a nightmare journey through hell itself. . . .

The trouble starts when Perley and his men meet some
damsels in distress—a lovely group of saloon girls with a
broken wagon wheel. Being a good Samaritan,
Perley feels honor-bound to help them.
But when the travelers cross paths with an ornery gang
of vicious outlaws, things turn deadly—and fast.
It only gets worse from there. Angelina County is infested
with a special breed of vermin known as the Tarpley family.
And this corrupt clan has a gunslinger of their own—who'd
love nothing more than to take down a living legend
like Perley Gates. . . .

**National Bestselling Authors
William W. Johnstone and J.A. Johnstone**

THE LONESOME GUN
A Perley Gates Western

On sale now wherever Pinnacle Books are sold.

Live Free. Read Hard.
www.williamjohnstone.net

Visit us at www.kensingtonbooks.com

CHAPTER 1

"Becky, another hungry customer just walked in," Lucy Tate said. "I'm getting some more coffee for my tables. Can you wait on him? He looks like trouble." She looked at Beulah Walsh and winked, so Beulah knew she was up to some mischief.

"I was just fixing to wash up some more cups," Becky said. "We're about to run out of clean ones. Can he wait a minute?"

"I don't know," Lucy answered. "He looks like he's the impatient kind. He might make a big scene if somebody doesn't wait on him pretty quick."

"I don't want to make a customer mad," Beulah said as she aimed a mischievous grin in Lucy's direction. "Maybe I can go get him seated."

"Oh, my goodness, no," Becky said. "I'll go take care of him." She was sure there was no reason why Lucy couldn't have taken care of a new customer, instead of causing Beulah to do it. Beulah was busy enough as cook and owner. She dried her hands on a dish towel and hurried out into the hotel dining room. Lucy and Beulah hurried right after her as far as the door, where they stopped to watch Becky's reaction.

"Perley!" Becky exclaimed joyfully, running to meet him. Surprised by her exuberance, he was staggered a couple of steps when she locked her arms around his neck. "I thought you were never coming home," she said. "You didn't say you were gonna be gone so long."

"I didn't think I would be," Perley said. "We were just supposed to deliver a small herd of horses to a ranch near Texarkana, but we ran into some things we hadn't counted on, and that held us up, pretty much. I got back as quick as I could. Sonny Rice went with Possum and me, and he ain't back yet." She started to ask why, but he said; "I'll tell you all about it, if you'll get me something to eat."

"Sit down, sweetie," she said, "and I'll go get you started." He looked around quickly to see if anyone had heard what she called him, but it was too late. He saw Lucy and Beulah grinning at him from the kitchen. Becky led him to a table right outside the kitchen door and sat him down while she went to get his coffee. "I was just washing up some cups when you came in. I must have known I needed a nice clean cup for someone special."

He was both delighted and embarrassed over the attention she gave him. And he wanted to tell her he'd prefer that she didn't do it in public, but he was afraid he might hurt her feelings if he did. Unfortunately, Lucy and Beulah were not the only witnesses to Becky's show of affection for the man she had been not-so-secretly in love with for a couple of years. Finding it especially entertaining, two drifters on their way to Indian Territory across the Red River spoke up when Becky came back with Perley's coffee.

"Hey, darlin'," Rafer Samson called out, "bring that coffee-pot out here. Sweetie ain't the only one that wants coffee. You'd share some of that coffee, wouldn't you, sweetie?"

"Dang, Rafer," his partner joined in. "You'd best watch what you're sayin'. Ol' sweetie might not like you callin' him that. He might send that waitress over here to take care of you."

That was as far as they got before Lucy stepped in to put

a stop to it. "Listen, fellows, why don't you give it a rest? Don't you like the way I've been taking care of you? We've got a fresh pot of coffee brewing on the stove right now. I'll make sure you get the first cups poured out of it, all right?"

"I swear," Rafer said. "Does he always let you women do the talkin' for him?"

"Listen, you two boneheads," Lucy warned, "I'm trying to save you from going too far with what you might think is fun. Don't force Perley Gates into something that you don't wanna be any part of."

"Ha!" Rafer barked. "Who'd you say? Pearly somethin'?"

"It doesn't matter," Lucy said, realizing she shouldn't have spoken Perley's name. "You two look old enough to know how to behave. Don't start any trouble. Just eat your dinner, and I'll see that you get fresh coffee as soon as it's ready."

But Rafer was sure he had touched a sensitive spot the women in the dining room held for the mild-looking young man. "What did she call him, Deke? Pearly somethin'?"

"Sounded like she said Pearly Gates," Deke answered. "I swear it did."

"Pearly Gates!" Rafer blurted loud enough for everyone in the dining room to hear. "His mama named him Pearly Gates!"

Lucy made one more try. "All right, you've had your fun. He's got an unusual name. How about dropping it now, outta respect for the rest of the folks eating their dinner in here?"

"To blazes with the rest of the folks in here," he responded, seeming to take offense. "I'll say what I damn-well please. It ain't up to you, no how. If he don't like it, he knows where I'm settin'."

Lucy could see she was getting nowhere. "You keep it up, and you're liable to find out a secret that only the folks in Paris, Texas, know. And you ain't gonna like it."

"Thanks for the warnin', darlin'. I surely don't want to learn his secret. Now go get us some more coffee." As soon as she walked away, he called out, "Hey, tater, is your name Pearly Gates?"

Knowing he could ignore the two no longer, Perley answered. "That's right," he said. "I was named after my grandpa. Perley was his name. It sounds like the Pearly Gates up in Heaven, but it ain't spelt the same."

"Well, you gotta be some kinda sweet little girlie-boy to walk around with a name like that," Rafer declared. "Ain't that right, Deke?"

"That's right, Rafer," Deke responded like a puppet. "A real man wouldn't have a name like that."

"I know you fellows are just havin' a little fun with my name, but I'd appreciate it if you'd stop now. I don't mind it all that much, but I think it upsets my fiancée."

Perley's request caused both his antagonists to pause for a moment. "It upsets his what?" Deke asked.

"I don't know," Rafer answered, "his *fi-ant-cee,* whatever that is. Maybe it's a fancy French word for his behind. We upset his behind." He turned to look at the few other customers in the dining room, none of whom would meet his eye. "We upset his fancy behind."

"I'm sorry, Becky," Perley said. "I sure didn't mean to cause all this trouble. Tell Beulah I'll leave, and they oughta calm down after I'm gone."

Beulah was standing just inside the kitchen door, about ready to put an end to the disturbance, and she heard what Perley said. "You'll do no such thing," she told him. "Lucy shouldn't have told 'em your name. You sit right there and let Becky get your dinner." She walked out of the kitchen then and went to the table by the front door where the customers deposited their firearms while they ate. She picked up the two gun belts that Rafer and Deke had left there, took them outside, and dropped them on the steps. When she came back inside, she went directly to their table and informed them. "I'm gonna have to ask you to leave now, since your mamas didn't teach you how to behave in public. I put your firearms outside the door. There won't be any charge for what you ate if you get up and go right now."

"The hell you say," Rafer replied. "We'll leave when we're good and ready."

"I can't have you upsettin' my other customers," Beulah said. "So do us all the courtesy of leaving peacefully, and like I said, I won't charge you nothin' for what you ate."

"You threw our guns out the door?" Deke responded in disbelief. He thought about what she said for only a brief moment, then grabbed his fork and started shoveling huge forkfuls of food in his mouth as fast as he could. He washed it all down with the remainder of his coffee, wiped his mouth with his sleeve, and belched loudly. "Let's go, Rafer."

"I ain't goin' nowhere till I'm ready, and I ain't ready right now," Rafer said, and remained seated at the table. "If you're through, go out there and get our guns offa them steps."

"Lucy," Beulah said, "Step in the hotel lobby, and tell David we need the sheriff."

"Why, you ol' witch!" Rafer spat. "I oughta give you somethin' to call the sheriff about!" He stood up and pushed his chair back, knocking it over in the process.

That was as far as Perley could permit it to go. He got up and walked over to face Rafer. "You heard the lady," he said. "This is her place of business, and she don't want you and your friend in here. So why don't you two just go on out like she said, and there won't be any need to call the sheriff up here."

Rafer looked at him in total disbelief. Then a sly smile spread slowly across his face. "Why don't you go outside with me?"

"What for?" Perley asked, even though he knew full well the reason for the invitation.

"Oh, I don't know. Just to see what happens, I reckon."

Finding a game that amused him now, he continued. "Do you wear a gun, Perley?"

"I've got a gun on the table with the others," Perley answered. "I don't wear it in here."

"Are you fast with that gun?" When Perley reacted as if he didn't understand, Rafer said, "When you draw it outta your holster, can you draw it real fast?" Because of Perley's general air of innocence, Rafer assumed he was slow of wit as well.

"Yes," Perley answered honestly, "but I would only do so in an emergency."

"That's good," Rafer said, "because this is an emergency. You wanna know what the emergency is? When I step outside and strap my gun on, if you ain't outside with me, I'm gonna come back inside and shoot this place to pieces. That's the emergency. You see, I don't cotton to nobody tellin' me to get outta here."

"All right," Perley said. "I understand why you're upset. I'll come outside with you, and we'll talk about this like reasonable men should."

"Two minutes!" Rafer blurted. "Then if you ain't outside, I'm comin' in after you." He walked out the door with Deke right behind him.

Becky rushed to Perley's side as he went to the table to get his gun belt. "Perley, don't go out there. You're not going to let that monster draw you into a gunfight are you?"

"I really hope not," Perley told her. "I think maybe I can talk some sense into him and his friend. But I had to get him out of here. He was gettin' too abusive. Don't worry, I'll be all right. He oughta be easier to talk to when he doesn't have an audience."

He strapped his Colt .44 on and walked outside to find Rafer and Deke waiting. Seeing the expressions of gleeful anticipation on both faces, Perley could not help a feeling of uncertainty. If he had looked behind him, he would have seen everyone in the dining room gathered at the two windows on that side of the building; that is, everyone except Becky and Beulah. All of the spectators were confident of the unassuming young man's gift of speed with a handgun. As far as Perley was concerned, his lightning-fast reactions were just that, a gift. For he never practiced with a weapon, and he honestly had no idea why his brain and body just reacted with no conscious direction from himself. Because of that, he was of the opinion that it could just as easily leave him with no warning. And that was one reason why he always tried to avoid pistol duels whenever possible. He took a deep breath and hoped for the best.

"I gotta admit, I had my doubts if you had the guts to walk out that door," Rafer said when Perley came toward them. Aside to Deke, he said, "If this sucker beats me, shoot him." Deke nodded.

"Why do you wanna shoot me?" Perley asked him. "You've never seen me before today. I've done you no wrong. It doesn't make any sense for you and me to try to kill each other."

"You ain't done me no wrong?" Rafer responded. "You walked up to my table and told me to get outta there. I don't take that from any man."

"If you're honest with yourself, you have to admit that you started all the trouble when you started makin' fun of my name. I was willin' to call that just some innocent fun, and I still am. So, we could just forget this whole idea to shoot each other and get on with the things that matter. And that's just to get along with strangers on a courteous basis. I'm willing to forget the whole trouble if you are. Whaddaya say? It's not worth shootin' somebody over."

"I swear, the more I hear comin' outta your mouth, the more I feel like I gotta puke. I think I'll shoot you just like I'd shoot a dog that's gone crazy. One thing I can't stand is a man too yellow to stand up for himself. I'm gonna count to three, and you'd better be ready to draw your weapon when I say three 'cause I'm gonna cut you down."

"This doesn't make any sense at all," Perley said. "I don't have any reason to kill you."

"One!" Rafer counted.

"Don't do this," Perley pleaded, and turned to walk away.

"Two!" Rafer counted.

"I'm warnin' you, don't say three."

"Three!" Rafer exclaimed defiantly, his six-gun already halfway out when he said it, and he staggered backward from the impact of the bullet in his chest. Deke, shocked by Perley's instant response, was a second slow in reacting and dropped his weapon when Perley's second shot caught him in his right shoulder. He stood, helplessly waiting for Perley's fatal shot, almost sinking to his knees when Perley released the hammer and returned his pistol to his holster.

"There wasn't any sense to that," Perley said. "Your friend is dead because of that foolishness, and you better go see Bill Simmons about your shoulder. He's the barber, but he also does some doctorin'. We ain't got a doctor in town yet. You'd best just stand there for a minute, though, 'cause I see the sheriff runnin' this way." Deke remained where he was, his eyes still glazed with the shock of seeing Rafer cut down so swiftly. Perley walked over and picked up Deke's gun, broke the cylinder open and extracted all the cartridges. Then he dropped it into Deke's holster.

"Perley," Paul McQueen called out as he approached. "What's the trouble? Who's that?" he asked, pointing to the body on the ground, before giving Perley time to answer his first question.

"I think I heard his friend call him Rafer," Perley said. "Is that right?" he asked Deke.

Deke nodded, then said, "Rafer Samson."

"Rafer Samson," McQueen repeated. "I'll see if I've got

any paper on him, but I expect you could save me the trouble," he said to Deke. "What's your name?"

"Deke Johnson," he replied. "You ain't got no paper on me. Me and Rafer was just passin' through on the way to the Red."

"I don't expect I do," McQueen said, "at least by that name, anyway. You were just passin' through, and figured you might as well cause a little trouble while you were at it, right?" He knew without having to ask that Perley didn't cause the trouble. "How bad's that shoulder?"

Deke nodded toward Perley. "He put a bullet in it."

"You musta gone to a helluva lot of trouble to get him to do that," the sheriff remarked. "Perley, you wanna file any charges on him?" Perley said that he did not. "All right," McQueen continued. "I won't lock you up, and we can go see Bill Simmons the barber about that shoulder. He's doctored a lotta gunshots, so he'll fix you up so you can ride. Then I want you out of town. Is that understood?"

"Yessir," Deke replied humbly.

"Perley, you gonna be in town a little while?" McQueen asked. When Perley said that he was, McQueen told him he'd like to hear the whole story of the incident. "I'll tell Bill to send Bill Jr. to pick up Mr. Samson." He looked around as several spectators from down the street started coming to gawk at the body. "You mind stayin' here awhile to watch that body till Bill Jr. gets here with his cart?"

"Reckon not," Perley said.

Bill Jr. responded pretty quickly, so it was only a few minutes before Perley saw him come out of the alley beside the barbershop, pushing his handcart. Perley helped him lift Rafer's body up on the cart. "Sheriff said he called you out," Bill Jr. said. "They don't never learn, do they?" Perley wasn't sure how to answer that, so he didn't.

CHAPTER 2

When he turned back toward the dining room again, he saw the folks inside still crowded up at the two small windows on that wall, and he thought maybe he'd just skip his dinner. But then he saw Becky standing in the open door, waiting for him to return. He truly hated for her to have seen the shooting. The incident she just witnessed was the kind of thing that happened to him quite frequently. There was no reason for it that he could explain. It was just something that had been attached to him at birth. The same as his natural reaction with a handgun, he supposed. He often wondered if when the Lord branded him with the cow-pie stigma, He thought it only fair to also grant him with lightning-fast reactions. He had his brother, John, to thank for the saying, "If there wasn't but one cow pie in the whole state of Texas, Perley would accidentally step in it."

Then Becky broke into his fit of melancholy when she became impatient and stepped outside the door. "Perley, come on in here and eat your dinner. It's almost time to clean up the kitchen." He reluctantly responded to her call.

Inside, he kept his eyes focused on the space between Becky's shoulder blades, avoiding the open stares of the customers as he followed her to the table by the kitchen door.

"Sit down," Becky said, "and I'll fix you a plate." She picked up his coffee cup. "I'll dump this and get you some fresh."

When he finally looked up from the table, it was to catch Edgar Welch's gaze focused upon him. The postmaster nodded and calmly said, "Attaboy, Perley." His remark caused a polite round of applause from most of the other tables. Instead of feeling heroic, Perley was mortified. He had just killed a man. It was certainly not his first, but it was something he was most definitely not proud of.

Becky returned from the kitchen with a heaping plate of food. She was followed by Beulah, who came to thank him for taking the trouble outside her dining room. "There ain't no tellin' how many of my customers mighta got shot, if you hadn't gone out there with him. He was gonna come back in here if you hadn't. There certainly ain't gonna be no charge for your dinner. Becky, take good care of him."

"I will," Becky said, and sat down at the table with him. She watched him eat for a few minutes after Beulah went back into the kitchen before she asked a question. "Before all that trouble started, when you first came in, you said you came by to tell me something. Do you remember what it was?"

"Yeah," he answered. "I came to tell you I've gotta take a little trip for a few days."

"Perley," she fussed, "you just got back from Texarkana. Where do you have to go now?"

"Rubin wants me to take a contract he signed down to a ranch somewhere south of Sulphur Springs. It's for fifty head of Hereford cattle. Him and John have been talkin' about cross-breedin' 'em with our Texas longhorns to see if they can breed a better meat cow."

"Why can't one of them go?" Becky asked.

"John and Rubin both work pretty hard to run the cattle operation for the Triple-G. I never cared much for workin' on the ranch, and there wasn't anything tyin' me down here, till

I found you. So, I have always been the one to do things like takin' this contract, and takin' those horses to Texarkana." He saw the look of disappointment in her face, so he was quick to say that there would surely be a change in his part of running the Triple-G after they were married. Judging by her expression, he wasn't sure she believed him. Their discussion was interrupted at that point when Paul McQueen walked in the dining room. He came straight to their table.

"Mind if I sit down?" Paul asked.

"Not at all," Becky answered him. "I've got to get up from here and help Lucy and Beulah. Can I get you a cup of coffee?" She knew he had been in earlier to eat dinner.

"Yes, ma'am, I could use a cup of coffee," he said. When she left to fetch it, he said to Perley, "Bill's workin' on that fellow to get your bullet outta his shoulder. I asked him how it all happened, but I swear, he seemed to be confused about how it did happen. I asked him why he pulled his weapon, if it was just you and his partner in a shootout. He said he wasn't sure why he pulled it. Said maybe he thought you might shoot him, and damned if you didn't. I don't think he really knows what happened, but I can pretty much guess. Anyway, I don't think you have to worry about him. I told him I wanted him outta town as soon as Bill's finished with him, and I think he's anxious to go. Bill Jr. was already back with the body before I left there."

"If you're wonderin' about that business at all, you've got plenty of eyewitnesses," Perley suggested. "Everybody you see sittin' in here now was at those two windows up front. So they can tell you better than I can. I'm a little bit like the one I shot. It happened so fast, I ain't sure I remember what happened."

"Don't get me wrong, Perley, I don't doubt you handled it any other way than you are about everything, fair and square. I just wanted the whole picture, in case the mayor asks me."

McQueen didn't have to wait long before he received the first eyewitness report. It came when Edgar Welch finished his dinner. Before leaving, he walked over to the table. "That was one helluva bit of shootin' you done today, Perley. Sheriff, you shoulda seen it." He then took them through the whole encounter. "Perley wasn't even facing that devil when he drew on him, and he still beat him."

"Maybe it ain't such a good idea to tell too many people about it, Edgar," McQueen said. "You might not be doin' Perley or the town any favors if we talk about how fast he is with that six-gun of his. We might have the kind of men showin' up in town that we don't wanna attract, like them two today."

"I see what you mean," Edgar said. "And I agree with you. We might have more drifters like those two showing up in town. Point well taken. Guess I'll be gettin' back to the post office."

The sheriff left soon after the postmaster, leaving Perley to finish up his dinner with a brief word here and there from Becky as she helped Lucy and Beulah clean up the dining room. He promised her that he would stay in town the entire day and eat supper there that night before going back to the Triple-G. She gave him a key to her room on the first floor of the hotel, right behind the kitchen, so he could wait for her to finish her chores. She would have a couple of hours before it was time to prepare the dining room for supper. He was concerned about Buck, so he took the bay gelding to the stable so he could take his saddle off and turn him loose in Walt Carver's corral.

He suspected that Possum was going to give him a goodly portion of grief for slipping out that morning without telling him where he was going. He was halfway serious when he wondered what he was going to do with Possum after he and Becky were married.

It was after two o'clock when Becky showed up at her room. They embraced briefly before she stepped away, apologizing for her sweaty condition, the result of just having cleaned up the kitchen. She seemed strangely distant, he thought, not like her usual lighthearted cheerfulness. "Maybe I ought to go on back to the ranch now," he suggested, "and let you get a little bit of rest before you have to go back to the dining room."

"I guess I'm just a little more tired than I thought," she said. "But I don't want to rush you off. I know you stayed in town because of me." She didn't want to tell him that the incident that took place right outside the dining room made a tremendous impact upon her. She had sought the counsel of Beulah Walsh, the closest person to a mother she had. Her own mother had passed seven years ago, leaving her father a widower living alone in Tyler. While they had worked cleaning up the kitchen, Beulah, and Lucy, too, had tried to help her understand the man she had fallen in love with.

"The thing that happened in the dining room today is not that unusual in Perley's life," Beulah had told her. "His skill with a firearm is a curse that he has to live with," she said. "To Perley's credit, he tries to avoid it, but it always finds him sooner or later. And like you saw today, even his name is a curse and an open invitation to a troublemaker. So you have to be prepared for that day when Perley's not the fastest gun."

"I know how you feel, honey," Lucy had suggested. "But why don't you wait to see if he's gonna be working full time at the ranch before you marry him? The way it is now, him and Possum are gone who knows where most of the time. You said he's leaving tomorrow to go somewhere for a few days, and that ain't good for a marriage. You don't wanna spend your life wondering if your children's daddy is coming home or not."

Those words were still ringing in her mind now as she tried to sort out her true feelings, and she could see the confusion in Perley's eyes as they searched hers. This was the first time since she had met Perley that she wondered if she was about to make the wrong decision. In spite of her love for the man, she reluctantly decided that Lucy's advice might be best. "Perley," she finally managed to say, "you're leaving tomorrow to take that contract for the cows. Why don't we wait till you get back to talk about any plans we want to make? I must confess, that business today really got to me. And working in the kitchen afterward just seemed to drain all the energy I had. I hope you understand. I love you."

He didn't understand at all, but he said that he did. She seemed to be a Becky he had never met before. "That's a good idea," he said. "I'm gonna go now, so you can rest up before you have to go back to work tonight. We'll talk about everything when I get back. I love you, too." She stepped up to him and gave him another brief embrace, a fraction longer than the one she had greeted him with. He reached in his pocket and pulled out her door key. "Here," he said, "I don't reckon I'll be needin' this."

She stood in the door and watched him walk down the hallway to the back door. "Perley," she called after him, "be careful." He acknowledged with a wave of his hand.

"That last kiss felt more like a goodbye kiss," he told Buck as he followed the trail back to the Triple-G Ranch. "It sure didn't seem like Becky a-tall. I feel like I just got fired." Walt Carver was sure surprised when he showed up at the stable to get Buck. Perley gave him no reason for returning so soon, other than the simple fact that he changed his mind. Without pushing Buck, he arrived at the ranch in plenty of time to get supper at the cook shack, which was where he generally ate his meals. His eldest brother, Rubin, and his family lived in the original ranch headquarters. His other brother, John, had built a house for him and his family. Perley was welcome to eat at either house, but he found it more to his liking to eat with the cowhands at the cook shack. He always felt that he was imposing, even though he knew he was a favorite with his nephews and nieces. Since he had time, he decided to stop by the house and pick up the contract and the money for the Herefords from Rubin.

"Howdy, Perley," Link Drew greeted him when he rode up to the barn. Young Link had grown like a weed since Perley brought him home with him, after the brutal death of Link's mother and father in the little store they operated. Link was nine when he came to the Triple-G. Looking at him today, Perley couldn't remember if he'd had one or two birthdays since he had arrived. "You want me to take care of Buck for you?" Link asked.

"I think Buck would appreciate it," Perley replied. "If you'll do that, I'll run up and get something at the house, and I'll see you at supper." He climbed down out of the saddle and handed Link the reins. He hesitated half a minute to watch the boy lead the big bay gelding away before turning to walk up to the house. "Knock, knock," he called out as he walked in the kitchen door. In reality, the house was as much his home as it was Rubin's, but being practical, he didn't want to surprise anybody.

"Oh, hello, Perley," Lou Ann, Rubin's wife, greeted him. "If you're lookin' for Rubin, he's in the study."

"Thank you, ma'am," Perley said, and headed for the hallway door.

"You stayin' for supper?" Lou Ann asked. "You're welcome, you know."

"No, thank you just the same, Lou Ann. I'm just gonna pick up a paper and some money from Rubin, and I'll be outta your way." Just as Lou Ann said, he found Rubin at his desk in the study. "You got that contract and the money for those cattle?" Perley asked as he walked in.

"Thought you weren't comin' back till after supper," Rubin

said as he opened a drawer and pulled out a big envelope. "What happened? Becky kick you out?" he joked. "When are you gonna bring her down here to officially meet the family?"

"I don't know," Perley answered. "Might be a while. There ain't no hurry."

"Well, you might be wise to take your time and be sure it's what you really want. You stayin' for supper?"

"Nope," Perley answered. "I just came to get this." He picked up the thick envelope and tested its weight. "You got a thousand dollars in here?"

"Plus a contract that Weber has to sign, sayin' he got the money," Rubin answered. "He wouldn't deal with anything but cash. Take Possum with you. That's a lot of money you're carrying."

Perley couldn't help chuckling when he thought of the remote possibility of getting away without Possum. "I'll tell him you said to take him. That way, he'll feel like he has a right to complain if something doesn't suit him. We'll leave right after breakfast in the mornin'." He turned and headed for the door.

"You take care of yourself, Perley," Rubin called after him.

"I will," Perley replied, and went out the front door in time to hear Ollie Dinkler banging on his iron triangle to announce supper was ready.

"Beans is ready, Perley," Ollie said when Perley walked on past him.

Perley replied. "I'll be right back, soon as I put this in the barn. He folded the thick envelope Rubin gave him, took it in the barn, and stuck it in his saddlebag. When he returned to the cook shack, he found Possum waiting for him.

"I thought you said you was gonna eat supper in town with Becky," Possum said. "What's wrong? And I know somethin' is, so tell me what happened."

"What makes you think somethin's wrong?" Perley asked. "She just had a hard workin' day and I thought she could use a little rest. Besides, we gotta get an early start in the mornin', and I didn't wanna get back too late tonight."

"You stickin' with that story?" Possum asked.

"I reckon," Perley answered. "Let's eat while there's still some beans in the pot."

Possum followed him inside where Ollie was serving. "You think you can find that Weber Ranch?" he asked Perley.

"I expect so," Perley answered. "I wouldn't think it would be too hard." He paused to let that simmer a little while in Possum's brain until he saw him working up his argument for the wisdom of accompanying him. "Oh, and Rubin said it might be a good idea to take you along." Possum sighed as he exhaled his argument.

"That brother of yours knows what's what," Possum said.

They carried their plates and cups of coffee to the table and sat down across from Fred Farmer, who at forty-four was the oldest of the cowhands. Were it not for the fact that Perley's brother John filled the role as foreman, Fred would most likely have been the best candidate. "Did I hear Possum say you and him are ridin' down below Sulphur Springs in the mornin'?" Fred asked.

"That's a fact," Perley replied. "So, it might be a little hard to keep things runnin' smooth without Possum and me," he joked.

"That's true," Fred came back. "'Course, you two are gone somewhere half the time, anyway, so we're kinda used to it. Besides, we picked up another man today."

"Is that right?" Perley asked. Fred nodded toward the door, and Perley turned to look. "Well, I'll be. . . ." he uttered when he saw Sonny Rice walk in. He looked at Possum. "Did you know?"

"Yeah, I was fixin' to tell you Sonny came back. I just ain't had a chance to," Possum said.

Sonny filled a plate and brought it and a cup of coffee to

join them. Fred slid down the bench to make a place for the young man. "Howdy, Perley," Sonny greeted him.

"Sonny," Perley returned. "I swear, I never expected to see you again. Are you back for good, or just a visit?" The last time he saw Sonny was when they were on their way back from Texarkana. Sonny left him and Possum to escort pretty young Penny Denson and her brother to their farm on the Sulphur River.

"I'm back for good," Sonny answered. "You know there ain't no way I could ever be a farmer."

"The way the sparks were flyin' between you and that young girl, I thought love conquers all, even walkin' behind a plow," Perley commented. "She was hangin' on you like a new pair of curtains on the window."

"I reckon I thought so, too," Sonny confessed. "And things was lookin' pretty good there till the feller she's engaged to marry came to supper the next night after we got back. She introduced me as her brother Art's new friend. I started back to the Triple-G the next day. End of story."

"Sonny, you're better off in the long run," Fred told him. "You'da missed all this good companionship you get at the Triple-G."

"The mistake you made was goin' back to that farm with her and her brother," Possum remarked. "If you was so danged struck by her, you shoulda just picked her up and run off with her."

"Now, there's some good advice," Perley declared sarcastically. "What would you do with a wife right now, anyway. You're better off without the responsibility."

"I reckon that could apply to everybody settin' here," Possum said.

The remark was not lost on Perley. He knew it was aimed at him, and Possum wasn't buying the story he told him about coming back early to give Becky some rest.

Visit our website at
KensingtonBooks.com
to sign up for our newsletters, read
more from your favorite authors, see
books by series, view reading group
guides, and more!

BOOK **CLUB**
BETWEEN THE **CHAPTERS**

Become a Part of Our
Between the Chapters Book Club
Community and Join the Conversation

Betweenthechapters.net